The Thief's Daughter

THE KINGFOUNTAIN SERIES

BOOKS BY JEFF WHEELER

The Kingfountain Series

The Queen's Poisoner
The Thief's Daughter
The King's Traitor

The Covenant of Muirwood Trilogy

The Banished of Muirwood
The Ciphers of Muirwood
The Void of Muirwood

The Legends of Muirwood Trilogy

The Wretched of Muirwood
The Blight of Muirwood
The Scourge of Muirwood

Whispers from Mirrowen Trilogy

Fireblood
Dryad-Born
Poisonwell

Landmoor Series

Landmoor
Silverkin

The THIEF'S DAUGHTER

THE KINGFOUNTAIN SERIES

JEFF WHEELER

47NORTH

This is a work of fiction. Names, characters, organizations, places, events, and incidents are either products of the author's imagination or are used fictitiously.

Published by 47North, Seattle

www.apub.com

Amazon, the Amazon logo, and 47North are trademarks of Amazon.com, Inc., or its affiliates.

ISBN-13: 9781503935006
ISBN-10: 1503935000

Cover design by Shasti O'Leary-Soudant/SOS CREATIVE LLC

Printed in the United States of America

To Victoria

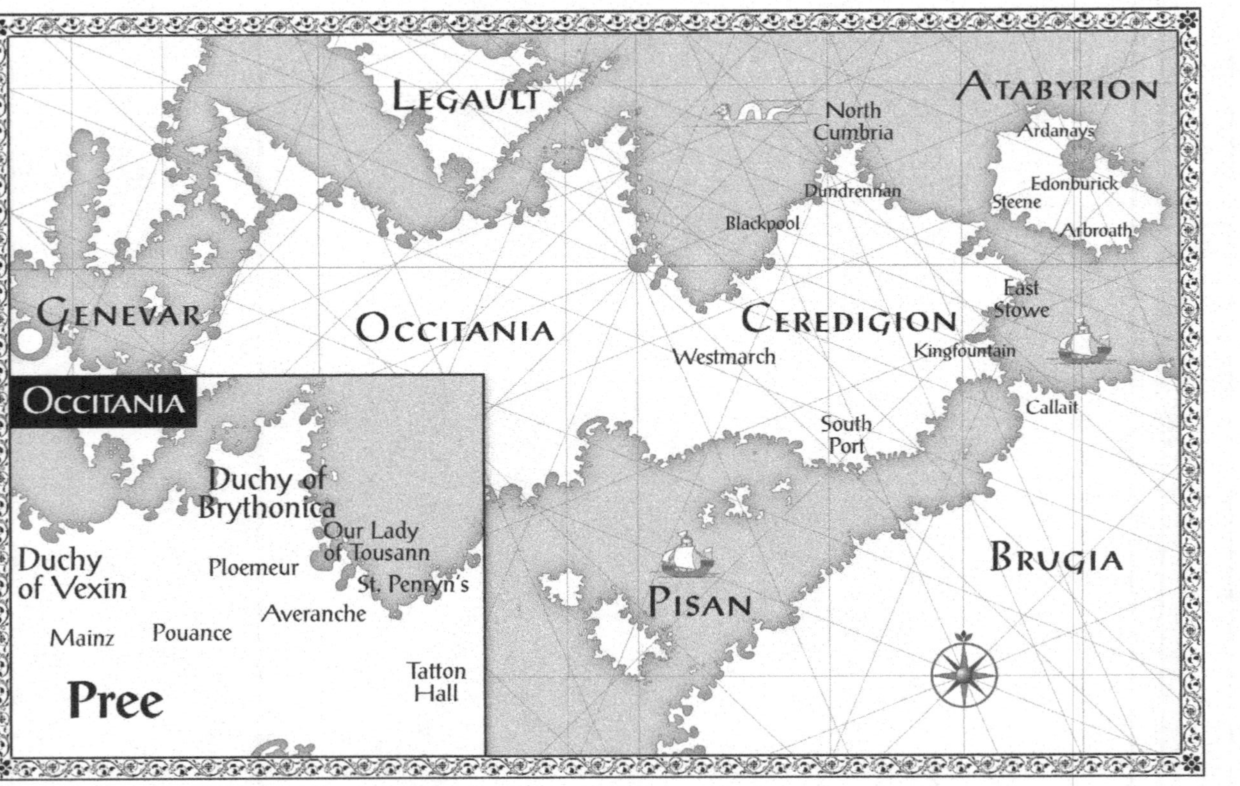

Legault
Atabyrion
North Cumbria
Ardanays
Edonburick
Steene
Dundrennan
Blackpool
Arbroath
Genevar
Occitania
Ceredigion
East Stowe
Westmarch
Kingfountain
Callait
South Port
Occitania
Duchy of Brythonica
Our Lady of Tousann
Duchy of Vexin
Ploemeur
St. Penryn's
Averanche
Mainz
Pouance
Tatton Hall
Pree
Pisan
Brugia

REALMS & CHARACTERS

MONARCHIES

Ceredigion: Severn (House of Argentine): usurped throne from his brother's sons who are missing and presumed murdered. He is forty years old and has reigned over his troubled kingdom for over a decade.

Occitania: Chatriyon VIII (House of Vertus): succeeded his father at age thirteen and ruled under the regency of his older sister until age twenty-one. Upon assuming total control of the throne, he began interfering with the sovereign rights of his cousin, the Duchess of Brythonica, with the intention of forcing her into a marriage alliance with him.

Atabyrion: Iago IV (House of Llewellyn): known for personal courage and bravery. His father (Iago III) was an ineffective king and plagued by the revolts of his own earls and a history of conflict with Ceredigion, the last being in the final year of Eredur's reign, in which Eredur's brother (Severn) and Duke Horwath defeated the Atabyrions in a decisive battle. During a subsequent rebellion, Iago III was killed and Iago IV became king at age fifteen. He is now nineteen and still unmarried.

LORDS OF CEREDIGION

Owen Kiskaddon: Duke of Westmarch

Stiev Horwath: Duke of North Cumbria

Jack Paulen: Duke of East Stowe

Thomas Lovel: Duke of Southport

Dominic Mancini: master of the Espion, the king's spy service

♦ ♦ ♦

Documenting the history of Ceredigion will take, in my estimation, ten years to complete. I am entranced by what I have learned in my stay thus far and do not intend, for the foreseeable future, to return to Pisan. I have started my history at the beginning of the reign of Severn Argentine and will proceed backward to document the reign of his brother, Eredur Argentine, and then delve into the civil wars that occupy a great portion of the histories. I have found a kindred spirit and great wealth of knowledge in the person of the Duke of North Cumbria's granddaughter, Lady Elysabeth Victoria Mortimer, who shares my fiery passion for history and has a surprising command of the details for a girl of seventeen. It will not be long, in my estimation, before King Severn secures a formal marriage alliance for her.

—Polidoro Urbino, Court Historian of Kingfountain

♦ ♦ ♦

CHAPTER ONE

The Duke of Westmarch

Owen Kiskaddon wasn't comfortable wearing a full suit of armor. It made him feel constrained, like he was wearing someone else's boots, so he rarely put on more than a chain hauberk. He was dressed that way now, his hand resting on his sword pommel, as he walked through the camp of soldiers on the eve before his first battle as commander. The night was settling in quickly, and even in the early twilight, he could see a few stars winking at him.

He missed the cold and beautiful North, which had become his home for nearly ten years. And he missed his closest friend, Evie, the Duke of North Cumbria's granddaughter. She would be desperate for news about his first battle, and he was both nervous and excited for what was to come. Although he was expecting blood, he wasn't looking forward to seeing the crimson stain. He knew the techniques of battle, but he had not yet tested them. For years he had trained in the saddle, trained with swords, axes, bows, and lances. Most importantly, he loved reading about battles, studying the accounts of the famous ones, ancient and modern. He could recite, from memory, how many soldiers had marched onto the muddy fields of Azinkeep and how the king had used a mixture of sharpened stakes, archers, and well-chosen ground to defeat a much larger force. But while everyone studied the histories, Owen brought it a step further. He liked to re-invent them.

What would he have done, as the battle commander of the Occitanian army, to defeat the King of Ceredigion at Azinkeep? Like the game of Wizr, he didn't just look at opportunities from his own side's perspective. He looked at it from the other sides too. And long ago, he had realized that there were more than just two sides to any conflict in the game of king and crowns, and there were always unexpected pieces waiting to be introduced to the board.

"Evening, my lord," said one of Owen's soldiers as he passed the man's campfire, lost in thought.

Owen paused and stared down at the man, whose name he could not remember. "Good eventide. Who do you serve under?" Owen asked. Even though the man was twice his own age, he looked up at Owen with reverence and respect.

"Harkins, my lord. My name is Will, and I serve under Harkins. Do you think this weather will hold for the battle tomorrow?"

"Well met, Will. Hopefully it does with a little luck, eh?"

Owen gave him a tired smile, a grateful nod, and continued on his way toward the command tents. He did not think he would sleep at all. How many of the soldiers were feeling jitters and nerves over putting their trust in such a young man? King Severn had led his first battle at the age of eighteen. Owen was a year younger than that. He felt the weight of the responsibility on his shoulders.

It bothered Owen a little, more than a little actually, that his men had such blind faith in him. Very few people could sense the ripples of Fountain magic, but those who did were endowed with magical abilities that amplified some of their natural talents. These gifts were so rare that everyone knew the stories of how Owen's ability with the Fountain had been discovered when he was just a child. What they didn't realize was that while he *was* Fountain-blessed, his supposed gift of seeing the future was a total deception. The cunning Ankarette Tryneowy, the queen's poisoner, had helped him perpetuate the ruse when he was a child in order to make him indispensable to the king. Together, they had misled the entire kingdom. After Ankarette's death, the deception had continued with the help of Dominic Mancini, the king's master of the Espion, who fed him some of the larger political developments before they were commonly known, cementing Owen's reputation for future-seeing both within Ceredigion and abroad. Although the king had said Mancini's appointment would only be temporary, the spymaster had an uncanny way of improving the king's interests, and had managed to hold on to his position for years. Owen and Mancini had a mutually beneficial partnership, one that served both of them well.

Sometimes Owen had already guessed the news the Espion snuck to him because of his keen ability to predict the cause and effect of things. For example, Mancini had not told him that King Iago Llewellyn of Atabyrion would strike an alliance with Chatriyon of Occitania, uniting the two kingdoms against Ceredigion, but he wasn't surprised in the least that it had happened. It wasn't being Fountain-blessed. It was being smart.

As Owen approached the command tent, the guards protecting it lifted their poleaxes to let him through. At seventeen, Owen had not finished growing yet, but he was already a man's height, and he was wearing his family badge, the Aurum—three golden bucks' heads on a field of blue.

The instant he ducked under the entryway, Owen saw Duke Horwath, who was wearing his battle armor and holding a goblet of sweet-smelling wine. His hair had gone grayer over the past few years, but he still had the same calm, unflappable demeanor that had always impressed the young man. He was a soldier, through and through, and had fought in numerous battles over the last fifty years. His steady presence filled Owen with confidence.

"Evening, lad," Horwath said, dipping his head, giving him a wry smile.

"You don't look at all nervous," Owen said, hardly able to suppress a smile.

Horwath shrugged, took another sip, and set his cup down on a small table near a fur rug.

"Any word from your granddaughter?" Owen asked hopefully.

"She said she'd hold the North if the Atabyrions invade while we're here doing battle with the Occitanians. I think she's hoping they do. She's a little jealous, you know, that you get to be part of a battle before *she* does."

Owen smiled at the sentiment, picturing her in his mind. Doing so always made him feel strangely excited, as if a cloud of butterflies had all clustered inside his stomach. He didn't know whether the feeling was battle jitters or the simple longing to see her again. He did his best not to mope, but he did miss her. She had lovely brown hair that was long and thick. Sometimes it was braided. Sometimes not. She had eyes that were the most transfixing shade of blue . . . no, they were green . . . or gray. It really depended on the light and her mood. He missed her way of chattering on and on, her quick wit, and her wickedly delightful sense of humor. Elysabeth Victoria Mortimer—Evie—was his best friend in the entire world and the only other person aside from Mancini who knew his deepest secret.

"Careful, lad," the duke warned, seeing Owen's faraway look. "Keep your thoughts here in Occitania, where they belong. You don't want to be daydreaming when a sword comes at your helmet."

Owen had indeed been daydreaming, so he smiled ruefully. The duke meant him well—after all these years, he was almost a grandfather to him too. Owen could see the grizzled duke hoped for an alliance between their duchies. Though Owen and Evie were never allowed to go off alone together, not without Evie's maid, the three of them were known to plunge off rocks into the river at the base of waterfalls and take some unnecessary risks to their health.

"When do we call in the captains?" Owen asked, chafing his gloved hands. He was impatient for dawn.

"They are settling down the soldiers for the night. They'll be here shortly. You keep pacing. Should have brought your tiles to stack."

Owen grinned. One habit that had survived boyhood was his love for stacking tiles into intricate patterns. Now that he was older, the patterns were even more ridiculously complex, and his collection had grown to an impressive quantity of tiles.

Owen's herald, an officer by the name of Farnes, ducked into the tent. He was in his mid-forties and already had some gray in his reddish hair. He knew protocol better than anyone and had served Owen's father in many battles. "My lords," he said after a stiff bow. "The herald from the King of Occitania just arrived in camp. He wishes for an audience with you both."

Owen looked over to Horwath, who frowned slightly. But rather than offer his opinion, the grizzled duke just said, "It's your army, lad."

"Well, send him in, Farnes," Owen said. As soon as the man left, Owen clasped his hands behind his back and started pacing again. "My guess is he's here to bribe or threaten us. A bribe is more likely. He can always pay us with the coins he's planning to rob from the Duchess of Brythonica's coffers." The current hostilities had been sparked, in part, by the King of Occitania's attempts to force the duchess to marry him against her will. The duchess had begged assistance from all the neighboring kingdoms, and Severn had heeded her call to secure an ally. "How much do you think he'll offer to send us away without a fight?" Owen continued.

Duke Horwath chuckled to himself. "Does it even matter how much it is?"

"Of course not. He doesn't understand us . . . or Ceredigion. I just want to get a sense of whether I should feel insulted or not." Hearing the sound of boots approaching, he paused to listen. "Here they come."

The herald announced the visitor as Anjers, and the Occitanian proceeded to enter the tent, striking his head on the tent flap when he didn't duck low enough while entering. It mussed up his hair somewhat, making Owen stifle a smile.

There was something about Occitanian fashion that Owen hated. The man's tunic was puffed velvet, a lavender color with lilies on it. The collar was stiff, straight, and high, making it almost look like a chain around the man's neck. The hair, as always, was combed forward, regardless of whether a man was balding or not, making the front point out. It was combed forward on the sides as well, making the tips look like feathers. No matter the fashion, the Occitanians were darkly handsome, and Anjers was no exception, even at twice Owen's age.

"Ah, the young duke," Anjers said, trying to fix the hair that had been mussed by the tent flap. He spoke Owen's language flawlessly. Commenting on Owen's age was not the best way he could have begun his speech.

"You have a message from your master?" Owen asked in a bored tone. He folded his arms and gave Duke Horwath a sidelong look.

"Yes, my name is Anjers, herald to Chatriyon, King of Occitania. Once again he is making an invocation of peace to Ceredigion. The affair with Brythonica is a matter of no concern to you. The king would be your ally and friend. As such, he proposes to pay the expenses for your campaign. If a battle is required to appease your bloodthirsty king, then he will allow the slaughter of three thousand men of his ranks to appease the Butcher of Ceredigion. It is my master's hope, however, that as princes, a truce can be signed between our realms without shedding any blood. The king rightfully seeks the hand of Lady Sinia, one of his own subjects, and a unified realm. At what price may my master be assured that this meddling will end?"

Owen listened patiently to the speech, but he was bristling inside at the words being used, both the accusations against his king and the brutal offer of collusion. He released some of his pent-up Fountain magic to discern the man's weakness and saw that he was a diplomat, not a soldier. He wore no armor beneath his puffy sleeves and was completely vulnerable. Owen had learned much about his abilities over the years from the king himself, who had tutored him on drawing his magic from the Fountain. The two had learned that Owen's well of capability had greater depth than the king's, which may have been a result of the fact that the king hadn't discovered his own gifts until much later in life.

Though Owen knew from Mancini that King Severn was deprecated in foreign courts as a ruthless tyrant, a villain, and a child killer, that version of him was no more the real King Severn than a toy sword could create true slices. Though the king's nephews had indeed disappeared, he was not responsible for their deaths. His mistake had been to allow untrustworthy men to take the children into custody.

The herald had long since finished speaking, and the silence grew awkward. Owen stared the man in the eye, letting the silence draw out longer, increasing the herald's discomfort. Men always felt uncomfortable in silence. He stared at Anjers all the while.

"I don't know which offends me more," Owen said evenly. "That your master believed he could buy us with a battlefield victory. Or that he thought we could be *bought* at all. Especially after his father tried to purchase my death at the hands of our former spymaster when I was a child." Owen paused a moment to let his words sink in. His supposed ability to see the future had been perceived as a threat by the realm's enemies, which had led to the assassination attempt. "I *knew* you were coming tonight," Owen said, letting his voice develop a mystical quality. "You tell your master this. When the sun dawns over this field, he will know the true measure of the men of Ceredigion. There is no gold that will turn us away from our purpose. My king and master made an oath to the Duchess of Brythonica that he would defend her realm. Your master will see that we do keep our vows. Tell him this, Herald. And return to this camp again at your peril. My king has not forgotten that this land was once ours. We have every right to come to the defense of *our* true subjects."

The herald's expression flickered with rage and contempt. "By your leave then. Boy."

He turned and marched back out of the tent, smacking against the tent fold again. This time he nearly knocked himself down, and it was all Owen could do not to laugh. He would have to tell Evie all about it later.

After Anjers was gone, Owen turned to give the old duke a questioning look.

"I think he meant to offend you with that parting comment," Horwath said.

Farnes chuckled to himself, shaking his head slowly, recognizing Anjer's blunder of almost criminally underestimating Owen.

"Farnes," Owen said, turning to face his herald. "Fetch Clark. I want the Espion to tail Anjers back to his camp and report on the reaction of the king."

"As you wish," Farnes said, ducking out of the tent without ruffling a hair on his head.

"What mean you to do, lad?" Horwath asked, wrinkling his brow.

Owen smirked. "What the King of Occitania least expects us to do. We're going to attack him tonight."

The duke's eyebrows furrowed more. "That is a very risky move, lad."

"Well, I did *warn* him I would," Owen said, holding up his hands. "Remember? Come morning, he would see the true measure of the men of Ceredigion? By morning, it'll all be over. In the panic, his own army will probably start attacking itself. Let's call in the captains now. I'm impatient to knock down the first tile."

♦ ♦ ♦

It is a common misunderstanding that kingdoms are defined places with fixed borders. A kingdom can be a city. It can also spread across a continent. Much depends on the ambition and ability of the kingdom's ruler. Weak rulers lose ground; strong ones gain it. It is the historian's purpose to shed light on the lives of the great people of time. Truly, it is the great ones and their decisions who guide the course of events—they are the cogs in the wheel.

Severn Argentine is feared by his people but also respected for his military prowess. He is sarcastic, impatient, and immune to flattery because he is not comely and has some acute deformations of the body. In the twelve years since he rose to power, he has consolidated his strength, placed trusted dukes throughout his domain, and he now seeks to expand his hegemony. The King of Occitania has only come into his rights as king since turning twenty-one a year ago. He is young and untested and half the age of his rival. Chatriyon loves fashion, music, dancing, falconry, and he is only now learning the arts of war. His eagerness to prove himself may play into King Severn's hands. It will be interesting to see how the maps change once this rivalry has ended.

—Polidoro Urbino, Court Historian of Kingfountain

♦ ♦ ♦

CHAPTER TWO

Marshal Roux

The night was lit by a pale moon, and it only took a moment for Owen's vision to adjust to the meager light. He swayed slightly in the saddle, feeling his nerves tingle with excitement at the prospect of the upcoming night raid. He carried his helmet in the crook of his arm because he did not want anything to obstruct his hearing. The hooves of the horses were making an incredible racket, but they were going to ditch the horses and approach on foot to minimize the risk of discovery. The maneuver was dangerous, but it would not endanger his entire army.

Owen's plan was simple. His main force, the one he was leading personally, consisted of one hundred men, of which only two dozen were archers. The archers were to send a hail of arrows into the Occitanian camp first to cause confusion and panic, and then the soldiers would rush in with swords and shields, trying to stir up enough noise that the Occitanians would think Owen's entire army was upon them. Two more groups of fifty each had taken different roads, and they would await the sounds of fighting before doing the same thing on the flanks of the army. Owen wanted to catch the Occitanian king off guard and trick him into thinking he was outnumbered. Basically, he hoped to frighten him into running away. Of course, the king could be held for ransom if captured, and Owen wasn't opposed to that outcome.

He ran the risk, however, that his men would make too much noise and the Occitanians would be waiting to ambush them. But he felt that was unlikely, for they had given the Occitanians no reason to predict his night raid. Owen had also set Espion up along the roads to catch any stragglers who might blunder into them by mistake. They were going to take out the other side's night watch as well, allowing Owen to get as close as possible.

Duke Horwath rode next to him, silent and unobtrusive as always. He had picked at Owen's plan repeatedly, telling him everything that could, and likely would, go wrong. The ground was unfamiliar. The scouts had not been precise in determining how far away the Occitanian army was. Rivers or streams might obstruct the way. Owen was grateful for the reasoning, but his own logic had held up. They were risking only a fraction of their army, and if they succeeded, the rewards would be well worth it.

A night bird called out from the woods to the left, and Owen jerked his head in response to the sudden sound. He felt a slight fluttering in his heart that reminded him of when he was a young child and he had been brought to the palace at Kingfountain, as a hostage to King Severn. Everything used to frighten him then. His courage had improved, but he still remembered being that scared little boy with the patch of white in his mouse-brown hair.

Like most memories, this one led the way back to Evie. That white patch she so loved was still in his hair, but it was partially hidden by the rest of his thick locks. She would reach up and touch it sometimes as they wandered the mountains of North Cumbria together, looking down on the vistas that filled him with awe and wonder. They longed to explore the ice caves together, but they had not had the chance; pressing affairs of state always kept them moving from castle to castle.

Sometimes a celebration would require them to go to Kingfountain. Sometimes trouble in Owen's lands meant he had to return home to judge a matter of land between lesser nobles or farmers. He was treated with great dignity and love at Tatton Hall, and always returned there during the winter months when North Cumbria was blanketed in ice. In his mind's eye, he could see Evie kneeling in front of the hearth fire, reading one of her histories, chewing a bit of her hair as she let herself be engrossed by the stories of kings and battles and plagues, which she would later tell him about or share with him. She was unpredictable, lively, and heartbreakingly pretty. Sometimes she would catch him looking at her and her cheeks would flush. When that happened, it made his heart ache in a way that felt almost soothing.

"You'll be needing your wits soon," Duke Horwath said, riding so close their legs nearly rubbed together. "Stay focused."

Owen wondered what had given him away, but Horwath was an observant man. While he was as tight-lipped as a turtle shell, he was always watching. He was one of the few people the king's barbed tongue could never injure.

"My lord," came a low voice from the darkness ahead of them. Owen reined in his stallion and waited as the man approached. It was one of the Espion, a trusted man named Clark. He was a lean, hatchet-faced man, his dark hair shorn to stubble. He was an excellent woodsman and tracker.

"What news, Clark?" Owen asked, trying to calm his restless mount.

"I recommend securing the horses here," he said in his usual formal way. "The outer edge of the army is five furlongs away. It's a short walk, but if you ride any closer, you'll be heard in their camp."

Owen nodded and slid on his helmet before dismounting. Clark held the reins for him and then led the stallion to the trees and secured the beast. The other men dismounted as well. The horses were given some provender to keep them quiet, and several handlers were left behind to tend to them. Owen saw the archers flexing their bows to fit the strings. Each one carried three quivers full of arrows. The archers were all talking amongst themselves.

"How long until dawn, Clark?" Owen asked, gazing up at the stars, but he was never good at constellations.

Clark sniffed, gazing up. "Few more hours, my lord. Some were up drinking recently, but most are fast asleep, except the sentries."

"Well, let's wake them early," Owen said with a grin. His hand dropped to the pommel of his longsword. He also had a short sword and a dagger. The hauberk felt comfortable enough, and he was warm despite the puff of fog issuing from his lips.

The men started marching to close the distance separating them from the Occitanian camp. Owen's heart began to race. He had trained and trained in the castle yard, but this was the deciding moment when he would learn if that training held true. It made him feel more confident that he had certain unfair advantages working in his favor. His ability to use Fountain magic permitted him to discern his opponent's weaknesses. It also provided him with an uncanny resistance to the magic of others who could tame the power. Turning, he was grateful to see Horwath by his side, even though he knew the old man would rather have been abed than hiking down a strange road in Occitania. Owen found himself gritting his teeth as he marched. Clark kept stride with him. He imagined the Espion had orders to keep him alive. But one does not lead from the back, so Owen was the first among his men.

They pulled out their weapons, preparing to fight, and left the shelter of the woods. The land before them opened up into a rolling plain, and the lights of the Brythonican castle under siege—Pouance—could be seen in the distance. Owen had studied the few maps they had at their disposal, so he knew it was part of the outer defenses of the duchy rather than the capital Ploemeur.

"Get ready to light the torches," Owen said to one of his captains. "Each man carries two. It'll double our numbers in their eyes. Archers, at the ready."

His nerves were calming, and a strange sense of peace washed over him. Then he heard it—the murmuring waterfall sound of the Fountain. He had not summoned the Fountain, but he felt it rushing through him. It had come to him, as if it were anxious to help him achieve his victory.

"Lads, let's teach these fools what we're made of," Owen said in a firm, clear voice. He looked over at Horwath, who gave him a crooked smile beneath the nose guard of his helmet. There was an excitement in the air, a feeling of confidence.

"Hand me a torch, Clark. Would you?" Owen asked.

The Espion nodded and struck two stones over the torches he'd tied together. The wet oil flared to life and Clark thrust the smoking brand into Owen's hand as the fire leaped and sizzled in the night. Owen lifted it high in the air and then shouted, "Ceredigion!"

It was like unloosing the waters of a dam. The roar from the men nearly drowned out the twang of bows as the sky filled with arrows. The archers dropped into low, taut crouches, then almost leaped into the air as their arrows went skyward. Another deadly wave was sent out before the first had even landed. The arrows began thunking into the camp. Shrieks of surprise came from the bewildered Occitanian army.

Owen started to run down the road, waving the torch over his head in circles. Clark was at his heels, still keeping pace with him. A wall of firebrands came behind him. It seemed like five hundred were charging with him, though his force was less than a hundred. Giddiness swelled in Owen's breast as he ran. The long hikes in the mountains had filled him with energy and stamina. Ankarette's medicinal tea had completely cured his lungs of their childhood weakness.

The camp below bobbed to life. Men were rising, hurrying to grab weapons and don armor, but it was too late for preparations now. The arrows were showering into the camp like rain, and the night sky was cleaved by shrieks of agony. Owen approached the first rows, where a few pikemen were shivering with their poleaxes. Then the pikemen dropped their weapons and bolted.

Owen knew he had won before the first stroke of hand-to-hand fell.

The archers stopped the deadly rain as Owen's men smashed into the panicked defenders. Owen watched as Clark moved with grace and skill, using the two short swords in his hands to cut down the soldiers who rushed at them. He had a businesslike look on his hatchet-face as he dropped, spun, and plunged his blades.

Owen felt the rush of the Fountain all around him, as if he were the floodwaters himself. Men were fleeing the other way, some with arrows sticking from their bodies. Tents collapsed in tangled heaps with ropes still whipping about. Horses screamed and charged. Owen thought he saw one with the flag of Occitania attached to the skirts, bearing its rider away.

Another set of screams sounded as the two other groups of soldiers joined the battle. In his gut, though, Owen knew they had already won.

A soldier with a pike charged at Owen from behind a tent and jabbed the sharp tip of his weapon at his chest. Acting on reflex alone, he blocked the pike with his sword and then threw his torch into the man's face. The pikeman flailed with pain and dropped his weapon. He too fled.

Another man came at Owen with a shield and tried to bull into him and knock him down. Owen ducked to the side and extended his leg to trip the man, who crashed face-first into his own shield. He slumped and didn't get up.

Owen watched his men raze through the camp like farmers' scythes through wheat. Strangely, he felt like laughing.

"Lord Owen!" one of his captains—Ashby—shouted, running up to him eagerly. "They are fleeing! Some of them barefoot! We tried catching the king, but he's on horseback and riding away, surrounded by his knights. He was the first to flee. You did it, my lord!"

The air filled with the sound of trumpets coming from the other side of the camp. It was a harsh wailing sound, one that sent a shiver down Owen's back.

"What was that?" another captain shouted in confusion.

"I'll check on it," Clark said stiffly. He ran off into the chaos of soldiers who were now beginning to plunder the tents. Some grabbed Occitanian flags or badges as souvenirs.

The trumpets blared again—a haunting sound.

"Gather the men to me," Owen ordered. "Stop rifling through their braies! Now's not the time to plunder. Pull the men in. Have the archers stand ready."

There was a ripple in the magic of the Fountain, and it made Owen clench his teeth with dread. Something was not right. He was sweating, casting his eyes around amidst the chaos for some sign of the source of the trumpeting.

Clark returned in moments, his face dark with concern. "Brythonic knights," he said gruffly. "They attacked the other side of the Occitanians' camp. The army is scattering."

Horwath walked up to Owen, sword in hand. "We're in a vulnerable position if those knights turn on us."

"Agreed," Owen said. He felt that strange, jarring pulse of the Fountain again. "We did what we came to do. Call all the men back. Bring them to me."

The commotion of the night only increased as more sounds of fighting came ghosting in from across the camp.

"My lord," Clark said in his ear, "I have a horse ready for you."

Owen turned and shook his head. "If I abandon these men, I'm no better than Chatriyon."

The Espion scowled, giving him a fierce, weighing look. It was clear he was deciding whether to risk Owen's wrath by insisting again that he flee.

"Here they come," Horwath said, tightening his grip on his sword.

Owen saw the flag before he saw the man. The standard was a field of white with black trim made from a quarter circle. The symbol amidst the white was a black-feathered bird, a crow or a raven, with a hooked beak. It struck Owen that King Severn's standard—a white boar on a black field—had a mirrored element.

The man riding the horse with the standard was middle-aged, about the same age as Severn. Although he was not an old man, his hair was slate gray and combed forward in the Occitanian style. He had a stern, brooding look in his eyes as his mount approached Owen's men, who gathered around him like a wall. The rider did not have any weapons drawn, and a long, white cape came down from his shoulders, covering the withers of his steed.

"Marshal Roux," Duke Horwath said evenly.

The stern man seemed to notice Horwath for the first time. "Duke Horwath," he said with a stiff nod and a slight accent. He adjusted himself in the saddle. "You're a little *far* from North Cumbria, my lord. Aren't you afraid of melting this far south? You lead this band? I thought it was Kiskaddon."

"It is," Owen said, feeling the Fountain's force ebb to a trickle now. He could discern that although the man was gruff, he did not intend to attack. The young duke kept his hand on his sword hilt anyway. He did not trust in coincidences.

The marshal turned toward the sound of Owen's voice, seeming to notice him for the first time. "Oh, you *are* here. I hadn't recognized you in the dark. My lord duke, I have a message for you from my lady, the Duchess of Brythonica. She thanks you for your pains in defending her sovereign rights. Your timely involvement has routed Chatriyon's army. We'll take it from here. I've ordered my knights to harry them back to their own borders. She bids me to thank you and your king for interceding on her behalf. You have a loyal ally in Her Majesty. When war comes to Ceredigion, you may be assured she will not forget the favor done to her and she will repay your kindness with her own. Thus speaks my lady." He bowed his head respectfully to Owen. He extended his arm and waved it ceremoniously. "Please divide the spoils amongst your men. Your bravery has earned you that right. I am Brendon Roux, marshal and protector of Brythonica. By your leave."

"Tell your lady," Owen said, nodding respectfully in return, "that it was our honor and privilege to come to her aid. Our lands border each other. We should be allies."

The marshal's brow knitted darkly. "I will tell her you said so," he said stiffly. Then he turned and rode back, his armed knights following him back into the maze of flapping tents and groans.

Owen turned to Horwath, whose eyes bore a distrusting look.

The grizzled duke rubbed his chin. "It was interesting that his knights attacked Chatriyon's army at exactly the same time as ours did. It was almost as if . . ."

"They were expecting us," Owen said softly, frowning.

CHAPTER THREE

Resurgence

Later that morning, Owen's pavilion was full of men, and it was all he could do to curb their enthusiasm. King Chatriyon VIII's army had been routed and was still fleeing, nipped at the heels by Brythonic knights. The king had made it to the safety of a castle deeper in his own territory, and word of the victory was spreading throughout the hamlets of eastern Occitania. Owen's captains had achieved victory without a single injury, a feat that had earned him enormous respect and gratitude. Young Kiskaddon's gifts from the Fountain did not just extend to dreams of the future, it was whispered; he had an unparalleled ability for combat too.

"My lord," Farnes said as the herald butted his way through two captains. He swiped his hand through his graying reddish hair. A grin threatened to break through his normally placid composure—and then did. "My lord, the mayor of Averanche has arrived with a delegation from the city." His lips quivered with suppressed delight. "They've come . . . well, they've come to surrender their castle and city to you and swear loyalty to Ceredigion."

Owen was taken aback. “Did I hear you correctly, Farnes? A town wants to surrender *before* we’ve attacked it? Where is Averanche? I need a map.”

“Over here, my lord,” said Captain Ashby.

Owen looked at Duke Horwath in disbelief, shrugging his shoulders and stifling a chuckle. Ashby brought over the map, and several men crowded around the precious document, trying to find the location of Averanche.

Owen shooed them away and motioned for Farnes and the duke to join him, and together they pored over the cartographer’s map. There was so little they knew of Occitania and her cities and duchies. The coastal ports were well marked, but the information about the interior castles and towns was vague. King Severn had a host of mapmakers under his employ, and the Espion had the most accurate maps of anyone, but they were guarded as state secrets. He couldn’t find Averanche.

“Well, Farnes, bring them in and they can point it out to us,” Owen said, clapping the herald on the back. Farnes chuckled and quickly left the tent.

Owen looked up at the captains clustered around the small space. “Start to break camp,” he ordered. “Change the guard and get ready to move. Await your orders.”

“Yes, my lord,” Captain Ashby said. The others hustled out of the tent, leaving only Owen and Duke Horwath.

“I can’t abide crowds,” Owen muttered. “Everyone wants to see you for some reason. There’s never a moment’s peace. What do you make of this development?”

Horwath frowned and gazed down at the map. “There is a long history of war between our kingdoms, lad. This could be a stronghold that benefits us later. Years ago we took Callait from Brugia, and it’s still a strategic port city for us on that continent. I’m sure the lord mayor doesn’t have enough men to defend his town, and what few he had fled with the king’s army last night. It’s like Wizr. You just made a strong move that your opponent wasn’t expecting. They’re vulnerable now, and we both know it.”

Farnes returned with the mayor of Averanche, a short, squat man with a gray beard and only a few strands of hair atop his waxy, sweating head. After a short, formal introduction, Owen learned that Averanche was a short distance away, with a castle along the coast, right on the border of the duchy of Brythonica. It was in the territory that Ceredigion had controlled centuries before, and the mayor was only too willing to discuss terms.

♦ ♦ ♦

By midafternoon the same day, Owen found himself walking the ramparts of the castle with Averanche's mayor, watching as the flag with three golden bucks on a field of blue flapped in the breeze. It was a surreal experience, to be sure, but Owen did not trust the hospitality of the local townspeople, and he had strictly forbidden his men to drink or carouse. He had soldiers patrolling the streets, learning the defenses in case they were attacked, and they were prepared to ride off at a moment's notice if Occitania's king should attempt to return with his hosts. Reports throughout the day showed that to be highly unlikely—the king was licking his wounded pride at being bested by a much younger man.

As Owen walked the battlement walls, he stared down at the lush valleys and farms below. In the distance, he could make out the coast, the flat gray waters too far for him to hear the rumble of the waves. There was an island off the coast, and he could see a fortress atop the crest.

"What is that place?" Owen asked the lord mayor as they walked, pointing out across the waters.

"Pardon? Oh, that is the sanctuary of Our Lady of Toussan. It is an ancient structure, the main sanctuary of Brythonica. The tide goes out once per day, allowing visitors in. Otherwise it is surrounded by water. It is the last defense of the duchess, our neighbor. The view is even better from the tower. Would you like to see it?"

"No," Owen said, pausing to gaze. The sanctuary clearly surpassed the size of Our Lady of Kingfountain, which was also built on an island, albeit a much smaller one, amidst a river. This island jutted out from the sea. It was hard to tell where the sanctuary ended and the island began. The walls came all the way down to the sea, and there were ships moored there. Owen's mind began working on how a person would go about conquering a place like that.

"What can you tell me of the Duchess of Brythonica?" Owen asked, clasping his hands behind his back.

"She is descended from an ancient house, my lord," the mayor said. "The house of Montfort has long ruled Brythonica. Her lord father died six years ago, when she was eleven. Her people will only have a Montfort rule them, even a girl. They are . . . independent spirits, my lord. Very stubborn."

"Very well, but that tells me of her people. What about her?"

The mayor frowned. "Well, I have only seen her rarely, my lord. I do not know her personality. She was twelve when I last beheld her, so I am really not to judge. She is fair, by all accounts. Is my lord . . . *interested* in getting to know her better?"

"By the Fountain, no!" Owen said, chuckling out loud. He had surrendered his heart to a water sprite in the North, and there was room for none other.

"That is wise," the mayor said, sighing with relief. "I hoped you did not carry any such notion. Even though you are her age, I can assure you that the Duchess of Brythonica will only marry a king. She has been very unlucky in her suitors, you know. Her first betrothal, as an infant, was to King Eredur's oldest son. That . . . did not end well. I hope I am being discreet enough in saying so. Her second betrothal was to a prince of Brugia. That did not end well either. The King of Occitania wants her lands for himself. Now that you have defeated his army, there will likely be a drawn-out negotiation for their marriage. Tell me, my lord. Is it true that your king is still unmarried after so many years?"

"It's no secret," Owen said in a neutral tone, but he was not about to reward the man's curiosity with court gossip.

"Does your king have *intentions* to woo Lady Sinia for himself?"

The king was very old compared to the girl, and the mere thought of such a match made Owen's stomach sour. There was no need to respond, however, for the mayor changed the subject. "It seems you have a visitor," he said with a gentle cough. "Excuse me."

When Owen turned away from the view, he saw Clark standing at a respectful distance. His posture was stiff and tense, full of foreboding. He looked like a hound at the gates before a race.

Owen dismissed the mayor and beckoned Clark to approach. The man hadn't shaved in a day, and the stubble on his cheeks matched the stubble atop his head.

"My lord, I apologize for interrupting you, but this could not wait."

"What is it, Clark?" Owen asked, concern blooming in his stomach. The Espion's demeanor meant there was dreadful news, and he wanted it out in the open.

"During our raid last night, I had a man go through Chatriyon's tent. This was just before Marshal Roux arrived. I've had several men reading his abandoned correspondence to see what information we could glean from it. There is a bit of news that must be reported to King Severn at once."

"You seem anxious because of it, Clark," Owen said, trying to curb his impatience.

"I'm anxious because of how the king may react," Clark said. "He's not a patient man. As you know."

"Tell me," Owen said, drawing closer to Clark and lowering his voice. He looked around, but there was no one anywhere close enough to overhear their conversation. The calm atmosphere belied the tension that had descended upon him. A few seabirds called from the sky overhead. The breeze caught the subtle tang of the ocean.

"My lord," Clark said, his voice low and serious, "Chatriyon received a letter recently from a man in Legault. A nobleman by the name of Desmond claims he holds King Severn's young nephew, the rightful ruler of Ceredigion. The king had two nephews, if you recall. The letter said that while the older nephew was indeed murdered in Kingfountain, the Fountain spared the younger one so that he could one day reclaim the throne. The letter was seeking Chatriyon's assistance to attack Ceredigion. Occitania would attack from the west under the pretext of subduing Brythonica, Atabyrion would attack in the East. That would leave the *North* vulnerable to the pretender and Legault. It's Ambion Hill all over again. We've known about the Occitanian treaty with Atabyrion for some time, but this one with Legault is a complete surprise. As I mentioned, the letter was recent. I believe our kingdom is on the brink of invasion. We disrupted this attack, but word of Chatriyon's defeat might not travel quickly enough to prevent the two other forces from acting."

Owen's heart skipped, realizing that Evie was defending the North alone.

"You're right, Clark. The king needs to hear of this straightaway. Another pretender has emerged."

Clark shook his head. "It gets worse, my lord." He squirmed with discomfort. "The king's sister, the dowager queen of Brugia, is supporting this plot. Four kingdoms have formed an alliance against us. Four." He shook his head in disbelief. "What I don't understand is why the king's own sister would believe the claims of an imposter? Which leads to the next logical question." Clark's voice fell to a whisper, his gaze earnest. "I was not part of the Espion at that time. I joined after. Well, what if it's true? What if one of Eredur's sons survived the murder attempt? He was just a boy then. Now he's a man. At least twenty or twenty-one by my reckoning. This is . . . this is a true blow to the king!"

Owen clapped Clark on the shoulder and looked him straight in the eye. "Tell no man of this. Prepare our horses. We will ride back to Kingfountain at once."

♦ ♦ ♦

King Severn Argentine has not remarried following the death of his first wife, Lady Nanette, daughter of the Duke of Warrewik. They had one child, who died of fever not long into Severn's reign. Then, shortly thereafter, his wife died. Some say she was poisoned, but that is always the first conclusion. The day of his wife's death there was an eclipse. Some say it was a sign from the Fountain that Severn should not have taken the throne. But others who know him well say it was a mark of his deep grief at his lady's passing. Some have nefariously insinuated the king secretly wishes to marry his niece, the lady Elyse. But those who have seen them together at court know their love is not romantic. They share a common bond of affection—a deep love of Eredur Argentine. Even after so many years, that ghost still casts a shadow.

—Polidoro Urbino, Court Historian of Kingfountain

♦ ♦ ♦

CHAPTER FOUR

Severn

Since becoming the Duke of Westmarch, Owen had become accustomed to sending messengers to deliver news and give instructions. But this was news that needed to be delivered in person, particularly since an invasion might be imminent.

Owen's feelings about King Severn were muddled and varying. The king was a hard man to serve, in part because of his razor-sharp tongue and characteristic moodiness, temper, and impatience. King Severn was Fountain-blessed too, and his power from the Fountain was the ability to persuade others with his words. He fueled that ability through diminishing others with his sarcasm and biting remarks. It was a strange combination of powers. Owen secretly wondered what would happen if the king switched to praise instead of ridicule. Would his gift be amplified? Or was giving a compliment even possible for such a hardened man?

Still, Severn valued loyalty above all else—his personal motto while serving his brother had been Loyalty Binds Me—and Owen admired the way he had surmounted the natural difficulties that arose from some defects of his birth. His shoulders were crooked, one of his arms a little bent. He often walked with a limp, though he tried to mask it.

The king had snatched the crown of Ceredigion after learning that Eredur had previously contracted a marriage, thus making his large posterity illegitimate. The boys had gone missing not long after, and there was a widespread belief that Severn had murdered his nephews in a grab for power. The knowledge of this public misperception tormented the king. Although he had not ordered the boys' murders, it had happened under his reign, and he held himself responsible for their deaths. There had been no official proclamation of the event either.

That was a mistake.

Some conjectured the boys were alive and had been sent to the North to live in one of the king's castles. Having been to all the king's castles in the North, Owen knew the lads weren't in any of them. It was a secret grief. Even after over a decade, it was a wound that still festered. Owen could scarcely imagine what emotions Severn would experience when he heard about the pretender's claim, and the fact that four kingdoms were rallying to aid the imposter.

Owen and Clark rode hard from Westmarch, changing horses at several waypoints along the way and sleeping only for snatches to preserve their strength. Duke Horwath would remain in Averanche to make sure Westmarch was secure before joining Owen at Kingfountain. Of course Owen had shared the news with him, and Horwath had agreed the king needed to be told immediately. They were both anxious about Evie and the possibility of an invasion deep in the North.

It had been several years since Owen had last been to Kingfountain, and his heart churned with strange, conflicted feelings as he made his approach. He remembered being a little boy and riding to the castle in Duke Horwath's saddle. Now his own men were riding with him, bearing his standard and badge for all to see. He was greeted with enthusiasm by the people, many of whom doffed their hats and waved them at him. Some of the women threw flowers as well, hoping to catch his eye. Word of his victory in Occitania had barely preceded him.

As he rode through the city and crossed the bridge to the sanctuary of Our Lady, he stared up at the spires and turrets, thinking about the time he had snuck away from the palace to try to claim sanctuary there. That was when he had first met Dominic Mancini, only a lowly Espion then, and the queen dowager, who still resided there. The thought sparked another—an idea he would mull upon until he saw the king.

They reached the palace hill and rode up swiftly, their horses exhausted from the long journey. It was a three-day ride from the borders of Occitania, and Owen was saddle-weary and hungry. He was tempted to sneak down to the kitchen to get some wafers from the cook, Liona, who had offered him so much comfort when he was just a boy.

Owen dismissed his escort and walked, hand on hilt, into the darkened halls of the palace. He was met, almost instantly, by Mancini.

"I'm surprised to see you here," the fat man said with a cunning smile. "But it must be the Fountain's will, for I have news." Mancini had a few streaks of gray through his hair. He had lost weight in his new role, but while he no longer had the girth of the past, he would always be a big man. Dressed in the fashionable clothes of a courtier, he bore the badge of the white boar on his tunic and the chain of office around his neck. In the ten years since he had been named head of the Espion, he had increased his influence with the king through his expert advice and his knowledge of foreign lands. His knowledge of the trading nation Genevar had increased the king's coffers significantly. Severn had sponsored several shipmasters in recent years and funded exploration to find new trade routes to the south. Some had been quite profitable.

"I wonder if our news is the same," Owen said, not slowing his pace.

"Judging by the urgent pace you young people like to keep, it may well be. Have you had any *dreams* lately, my lord?" Mancini asked with an oily smile.

"I have, in fact," Owen said. While he appreciated Mancini's abilities, he was always wary of the man, for he knew he kept most of what he heard to himself. "I dreamed of the land of Legault."

Mancini pursed his lips. "Then you've heard about the imposter. I've already told the king. Don't look angry, lad, it's my *job* to tell him something before he finds out another way. Had I known you were coming, I would have waited another day. But such news cannot be delayed."

"I understand, Mancini," Owen said, though what he understood was that Mancini would always look out for himself first and foremost. "Where is the king?"

"Where he usually is when he's angry. Come with me."

They walked together to the throne room of the palace. Owen was sticky with sweat and irritated from lack of sleep. He needed a bath and a meal desperately, but he was anxious about Evie and wanted to head north to ensure she was well. The possibility of an army landing in the North in a surprise attack by the false prince caused a twist of anxiety in his gut.

They were announced by trumpet before entering the hall, a ceremony that Owen hated and knew the king did as well. Owen's eyes found Severn as soon as he and Mancini strode into the throne room together.

Owen could not help but think how much things had changed since he had been presented to the king all those years ago. The king had aged quite a bit. His black hair now had a few silver glints near his ears, but it was still long, as was the fashion in Ceredigion. He wore black, though his tunics were becoming more and more elaborate as his wealth increased. Owen saw he was twitching with his dagger still—loosening it in its scabbard, drawing it out a bit, and then slamming it back down. It was an unconscious habit that gave one the perception he was accustomed to stabbing people. The way he was leaning forward on the throne—his chin resting on one fist—disguised the deformity of his back.

"Owen," the king said in surprise, his look softening as the young man knelt in front of the throne. He gestured impatiently for him to rise.

"My lord, I rode as hard as I could," Owen said, feeling sweat trickle down his back.

"Your arrival couldn't be more opportune," the king said gravely. "I applaud your victory. Word arrived only yesterday. You did well, lad. I expected nothing less. But there is trouble. A storm is brewing out at sea." His look darkened again, his mouth turning into a frown.

"I know," Owen said, drawing closer to the king. Mancini kept a respectful distance away. After clearing his throat, Owen continued, "Pardon me, my lord, but I'm weary from the journey. I had a dream in Westmarch. One I had to tell."

"You did?" the king asked. "Tell me!" He seemed very agitated, his eyes wide with a keen desire to hear about Owen's supposedly prophetic dream.

"It was a short dream," Owen said. "I dreamed I was walking in a garden. There was a withered rosebush, but when I passed it, I noticed there was a single white rose on it. I plucked the rose and smelled it, but in dreams you cannot smell. I could not tell if it was living or not."

The king's eyes narrowed. "A white rose."

Owen nodded. He had used the imagery of the rose deliberately because the Sun and Rose was the battle standard of Eredur. Reaching into his vest, he withdrew the letter found in Chatriyon's tent. "Then we faced Occitania's army and my man Clark found this in the king's tent. The dream made more sense to me after I read it."

The king snatched the paper away and unfolded it, scanning the contents feverishly. His countenance burned white with livid fury as he read it.

"Blast the Fountain!" the king thundered, throwing the letter down to the ground. He rose from his throne, quivering with rage. Servants were already slipping out the doors to escape the great hall before the coming storm. Owen felt his heart rattled by the king's blasphemy, but he said nothing. He knew from long experience that it was best to ride out the weather silently.

The king's boot trampled the letter as he walked off the dais. "Must I always be plagued by malcontents and whisperers? Am I never to have a moment of peace? I had two enemies, two *wolves* snarling and snapping at my boots. Now a hunter comes with a long spear aimed at my heart. And my sister, no less, is behind this. My own sister."

Owen stared at him, knowing it wasn't yet time to speak. The king's wrath was still flaming.

Severn muttered dark curses under his breath. "I am hated everywhere," he said. "Hated, feared, despised. Dogs yap at me as I pass. Once, the house of Argentine commanded such respect and devotion. Nations quivered in dread of offending us. Now look at them. Conspiring and plotting to bring me down. Like a boar." His voice deepened to a growl. "But I won't be captured. I won't be speared."

He seemed to become aware that he was talking to himself. Straightening, he turned back to look at Owen and Mancini, who were staring at him.

"It's hard to be dispassionate in such a match of wits," Severn said darkly. "That is why I need you, Owen, Dominic. I cannot see through the haze of my anger right now. Three enemies, four if you include Brugia. May as well bring back the Dreadful Deadman prophecy and have all *six* kingdoms attack us at once." He tapped his lips and shook his head worriedly. "The Dreadful Deadman prophecy. I hadn't thought of that. What if *this* is the fulfillment of that prophecy? A king rises from the dead and unites Ceredigion. My brother thought it was himself. So did I at one time. But what if it is this pretender? What if this is a game I cannot win?"

"My lord," Mancini said patiently. "It is no use clinging to the ravings of dead men. There are plenty of living ones who threaten you. Princes play Wizr and kingdoms are the prize. Your protégé just handed a nasty defeat to Chatriyon VIII in Occitania. He wanted to increase his power by marrying the Duchess of Brythonica, and you've blocked him. Why else would he be supporting this . . . this . . . draper's boy in Legault as King of Ceredigion! He fears you, my lord, and he fears losing to you in a fair battle. He may as well have crowned an ape! The imposter won't last the month, let alone a year. It's a game. A maneuver. You will have time to punish Occitania for its treachery."

"And Legault?" the king demanded hotly.

"And Legault," Mancini said. "And Atabyrion too. The way you win this game of Wizr is by being ruthless and bold. As I've told you time and again, you will not be loved by your people as your brother was. You must stop expecting this of yourself. It is better to be feared than loved."

The king's angry look was softening. "You speak wisely, Dominic. And I assure you, I intend to punish those who defy me. If I am too lenient, I will only risk more defiance."

"The last time it helped," Owen said in a subdued tone, "that you had the real Dunsdworth here at the palace. That was easy to prove. This one will not be. But I have an idea you might consider."

"I treasure your ideas, lad. You know that," the king said with a nod.

Owen looked around to ensure that all the servants were indeed gone. As soon as he was sure the three of them were alone in the throne room, he said, "A thought struck me as I rode past Our Lady on the way to Kingfountain. The prince's mother still resides there. So does John Tunmore. They might be behind this resurgence. You remember the lies in that book Tunmore wrote about you? You let me read it all eventually because, for some reason, the magic of the other Fountain-blessed doesn't work on me." Owen looked steadily at the king. Both men knew that Owen's innate resistance to the magic was not typical. He could not be easily deceived, which made him a great asset. "Tunmore's gift from the Fountain is his ability to convince people through his writing." Owen bent down and picked up the crumpled letter. "I have a feeling he may have written the original. He cannot get himself out of sanctuary, but it would only be too easy to smuggle something he's written out of Our Lady. He may be persuading others to believe in the upstart."

The king looked at Owen, impressed. "I had not thought of that."

"Neither had I," Mancini said, giving a little nod of acknowledgment.

Owen felt a little flush rise to his cheeks. "With your permission, Your Majesty, may I visit the sanctuary to see what I can learn? Perhaps he knows more about the pretender's designs."

"Or, as an alternative," Mancini said eagerly, "I could have him removed from the sanctuary. Just give the command. I will have him here before you by supper."

Owen scowled.

The king noticed. "You don't approve, Owen. Even though you know the legends of the Fountain's divine protection are false?"

Owen shook his head. He tightened his lips, not sure he wanted to speak.

"Tell me," the king said.

"I'm not a child anymore," Owen said. "Yes, I know that the sexton rakes the offerings thrown into the fountains and fills your coffers with them. But even that happens at night, not in front of the people. You cannot change the rules of Wizr just because you want one piece to move four places instead of two. If you change the rules, others will do the same." Owen shook his head. "You might not like the consequences. Don't risk the deconeus speaking out against you. The people wouldn't take it well."

The king's eyes narrowed. He approached Owen and reached out to put a hand on the younger man's shoulder, like a father would to a favored son. "You speak wisdom for one so young. I trust you, Owen. Go have a discussion with Tunmore." His lips wrinkled into a sneer. "I grow more and more impatient with that man. While you are there, see if you can persuade the queen to leave sanctuary. It's been twelve years. I won't seek vengeance for the plots she has spun against me. Tell her that."

"I will, my lord," Owen said, pleased to see the king's trust in him.

The king patted him fondly on the cheek. "Get you a bath first, though. You're in need. Be quick about it, lad. I'll be sending you to the North tomorrow morn to catch a pretend king!"

♦ ♦ ♦

The best poisoners, they say, are trained in Pisan. Whoever comes to lead in that island kingdom is subject to the petty whims of the nobles who would betray their own fathers for a chance to rise in power. The diplomacy of poison is practiced there with an almost religious fervor. Even the most circumspect of princes must keep a poisoner in their employ. If only to counter those who are sent to murder them.

—Polidoro Urbino, Court Historian of Kingfountain

♦ ♦ ♦

CHAPTER FIVE

The Poisoner's Tower

Liona was still the best cook in all of Ceredigion, and she kept a jar of fresh wafers ready for those who visited the kitchen. She had always spoiled Owen horribly, which was why he liked going there.

"Bless me, child, but how you've *sprouted*!" Liona crooned, mussing up his freshly washed hair as he sat on a barrel's edge eating a wafer. "When you first came here, I didn't need a ladder to kiss your cheeks! Look at you, a man grown." She stroked the edge of his arm, smiling at him with tenderness.

Her husband, Drew, whose hair was more silver than red now, smiled fondly. "Do you still have that satchel, Owen? With all those tiles for stacking?"

Owen chuckled and nodded, dabbing a crumb from his mouth. "Of course! Only the collection has grown. Sometimes Evie and I bring them into the great hall when her grandfather is away and build our designs there."

"In the great hall?" Liona asked, surprised. "Bless me. I'd like to see that."

After Owen finished off the wafer, Liona offered him the jar again, and he eagerly took another. The kitchen looked smaller than in his memories. When he glanced at the corner where he used to play by himself, he could almost see the ghost of the little boy he had been. So shy and bashful, afraid to speak to anyone. Owen was rarely tongue-tied now, and his good looks and confidence made him approachable. There was still that solitary little boy inside him, though, and he would always prefer the company of a few to the company of many.

It felt good to be back in the kitchen with his dear friends, but there was a feeling of sadness as well. The kitchen invoked memories of Ankarette, and in so doing, freshened the hurt of losing her.

He glanced at the wall that concealed the secret door leading to the maze of tunnels that could be used to secretly navigate the palace. Through the upper window in the kitchen, he could still see the poisoner's tower, Ankarette's former home. In that tower, she had coached him in the ways of her arts and the arts of the Espion. He remembered her lessons well, but he had not ventured up there since.

Drew clapped his shoulder. "I've a tree that needs to be felled. Off I go before Berwick complains. It's great seeing you, Owen."

"Berwick's still alive?" Owen asked, chuckling. The butler had seemed ancient to Owen when he was a boy.

Liona pursed her lips. "He's got gout now and waddles when he walks. But he's determined to keep serving. Bend down so I can kiss you, my boy. I'm not fetching a stool!"

Owen complied and bent his head down. She kissed him on the forehead, patted his cheek as if he were still eight, and then bustled around the kitchen. Breathing in the comforting smells of baking bread and yeast, he sat there for a while longer, but his gaze kept returning to the secret door.

Owen scooted off the barrel and walked over to his old corner. Though he'd spent many hours playing there alone, he'd spent many more with Elysabeth Victoria Mortimer. The thought of the danger she was currently facing made him frown. If anything happened to her, he would never forgive himself for not being there. At the thought, a spark of pain shot through his chest that turned into a dull, throbbing ache. He clenched his teeth, anxious to fulfill his duties and get into his saddle again.

But first, he needed to visit a ghost.

Owen looked around to make sure no one was watching, then tripped the latch of the secret door and stole into the secret corridor beyond. He walked quickly. He wasn't afraid of being caught by the Espion now, for they all knew that the Duke of Westmarch was part of the spy ring himself. The corridor was small and dusty, and it felt more cramped than it had when he was a little boy.

Soon he was tramping up the tower steps, listening to the sigh of the wind through the arrow slits as he continued his upward trek. His heart began pounding with the effort, but it wasn't just from the physical exertion—a feeling of dread and nervousness began to bore into his heart. Was he ready to face the memories of Ankarette again? He owed so much to her—the chain of office around his neck, his arrangement with Mancini, even his continued life. Everything he was today could be ascribed to her subtle influence and care. He slowed as he reached the pinnacle of the tower. He looked forward to seeing her things—the intricate embroideries she had done, her lovely dresses—but he reminded himself that the tower room would be covered in dust.

Owen reached the door and steeled himself, his hand tightening on the latch. Sweat clung to the roots of his hair. He sighed deeply and clutched the handle and unlatched it, giving it a firm push.

He was almost blinded when he entered. The curtains had always been drawn, for Ankarette had slept during the day, but now they were wide open. He saw the outline of the bed and a few tables, but there were also things that should not be there. Gowns that hung from wooden frames, and casks of jewels that winked in the radiant light. A few pairs of slippers were arranged under the bed, a washbowl full of water, and a brush with gold strands of hair clinging to it. The room didn't smell of roses. It smelled of something more subtle . . . lavender, perhaps?

He found himself standing in the middle of the room, one hand shielding his eyes from the sunlight as he took in the change of scene. Except for the white-and-purple Wizr set, the room was not as Ankarette had left it. It belonged to someone else. Another woman.

He heard a faint scuff on the floor, the deliberate tread of someone trying to sneak up on him. His ears had always been sharp, alert to the sound of anything out of place. There was someone behind him, someone who had hidden behind the open door.

Owen jumped toward the table with the washbowl and ewer, turning as he landed. A slender arm with a dagger was thrusting at him. As he grabbed the woman's wrist, he barely had time to notice the purple powder on the blade's tip—*poison*—before she tried to strike his throat with her other hand. He warded off the blow with his free hand, not budging the hand restraining her wrist. He was fighting by instinct now, and he knew it would all be over if she stabbed him with the poisoned dagger.

She hooked her slippered foot around his heel, and he felt her body shift to trip him. Grabbing a fistful of her golden hair with the hand he'd used to block her throat jab, he shouted, "Peace! I don't want to hurt you!"

And suddenly the room was spinning and Owen landed on his back, hard, the blow knocking the wind from him. He grunted with pain, still clutching her hair, only then realizing he was holding a wig.

She stood over him, knife at the ready, her shorn hair giving her a boyish look despite the pearl-colored gown and necklace that were clearly Ankarette's.

"Hurt me?" she said disdainfully. "You flatter yourself. Stay down, boy, or you'll bleed."

Owen did not want to lose sight of that dagger, but he also wanted to get a better look at her. From his position on the floor, he could kick her legs, but he expected that she was anticipating that. Being called a *boy* was deliberately offensive, which he also thought was part of her plan. He propped himself up on his elbow, but did not try to sit.

"I'm sorry if I startled you," he gasped, trying to calm his racing heart.

"You made enough noise, but you didn't startle me at all. Now give me my hair back before you ruin it." She extended her free hand, gesturing for it.

He felt rather silly holding the wig, so he leaned forward slowly and offered it to her. She snatched it from him and then set it on the table.

She was older than him by just a few years. She was beautiful, even with the shorn hair, in a way that was calculated to drive a man to desire. Her haughty look told him she felt completely in control of the situation. It irked him to see this stranger wearing Ankarette's gown, her jewels.

Owen licked his lips, trying to keep himself calm and focused. "Can I sit up without getting stabbed? I won't attack you. You have my word."

"Turn your head to the side," she commanded. He complied, but didn't let her out of his sight. "No," she said impatiently, "turn the other way!"

He did, and her look changed immediately, wilting into surprise.

"Oh dear, you're the Duke of Westmarch," she said, then smiled. "Look who I've caught in my web."

"And who are you?" Owen asked, feeling his stomach twist and clench.

"I'm the King's Poisoner obviously," she answered. Then she lowered the dagger. "Get up, my lord. You're fortunate I didn't kill you on accident. This tower is forbidden. Even for you. And haven't you the least sense of courtesy to *knock* before entering a woman's chamber?"

Owen was flustered a moment, his cheeks turning pink. "I assure you that I believed this tower was deserted."

"Stand up, I said. You look ridiculous sprawled on the floor. I'm not going to hurt you now that I know who you are."

Owen rose cautiously to his feet, his eyes still narrowed on the purple dust on the dagger tip, but at least the blade was pointed away from him. The girl scrubbed her nails through her shorn hair, then hurled the dagger into the wooden beam on Owen's left. It made a loud thunk sound, the pommel shuddering under the force of the throw.

She held her hands open. "You are too trusting. If I had wanted to kill you, it would have been easy. Remember that in case another poisoner is sent to threaten you."

"You serve King Severn?" Owen demanded, reining in his anger.

She nodded imperiously.

"Who are you? What is your name?"

"If they wanted *you* to know that, they would have told you about me. Now if you would please get out of my tower."

Owen felt he was losing control of his anger. "This was *hers* before it was ever yours."

The girl started, giving him another look of utter surprise. "You knew about Ankarette? Ankarette Tryneowy?"

"She saved my life," Owen said fiercely, trembling slightly at the rush of feelings. It dawned on him that he should have kept his mouth shut. It was clear she had not known about his connection with Ankarette. He cursed himself.

"I see," the poisoner said in an offhand tone that was belied by the intelligent gleam of her eyes. Some of the haughtiness faded. "So you used to come up here back when you were a hostage?"

He nodded sternly, saying nothing more.

"That explains some mysteries then."

"What do you mean? What mysteries?"

"She left a note. I think it was meant for you. And one of her embroideries had your name and badge on it."

"There was a note?" Owen asked eagerly.

"Mancini has it. I only read it once, years ago. When I was brought here from . . . well, never mind that part. Now, please leave, my lord. My gown is wrinkled now, so I must change before going downstairs." She gave him another imperious, haughty look and fidgeted with the lacings of her bodice, challenging him to obey her. As a duke of the realm, he outranked her in every possible way. She should not be dismissing *him*. He could tell she had not the slightest intention of telling him what the note had said, and he would not demean himself by asking her.

"I thank you for not stabbing me," Owen said guardedly. He glanced around the room, feeling both foolish and offended. "I won't bother you again."

He turned and marched out of the tower, resisting the urge to slam the door childishly behind him. He felt at once embarrassed, flushed, and bewildered by the encounter. Why hadn't the king told him about the poisoner? Or the spymaster for that matter?

Owen fumed as he walked down the steps, realizing now that Mancini had kept something from him that he should not have. Perhaps they were training a new poisoner in case they needed to use one against someone who was Fountain-blessed.

Someone like Owen.

CHAPTER SIX

The Eel of Ceredigion

One had to look the part of a prince to be convincing in that role. As Owen rode his stallion to the sanctuary of Our Lady, followed by a few attendants, he realized he had gotten used to the stares and deference from the people milling about the streets buying mincemeat pies and muffins. His tunic was not ostentatious, but his fashionable clothes set him apart and identified him as one who should be obeyed. A woman with a small child steered the lad out of his path, speaking in low tones to the boy, training him to give way to someone who was highborn. The bucks' head badge was respected and recognized; those who saw it knew the owner of that standard was Fountain-blessed, a rare gift to anyone.

As they reached the gate, Owen saw the sanctuary men appraising him. The gate was open, so Owen dismounted and handed the reins to one of his retainers. As he marched into the yard, he stared up at the beautiful arches of the sanctuary, admiring the craftsmanship that had gone into the structure. After jogging up the steps, he approached the main door and discovered the deconeus of the sanctuary, a man by the name of Kenilworth, awaiting him with attendants.

"You honor us, my lord duke," the deconeus said ingratiatingly. "You have come to worship at the Fountain?"

Rather than wait for the man, Owen continued into the main hall. The black and white tiles on the floor had always reminded him of a giant Wizr board, and indeed, his visit here was akin to his next move in an especially long, difficult game. The deconeus hurried to keep up with him.

"Is there a particular purpose for your visit then?" the deconeus asked hurriedly. "Is all well, my lord?"

"Perfectly," Owen said in a curt, impatient voice. "Where is John Tunmore, erstwhile deconeus of Ely?"

The deconeus paled. "My lord, you *know* he has claimed sanctuary at Our Lady."

"Why else do you think I came *here* to speak to him? Fetch him at once."

"With all due speed," the deconeus answered, bowing reverently.

Owen had paused by the interior fountain in the main hall, the largest of the fountains on the grounds. There were three main jets of water accompanied by many smaller ones around the rim. The sound of the fountain was soothing, and its warbling masked the various conversations happening around the vast hall. Commoners, merchants, sailors, and even a few lesser nobles were all walking around the hall, speaking amongst themselves. Owen stared into the waters, his eyes darting to the dark coins settled on the basin floor.

Out of the corner of his eye, Owen saw the deconeus speaking to some underlings, and he felt his impatience stirring. When he was younger, Ankarette had urged him to describe the Deconeus of Ely as an eel in one of his false visions. The analogy was fitting. Owen was eager to ride north to prevent more trouble from brewing. But he knew his mission here was important. Even if there were a hundred little ways to prove this supposed prince was an imposter, the magic of the Fountain was too powerful to be ignored. If Tunmore had played a role in convincing others of the prince's legitimacy, they needed to know. Besides, it was possible he had useful information about the plot as a whole.

Deep in thought, Owen continued to stare down at the coins in the fountain. Then, beyond the dark smudges of the coins, he saw something more substantial. Yes, there was something in the waters.

It was a chest, with four sturdy iron legs, a rounded top, and a handle. The handle almost protruded from the surface of the waters, but it remained completely submerged. As Owen drew nearer to it, he saw the designs crafted into the lid and box. Eager to touch it, he tugged off his riding gloves and stuffed them into his belt, hiked up the sleeve of his tunic, and reached into the water. The iron chest was real. He rubbed his hand over it, feeling the handle lying flat against the top. There was a hasp and a lock on one side, a groove opening in it for a key. There was no key.

He felt the Fountain rush through him, triggering memories from long ago. He had seen this chest amidst the treasures the Fountain had revealed to him at the bottom of the palace cistern. The treasures consisted of casks of jewels, shields, armor, and the like. The day he and Evie had almost drowned there, he had noticed an empty space in the piles of phantom riches, a path showing where the chest had been dragged toward the opening of the cistern. So much had happened immediately after that incident, he'd almost forgotten. But now, amidst the shushing noise of the waters, he remembered it with clarity.

Over the years, he had read everything he could find about the mysterious treasures that some Fountain-blessed saw in the water, but he'd discovered very little. According to some accounts, seeing the treasures of the Deep Fathoms was a precursor to death. Others claimed the treasures were gifts or boons the Fountain granted to mere mortals. The most famous story was how King Andrew had drawn a blessed sword from the fountain waters of Our Lady. A sword he had taken out to sea with him upon his death. But Owen believed the treasure was real. He had touched it with his own hands in the cistern. And now, at this very moment, he could feel the hard edges of the chest as he groped it in the waters.

"It's considered sacrilegious to wash your hands in the fountain. If you believe in that sort of thing."

The voice caught Owen completely off guard. He had been so immersed in the memory that he had not heard Tunmore make his approach.

Owen was stooped over the waters, but he turned and straightened. John Tunmore was a tall man, and his voice betrayed a slight Northern accent. Owen had caught glimpses of him before, but they had never met in person. Tunmore was in his early fifties, and his hair was shorn almost to the skin. It was dark brown with flecks of gray. His size gave him an intimidating bearing, and he radiated a snide aura, as if he had contempt for the world in general and Owen in particular. But the sparkle in his eyes hinted that he was intrigued too.

"You wished to see me?" the Eel reminded him.

"I was not washing my hands," Owen said tautly.

"It looked like it from my perspective." His eyes narrowed, his lip curling into a barely suppressed sneer. "Or were you trying to steal a coin?"

"I leave that work for the sexton," Owen quipped. "No, I thought I saw something in the water. No matter."

"What, if I may ask?" Tunmore probed.

"I saw a chest."

"You *thought* you saw a chest," Tunmore corrected. "There clearly isn't a chest in the fountain."

"It was there, and I was about to pull it out when you startled me."

"Indeed," Tunmore said, his voice betraying a hint of uneasiness. "As you can see, it is not there now. What did you come here for, my lord?"

Owen glanced back at the water, and the chest was indeed gone. He bristled with frustration. "To speak with you," he said. "I've recently returned from Westmarch. From Occitania, actually."

"So it would seem," Tunmore said. "I heard you arrived yesterday. What news from the borderlands?" He looked like a starving man seeking crumbs from a rich man's table. Though he tried to keep his voice smooth and unconcerned, Owen could sense he was restless.

"Would it interest you to know that Lord Horwath and I sent King Chatriyon fleeing? His army was completely routed."

Tunmore's face grew visibly pale. "Indeed? What a surprise. How fortunate for you. I'm flattered you came all this way to tell me about your *exploits*."

Owen shook his head. "That's not the fortunate part, Deconeus. We found something in Chatriyon's tent. A letter."

Tunmore frowned. "Are you suggesting I wrote a letter to the King of Occitania?"

"No, I am not. It's what was *in* the letter that was so interesting." Owen tugged his belt and withdrew the letter. He had requested that one of the Espion forgers copy it during the night. To Owen's untrained eye, it looked identical to the original. He offered the letter to the other man.

Tunmore took it and pursed his lips. He opened the letter and began to devour the contents. As Owen watched the other man's eyes move over the words, he felt the subtle churn of the Fountain. It was as if a winch had turned and opened a sluice gate, rushing water into the deconeus's reserves. And Owen realized in an instant that *this* was how Tunmore fed his magic with the Fountain. It was through news, gossip, lurid intrigue, treason—the machinations of courts and politics fed him, sustained him, and gave him his power. Being trapped in the sanctuary of Our Lady had deprived him of his main sources of information. Owen's own source of power was more flexible. He derived it from stacking tiles, playing Wizr, or reading challenging works—anything that taxed his wits and made him think intently.

Owen snatched the letter from the Eel's hand and literally felt the sluice gates slam shut.

The deconeus's eyes were wide with panic, and he almost tried to grab the letter back from Owen. It was the food the hungry man craved.

"I was not . . . quite done reading that yet," Tunmore said, stammering, his hand trembling.

"I know you are Fountain-blessed," Owen said softly.

The deconeus stiffened, seemingly shocked at Owen's words. "How can you suggest such a thing? I am close to the Fountain by virtue of my office, but I assure you that your understanding of me is quite mistaken."

"And I assure you that it is not," Owen answered evenly. "Just as I am sure you know about the chest that disappeared from the fountain. You're the one who put it there. You took it from the cistern at the palace, did you not?"

Tunmore's face was white. "How could you possibly know that?" he said through clenched teeth.

"Because I too can see the treasure in the cistern, and that chest was dragged away right before you made your escape to Our Lady. And these *lies* you've written," Owen continued, holding up the wrinkled note, "will be brought to light."

Tunmore's face sank into a mask of fear and dread. He looked like a man standing on a precarious bridge, one that was about to collapse. "You have no idea, little *pup*," Tunmore whispered harshly, "what is truly happening here. What you *risk* in supporting that monster. This is not about kings and courts and Espion. There is more at stake here than you can even comprehend. You pretend to have the sight, but you see nothing!"

Just then Clark walked up to them. His face was composed and neutral, but his eyes were gleaming. There was a folded note in his hand, the wax seal broken.

"My lord, I found it," Clark said as he handed the note to Owen.

"Where did you . . . ? That is *mine*!" Tunmore blustered. He reached for the note, but Clark seized his wrist and applied pressure to a sensitive spot. Suddenly the deconeus was wobbling on his feet, his features tight with pain.

Owen took the note from Clark and opened it. As the first words met his eyes, he felt the force of the Fountain again, but this time it was as strong as a river. Before Owen could be swept away by it, he steadied himself. When he looked down at the words again, it was as if he had become a boulder dividing the river. It went around him on both sides, making him a little dizzy from the rushing noise, but it could not budge him.

"How are you *doing* that?" Tunmore snarled, staring at Owen in amazement.

"Though it is your gift to sway others, you cannot force me to believe something against my will," Owen said with scorn. "I see it clearly. You wrote the original. Now the information is being copied. The one we found in the king's tent was a copy of a copy. You're spreading lies to weaken King Severn just as you attempted to do years ago. This is misprision in the highest degree. Believe me, Deconeus, if you leave this sanctuary, you will not be thrown into a river to judge your guilt. We both know most Fountain-blessed would survive such a test. No, you will be taken to a mountaintop to freeze to death. Yes. I know *that* too!" Tunmore's face went wild with disbelief and fear.

"You are guilty of treason, and everyone who has supported you and sent you messages is also guilty. If you wish me to intercede on your behalf with King Severn, there is one piece of information you must give me this very moment. Where will this pretender's ships land? Where will they strike first? I know about Atabyrion striking the East and Occitania striking the West. Where in the North is the pretender going to land?"

Tunmore's face was like dripping wax. "Despite what you may think, I have not committed treason. It is not treason to support the *true* king."

"I may be young, but I am not a fool," Owen said sharply. "Do you think I believe any of this rubbish?" he asked, wagging the papers in front of Tunmore's face.

Tunmore shook his head. "It is not rubbish, you little upstart. *I* am the one who persuaded the king's simpering former spymaster, Bletchley, to make the princes disappear. It was always my intent to keep the throne of Ceredigion unstable until the surviving lad was old enough to take the crown himself. I've hidden him in Brugia. I've hidden him in Legault. He's been to every kingdom except his own. And he is returning, our true king! When he lands, the people will rise up and throw the tyrant into the river. You cannot stop the destiny of the Fountain, lad. You might as well try and turn a river with your hand!"

"Where is he landing?" Owen demanded.

"Even if I told you, you would not get there quickly enough," Tunmore snarled.

Blackpool.

Owen heard the whisper in his mind. Tunmore stiffened, indicating he had heard it as well. Blackpool was one of the coastal cities in the north of Westmarch, the largest trading city.

"This explains why the queen dowager hasn't been eager to leave sanctuary," Owen said rudely. "I had come with a commission from the king to pardon her. I can see now that she is also behind the plot."

"The queen is deathly *ill*," Tunmore said roughly. The tone of his voice hinted that the man did not believe the ailment was natural. In light of Owen's discovery in the tower, he wondered if Mancini was behind it.

Owen nodded to Clark, who was still gripping Tunmore's wrist. Returning the nod, Clark released the man and shoved him toward the edge of the fountain, causing him to totter and then splash into it. The man sputtered and choked, coming up dripping wet, small beads of water dripping from his short hair.

"It's considered sacrilegious to bathe in the fountain," Owen said before turning on his heel and storming out.

♦ ♦ ♦

The history of Ceredigion and the myths of the Fountain go back for almost a thousand years. Some historians have written that the Fountain myths go back even further, to the very creation of the world. They tell of a land birthed amidst ash and fire from a tumultuous sea called the Deep Fathoms. Boundaries were invoked by the great Wizrs of old to hold the Deep Fathoms at bay. The myths say that the kings of old came from the sea to learn how to tame the land. But one of those kings defiled the boundaries, and then there came a flood.

—Polidoro Urbino, Court Historian of Kingfountain

♦ ♦ ♦

CHAPTER SEVEN

The Earl's Daughter

The king's army rode north as if the hooves of their steeds were on fire. Messengers had been loosed ahead of them to warn Evie of the danger, but Owen had insisted on riding at once. After hearing what Owen had learned in his confrontation with Tunmore, Severn had not only permitted it—he'd chosen to join him. They rode like thunder and lightning, a storm that swept across the kingdom in a sea of black flags bearing the white boar.

Owen's confrontation with Tunmore played itself over and over in his mind. Facing another Fountain-blessed had been intimidating, but the young duke believed the deconeus had come away even more shaken by the encounter. He remembered Ankarette saying that Tunmore had been her mentor. The man had tutored her in the arts of deception and court intrigue, just as the king had trained Owen after Ankarette's death. But Tunmore was not the adversary he had once been; his well of magic was nearly dry, and he had been deprived of opportunities to replenish it fully.

Their company changed horses frequently to gain more ground. The king had brought five hundred men and mounted archers. It would probably not be enough to defend his kingdom, but it was more urgent to get to Blackpool quickly than it was to do so en masse. Owen's captains would be coming to Blackpool from Occitania, but they would likely not arrive for several days. However, Owen knew that the kingdom's main fortress in the North could withstand a long siege, and if they managed to trap their enemy against its walls, they could expect victory in the end.

His mind was constantly plotting and assessing the situation, thinking of ways they could defend themselves if the kingdom faced attacks on all three sides.

On midday of their third day riding north, a horseman came with news that a fleet, bearing a man who claimed to be Ceredigion's rightful king, had drawn ashore north of Blackpool. The pretender called himself King Eyric Argentine, and he had pitched Eredur's standard—the Sun and Rose—on the beach.

The look on King Severn's face was dangerous when he heard the news. He wiped his forearm across the stubble on his chin, his eyes dark with rage. "My brother's standard? Well, we will see if he deserves to *keep* it."

The messenger said at least three hundred men had disembarked from the fleet with horses, pavilions, and poleaxes.

After receiving the news, Owen and King Severn rode the remainder of the night, without rest, to reach the town of Blackpool. Owen's stomach seethed with worry. He had not suspected he would be riding into another battle so close on the heels of the previous one.

♦ ♦ ♦

Dawn found them at the beaches of Blackpool amidst the carnage of a battle.

It had ended before they arrived.

Owen sat in his saddle, gazing down at the dead men, punctured by arrows and lying in the frothing surf. Battle standards with the Sun and Rose were splayed here and there, mostly soaked, torn, and broken. His mind was still reeling from the news.

Elysabeth Victoria Mortimer had ridden to Blackpool from Dundrennan, and she had defeated the pretender's army.

Prisoners were being held in stockades at Blackpool, awaiting the king's justice. The pretender, Eyric, had escaped with the remnants of the fleet, but his army had been bested by a seventeen-year-old girl.

"My lord!" someone shouted from afar. Owen turned in his saddle to watch as a messenger wearing the lion badge of Duke Horwath hastened to him. It was Evie's chamberlain, a man named Rigby whom Owen knew well.

"Rigby!" Owen shouted in surprise, smiling at the man's obvious enthusiasm.

"My lord," Rigby said with a formal bow. "My lady awaits you and the king at the Arthington, one of the nicer inns in town. I thought it best I should tell *you* first. She's anxious to see you, my lord. I'm to fetch the king next. Go."

Owen didn't need any persuading.

His heart beat more furiously as he rode into town. The streets were in commotion, and people everywhere were waving Duke Horwath's banner of the pierced lion with jubilation. Owen quickly found the Arthington, a cheerful two-story dwelling. After entrusting his weary horse to a page, he hurried toward the common room of the inn, which had been emptied in anticipation of the king's arrival. People in the streets began to shout about the imminent arrival of Severn, and the crowds suddenly swelled and moved toward the ruler, like a river of bodies flooding the town. Cheers and acclaims rang out.

Before Owen even reached the door to the inn, it flung open. There she was on the threshold, as if stepping out of a dream. She looked like she had not slept. Her dark hair was a bit windblown, but it was freshly braided. He saw a bit of goose down woven into the braid by her left ear. As part of an ongoing jest between them, she sometimes did that to mimic the white patch in his hair. Her eyes, the same green as her gown today, were eager to find his. There was a dagger fastened to her girdle, which was new, and she had on the sturdy leather boots and scarf she always wore when they climbed up into the waterfalls together.

"Owen," she breathed, staring at him with relief, like she had been the one worrying about him all along.

She ran into his arms and hugged him so tightly it hurt, pressing her cheek against his chest and swaying slightly. After days in the saddle, nights under the stars, and rations only a soldier could eat, she felt too good to be real. She was soft and warm, and her hair smelled like home.

"Are you all right?" he demanded, grabbing her by the shoulders to look her in the face.

His eyes found the dimple at the corner of her mouth. He sometimes imagined what it would be like to kiss that dimple, but he didn't dare do it.

"Come inside—there is so much to tell you!" Evie said, hugging him once more and squeezing him even harder this time. "I was not expecting you for another day. I'm hardly presentable."

"You're hardly presentable!" Owen said in dismay. "I smell like the stables!"

"Yes, you *do*," she said, crinkling her nose. "You can bathe later. The king will want to hear this too, but I have to tell you! I don't mind saying it twice. Come with me!"

She tugged at his hand, and Owen caught sight of Justine, Evie's maid, standing just within the threshold of the inn. She was Evie's constant companion and chaperone, always there to keep the two young people from being alone. Dark-haired and rather serious, she was the daughter of Lord Camber, whose father served Horwath. Justine was the guardian of Evie's virtue, a constant and subtle reminder that, although Owen and Evie had been friends since they were children, there were certain prohibitions between the sexes.

Justine gave Owen a shy smile, as she usually did, and inclined her head in respect. He returned that smile with a nod as Evie flew past her friend and dragged Owen into the common room by the hand.

"Sit there while I tell you!" she said breathlessly, flinging him toward a large stuffed couch. Her hands were shaking a little, as if her excitement were too keen to be contained inside her body. Justine quietly took a seat in a nearby chair, folding her hands in her lap.

Owen was starving, but he was too interested in hearing Evie's story to consider eating.

"What happened?" he demanded. "When I first saw the battlefield, it made me worry even more."

She shook her head. "There's no need. The dead are Legaultan mercenaries mostly. More eager to get back to the boats than they were to fight the stout men who serve my grandfather. Many of the poor souls drowned trying to escape. So let me tell you about this imposter. I loathe the man. What fools does he take us for? His ships were sighted off the coast, so I gave the order that any who came upon them were to welcome them as if the imposter did indeed have the right to the crown."

"You did *what*?" Owen demanded, astonished.

She grinned mischievously. "How many times have we discussed history, Owen? How many princes were duped by the promises of others? This pretender is trying to dupe the world into believing he's truly Eyric Argentine! Well, two can throw dice, as Mancini likes to say. As soon as they landed, I had one of my trusted men ride into the camp to demand to know who kept the standard of the Sun and Rose. They said it was for King Eyric Argentine, who was aboard the ships. My man claimed that if Eyric came to camp, he'd be welcomed by the citizenry as the new king." She frowned. "But he was too wary. He refused to come ashore. I think he just didn't trust we were sincere. There were at least three hundred of his men ashore by this time, and more coming every hour. I knew that if I waited until all their full force had disembarked, we'd be outnumbered."

"But why aren't you at your grandfather's castle?" Owen asked. "Evie, truly! You put yourself in great danger by coming here. What if they'd caught you?"

"How sweet of you to worry about me!" she said, delighted, cupping his cheek with her warm palm. "I've been fretting, you ask Justine—she'll tell you—about you facing that snob Chatriyon and his army. You didn't let him force the Duchess of Brythonica to marry him, did you?"

"Of course not. We scattered his army in the middle of the night and sacked his camp. That's when we learned about Eyric and the threat to the North."

She nodded, sidling closer to him on the couch. "Brilliant! A night attack is very dangerous, but the rewards can be great. Ulbert IV tried that maneuver at the Battle of Cecily, remember?"

"Stop!" Owen said, laughing. "What happened? You get distracted. Tell me!" He took her hand, rubbing his thumb across her knuckles.

"I forgot where I left off," Evie said, smiling awkwardly.

"Why did you even come to Blackpool? Why not stay at the castle and prepare for a siege?"

Her brow furrowed. "Why would we let him get that far before resisting? The longer he stayed ashore, the more miscreants would rally to his banner. What would *you* have done if you'd been in the castle and heard someone was invading Westmarch?"

"Well, I would have led an army to stop him," Owen said.

"Which is exactly what I did!" she said, exasperated. "Do you think for one *moment* that my grandfather's soldiers would have let me come to harm? The fact that I'm a woman only made them more determined to come to blows with the interlopers' men. Men are eager to please when you smile and praise them," she said with a wry smile. "Except for *you*, who are a rogue and won't abide flattery." She tried to tickle his ribs, but he blocked her with his arms.

"Mistress, the king is here," Justine urged in a small voice.

Owen wanted to take advantage of this last moment alone together by wrapping Evie in his arms and kissing her. The eager look in her eye and the way she sat so near him told him she wanted that too. But he was so travel-stained and sweaty, and the timing was not right. No, their first kiss should happen at the waterfalls near her grandfather's castle. On the bridge, perhaps, when the snow on the peaks changed color near sunset. That was what she deserved.

He rose from the comfortable couch and extended his hand to her. She gazed up at him, smiling coyly at his show of gallantry, and then accepted his hand. Her eyes had been green when he'd first seen her, but now they looked a peaceful blue. Maybe she was a water sprite, as Mancini had often joked. All Owen knew was that she had some kind of magic that made him ache inside.

"I'm glad you are safe," Evie whispered, looking at him with brooding, worried eyes.

He almost brought her fingers to his lips, but a soldier opened the front door of the inn just then, and Owen saw Severn striding toward it. The king's boots were mud-spattered, but he looked elated at the victory at Blackpool.

Owen used those last moments before the king entered the room to squeeze Evie's fingers gently and give her a tender smile. "You were brilliant," he confessed, winking at her.

She flushed with pleasure at the compliment and turned to curtsy to King Severn. Owen bowed formally beside her.

"My lord," Evie said. "You are the true sovereign of Ceredigion. Your people were faithful to you. I wish I could have delivered up the pretender in person, but he was too afraid to come ashore and face me in battle. 'Tis a pity, for I would have liked to beat him. In the language of Wizr, I believe the *threat* has been *blocked*."

The king looked at her with satisfaction; his gray eyes were lit with gratitude. "Well done, Lady Mortimer. Lady Elysabeth Victoria Mortimer, pardon me," he added, seeing she was about to correct him. "You've shown great sense, bravery, and pluck, and you will be rewarded. I promise you that. To also use the parlance of Wizr, you have proven you are more than a pawn. I best make good use of you then. Tell me all that happened. Leave nothing out."

♦ ♦ ♦

The Duke of North Cumbria oversees a vast land in Northern Ceredigion. It is a land of towering mountains wreathed with snow and ice. There are glaciers there that are older than time and riddled with ice caves from the melt. I have spoken to the palace mapmaker, who informs me that the river feeding Kingfountain comes from this land of ice and snow. The winters in North Cumbria are harsh, and there is little travel in or out during those months. The people are used to it. They are hardy folk with a queer dialect not dissimilar to that of Atabyrion. There is belief that Atabyrion was once part of Ceredigion. The lands are only separated by narrow gaps of water. The Dukes of the North have been loyal to the Argentines for generations. King Severn himself was raised in the North when his uncle Warrewik governed the land from the mighty stronghold of the North. The fortress is called Dundrennan.

—Polidoro Urbino, Court Historian of Kingfountain

♦ ♦ ♦

CHAPTER EIGHT

Dundrennan

Owen could hear the fire in the hearth crackling and feel the warmth of its flames on his shoulders. But his eyes were fixed on the Wizr board. It was the beautiful, handcrafted set that King Severn had given to him when he was eight years old. And this time he was playing the king himself.

Severn's eyes were as gray as storms as he bent over the board, his gaze intense and his lips pressed hard together. He was losing. Again. Owen knew it rankled the king that a seventeen-year-old could best him half the time. Sometimes Owen let him win and the king would look at him suspiciously, never certain if his victory had been hard-won or yielded out of graciousness.

"Hold nothing back," Severn admonished him, bringing forward a piece shaped like a knight on horseback. The king's free hand fidgeted with his dagger. "If I win, I want to earn it."

The king let go of the piece.

When Owen played Wizr, he deliberately kept his face neutral. He had learned from playing with Evie that he tended to smile when his opponent was about to make a mistake. She used to keep watch on his mouth from start to finish, which had lost him plenty of games. He had trained himself not to give anything away.

Owen lifted his hand and moved his Wizr piece forward from across the board. "Threat and . . . defeat." *Then* he smiled.

The king's face darkened with a scowl. "By the Fountain!" he growled. "Do you use your gift of second sight in games? Who taught you to play so well?"

Owen met the king's gaze, but he dared not reveal the truth. That he had been taught to play Wizr by a woman the king had feared would poison him.

"Never lose sight of the Wizr," Owen said with a hint of smugness. "But as a practical matter, my lord, I'm just very good at this game."

The king snorted and chuckled. "When I said hold nothing back, I didn't realize it would be prophetic. You have a keen mind, Owen. Do you agree, my dear?" he said, addressing Evie. "I would like to see the two of you play Wizr."

Evie was curled up on the couch near Owen, her nose in a book. She did not look up as she turned the page. "Why do you think he is so good, my lord? He plays against *me*."

The king chuckled at her haughty tone and then stood, wincing as he came to his feet. He limped to the huge window and watched the fluffy flakes of snow coming down. His expression softened as he ran his hand across the pane of glass, and the gray skies above chased away the shadows on his face. Though it was not yet winter, the mountains were notorious for bizarre snowstorms that could strike unpredictably.

Owen sorted the pieces and returned them to their wooden box. He stared at Evie, who seemed to sense his attention and shifted her eyes back to his. She was giving him her *I'm proud of you* look, then winked at him and returned to her book.

"I have many a fond memory of Dundrennan," the king said in a brooding voice, still staring out the window at the gentle snow. He turned away, folding his arms and leaning against the crook on the wall near the window seat. "I used to play Wizr in this very room with my cousin, Nanette." His voice fell as he mentioned the name of his dead wife. "As children, we'd catch snowflakes on our tongues. I think every child does that." He chuckled softly to himself, and Owen felt he could see the oozing wounds of the king's heart.

Evie put the book down, her attention drawn to the king's raw grief. The light from the window made his black hair look like it was glowing. He stared down at the rushes that covered the floor, lost in a storm of memories.

"How old was she when she married the Prince of Occitania?" Evie asked. It was a sensitive question to pose. Lady Nanette's short first marriage was likely a bitter memory for him.

The king's eyes were as sharp as sword blades. His mouth twisted in shape, the expression somewhere between a smile and a frown. "You know your history, my dear. Many have forgotten those dark years. Those months my brother and I spent in exile in Brugia. Those months she spent married to that *princeling*." His voice was so thick with scorn that Owen could see the wound had not fully healed. "She was seventeen."

Owen glanced at Evie, who was the same age that Nanette had been. The possibility of losing her to another man made him grow warm with anger.

"It was a marriage that would have made her Queen of Occitania," Evie said. "But it was a reckless match. Your uncle lost his life because of it."

"We all lost much that year," the king said bitterly. "And gained much. She lost her father and the throne of Occitania. And she gained another husband and the throne of Ceredigion. For a time."

There was so much hurt in his voice that Owen wanted to steer the conversation away from such painful waters. Evie's eyes were full of so much sympathy, she looked liable to go hug the king.

"You have not married again, my lord," she whispered softly. "Is it because you truly loved her?"

Owen gaped at her audacity, but she was one who tended to jump into cisterns without a second thought. Perhaps it should not have surprised him.

The king looked taken aback, but he did not appear offended. He folded his arms across his chest and walked away from the window. "Aye, I loved her," he said, breaking into a subtle Northern accent, as if honoring the memory of his late wife. "You can imagine it was awkward between us at first. We were raised together in this very place, this idyllic mountain valley. Dundrennan. I fought her father and bested him. I fought her husband, that little *princeling*, and bested him not far from Tatton Hall, where he was trying to escape back to Occitania. Scampering away like Chatriyon." He chuckled mercilessly, glancing at Owen. "You've made an enemy there, Lord Kiskaddon. No king likes losing a game of Wizr. And losing a fight is every bit more galling. But I see how you play the game. You're more than a match for that runt."

She was not to be deterred. "But why haven't you remarried, my lord?" she pressed. "It's been ten years since your lady died. You have no heir. Surely it is time to set aside your grief?" Her look was sad but sincere, and very sympathetic.

The king stared at her for a moment. "You do speak your mind," he said with a chuckle. "And like a dog with a bone, it won't be wrested from you."

She dimpled slightly. "If I'm being too presumptuous, forgive me. But I cannot believe your council hasn't mentioned this to you."

"My council!" he snorted with a bark-like laugh. "They wanted me to force the Duchess of Brythonica into a marriage alliance. She's of an age with you and Owen." He wrinkled his nose in disgust. "It has been forty years, this month, since I received the water rite and my name. How could I look on the duchess . . . and not see *you*, Elysabeth Victoria Mortimer?" He frowned deeply, shaking his head. "No, my council has not yet persuaded me to take a wife. It is customary, you know, for a king to marry the princess of another realm. My brother's choice of a bride offended many, including my uncle, who committed treason because of it."

He paced as he spoke, his voice throbbing with strong emotion. "Let me count the options. They are few. Save for the Duchess of Brythonica, there are no princesses in Occitania. Chatriyon has been vying for her himself, as Owen can attest. She has made it perfectly clear she wants nothing to do with him. She rules in her own right, and I cannot blame her for not yielding to a man who wants her domain perhaps more than he wants her hand. Even if Chatriyon were to succeed in marrying her, they will not produce children for several years, so there are no prospects for me there. And to boot, the duchess *fears* I am a child murderer and a misbegotten demon. *That* tree of opportunity is quite barren."

He took another step, using his fingers to tally. "Let us move on to Atabyrion. King Iago is nineteen years old and unmarried himself. He has many damsels to choose from in his own realm, the Earl of Huntley's daughter, Kathryn, is the most beautiful in Mancini's estimation, but he wishes to expand his domain rather than empowering one of his nobles even more. Iago Llewellyn would also love to woo the duchess if he could, but his domains are even smaller than Occitania's. Then there is Brugia. There was no legitimate heir, so the many princes of that realm are preoccupied with slaughtering each other in an effort to unify the realm. I could throw the gauntlet down and marry one of their daughters, but that will entangle me in wars, over land that I care nothing for, and irk a possible ally. I think Duke Maxwell to be the likely victor. He is shrewd, cunning, and utterly ruthless." He rubbed his hands together vigorously. "Pisan . . . too small. That leaves Genevar, which earns its coins trading and exploring. The council once tried to persuade me to marry my niece, Lady Elyse, but that would cause no end of trouble for me. Besides, it would repulse my subjects if I were to marry my brother's daughter, whom I disinherited. To be honest, my dear . . . I have very few options, and all of them are unsavory to me. Is there anyone I am missing, my dear? Do *you* have any suggestions?"

She looked crestfallen and sad. "I . . . I don't, my lord."

"Then I trust you will not *pester* me about this again," he said with just enough of a barb to sting. His mood was always mercurial, and Owen could see the anger thrumming through him now. It was common for countries to seal alliances with marriage. That none had tried or dared to offer one with Severn Argentine had to rankle.

The king turned back to the window. "Well, I'll be blessed by the Fountain," he said, his expression changing. "Your grandfather has ridden through a storm to get here."

♦ ♦ ♦

Before long, after a greeting delivered amidst a chorus of barking hounds, Duke Horwath was sitting in his favorite chair in front of the crackling hearth, savoring the mug of steaming broth in his hand. His cloak was dripping from a hook nearby, the plops sizzling when they hit the warm stone floor. The snow was melting from the cloak, and chunks of ice pattered off it.

Evie knelt by her grandfather's chair, her face beaming with relief. He looked haggard and uncomfortable, but he did not complain, and the lines of weariness were slowly fading from his face.

Horwath rested his hand on the girl's on the thick armrest, patting gently. "I heard what you did at Blackpool, child," he said with warm affection. He patted her again. "You've my blood in you!"

She beamed at the soft-spoken praise and picked some dust or lint from his doublet. "You left me in *charge*, Grandfather. I didn't want to disappoint you."

He chuckled softly, then hooked his hand around her neck and pulled her close, kissing her hair in a mark of tender affection that made Owen swallow. How he wished he could be that open in his feelings for her.

Then Horwath tipped her chin up and gazed into her eyes. "You are beautiful. And the king is proud of you." He looked over at Owen. "He's proud of you *both*. He couldn't ask for more loyal young people to serve him. Mark my words. You two are special. And you will both make Ceredigion stronger. I know you will."

Owen felt his heart burning with pride. He walked up to the other side of the duke's chair, glancing down at Evie. She looked so beautiful at that moment, the firelight shimmering in her dark hair, her eyes glowing with happiness. There was that familiar ache again, that growing impatience.

"The king was surprised you rode through the snow," Evie said with an impish smile. "I think he's forgotten he's from the North as well."

Horwath smiled as he stroked his gray goatee. "He'll never forget that, lass. Not until the waters stop falling at Kingfountain. He has ice in his veins, as we like to say. Even young Kiskaddon here is a little frostbitten, I think. What say you, lad?"

Owen folded his arms, still gazing down at Evie. "I do love the North," he murmured.

Her cheeks flushed a little, and she couldn't hold back a grin.

The grizzled duke took one of her hands and then one of Owen's, and for a moment, he looked as if he would join them together.

"It's my deepest wish," he said huskily, "to unite our houses and duchies. Before the king rides back to the palace, I plan to petition him for a boon. But only if you both are still willing." He smiled wryly. "I've seen the way you look at each other. I'm old, not blind. I'd like to speak to the king on your behalf, Owen. He may take it better coming from me. But I didn't want you to be startled in case he asks about your feelings." His smile slipped a little. "His heart is so wounded, he may not have noticed the signs as I have."

From the look on Evie's face, Owen could tell she was trying to quell her excitement and enthusiasm. He could tell she wanted to burst out with her answer, but she was waiting for Owen to say something first.

"I would prefer to ask him myself," Owen said, still looking at her, his heart so full he almost couldn't speak.

Evie jumped to her feet and into his arms, quivering with joy. It was only when he felt the wetness on his neck that he realized she was crying.

♦ ♦ ♦

After the defeat at Blackpool, King Severn sent warships to ravage the coast of Legault. They are on the hunt for the pretender's ship. Their orders are to punish the Legaultans and prevent them from creating a safe haven for the pretender. A sizable reward has been offered for the capture of the man masquerading as Eyric Argentine, the lost son of King Eredur. I think it is far more likely that the pretender has sought haven elsewhere. The question is—which of the king's enemies would shelter him?

—Polidoro Urbino, Court Historian of Kingfountain

♦ ♦ ♦

CHAPTER NINE

The Duchess's Warning

Owen walked with Severn across the bailey to where the king's horse awaited him. The host of riders all wore the badge of the white boar and one carried a spear with a pennant that flapped in the cold wind. Their boots crunched on the thin cakes of snow in the yard. The king seemed invigorated by the cold, and there was no sign of a limp as he walked.

"My lord," Owen asked, clearing his throat.

"What is it?" the king asked curtly, scanning the feathery clouds that crowned the massive mountains to the north.

A groomsman positioned a mounting block as they neared the king's charger, and Severn swung up effortlessly into the saddle. The horse grunted with familiarity, and the king stroked his neck, smiling fondly at the beast.

Owen felt a tightening in his chest, a familiar sensation he had rarely experienced since childhood. His tongue became swollen in his mouth, preventing the words from coming out.

"Well?" the king demanded, his brows knitting. His gloved hand tightened on the reins.

"It's a small matter," Owen stammered, feeling a blush creep to his cheeks. By the Fountain, why did he have to get tongue-tied still!

"I'm not interested in small matters," the king said petulantly. "We must away. Now that Horwath has returned to the North, I'd like you to return to Kingfountain in a fortnight. No more. I don't think this pretender will strike the North twice, now that we've disrupted his plan. It is getting nearer to winter." He gazed up at the clouds again. "Although here it is always winter. I miss it." He looked down at Owen sternly. "A fortnight. No more. Then come."

"I will, my lord," Owen said, chafing with impatience.

The king nodded in dismissal and then yanked on the reins of the charger. There was a thunder of hooves as the king's soldiers rode out of the bailey. Owen gazed up at the battlement wall, where he saw Duke Horwath wrapped in a bearskin cloak, arms folded imperiously. His stern look implied he had discerned from afar that the conversation had failed to happen. Owen's cheeks mottled with discomfort as he listened to the sound of the clacking hooves change once the horses crossed the drawbridge and hit the cobbles. Even if he had not ridden in with the king, he would have instinctively known Severn was traveling with a hundred men from the sounds made by the party.

Turning, he walked back across the bailey amidst the grooms who brought shovels and barrows to begin clearing away piles of steaming manure. He hated the sound the shovels made in the muck and stone, so he quickened his step.

He found Evie in the solar, pacing nervously. The look on his face gave him away before he could say a word. He felt sick inside, wounded that he had let her down.

Justine glanced up from her needlework, her black hair hanging over her shoulder. She looked at Owen, also saw the unspoken news, and a small frown twisted her mouth.

"I *knew* I should have gone with you," Evie said darkly, her eyes suddenly an intense shade of green.

Owen shrugged helplessly.

♦ ♦ ♦

The snows vanished by midday, and Evie suggested they leave the stifling solar and walk amongst the mountains. Owen had spent the morning arranging over two thousand tiles that he was not yet ready to topple, so he agreed to the plan. He too was restless. So, pausing only to grab their cloaks and their chaperone, they ventured onto the mountain trails that led to majestic views of the valley floor. Owen's legs were tired, but he loved the firmness and steadiness of the rocks and cliffs, and years of experience had inured him to the alpine air and the rigors of a long hike. The air was crisp and redolent with the lovely scents of nature. Part of the trail was rugged and steep, with switchbacks broken in after centuries of use. They could hear the distant roar of the huge valley waterfalls as they moved.

Owen and Evie walked side by side, and he kept glancing at her, enjoying the way her eyes were shining with joy as they passed the mountain flowers and pines. They had to stand aside as a shepherd drove his flock down the trail, pressing their backs into the craggy wall to leave room for the bleating woolly beasts. Owen's shoulder brushed against Evie's, and he felt the point where they touched as if it burned his skin. Justine was on her other side, lower down the trail, and she sighed a little at the delay.

Shifting his position a little, Owen felt Evie's fingers brush his. She glanced up at him, her tender look telling him she forgave him for his earlier blunder. He felt one of her fingers hook around his and his heart began to hammer wildly in his chest. His mouth went dry.

Taking the hint, Owen grasped her hand, which he found surprisingly warm. Justine could not see their clandestine act, and Owen relished the feeling of her fingers mingled with his. A pleased smile crossed her lips, making her look even more beautiful. A burly sheep waddled past, brushing against them both, and Evie sidled a little closer to Owen to give the beast more room to pass. Once again, Owen felt the urge to kiss her. He had been thinking about that so often lately.

After the sheep passed, they continued down the mountain trail, their hands occasionally touching. Evie was an endless source of chatter.

"Do you remember the night we ambushed Ratcliffe with that pillow fight?" she asked with a wicked laugh. "How the down stuck to his sweaty bald head?"

"And he started to choke on the feathers while trying to scold us?" Owen added with a grunt of laughter.

"I *still* laugh at the memory," she said lightly. "To be a child again. I still want to dance around the fountain's edge and fall into the water."

"That would be unseemly, my lady," Justine broke in.

"I know! But when you're little, you can get away with so much more. We are only seventeen and now we have to *pretend* to be older. I admit there are certain pleasures at our age—going to festivals and tournaments. I can't wait to see you at your first one, Owen!" She bumped into his arm deliberately. "I've seen you practice in the training yard. You always catch the rings on your lance, and you make the sword master wheeze because you drive him so hard."

"I make him wheeze because he has an arthritic knee," Owen said, scooping down to pick up a stone, which he then hurled off the trail down into the valley. He watched it arc and then plummet.

"That could hit a peasant, you know," Evie scolded.

"He might take it as a sign from the Fountain to mend his ways," Owen retorted.

"How do you know Clifford has an arthritic knee?" she asked. "I've not seen him limp."

Owen shrugged. "I just know."

That wasn't entirely true. Owen's gifts from the Fountain had manifested in multiple ways. He had a keen sense of hearing, and his eyes noticed weaknesses of all varieties. It happened when he played

Wizr—he could see the weaknesses in his opponent's defenses just from looking at the board—and it also happened in the training yard. Even though Clifford was so much more experienced, Owen frequently bested him. He knew that the older man's left knee was injured and aching, so he always forced him to defend on that side. The flow of the Fountain also ensured that Owen always knew where to put his lance to catch the ring. He had gained a reputation for his skills with sword and shield. He did not wish to disabuse people of their notions, but he knew the praise wasn't truly earned. It felt like cheating.

As soon as they returned to Dundrennan after their long hike, they were approached by Owen's herald, Farnes.

"What is it?" Owen asked the older man, seeing the worried look in his eyes.

"We have guests," Farnes announced, bowing formally to Owen. "There is a lawyer here from Averanche who wishes to see you. He was escorted by one of the Duchess of Brythonica's knights, who happens to be your new neighbor. One of Roux's men."

"When did they arrive?" Evie asked.

"Shortly after you both left," Farnes said, sniffing. "They've been awaiting your return for several hours."

"I never get a moment's peace," Owen said to Evie, shrugging. "Let me change first, and then I'll meet them . . . in the solar?"

"Very well, my lord," Farnes said, bowing again.

"Odd that he's come all this way," Evie whispered to Owen. "Do you think he's spying on us?"

"Which one?" Owen asked. "The lawyer or the knight?"

"Both," she answered.

They separated to change clothes, and Owen picked one of his more princely costumes. When hiking in the mountains, he opted for comfort and warmth rather than fashion. He changed into a stylish dark-blue velvet doublet with ribbed sleeves. As he looked at himself in the mirror, he tugged on the collar of his shirt and gave himself a self-assured grin. Then, satisfied that he looked the part, he walked to the solar.

The lawyer was a handsome younger man, probably in his early thirties. If his relaxed demeanor was any indication, he was apparently used to traveling long distances. He was wandering around the room and sampling from a platter of various roasted nuts. The knight, on the other hand, was stiff and straight and nearly seven feet tall. He was older than the lawyer, and his hair was arranged in the Occitanian fashion of being combed forward. He had a stiff, high collar and an overly long belted tunic, which again paid homage to his country of origin. Owen gave the knight a disdainful look, feeling a preternatural sense of enmity for that kingdom and its fashions.

"Greetings, my lord," said the lawyer. "My name is Julliard. I serve the mayor of Averanche, who bids you great kindness. I am here on a *delicate* matter, if you will. The lord mayor was attainted of treason for surrendering Averanche to you. King Chatriyon has summoned the lord mayor to the palace to stand trial for his crime."

Owen wrinkled his brow. "That is presumption," he answered with a hint of sarcasm. "The entire land of Averanche and its surroundings was once part of Ceredigion. So was Brythonica, if I recall my history lessons." Owen glanced at the knight to see if he would react to the poke.

The knight said nothing and did not lose his mask of composure.

"Yes, indeed!" said Julliard. "That is why my lord sent me—to be sure you intend to . . . ahem . . . *maintain* your claim on Averanche. The King of Occitania sent an ambassador to negotiate a pardon with the lord mayor if he will return to the fold. So to speak."

Evie entered the solar, followed by Justine. She glanced at the two visitors curiously.

Owen nodded her over. "Gentlemen, this is Lady Elysabeth *Victoria* Mortimer, the duke's granddaughter." Then he gave her a conspiratorial look. "Chatriyon has charged the mayor of Averanche with treason, and now he's trying to bribe him with a pardon to win him back."

She nodded and slowly paced around the room while Justine found her favorite seat and began embroidering again.

"And why are you here, sir knight?" Owen asked, clasping his hands behind his back and looking up at the hulking figure. As he stared at the man, he silently sent out a little trickle of magic to probe him for weaknesses. The thought of fighting someone so huge terrified him.

Owen's magic was like water, for it could find the tiniest chinks and cracks. He saw immediately that the huge knight was blind in his right eye. He noticed the puckered scar hidden by a shaggy eyebrow. He was completely vulnerable to attacks on that side. Add a helmet, and he would be even more hampered. Owen smiled to himself and released the magic. He felt the loss of the power, but there was still much in his reserves, which he had filled earlier by organizing his tiles.

"I am here on orders of Marshal Roux," the knight said in a thick Occitanian accent. "My name is Loudiac."

"Welcome to North Cumbria, Sir Loudiac," Owen said, nodding.

The knight bowed formally. "My master bids me to tell you there are lands in dispute between Averanche and Brythonica."

"I was just getting to that," the lawyer broke in, but Loudiac gave him a scowl sour enough to silence him.

"I think it's important that I understand these disputes," Owen said, nodding to Loudiac to proceed.

"The duchess has several royal forests that she has reserved for hunting. Because of a history of poachers, there are sharp penalties for intruders."

"And by *sharp*, do you mean arrows or spears?" Owen asked with a grin.

Sir Loudiac bristled at the informality of Owen's banter. "The duchess has seven such forests in her realm. One is also claimed by

Averanche. There have been incidents in the past. The King of Occitania likes to hunt. Do you, my lord?"

Owen gave the lawyer a curious look.

"My lord," Julliard said. "Occitania has always sought to enlarge its hegemony."

"As most princes do," Owen said knowingly.

"Yes, so what Sir Loudiac says is true. There have been disputes about the royal forests when the King of Occitania would illegally hunt in the duchess's forests, thus causing strife. It challenges her authority in her own dominions and threatens the borders of Brythonica. There have inevitably been accidents."

Owen pursed his lips. "What sort of accidents?"

"The duchess will defend her territory," Sir Loudiac said sternly. "I was sent to warn you not to follow in King Chatriyon's footsteps. It would only cause needless contention."

"I see," Owen said. "And your master, Marshal Roux, sent you to warn me? Or was it the duchess?"

"They speak with one voice, my lord," said Loudiac grimly. "He was her father's most trusted lord, and he protects Brythonica on her behalf."

"Well, then," Owen said, turning toward Julliard. "Tell the lord mayor that I am quite ready to defend my new territory. He has proven his loyalty by revealing the offer of a pardon, so please thank him on my behalf. You may go."

The lawyer looked startled, surprised. "I . . . I thank you, my lord, for being decisive. By your leave. When shall I tell the lord mayor you intend to next visit Averanche?"

"I have no idea," Owen said with a short laugh. Then he nodded curtly for the man to leave, which he did.

He turned his gaze to the massive knight. "I do not seek a quarrel with my new neighbor," Owen said in a low voice.

"Not yet," the knight said in a tone that could almost be called a sneer.

Owen chuffed a bit at that. "I don't care for the sport of hunting. I'm stronger at playing Wizr. Does your master like to play?"

The knight nodded slowly, warily.

"Excellent," Owen said. "I would like to challenge him to a match upon our next meeting."

The knight's mouth betrayed a smile of approval. "I will issue your challenge to him."

"Farewell, then. I'm sorry you had to travel all this way to deliver your message. Or should I say . . . your *warning*."

Sir Loudiac smiled warily. "The trip was not wasted."

"Sir Loudiac," Evie said, eyes narrowed curiously. "There was a duchess of Brythonica many generations ago. Her name was Constance."

"Aye, my lady. You know our history well."

"She married the first Argentine king's third son. They had a child, a son, whom she used to try and claim the right to rule Ceredigion. Does Her Highness still press this claim?"

Sir Loudiac's smile faded. "That was many hundreds of years ago, my lady. We Brythonicans have since learned that the *men* of Ceredigion are not known for keeping their promises."

"You are *bold* to say it," Owen muttered under his breath.

Sir Loudiac bowed to them both and then stomped his way to the door.

After he was gone, Owen gave Evie a curious look. "You have a knack for remembering stories. I had not thought of Constance and Goff. That was back at the beginning of the Argentine dynasty, you say?"

Evie nodded. She looked very somber. "The very beginning. Ours is a kingdom where the stories keep repeating themselves over and over. It's odd, Owen. It's almost as if history were a waterwheel that keeps coming back to the same point in the river."

"Why do you say that?" Owen pressed. Justine looked up as he approached Evie near the table.

"Constance and Goff had a son they named Andrew, who should have been king. But his uncle claimed the throne for himself. And he put the young man to death."

Owen felt his skin crawl. "How . . . how old was Andrew?"

She blinked up at him, her eyes a mix of green and gray. "Our age."

CHAPTER TEN

King of Atabyrion

The king had given Owen a fortnight to remain in North Cumbria. But not even a fortnight was permitted, as events in the world began to unravel.

Owen was fighting in the training yard with Clark from the Espion. He liked practicing with Clark because the man had no chronic weaknesses, meaning Owen did not have his usual easy advantage. In his late twenties, he was strong and fit and had been training his entire life, which gave him the grace and skill to help Owen improve. In addition, he taught Owen how to fight with daggers, how to block with elbows and forearms, how to trip a man and wrestle him to the ground. He was bigger than Owen, so he usually won.

The two men were taking a rest, dripping with sweat, when a messenger arrived in the training yard. As he approached, he made a subtle hand gesture identifying himself as part of the Espion. Though he was not old by any means, he had dark brown hair with streaks of premature silver.

"What is it, Kevan?" Clark asked. The Espion saw Owen and nodded to him as well.

"I have news from Mancini," Kevan said as he approached them.

"For both of us?" Clark demanded, his frown deepening.

"Aye. You are both wanted back at court immediately. The king wants Lady Mortimer to come too."

Owen looked between Clark and Kevan in surprise. "Evie?"

"The very one," the man said with a chuckle. "Mancini requested her specifically."

"What for? Do you know?"

"Well, something is afoot," Kevan said. He looked around cautiously, making sure no one else was close enough to overhear. "Duke Horwath isn't to know everything, but I was told to share the full truth with you. The king is sending her on a mission to Atabyrion."

Owen's stomach dropped suddenly. "Whatever for?"

"It's a mission requiring some modicum of diplomacy," Kevan said. "She's an earl's daughter, and she's of an age. The king is taken with her sharp wit, her bravery, and her studies, so he's sending her to negotiate a truce with Atabyrion's king, Iago Llewellyn. King Severn has already spent too many resources defending against an attack that didn't come from the east as we were expecting. That's what I'm to tell the duke. But the true story is this. Mancini found evidence that the pretender may in fact be the son of a fisherman in Brugia. A cub by the name of Piers Urbick." Kevan looked around again and then dropped his voice even lower. "My lord duke, the king wants you to go to Atabyrion too. In disguise. We have reason to believe this Urbick fellow is hiding in Atabyrion. Lady Mortimer discusses an alliance. You fetch the lad. We'll tell Duke Horwath that you will go in disguise as added protection for his granddaughter. The king trusts you, my lord, to figure out what needs to be done in a place that he can't go himself. That's your mission, and my mission was to tell you. You will get more information at the palace. For now, you are *both* Horwath knights escorting her ladyship and her maid to Kingfountain," he said, shaking his finger at Clark and Owen.

♦ ♦ ♦

It was strange for Owen to wear the tunic of the Duke of Horwath. He hadn't realized how much of his own sense of self derived from his dukedom's badge until now. He wore it still, hidden beneath his chain hauberk and tunic. It was exciting to be in disguise, though, and as a knight wearing a chain hood, he was nameless, faceless, and practically invisible.

Of course, Evie was wild with eagerness to embark on her secret mission to Atabyrion. She had never left Ceredigion before. Justine was cautious and worried, as she tended to be, but it did little to douse her companion's spirits. Evie gave instructions for what books she wanted packed, which gowns and jewels she would wear to the court of Iago Llewellyn. But those items would be sent by cart. She was determined to ride to Kingfountain on horseback rather than be trundled along with the baggage.

There were no secrets between Evie and Owen, so he had shared the part of the message that he was supposed to keep to himself. The journey from Dundrennan to Kingfountain took five days, and though Evie attempted to convince the others to spend one of the nights camping, they stayed at comfortable inns along the way to ease the burden of the journey.

They reached Kingfountain and found everything as chaotic as Owen had expected. His heart was churning with emotions and excitement. He had always wanted to take an adventure, and the idea of traveling with *her*, of being truly alone and away from court and their lives in Ceredigion, was sweeter than treacle. As they crossed the bridge leading to the palace, he saw the ships docked at the lower portion of the falls and wondered which vessel would be taking them across the sea.

They arrived with pomp and fanfare and were ushered into the throne room to see the king, who was pacing, limping slightly, and brooding. Owen saw the king's niece, Elyse, sitting on a nearby bench, her eyes puffy and swollen from crying. His heart panged to see her this upset, particularly since he had not seen her in many months, but she did not give him a second look as he entered. His disguise saw to that.

"My lord," Evie said with a gracious and formal curtsy. "I am here at your command to do your bidding."

Justine curtsied as well, not daring to look the king in the eye.

Mancini was leaning against the fireplace. His pose was all easy relaxation, but Owen noticed he did not sip from the goblet in his hand.

"Leave us," the king ordered his servants, dismissing the cupbearers and butlers and hangers-on. Lady Elyse started to rise as well, but the king curtly shook his head, gesturing for her to stay.

In a few moments, the hall had been cleared for the king, except for the new arrivals, Mancini, and Elyse. The king sighed deeply, then turned to Owen.

"Take off the hood, lad," he said with a chuckle. "Even *I* hardly recognize you with it. If I, who know you so well, am deceived . . ." He stopped, his lips quivering. He glanced at Elyse, his eyebrows knitting with worry, but a warm, welcoming smile had spread across her face at the sight of Owen's face.

"I will be honest with you all," the king continued. "Things are difficult right now. The attack at Blackpool has the people talking. And thinking." He continued to pace, looking down at the ground, tapping his lips with his black glove. "I haven't been this vulnerable since before Ambion Hill." He wiped his mouth. "Every day, Mancini and his Espion are finding new traitors. I haven't acted on them yet. He bids me to refrain."

"If you act too soon, my liege," Mancini said deftly, "the others will go underground. I'm pulling in the nets slowly, lest I lose more fish before the rope cinches."

"Who?" Owen said, feeling his blood boil.

"My own chamberlain," the king said bitterly. "When I found out, I nearly threw him into the river myself. I've rewarded that man. I've trusted him. And he's betrayed me." The king's eyes turned to molten silver. "But I heed you, Mancini. Your advice has been sound. Know who the traitors are before acting. That is one reason I cannot go to Atabyrion myself. That is why I must trust *you*." His gaze fell on Evie and a proud smile stretched across his mouth. "You've proven you have courage, my dear. You are sensible. Polidoro tells me you know the history of our kingdom better than anyone, including himself. You know the history of our troubles with Iago Llewellyn's father. Your *grandfather* and I defeated him last time."

"I know," Evie said, clearly chafing with excitement. "I am ready to perform any service I can, my lord. You wish me to negotiate a truce? To cease hostilities between Iago and yourself? To convince him to break the alliance he made with Occitania?"

"Indeed," the king said. "But there is more."

Her eyebrows lifted curiously.

"This is a game of Wizr I intend to win," the king said. "A strong alliance with Atabyrion would change things in my favor. Iago has asked me, repeatedly, to provide him with a marriage partner befitting his rank. Who he has asked for . . . well, it's not possible . . ." He could only mean Elyse. It made sense that he would not support such a union. Any offspring they had could be used to make a claim for the throne of Ceredigion.

"The lad is ambitious and reckless," the king continued. "He needs someone to tame him. If I'm to have a partner to watch my flank, I need to be able to rely on that partner. Can I count on your loyalty, Elysabeth Victoria Mortimer?"

Her lip trembled. "Count . . . count on me for what, my lord?"

"I have ulterior motives for sending you to negotiate this truce with Iago."

Owen's stomach was turning over and over as he realized the direction the current was headed. He deduced what the king was going to say next. He saw what was happening, but felt as powerless against it as he had been to speak his truth to the king before Severn left the North. He wanted to cry out a warning, but he knew he could not.

"What would you have me do?" Evie asked in confusion.

Owen glared fiercely at Mancini, who was watching him unflinchingly. Ah, so he knew. He knew and he hadn't warned Owen.

"It is my will," the king said, "that you marry King Iago of Atabyrion."

◆ ◆ ◆

Above all, King Severn of Ceredigion values loyalty. He is known to test the loyalty of those who serve him in ways that truly pierce the heart.

—Polidoro Urbino, Court Historian of Kingfountain

◆ ◆ ◆

CHAPTER ELEVEN

Etayne

As Severn said those words, Owen could only listen in shock and pain. Evie flinched as if she'd been struck. There were many things Owen wanted to say at that moment. None would have been prudent.

Evie's face was pale, and knowing her as he did, Owen was certain she was battling a fierce storm of emotions. Still, she rallied and bowed before the king.

"I am grateful to Your Majesty," she said in a quiet voice, "for the trust you have in me. I will go to Atabyrion as you have commanded." Though she looked crestfallen, stricken, she put on a submissive air.

"I knew that I could depend on you," the king said. "I would have you depart within a fortnight. But first, you must speak with my chancellor, who will explain the state of affairs between our two kingdoms. If you are to go there, you must be prepared to threaten Iago. At all times, you are to project strength rather than weakness. My chancellor will also provide you with the funds required to act as my emissary. I have *contacts* at the court of Iago, which Master Mancini will explain to you. You will go with a full diplomatic escort, including several of my court lawyers to serve as your advisors. But I would have it made clear that you represent *me* and are empowered to negotiate on my behalf. You must make him see that his interests are best served with me as a friend and Occitania as his enemy."

"It is . . . a great honor," she stammered.

"You have proven worthy of it." The king gestured her dismissal. "I would speak to Owen next. As you know, he will be going with you as one of your protectors. You may go."

Owen's heart was dark and brooding and sizzling with enmity. He cursed himself silently for not speaking to the king about his feelings back at Dundrennan. To expose them now would risk offending Severn to a catastrophic degree. There was only one hope: He was going with Evie to Atabyrion, so perhaps he could prevent the disaster simply by being there.

Evie bowed again, still pale with dread, and left the throne room. She glanced at him once before leaving, her eyes beseeching his. Though Owen ached to follow her, he could only stare at her with pain.

"You as well, Niece," the king said, though he spoke with compassion. Elyse looked at the king, a small frown on her mouth, but she rose and left as she had been bidden. Was she suffering because she knew what was happening to Owen and Evie? Or was it this business of the pretender that had her so twisted up inside?

As the door shut behind her, Owen turned to face Severn and Mancini. The spymaster gave a nod to tell Clark to stay put.

The king rose from his throne, wincing with discomfort, and began to pace the throne room. He glanced at Mancini. "Fetch her," he said curtly.

Mancini nodded and walked over to the doorway the king usually used to enter the throne room. The king's expression was guarded.

"Do you really seek a marriage alliance with Atabyrion?" Owen asked, trying to keep his tone neutral, but he felt his voice nearly breaking.

The king smiled deviously. "An alliance, if possible. If Iago is smart, he will bite at the bait. But *your* assignment in Atabyrion will be quite different from that of the earl's daughter. As you have no doubt noticed, the rumors about young Piers Urbick have rattled my court and stabbed at the heart of my niece." His face wilted with pain. "You can imagine it has affected me in an equally painful manner. I have long been under the impression that both of my nephews were murdered. Bletchley left no clues as to the whereabouts of their bodies or even how they were murdered. But my spies in the courts of Brugia and Legault have begun to piece together clues that make this situation very compromising for me. If the lad is who Tunmore claims him to be, then he does have a motive to instigate a challenge to the throne. However, the deconeus is a notorious liar, and he's using his gifts to propagate the boy's story. I might control the treasury and the reins of state, but there are clearly many who would prefer a change in government. And benefit from one. I wish to know for *certain* whether the boy is an imposter. Ah, there she is."

Owen saw movement from the corner of his eye, and then Mancini returned from the passageway with a young woman at his arm. He recognized the girl immediately as the one he had fought with in the tower. She had on a beautiful court gown and her hair was done up in a stylish coiffure—obviously another wig. She wore Ankarette's jewels still, and when she saw Owen, a sly smile turned the corner of her lips. Still, she did not give off the sense that she recognized him. Their secret would not be revealed by her—not yet.

A flush of heat bloomed on Owen's cheeks.

"Owen, this is Etayne," the king said by way of introduction. "She is the King's Poisoner. Etayne, my dear, this is Lord Owen Kiskaddon. You will be reporting to him, and to him only, on your assignment in Atabyrion. Is that clear?"

"Yes, my lord," she said. Her eyes were twinkling with mirth at the shared memory of their earlier introduction. "I recognized him—" She paused just long enough to make him squirm a little, then added, "—by the bit of white in his hair." She bowed gracefully to Owen.

The king scrutinized her, seemingly curious about her comment, but then he looked away. "The two of you will need to become acquainted. It was Mancini's idea to hire a poisoner. My brother had a girl working for him for many years by the name of Ankarette Tryneowy. You've probably heard chatter about her among the Espion." The name made Owen flinch, but he managed to nod mutely, even as sweat trickled down his ribs. The girl's eyes were watching him closely, studying him for a reaction. "Etayne is from our country. I won't go into her past, but we've had her trained in the arts over in Pisan. She is very persuasive, and talented in the art of disguise, but this will be her first . . . test. Mancini tells me you are up to the challenge, Etayne. Why don't you explain your mission to Lord Owen?"

Owen's heart turned a little darker, a little sicker. Before she even said her first words, he had already figured it out. But it would have been rude to interrupt her.

"My assignment, Lord Kiskaddon, is to help you infiltrate Iago Llewellyn's court and arrange a meeting between you and the pretender, Piers Urbick—or Eyric Argentine, if you believe his tale. My disguise will be as one of Lady Mortimer's ladies-in-waiting. If the story is true, we will seek a way to *persuade* him back to Ceredigion to meet the king in person. If the tale is false . . . well . . . then I will ensure that he no longer poses a threat."

Owen clenched his jaw, struggling to control his own surging emotions. He felt as if he were already aboard the ship to Atabyrion—and the pitching of the vessel was making him queasy. The glee he had felt about journeying alone with Evie was snuffed out like a candlewick.

"I still think the boy is likely an imposter," Owen said softly. "No matter how many he has managed to convince."

"He's not a boy," the king answered gravely. "He's older than you, and he has somehow persuaded several rulers in different realms that his claim is legitimate. It is a cruel game they are playing at. My niece is not the only one who is worry struck. There is more. Mancini . . . tell him."

"As you will, my lord," the spymaster said. Owen stared at him with loathing, but he was curious to hear him speak. "I've seen copies of Urbick's claims, just as you found in Chatriyon's tent. According to reports, he was smuggled out of Ceredigion as a boy after his older brother was murdered by one of Bletchley's men, a killer known as Tyrell. The boy was commanded not to reveal himself and was kept in the company of protectors who helped disguise his true identity. The lad has *sworn* this in front of lawyers. So my Espion stationed in Brugia began a search there. They found a town along a river where the lad's parents claim to be. I have their sworn statements. The boy is likely being used by the king's enemies in a great scheme of deceit, but the longer he remains protected by Iago Llewellyn and the other rulers, the more legitimacy he gains. We have a nobleman at Iago's court who informed us that Urbick did indeed journey to Atabyrion after his defeat at Blackpool. You and Etayne will go to *him* first, and he will try and get you close to the pretender without compromising himself."

The king came forward, standing before Owen. Sweat glistened on his upper lip. He gripped Owen's shoulders. "*Now* can you see why I must send you? I suspect he is an imposter. And I believe he has duped so many because he is either Fountain-blessed himself or is relying on the craftiness of Tunmore. But I must know the truth before I act. Elyse needs to *know*. I don't want to be accused of murdering my nephew a second time. You will be able to tell if he has access to the Fountain, Owen, and I trust that you can discern if he is lying. The pretender's life will literally be in your hands. You must be very sure. In this matter, I trust you absolutely."

♦ ♦ ♦

After the interview with the king and his new poisoner, Owen managed to get Mancini alone in the Espion tunnels.

"You should have told me this," he said angrily, grabbing the big man's arm and stopping him as they walked. "Why did you betray me?"

Mancini paused and glanced back at him. "I didn't betray you; I outmaneuvered you. That isn't easy to do with a *Fountain-blessed* boy, you know. Especially one who cheats."

"I can't believe you would do this to me," Owen said with growing agitation. "You know how Evie and I feel about each other. You've seen us together since we were little!"

Mancini snorted. "You fancy the girl. Anyone can see that. But Horwath has been deluding himself, and it seems you and Lady *Victoria* have been doing the same." His eyes were sharp as daggers. "There is no way in the Fountain the king would allow your two duchies to be controlled by a single couple. It would rival the king's own authority. I have consistently advised him to prevent it. Such a union would benefit the two of you, but it would be absolutely detrimental to the king's interests."

"I cannot imagine how!" Owen nearly shouted, shaking with rage.

Mancini pursed his lips. "You're wroth. We should discuss this after you've calmed yourself."

"We will discuss it now!" Owen insisted.

"Your wound is raw and oozing, but it will heal. You want the truth, eh? You and the Mortimer chit are two important powers in the realm. It would be an utter waste of potential to allow you two to unite instead of using you both to increase the *king's* power." He jutted his jaw at Owen. "Think on it, lad! Think on it from the king's perspective! If Iago marries her, then he must swear fealty to Severn in exchange for his domains in Ceredigion. And it brings Atabyrion under our control through their children. You, on the other hand, have lands that border Occitania. You've already succeeded in growing your domains through Averanche. It's only natural that the king wants an ally in Brythonica so that land can be used as a base to launch an invasion of Chatriyon's realm. That entire kingdom used to be ours until the Maid of Donremy drove us out like a whipped pup. She was Fountain-blessed. Well, so are you! The king has big plans for you, boy. And those plans do not include Elysabeth Victoria Mortimer!"

Owen felt the fires in his heart burn off into ash. He was sick inside. If there had been a bucket nearby, he would have retched into it. He sagged into the corridor wall, staring incredulously at the Espion master.

"I . . . I love her, Dominic," he said, his throat clenching with agony.

The spymaster gave him a rare pitying look. He reached out and tried to rest his hand on Owen's shoulder, but the younger man shoved it away.

"And what does *that* have to do with a political marriage?" Mancini said in a disquieting way. "I had begun to fear you'd spent too many years in the North. Horwath has trained you to be a duke. You are his equal, not his inferior. He's hinted to the king that you and Evie are fond of each other. But the king *never* supported such a match. Best you deal with this disappointing truth sooner rather than later, boy. It will only cause you pain if you hold out hope."

Owen shook his head defiantly. "I'll figure out a way," he said.

Mancini coughed a chuckle. "You do that, lad. But if I were in your place, I'd use this trip to Atabyrion to say good-bye. She is the proper marriageable age. She would make an excellent queen. You, on the other hand, haven't even reached your full potential yet."

"I thought we were allies," Owen said with suppressed fury.

"I never deceived you," Mancini said. "You did *that* to yourself." He turned to leave, then paused and looked over his shoulder. "Etayne will keep an eye on the two of you." He chuckled softly. "She is a masterpiece of treachery, Owen. I had her trained by the very best. Remember that she is loyal to *me*."

♦ ♦ ♦

When King Eredur was forced to leave Ceredigion, he took his younger brother Severn to the kingdom of Brugia with him. They were hosted by one of the princes of its great cities. King Eredur had a wandering eye, it is said. With so many rumors abounding about this pretender, one must simply consider all the possible options. Perhaps the boy has convinced so many he is Eredur's son because he is a child of the previous king and bears his likeness. But that does not make him a prince.

—Polidoro Urbino, Court Historian of Kingfountain

♦ ♦ ♦

CHAPTER TWELVE

Promises

Owen paced in his chambers, his mind whirling with schemes for how he could overthrow the king's plot to marry Evie off to Iago Llewellyn of Atabyrion. He needed to talk to her, needed to see how she was handling such ill tidings. He hated the fretfulness and consternation caused by this turn of events. Finally, the bustles and creaks in the palace started to wane.

After tripping the latch to the secret door in his room, he fetched a candle and started off toward Evie's chamber. He was grateful that he had spent so much time wandering the secret passages of the palace under Ankarette's guidance. His mind wandered to the King's Poisoner in the tower, Etayne, who had taken to wearing his friend's gowns and jewels. It made him uneasy that she would be traveling with them to Atabyrion. But what worried him even more was that King Severn had charged Owen with judging whether she should use her abilities. Defeating someone in battle was one thing. Murdering him in the dark was quite another. The prospect of being involved in such a thing did not sit well with him.

Owen traced his hand along the walls, pausing at each intersection to touch the Espion signs giving directions. These were ancient catacombs, showing centuries of use. The air smelled musty, and the wind blowing through arrow slits made little ghostly sounds that had once filled him with fear.

When he reached Evie's quarters, he tripped the latch and gave the door a little push. There was a midsized fire burning in the hearth and the sound of splashing water. Owen quickly realized he had walked into Evie's chamber while she was bathing.

He heard a sharp intake of breath, a gasp, and then Justine was rushing toward him, holding up a towel to block his view. "Owen! You should not be here!" the girl scolded. "Have the courtesy to knock before sneaking into my lady's room! Out, you must go!"

"Justine!" Evie said. "Don't shoo him away so fast. Let me dry off. I'll be but a moment."

"My lady," Justine said in a warning voice. "This is hardly proper!"

Owen heard the sound of water dripping on the floor rushes, and his cheeks went crimson with embarrassment. "No, I'll leave. I'm sorry."

"Wait for me!" Evie said, speaking in a voice that would brook no disobedience.

Justine stood there clenching her teeth, holding up the towel and giving him a look that was full of disapproval. Her voice dropped lower. "You should not have come, Owen. If you are caught here, there will be terrible consequences for you both."

"I know, Justine," Owen said. Although he couldn't see Evie, he could hear her drying herself with a towel quickly. His embarrassment grew in intensity, to the point where he was starting to forget why he had come.

"I'm behind the changing screen," Evie said. "Justine, help me. Grab my nightgown."

Justine's frown was more threatening than a spearhead. "You stay over there, my lord," she urged him, thrusting the towel into his hand.

Owen stepped back until he struck the wall by the Espion portal. His forehead was covered in a sheen of sweat, and he was almost tempted to flee for his life as Justine marched back to the changing screen. There were some muttered whispers from the other side, but not even his sharp hearing could make out what was said.

A few minutes later, Elysabeth Victoria Mortimer appeared from around the changing screen, finishing the final buttons of her nightdress. Her dark hair was damp from the water, and she was vigorously rubbing it with a small towel to dry it faster. She looked so pretty and intense, and the firelight revealed a little flush on her cheeks.

"Well, Owen Kiskaddon," she whispered playfully, "if you've come to suggest we jump into the cistern tonight, you're too late, I'm already wet."

Justine gave her mistress a scolding look, but Owen barely noticed—he was too transfixed by Evie. As he watched the firelight dance across her gown, his embarrassment began melting away, replaced by more interesting emotions.

"Don't be so shy, Owen," Evie urged. "You've seen me like this before, in Dundrennan. Why did you come tonight? We both know it's *dangerous* to be meeting like this."

His tongue was thick in his mouth, and he felt a bit muddled, seeing her that way. She flung the hair towel to Justine, who caught it and muttered something under her breath.

"I had to see how you were doing," Owen said awkwardly. "I've been miserable all day."

Evie shook her head. "I haven't. And you shouldn't be either."

He stared at her in disbelief. "But the king said—"

"Toss what he *said*, Owen." She walked up to him and reached for his hands. The smell of scented soap still clung to her. Her fingers were wrinkled from the bathwater, but the rest of the skin on her hands felt warm and soft. "You know how Severn is. We both know he's fond of testing his subjects' loyalty. That's exactly what I believe he's doing. He's testing our loyalty. Are we more loyal to him or to each other?"

Owen couldn't help but frown. Holding her hands made his stomach flip around. He had the unbidden, though certainly not unfamiliar, urge to lean down and kiss her mouth, but he didn't dare. She had been a part of his life for years now, and they had grown so close that the thought of her being another man's wife was unthinkable and unbearable. All those hours they had spent kneeling across from each other, knees touching, while he built with his tiles, all the hikes they had taken into the mountains of North Cumbria, trudging through snow. Always it had felt like they were making a promise to each other—a promise that they would be together forever.

"He may be serious," Owen said huskily, gazing into her eyes, which were now a calm shade of blue mixed with green.

Though he could see the worry in her eyes, she controlled it with a firmness of spirit. "I trust my grandfather," she said softly, confidently. "He has served the king for many years. When he finds out, he'll speak for us. We both know that he wants us to be together." She reached up and smoothed some of his hair by his ear. "As provoking as this situation may be, it does *please* me that you're upset by it. A little, anyway."

"A little?" Owen scoffed. "I can't imagine being more anxious if I were being tied up in a boat about to go into the river."

She gave him a pretty smile. "That's sweet, Owen. I suppose I'm more nervous than I'm letting on. But we've faced worse dangers in the past. He's trying our hearts. I believe that if we stay loyal to him, the king will reward us. I *believe* that." She squeezed his hands again.

Owen sighed, feeling more settled by her assurance. He wanted to believe that too. "There is something else I wanted to tell you. Something else that I learned."

Her eyes widened with eagerness. "Come sit down." She brought him over to a small couch and sat him down. For an instant, he thought she would come down on his lap, but she sat next to him, so close he could feel the warmth coming from her. Their hands were entwined.

Justine started pacing, casting furtive looks at the door and chafing her hands. She had always been an innocuous presence. But with her mistress now committed to another man—a king, no less—she clearly recognized the impropriety of their situation.

"What did the king tell you after I was gone?" In the firelight, her eyes had shifted to gray, reminding him of this magic that was only Evie's.

He explained quickly, telling her about the King's Poisoner, how she would pose as one of Evie's ladies-in-waiting, and what her role would be should the pretender prove to be false. He did not tell her about meeting the girl in the tower earlier and being thrown onto the ground by her. His pride demanded he keep that part to himself, though he felt a little nagging impression that he should tell her.

Evie's face darkened at the words. She looked down at their hands, considering it. "I guess I shouldn't be too surprised the king is planning to use the diplomacy of poison." She pursed her lips. "But he should have told me he was doing this." She looked into his eyes. "I'm glad you trusted me with it, Owen. So her name is Etayne. Is she as pretty as Ankarette?"

He blinked with surprise. "She's . . . she's much *younger*. Dunsdworth's age if I were to guess."

"But is she very pretty?"

Owen squirmed, wondering how best to answer the question. "Well, she . . . I don't think . . . it's hard to say . . . I don't think she's as pretty as you."

A pleased smile spread over Evie's mouth. "She's gorgeous then. Just as I feared. But that was a gentle answer. I know I'm pretty, Owen. But I'm not beautiful. Not in the way the girls from Occitania are, or the Earl of Huntley's daughter in Atabyrion. I've heard about *her* already today. Lady Kathryn the Beauty." She rolled her eyes. "I think I look too much like my father to be considered beautiful."

Owen had rarely seen her exude such self-doubt. He suspected she might be fishing for a compliment, though he wondered how someone so confident could still want assurance on such a point.

"You are the most beautiful girl in all of Ceredigion," Owen whispered softly, squeezing her fingers. He was so close to her, he saw the dimples as she smiled with pleasure. She looked up at him, her eyes misty with emotion, her lips slightly trembling. There it was again, the desire to kiss her. He could see that she felt it too. She even tilted her head, just a little, to make it easier.

Justine marched up to them. "You'd better go," she said to Owen in an urgent voice.

A kiss was a promise. A kiss was something couples did when courting, usually reserved for *after* a pact of marriage had been reached. In the eyes of her grandfather, they were already trothed—promised to each other. But how could he take such a liberty when the king had expressly promised her to someone else?

He saw her tongue dart to wet her bottom lip, and it made his bones burn with fire. Owen cleared his throat, his head a bit dizzy from the emotions surging through him. "Well, I'm glad we're facing this together, Elysabeth Victoria Mortimer." He brought her hand up to his mouth and pressed a gentle kiss on her knuckles.

He could see a shadow of disappointment in her eyes. His throat went dry when he saw her look change—with Evie, an impetuous look like that was always followed by a rash act. She was going to kiss *him.* A dominant part of him wanted her to do it.

"My lady," Justine whispered desperately, clearly coming to the same conclusion. "Don't."

Evie blinked a few times. Then she sighed. "Good night, Owen. My knight. My dearest friend." Her eyes burned into his, still willing him to kiss her. Discomfort held him back. This felt hidden and shameful and secret, which was not what he wanted for them.

Owen stood slowly, his knees nearly knocking together, and pulled his hands away. Now a demure lady in appearance, Evie rested hers in the lap of her nightgown. It was so hot in the room, Owen felt like tugging at his collar.

"I'll be your knight," Owen said, bowing. "And my heart belongs to you, my lady."

She looked pleased at the words, but her disappointment was still apparent. "You are dismissed, sir knight," she said, and Justine sighed with relief.

Owen left through the secret door in her chamber and shut it behind him. He leaned back against it, his heart pounding in his chest with feelings he'd never experienced this forcefully. They were delicious, dangerous, and thrilling. Now that he had seen Evie, he felt more resolved. He was going to outthink King Severn and defeat him in this matter, just as he would in a game of Wizr. He had to.

Owen was about to leave, but he had the idea of checking on her one more time. Turning back toward the door, he found the spy holes were already open.

But he did not remember opening them. No, the holes must have been *closed*, or else he wouldn't have burst in on her like that.

He hesitated, the ebullient feelings in his heart turning to the oil and sludge of suspicion.

"Go ahead and look," Etayne whispered from the dark corridor behind him. Her voice was silky and knowing. "I won't tell."

He whirled around to face her shadowy form in the dark tunnel.

"You were watching us?" Owen stammered in a low voice, feeling mortified as he realized the Espion girl had been spying on them the whole time.

He did not hear her approach, but he saw her silver gown in the dim light escaping a hooded lantern. "I'm not as *pretty* as her," she said slyly. "You struggled with that one. But it was a good answer. You should have kissed her, my lord. She wanted you to. Perhaps you need someone to teach you how?"

Owen was grateful for the dark to hide his flush. He wanted to be gone. To be anywhere other than that small confined corridor with the Espion girl who had observed him making a fool out of himself.

"So you are also coming to spy on us throughout the journey?" Owen demanded thickly, but he suspected he already knew the answer.

"Mancini suspected that you were going to tell her about me," Etayne said. "But no, he didn't send me to spy on you tonight. I did that on my own. Just as I didn't tell him that we had already met in my tower. I know that the *best* secrets are kept, my lord. And I will keep yours."

♦ ♦ ♦

One of the more difficult decisions a prince must make is what to do with the survivors of a rival. For certainly if the survivors are allowed to marry and have children, their heirs will become future threats. In the days of the first Argentines, one surviving son was locked away in the dungeons by his uncle and purportedly starved to death. There are no official court documents about how the lad met his fate. This is a more brutal example of how this dilemma may be approached. In this day, King Severn has chosen to deal with the survivors of his brothers thus. He keeps them close to him at the court of Kingfountain. They include his brother's child, Dunsdworth, now a man past twenty. And his older brother's daughter, Elyse, whom he keeps especially close to him. In both cases, he refuses to let them marry and keeps them under constant watch by the Espion. For all appearances, they may look free, but it is a cruel form of bondage for ones so young.

—Polidoro Urbino, Court Historian of Kingfountain

♦ ♦ ♦

CHAPTER THIRTEEN

Fate of Princes

In the days following the midnight meeting, preparations were made for the journey to Atabyrion. They were to leave on a ship called the *Vassalage*, which would be escorted by several of the king's warships, full of soldiers, lest Iago do something foolish. Owen did not return to Evie's room again, knowing he was being watched by the Espion girl.

As a knight in disguise, Owen spent time in the training yard working on his skills. He enjoyed swordplay, and the sweat and the sheer physical effort of it helped distract him from the nagging dilemmas pervading his mind.

Owen was in the middle of a bout with the palace sword master the morning of the day they were supposed to set sail for Atabyrion, when two men entered the training yard. He assumed they had come to share the space, but they only stood there and watched him spar. After the bout, Owen sheathed his blade and fetched a drink from a bucket ladle, then dumped some of the water over his head to ease the heat and wash away the sweat dripping down his cheeks.

The two men approached him from behind—he could hear the gravel crunching from their boots—and he quickly turned to assess them as potential threats. Not many in the castle had been informed Lord Kiskaddon was there, and most seemed to accept he was a household knight of Duke Horwath. It was interesting to Owen how a simple change in attire could deceive the senses of people who should have known him. When one looked like a prince, or dressed like a king, it led others to suppose it to be true.

"You're the new knight," one of the men said to Owen. It only took him an instant to recognize the young man as Dunsdworth, the enemy of his boyhood. Recognizing his face brought ugly memories to mind.

Dunsdworth had been the castle bully, but he had also been the most constant recipient of Severn's sarcasm and cutting wit. The treatment had probably deranged the young man's mind. Owen had rarely interacted with him since being declared Duke of Westmarch and Horwath's ward in North Cumbria.

Standing before him now, Dunsdworth still towered over him. He was a full-grown man, but beefy like a cow. His cheeks and neck were thick, and his left eye drooped. He had the unkempt beard of someone who was too lazy to go to a barber for a shave, and his thick brown hair was cropped just above the neck after the fashion of Ceredigion. He smelled of sour wine.

Owen gazed at him in surprise and growing disgust. It had been years since he'd seen him this close. It was clear Dunsdworth no longer had the discipline of a warrior. His bulk was caused by overeating and a lack of exercise. There was a vague memory that as a boy Dunsdworth had spent his free time at the training yard. Owen hadn't seen him there once in the days he'd been back.

Silence hung in the air between them for a moment as Owen sucked in these truths and found the taste bitter.

"I'm from the North," Owen said stiffly, warily, adding the touch of an accent. Dunsdworth's companion looked bored and unhappy. He had given Owen hardly a second glance.

"You're good with a blade," Dunsdworth said. "I could *swear* I knew you from somewhere." His mouth turned into a frown as his brain tried to reconcile the situation. But he was foggy, unused to thinking, and it was clear he couldn't place Owen's identity.

"I must go," Owen said, not wanting to be trapped in such a conversation any longer. He started to move away from the water bucket, but Dunsdworth shot out his hand and shoved Owen back. He wasn't ready to let him leave.

"I'm a prince of the blood," Dunsdworth drawled. "You'll leave when I dismiss you."

Dunsdworth's companion rolled his eyes at the comment, but he said nothing. Owen could see the contempt in the man's face. He was a minder, not an accomplice.

Owen scrunched up his eyebrows and tapped his lip. "Aren't you Lord Dunderhead?"

"What did you call me?" Dunsdworth spat angrily, his face contorting.

"Dungheap?" Owen tried again. "No, Dungworth. That's it. I thought I recognized you. Apologies, my lord, for not remembering you sooner."

Dunsdworth's companion started to guffaw, looking at Owen as if he were truly insane.

"Shut it, Corden," Dunsdworth growled, butting his elbow into his companion's ribs to try to silence him. His face was bright red with fury and humiliation.

Owen noticed Clark approaching them briskly from across the training yard.

"I'd love to stay and chat, but I must go," Owen said, walking away.

Corden could still be heard laughing behind him, muttering, "Dungworth, by the Fountain!"

"Mancini sent word to find you," Clark said as Owen fell into stride with him. "He wants you to inspect the *Vassalage* with him while she's being loaded. The sea storms have prevented our departure long enough. I'm anxious to leave."

Owen nodded, but his mind was still elsewhere. "I can't stand him," he said, nodding back toward Dunsdworth. "He used to torment me as a boy. He almost recognized me, but I think he's too addled to remember."

Clark looked distastefully at the two men arguing with each other in the training yard. "I pity the man assigned to him," Clark said. "That is a duty no Espion relishes."

"Corden is an Espion?" Owen asked with a chuckle. "I pity him too then. What a horrible companion."

Clark was always serious, but his face became even graver. "I had that duty myself a few years ago."

Owen stared at him in shock. "Was it a punishment?"

Clark frowned. "No. A duty. And it was miserable."

"I can only imagine. Did you train with him? Is that why you were chosen?"

"Dunsdworth lost his interest in swords years ago. He has one interest now, and it is something the king denies him. Most young men his age are already experienced . . . in the ways of the flesh, to put it delicately. The king denies him any companionship. Dunsdworth used to terrorize the serving girls, which is why he now has an Espion assigned to him at all times. He has to keep his hands off any lass, for the risk that one of them will bear his child." Clark looked disgusted.

"He'll never be allowed to marry, will he?" Owen asked, his voice softening. He glanced back at Dunsdworth with a flicker of pity. Owen could not imagine being permanently deprived of the company of women. It would be an easier fate to be thrown into the river.

"No. The lad is utterly miserable. He's a prince of the blood, but he's treated like a prisoner. When I suffered under that assignment, I had to sleep in bed with him at night to ensure he had no bedmates. It's loathsome work, my lord. He drowns his frustration in wine and hardly spends a day sober now."

"You had to sleep in his bed?" Owen asked with utter revulsion. "How did you bear the smell?"

"Someone has to clean the privies, my lord," Clark said darkly. "I much prefer your company, to be honest."

Owen glanced back at Dunsdworth one last time, and this time the man was staring after him with hatred in his eyes. He felt guilty about taunting him. According to the rights of succession, Dunsdworth was Severn's legal heir to the throne. But he was in no way being groomed to take on that role. He was not invited to take part in the king's councils, and had always been treated with nothing but contempt and disdain. His father had played the traitor twice, ultimately signing his own death warrant. Officially, he was put to death for convicting Ankarette Tryneowy on his own authority—even though she had survived the plunge down the falls. If anything happened to Severn . . . it made Owen shudder to think of Dunsdworth becoming King of Ceredigion. The thought of one of Severn's young relations inevitably turned his mind to another.

"Clark, I've not seen the lady Elyse since the day I arrived. I'd like to see her before I go." In his disguise as a household knight, he couldn't visit her rooms and ask to see her. Not without causing all sorts of gossip. A horrifying thought occurred to him. "Is she being treated like Dunsdworth? Is someone escorting her constantly? Is *she* a prisoner?"

"Oh no!" Clark said, shaking his head vehemently. "No, she is treated far better. The king trusts her implicitly. She's allowed to go wherever she wants, even to the sanctuary and back to see her ailing mother."

"So she has not improved?" Owen asked.

Clark shook his head. "The king has sent his physicians to treat her, but she continues to languish. The queen dowager's health has been pressing on Lady Elyse quite heavily. She's not been to court as often because of it. It's whispered amongst the Espion that the king is grooming her to be his heir in case he's poisoned or murdered. She's illegitimate, of course, but something like that can be overruled if need be. They have a close bond, the two of them." Clark gave Owen a worried look that spoke of the fear of having said too much. Owen nodded encouragingly and Clark continued in a lower voice. "For years, everyone expected him to take her as his wife. He would not, though. Not his brother's daughter."

"Will he let her marry, though?" Owen probed.

Clark shook his head. "No. For the same reason he won't let Dunsdworth. Any child of hers would be a potential threat to him."

"So she's given her freedom because she's been loyal to him."

"Exactly. Dunsdworth is a fool. There's no other word to describe him. His father was a fool too. Always scheming. Always hungering for the crown himself. There are those in the kingdom—lesser men—who would prefer a weak king like Dunsdworth to a strong one like Severn. It would ruin us all. Severn may be cruel and tightfisted, but he's brought prosperity. The royal treasury has recovered and then some. He's a formidable power. Atabyrion is about to learn that firsthand."

Owen was surprised to find his contempt for Dunsdworth had metamorphosed into compassion during their walk away from the training yard and into the castle corridors. The thought of not being able to marry Evie brought him anguish. But not being able to marry at all? To have a constant companion assigned to you, day and night, would be an unimaginable fate.

But a king held such power. A king could ruin a person's life. If Dunsdworth did become king one day, Owen could lose his duchy on a whim. He could be exiled as his own father had been. Or worse.

Owen's thoughts turned bleaker and bleaker. If Severn had not claimed the throne as his own, he would have lost everything. He would have risked murder or exile. He found himself thinking about the image Evie had drawn for him, about the wheel spinning around and around.

It was a long walk from the castle to the docks, which were downriver at the base of the waterfall. It gave Owen a lot of time to think about his upcoming encounter with Mancini. There was a lot he wanted to say to that man, but he realized prudence would be the best approach.

Etayne had revealed to Owen in the tower that Ankarette had left a message for him. The thought that Mancini had the message had been preying on him ever since. If Owen were to ask after it, the spymaster would know that Owen and Etayne had previously encountered each other. Did he want Mancini to know that? It had been Ankarette's greatest trick to keep her secrets secret.

His mind turned to the girl they had chosen to be the new poisoner. How had they found her? Owen still wished he had not been so unguarded about his relationship to Ankarette, but what other explanation was there for how he had ended up in her tower? Just being there had implicated him. How clever was this poisoner? Would she begin to deduce that Owen's reputation for being able to see the future was a sham? What would she do with that knowledge if she did realize the truth? Mancini knew it, of course. But he obviously hadn't told her.

Mancini was quite adept at manipulating the king. He always made sure that the Espion brought in news that the king would find interesting, news he would be able to act upon. While Ratcliffe had mostly responded to events, Mancini crafted them in his favor. He had made himself indispensable to Severn, always acknowledging with false humility that he served at the king's grace and pleasure.

Now that Owen was reaching the age of his manhood, he had learned that the world always felt like a dangerous, threatening place. A place where trust and loyalty were as rare as gems and even more valuable. Owen's loyalty to the king had resulted in his position as a duke of the realm. But trust was as fragile as eggshells. The king didn't know that Owen had conspired with Ankarette, and even Mancini, to dupe him. Their relationship of trust was based on that long-ago deceit. What if Etayne revealed the truth to the king to further her own ambitions?

And it was Owen's intention, even now, to use his Fountain-blessed abilities to thwart the king's plans for Evie. The king only believed that Owen had visions. He did not know about his true abilities.

"There she is," Clark said, huffing as they descended the stairs carved into the cliff walls. "There is your ship."

Owen's stomach prickled with excitement. He was going to make the most of this journey. He was going to make sure Elysabeth Victoria Mortimer did not marry anyone but himself.

Despite Mancini.

Despite the king.

♦ ♦ ♦

Of all the kingdoms, Ceredigion and Occitania share the most similarities in regards to heritage. While other kingdoms do espouse a belief in the Fountain, many have laid aside some of the traditions and beliefs. But both Ceredigion and Occitania still execute their traitors by means of waterfalls. Both enshrine the ideal of the female in the personage of Our Lady. They carve monuments to her of stone and build fountains around them. I have read many of the local histories regarding these traditions, dating back to myths regarding the first overking of Ceredigion, King Andrew. I use the word "myth" because there is no documented evidence that King Andrew ever lived, yet every person in every kingdom believes he was a historical person, a king who left Ceredigion in a small boat and vowed to return to power when his kingdom was besieged. This is known as the prophecy of the Dreadful Deadman. The Occitanians fear King Andrew's return. The Ceredigic people eagerly await it.

—Polidoro Urbino, Court Historian of Kingfountain

♦ ♦ ♦

CHAPTER FOURTEEN

The Vassalage

Mancini slapped the timbers holding up the roof in the cabin. He wrinkled his nose and then nodded to Owen with purpose. "She's a sturdy ship, lad, but not meant to withstand ballista fire."

"What's a ballista?" Owen asked, looking at the comfortable bed where Evie and Justine would be sleeping. Several chests had already been stowed in the room, and the rest of their belongings were being lowered into the hold with ropes. The creak and sway of the timbers made him grip a post to steady himself.

"An overgrown crossbow," Mancini said. "Edonburick has two fortresses commanding the lake, each with probably twenty ballistae. They are burdensome to load, but give deadly fire. Fortunately, they have a weakness: the string used to load them. My Espion in Edonburick has been assigned to infiltrate those fortresses and nick the ballistae strings. Imagine loading one of those when the string snaps." He shrugged. "It will only matter if you need to make a quick escape. I'm expecting," he added seriously, "that the negotiations will be successful."

Not if I can help it, Owen thought darkly, but he nodded in agreement.

Mancini folded his arms, looking annoyed. "You don't seem to accept the current state of affairs yet. At least you're not still sulking."

Owen could tell he was probing for weakness, and he didn't want to give himself away with an impulsive response. "If you're expecting me to be *happy* about it already, Mancini, then you've misjudged how I feel about the girl."

Mancini shook his head. "No, I'm not expecting you to be happy. Marriage isn't about happiness. It's about politics. Name me one happy marriage between nobles that *didn't* end in disaster. Marriage is power. It either increases, or it withers."

Owen pursed his lips, thinking on that for a moment. "By your same argument, Mancini, maybe it's *because* most marriages are political that they fare so badly. If you poison the well water, everyone who drinks from it gets sick."

The head of the Espion gave Owen an exasperated look. "Remind me next time that arguing with you is tantamount to playing Wizr. I always lose."

"If you need the reminder," Owen said with a mocking smile.

"Your quarters are over here," the spy continued, escorting Owen to the room next to Evie's. "A knight should be guarding his lady. You and Clark will take turns walking this corridor while she is in the chamber. Take shifts sleeping. At night, Etayne will watch from inside the girls' room, so don't get any *romantic* ideas. The poisoner's ability with the Atabyrion language is such that she can pass for a native quite deceptively, if needed, through one of her many disguises, and she's also been studying the Espion maps. She'll help you locate and apprehend the pretender."

Owen nodded, rubbing his lip with his finger. "So you believe he truly is a pretender, Mancini?"

The spy shrugged with cynicism. "It's highly suspicious that this young man should suddenly appear in the major courts of the continent. A man grown, instead of a boy. I've heard many say he *looks* like Eredur, but let's be honest. Eredur wasn't as faithful to *his* queen as Severn is to the mere memory of his." He wiggled his fingers together playfully. "I'm *still* trying to find a suitable wife for him. It's been ten years. Perhaps that is a lucky number after all."

Through the doorway, Owen saw Etayne walking down the aisle toward them, her skirts swishing as she moved. She was dressed as a lady-in-waiting, her gown showing her station to be lower than Evie's. Her wig was brown now, like chestnuts. The necklaces and jewels she had appropriated from Ankarette were gone, replaced by simpler fare. But there was no hiding her beauty.

"Is all well here?" she asked.

"Owen and I were just talking about you," Mancini said enigmatically.

She dimpled but said nothing in reply.

"Look at you," Mancini said, reaching out and touching her chin. He lifted it and angled her head to one side and then another, as if she were an animal being inspected. Owen saw her eyes glitter with disdain, but she did not resist him. "You are one of my finest accomplishments," he whispered in a low voice. "You will be one of *the* best poisoners in any kingdom. Even better than your predecessor. I've spared no expense in her training," he added as an aside to Owen. Then, fixing his gaze with hers, he continued, "And you look almost as innocent as the earl's daughter. Almost." He patted her cheek, his gaze openly admiring his handiwork. He shivered. "Do us proud, girl. The pretender must perish."

"*If* he's lying," Etayne reminded him, giving Owen a quick look. "If he's only pretending to be a prince."

Mancini smiled sardonically. "You and Owen are too alike. He *is* an imposter. I have no doubt of that. You could pass yourself off as an earl's daughter. Or a shepherdess. I've trained you to be anyone. This Urbick fellow could be anyone too—even a trained poisoner like you are. Be on your guard."

"I always am," she replied deferentially, but Owen could see shades of contempt in her eyes. Mancini thought this girl was tame, but she had a mind of her own.

A loud voice rang out from the deck. It was the captain calling attention to the arrival of Elysabeth Victoria Mortimer, the earl's daughter.

"Our lady has arrived," Mancini said. "I'd best start back for the palace." He turned back to Owen again. "Evie is in charge of the negotiations. But you are in charge of defending her and our forces. The king trusts you, lad. If you need to start a war with Atabyrion, you have the authority to do so. Severn wants this to be a display of his power, and he's authorized the girl to make quite a nuisance of herself. Make sure it is *memorable* enough for word to spread to the other courts."

"I will," Owen said, looking deep into Mancini's eyes. He had hoped the man would confide in him without being bidden, perhaps as a nod to the fact that he'd sabotaged Owen's life. But he had said nothing about Ankarette's letter, and Owen did not want to reveal that he knew about it. Not yet.

Mancini patted Etayne's cheek one more time and then sauntered back down the aisle so he could leave by the gangway. Owen watched him for a moment before turning his gaze back to Etayne. Her eyes were raw with disgust and contempt as she stared after the Espion.

"You don't like him very much," Owen said softly.

She gave him her haughty look again. It slipped on like a mask. "Would you like to be treated as if you were only a weapon, not a person?" Then she smoothed her gown, and a pretty smile tipped up the corners of her mouth. "I have to prove myself on this mission, my lord. I cannot fail. At anything, it seems," she added in a deceptively cheery tone. Her palm stroked her stomach. "I will enjoy working with you,

I think. We are not so very different in age. You look a little older than twelve." She winked at him to let him know she was teasing.

He didn't believe her banter for a moment. Was she a dangerous serpent to be avoided and feared? Or was she someone who could be trusted? She had kept their encounter in the tower secret. He thought he could see glimpses of her beneath the mask, but he would need to know more about her before he decided if he could trust her.

There was a commotion on deck as Evie made her way to the staterooms, the sailors cheering in welcome. She walked confidently, waving back at them, and her beautiful gown shimmered in the sunlight as the light caught the gems and silver thread.

Etayne was watching him watch her, a sly smile on her mouth. He knew it, but he still had a hard time taking his eyes off the girl who had carved a part of his heart away from him.

The poisoner put a hand on Owen's shoulder, and when she spoke, her voice was just a whisper. "I think it's harsh what they're doing to you both. For what it's worth." She patted his shoulder and then slipped into Evie's room quietly, letting Owen be the one to greet her first.

♦ ♦ ♦

Owen had never been to sea before. He had worried, based on the experiences of others, that he would be greensick like poor Justine, who spent nearly all her time aboard crouched over a bucket. She looked a miserable creature, and even had vomit in her hair. Evie was immune to the effects; she walked from one end of the ship to the other, asking questions and learning about the nautical terms, and basically charming the captain and his entire crew with her intense interest and curiosity. Owen walked in her shadow, a hand on his sword, and felt the salty breeze in his hair. He could almost feel the ocean beneath his boots, and the rhythmic sway was as gentle to him as a mother's lullaby.

They followed the coast of Ceredigion up to East Stowe before plunging into the open sea separating the two kingdoms, which were adjacent to each other. Sailors were always nervous being in open waters, but it was not a lengthy voyage. Land was sighted on schedule, and the weather, according to the captain, had been surprisingly calm compared to the previous fortnight. Upon reaching the coast of Atabyrion, they took the eastern approach to reach Edonburick on the other side of the island. There would be no hiding the fleet, and Owen knew word of their imminent arrival would precede them to Iago Llewellyn's court. The navigator was from the merchant fleet and knew the way to distinguish the fjords and rocks and how to maneuver the ship safely through them.

After nightfall, Owen found himself standing at the prow of the ship with Evie. She leaned over the railing, her hair whipping around as the wind caught it. She was beaming, her face soft as they faced the purple sky, the sun setting far behind them. Many in the crew had gathered to the stern to watch the sunset, as was their ritual, but Evie had wanted to face forward, toward their destination.

"Where is Justine?" Owen asked, joining her at the rail and planting his elbows next to her.

"In the cabin," Evie said, cocking her head at Owen. She shivered with delight, her eyes glowing. "I've never been at sea before. I could get used to this. I would love to visit each of the kingdoms and learn about them firsthand. Books are lovely, of course, but seeing Atabyrion fills me with anticipation. Look at those mountains! They are hauntingly beautiful."

"You wish to stay here then?" Owen asked a bit too snidely.

She gave him an annoyed look. "You don't understand. I love traveling and visiting new places. I don't want to come here to *stay.* I want to see Occitania, Genevar, and Pisan too. I want to see all the places I've only read about." She folded her arms beneath her breasts and leaned forward against the rail, breathing it all in. He was tempted, for just a moment, to grab her waist and startle her.

He looked around, saw that no one was looking their way, and succumbed to it.

She gasped with surprise and shock and then turned and hit him on the arm. "That wasn't kind!" she said. "I thought I was falling!"

Owen was trying to control his laughter, which only made it worse, and she hit him again. "Stop it. You're such a boy. We're not eight anymore, you know. What if I had fallen in?"

He had to wipe the tears out of his eyes. "You always said you fancied to know what it would be like falling off a waterfall. It isn't even that far down."

"You are contemptible," she chided, but there was her smile again, a warm knowing smile that went straight through his heart like a ballista bolt. She leaned back against the railing, her hands behind her, her head cocked to one side. The sun had set and darkness was settling in all around them, lowering like a bank of clouds preceding a storm.

Owen leaned his elbows against the rail again, inhaling the salty smell of the air.

"Why won't you kiss me, Owen Kiskaddon?" Evie asked in a small voice, only loud enough for him to hear her. It was almost a whisper. "I've tried to make it obvious enough, but you are either being stubborn or you don't want to."

He felt a blush rise to his cheeks and his stomach flipped around like a fish on the deck.

"You don't know how much I want to," he said, unable to stop the words from spilling out.

"That's comforting," she said dryly. "At least it's not because you don't want to. Why haven't you then?"

"Why are we talking about this?" he asked her.

"Because I'm a girl, and girls like to talk about kissing," she said with a mischievous smile. "I've wanted you to kiss me for *years* and you never have. I've almost kissed you first a thousand times, but I always wanted you to be the one to start it. Justine is vomiting in a bucket in my room. The crew is watching the sunset over there. And *your* thought was to startle me by pretending to push me overboard." She sighed with exasperation. "Sometimes I can't figure out how your mind even works."

Owen could hardly make sense of his churning emotions. They were a mix of delight, mortification, embarrassment, eagerness, wariness, and giddiness.

He hung his head and chuckled. She had the ability to talk about the most ridiculous things with candor. She was so open, so assured of herself. He envied her that. He was constantly riddled with worries and doubts.

"Sometimes I can't figure it out myself," he said honestly. "It was a perfect moment and I ruined it."

"Yes . . . you did." She reached over and touched his arm. When he looked up at her face, he saw tenderness there. A feeling of protectiveness came over him.

She clucked her tongue in regret. "Well, here comes the captain. Tomorrow we'll be in Atabyrion, in front of strangers who abide by savage customs. People there eat with their hands and throw cups of wine and scream at each other during meals." She wrinkled her nose. "They also start fights rather rashly. As one of my knights, I'm depending on you to defend my honor." She gave him an arch look.

Owen rose and bowed to her formally. "I will defend it with my life, my lady."

She pursed her lips at his gallant comment and then gave him a dismissing nod as the captain approached.

Later, after midnight, Owen was pacing the corridor outside her room, rebuking himself for having missed the perfect opportunity to kiss her. His conflicting emotions stymied him. He wanted to show her how he felt, to pledge his heart to her in a meaningful way. But to do so would feel disloyal to the king. This was a test, he tried to reassure himself. It was only a test. Part of him believed it, but a nagging voice in his head insisted the intended alliance with Atabyrion was real. If so, kissing her now would make things worse for them in the future. It could even damage their friendship.

He had promised Clark he would awaken him after midnight, but Owen did not know if he would even be able to sleep.

A sliver of light bloomed from her doorway, and he noted it immediately, his nerves taut and on edge. Swinging his head around quickly, he saw Etayne framed in the glow. She gestured for him to approach, and he hurried over to her.

"What is it? What's wrong?" he whispered.

Etayne shook her head. "Nothing's wrong," she whispered. "I gave Justine a sleeping potion for her seasickness. A strong one. She won't awaken until morning." Her eyes were full of mischief. "Shall we trade places?"

CHAPTER FIFTEEN

Edonburick

Owen stared at Etayne, the conflict within him growing fiercer. The thought of being alone with Evie, truly alone with her, kindled a feeling inside him akin to the roar of a waterfall. But at the same time, he felt distrustful of the Espion's intentions.

"What do you mean?" Owen asked, wrinkling his brow.

"I'll guard the door. You can be in here."

One of the strategies in Wizr was to move a piece for an easy kill. To an opponent, it would look like an error, but it was a deliberate move intended to provoke an action that would later be regretted. As Owen stood there in the dark corridor, he felt he would be making a crucial mistake if he accepted Etayne's offer. Perhaps *she* was testing *him*.

He shook his head. "Thank you, but no. I have a duty to perform. And so do you."

Etayne looked a little startled. She stared at him for a long moment and then gave him a nod of respect. "Not one young man in twenty would have said no. You *are* unique." She came out into the hall, shutting the door quietly behind her. With the absence of light, shadows engulfed them.

"I would never want to do anything to dishonor her," Owen said in the darkness. He didn't like that he couldn't see her face very well, as he would have to judge her by her words alone.

"Thank the Fountain you are not like Dunsdworth then," she replied with an edge in her tone. "If that man ever became king . . . well, I'd probably poison him first."

"I'm *nothing* like him. He used to torture me as a boy."

"He tortures anyone he can," she replied with a grunt, and Owen was suddenly suspicious that she had experienced a run-in with him before. "You have my respect. Sadly, it's been my experience that most young men *are* more like him than not. When I caught you sneaking into her room the other night, I had my suspicions about the two of you."

Owen leaned back against the wall. "When I went in to see her, Justine was there and fully awake. It wouldn't be . . . *proper* to see her without a chaperone. Not at night, anyway."

"You believe in the old code of chivalry? How quaint. You care about her honor and not just about gratifying your needs," Etayne said slyly.

"She's also my friend," Owen said simply. "Of course I do."

He was a little put off by the King's Poisoner. Or perhaps he was just comparing her to Ankarette. Maybe she too had been worldly and cynical when she was younger. Owen wondered again if he could trust her. He realized now that he wanted to.

"In addition to poison, what are your other skills?" Owen asked.

"I was fully trained," she replied evasively. She was not one to reveal anything about herself. "Tell me about Ankarette. I've only known her through Mancini's eyes. She was the standard, the mark I had to aspire to better. You were only a child, but what do you remember?"

Owen's vision was adjusting to the darkness and he saw her better and better—she was studying him just as he was studying her.

"I don't like talking about her," Owen said, trying to keep his voice neutral. "It was so long ago."

"Very well. When you are ready then. I would be grateful if you told me. It is difficult competing against a ghost."

"I imagine so," Owen said. He wondered about this girl, her defenses and weaknesses. What would his magic reveal about her? He opened himself up to the power of the Fountain, his source of power and insight. Letting the magic ripple through him, he extended it out to Etayne, probing for her weakness. Everyone had a characteristic weakness—except for Clark. Probing Clark was like testing the walls of a dam. He wondered whether Etayne had any chinks.

He learned, immediately, that she was left-handed and always disguised that fact out of embarrassment. She had trained herself to be almost equal with her right hand, but she definitely had a dominant hand, and it made her difficult to predict. She shivered suddenly as the magic probed her more deeply, looking for more.

"What are you doing?" she demanded in a quavering voice. Owen stopped the flow of magic, startled that she had noticed it.

"What?" Owen asked, feeling a little guilty that he had been caught at it.

She backed away from him, just slightly. "Did you . . . did you just use your Fountain magic on me?"

Owen stared at her, conflicted. There was no denying it. "Yes. You felt it?"

"I'd never felt it before." Her voice was just a whisper, a mix of awe and fear.

"Are you Fountain-blessed?" Owen whispered.

"I don't know," she said. "But I felt something. It was coming from you . . . like . . . like a river. How did you do that? What were you *doing* to me?" she asked, distrust seeping into her voice.

"I guess you could say I was testing you, in my own way."

She shuddered again. "It felt strange, yet pleasant. I almost didn't notice it with the ship rocking. How old were you when you learned you were Fountain-blessed?"

Owen hid his smile. "Very young. It usually begins with a habit, a task—something that you focus on and lose yourself in. Something that you love and are passionate about. It's different for everyone. That task fills you with the Fountain's power. Once you've stored it, you can use it in certain ways. I can sense it when someone else uses it. If you can, then maybe you are just discovering your power."

Etayne stepped forward suddenly, and he could see the scant light reflecting off her eyes. "Will you teach me?" she asked, so fervent he could only stare at her, speechless.

♦ ♦ ♦

The *Vassalage* reached Edonburick and everyone came on deck to watch as the ship navigated slowly through the mouth of the bay. The cliffs on each side were massive and crowned with timber battlement walls. What struck Owen immediately was that the defenses were primarily made of wood. The wood was nearly black, and the posts were all sharpened like stakes. Torches burned in iron sconces, belching black plumes into the air.

As the ship came into the bay, Owen stared out at the massive lakelike harbor. It was small compared to the one at Kingfountain, but there were ships from every kingdom there, including Ceredigion, so the *Vassalage* did not stand out. Craggy fingers of rock protruded from the bottom at certain places in the bay. A waterfall gushed down into the bay, and Owen could hear its roar even from a distance. The palace of Edonburick was built into the cliff near the falls, accessible by means of a series of wooden rails and stairs constructed along the side of the mountain. There were houses fitted vertically into the cliffs all around the bay, but they were rustic-looking, peak-shaped lodges, few larger than a single story.

Owen breathed in the salty air that reeked of fish. There were no structures made of stone, he suddenly realized. Not a single one. It did not even require his special ability for him to see the weakness.

Fire. A few ships with archers in the hold with pitch-tipped arrows could wreak havoc on such a place.

Their ship maneuvered around the tall columns of stone protruding from the lake, and Owen leaned against the railing, staring down at the waters. With the rushing noise of the waterfall in his ears and the sight of lapping waves all around him, Owen felt something *stir* inside him. It felt familiar, almost like a mother's soothing whisper. He stared down at the water, trying to see beyond the foam. He was trying to see because he suddenly knew without a doubt there was something down there. The memory of the ephemeral treasure in the cistern at Kingfountain flickered through his mind.

The true Edonburick was drowned.

The insight came to him with such startling clarity that he gasped. Visions bloomed in his mind, unbidden. Their ships were gliding over the ruins of a lost kingdom. It was all still there, submerged beneath the waves. Castles made of stone, cottages and wells and hedge walls. The buildings were all still down there, blanketed in seaweed and muck.

"What is it, Owen?" Evie asked with concern. She touched his arm, and the contact snapped him out of the vision's thrall.

Owen staggered back from the railing, breathing hard and fast. The inhabitants of the original settlement had all drowned. Only those who'd lived in the upper mountains had survived. Indeed, all that was left was the upper mountains. There were no stone buildings because the devastation had crushed Atabyrion into poverty. He did not know how long ago it had happened, but he could almost hear the screams of sorrow muffled by the water.

"Are you sick?" Evie asked again, looking at him worriedly.

Owen *felt* sick. He could not even comprehend the amount of water that must have come crushing down into the valley. This wasn't a bay at all. It was a deathtrap.

"I don't know," Owen said, wiping his mouth on his sleeve. Sometimes the Fountain spoke to him. It was rare and had not happened in a while. When it did, it left his bones feeling weak. He didn't want to frighten her, nor could he even find words to describe what he had seen. "I need to sit down."

Turning, he managed to sit down with his back against the side of the railing. How many had died? How many had been drowned? It felt like the roar of the waterfall was the only thing blocking out the shrieks of the dead.

Justine crouched next to him and offered her bucket to him, giving him a sympathetic look. She patted his shoulder.

"Don't hold it in," she said. "It only makes it worse. I felt it as soon as I got on board."

He wanted to laugh, but his throat was dry as sand. He wasn't seasick. He was horrified—it was as if he'd encountered a mass grave after an enormous slaughter.

"We're almost to Edonburick," Evie said sweetly, rubbing his shoulder.

After a while, Owen's shock began to subside. He thanked Justine for the bucket he hadn't used and made it back to his feet. They were approaching the docks to the right of the falls. The cliffs were jagged and broken, and large boulders peeked out of the waters. The ships had to move carefully, maneuvering by poles and oars until they reached the safety of the harbor. The cliffs, up close, were a mesmerizing shade of green from the moss clinging to the rocks. An abundance of pine and cedar trees crowned the mountains, which was undoubtedly another reason why so much of the city was constructed of wood. Part of the stone cliffs had a peculiar natural pattern that fascinated Owen. They looked like a bunch of slim columns, or strands, bunched together in cords. The pattern resembled a tiled wall, and there were mounds of broken pieces of stone at the base of the cliffs.

As the gangway was hoisted to connect to the ship, Owen watched as a nobleman shuffled his way down the pier with an entourage of knights. Rather than armor, they wore toga-like cloaks and skirts and boiled-leather bracers and girdles. Each had high leather boots covering pants that seemed to be made out of woolly sheepskin. Their hair was long and braided, and each was bearded. They looked like wild men. The effect was only heightened by the fact that each cloak and skirt bore a different patchwork pattern.

The nobleman leading them was a mature man, his hair only partially tamed, with a cropped beard and mustache. He was a handsome fellow, quite tall, and he stood with one foot planted on the dock, the other on the gangway, his hand resting on a huge sword that was hanging from straps around his shoulders like a longbow.

"Milady of Ceredijun," the nobleman said in a thick accent, giving her a bow and a flourish. He was looking up at Evie, who was standing by the captain. Owen and Clark stood just behind her. "Ye are most welcome to Edonburick. Word of your impending arrival came aforehand. Our most illustrious King Iago the Fourth bids you welcome and honor. Ye have come just in time to participate in the revels."

Evie's brow furrowed. "And what revels might those be, my lord?" she asked formally.

He gave another swooping bow, extending his arm in a broad sweep. "Why, the nuptials, my lady. The *marriage* of Ceredijun's true king to the daughter of the Earl of Huntley of our fine realm. I hope ye have a stomach for mead, for there is plenty of drink at hand. Come pay homage to your new king, my lady. He is expecting ye as well."

"Now this will be interesting," Evie muttered under her breath to Owen. Then she straightened imperiously and started down the gangplank.

CHAPTER SIXTEEN

Iago Llewellyn

They had to climb a huge series of wooden steps fixed with railings to reach the court of King Iago. Several members of their party were fatigued after mounting so many steps, but Owen and Evie were accustomed to long hikes. As they ascended the terraced planks, the rushing sound of the waterfall became part of the general noise, but it was still impressive to see the falls. They were birthed from a river that twisted and moved within a steep chasm of tree-topped growth. The falls seemed to start a bend in the river, forming a crescent-shaped drop that was both wide and steep. Owen saw a black-slicked tree wedged against rocks at the top of the falls. The force of the current pinned it there, preventing it from dislodging and careening down. Farther upstream, he could see timber rafts landing at river docks that were located a good way inland from the falls.

The climb brought them to the wide plateau where the king's lodge stood. *Lodge* was the word that best described it, for it had none of the majesty of the palace at Kingfountain. The structure was large, and there were several gabled wings attached to the symmetrical roof. A huge chimney rose from the center, belching a plume of soot. As he drew nearer, Owen saw the posts and beams were carved with an inlay of gold designs. The designs were of high craftsmanship and reminded Owen of the patterns found in leather weaving. At least two dozen armed warriors in leather and skirts were posted at the front of the lodge, equipped with thick spears and bronze helmets from which their braided hair and beards could be seen. Each man had half his face painted in blue woad.

Clark nudged Owen's elbow and nodded toward a nobleman who was standing to the side of the porch accompanied by a small entourage of servants with caps and quills. The man was balding with strands of black hair combed from the front of his dome down to the back.

"He's Espion," Clark whispered. "Just showed me a hand sign."

Owen nodded and followed Evie up the wooden steps of the lodge. The warriors guarding the entry peeled back, and the enormous wooden doors were yanked open by their stout iron handles, each taking a strong man to heave it open.

As the doors opened, the roar of the waterfall was overcome by the commotion of a lively celebration. There were flutes and pipes and the stomp of boots in fast dancing. Smoke billowed out, for every other man inside the room had a curved pipe to his lips, and an enormous fire burned in a sunken pit in the middle of the hall. Long spits of meat were hung over the pit, and lads were crouched by the edges, turning their hands to rotate the sizzling flesh. The air smelled of crisping fat, honeyed mead, and sharp cheese. The commotion and assault on the senses made Owen's head whirl. He rested his hand on his sword hilt, feeling threats and dangers were everywhere.

"Follow me this way!" shouted the nobleman who had escorted them from the docks. His voice barely rose enough to be heard over the noise. Evie nodded, and they followed him around the perimeter of the hall, under wooden arches and beams that held up the massive roof. In the center of the roof was a huge opening leading to the chimney, allowing smoke from the fire and pipes to escape. Still, Owen felt the fumes sticking to his clothes and skin.

They approached the head of the hall, where a wide dais led to an empty wooden throne. Torches hung on the walls behind the throne, revealing a mosaic of engraved sigils inlaid with gold. Next to the throne was a small pedestal and a goblet made of bronze that looked apt to tumble off the edge.

Owen tried to catch a glimpse of King Iago or the pretender, but with all the whirling bodies, clapping, and stomping, it was impossible to make any sense of the scene. The footwork of the dancing was impressively complicated, nothing like the more stately, solemn, and slow movements Owen was used to from the court at Ceredigion. Each man held an arm up in a half-moon shape while he danced, holding his partner's waist in a grip that mirrored the posture with the other arm.

How to describe the women? It was impossible to distinguish their hair color because each wore a stylish headdress of varying design that completely concealed her hair. No two headdresses were the same, or so it appeared to Owen. How they managed to keep them on was a mystery, particularly considering the velocity of the dancing. The small serving girls who scuttled in and out with trays of drink and food did not wear them, though their hair was meticulously braided, some even with flowers, but it was definitely a symbol of wealth or power or rank to have an ornate headdress. In contrast, the gowns of the ladies were far simpler than the fashions Owen had seen in his own kingdom.

Evie and her company were escorted to the empty throne at the head of the hall and made to wait. Then a tall, fat man who reminded Owen of Mancini raised a huge horn to his lips and let out a blast that nearly shook the walls. The horn came down and the man wiped his lips on his sleeve.

The dancing stopped midstep.

The nobleman who had escorted them raised his voice. "Lord King Iago, you have a visitor from the benighted realm of Ceredigion. Lady Mortimer has come to the great hall of Chambliss to seek your counsel."

Considering the press of dancers, it was impossible to judge whom the nobleman was addressing. Owen searched the faces, trying to identify the king from the rabble. And then he spied him, for heads all around the great room turned to look at him, and a small opening peeled off to provide him a view of Evie and her escorts.

Iago was short.

By Owen's reckoning, and from what he'd been told by Mancini, the young king was nearly twenty years old. He was sweating profusely, and his mane of black hair was disheveled by the dance. There was nothing in his Atabyrion garb that differentiated him from his peers at all except for a circlet of dark gold around his brow, which Owen had not noticed amidst the throng. The king held the hand of an exquisitely beautiful young woman in a white satin dress, so white that it appeared to be snow, with a dazzling silver girdle and billowing sleeves. Her ornate silver headdress concealed her hair but not her serious mouth, flushed cheeks, and hazel eyes. The king held her hand and escorted her down the tunnel of bodies until he reached another young man. As the king delivered the woman's hand into the awaiting grip of the young man, restoring the bride to her husband by all looks of it, Owen realized instantly that he was their quarry.

This young man was the pretender, and he did indeed *look* like an Argentine.

The king dipped his head to the young woman, saying something in the thick brogue of his native tongue, then brushed his hands together vigorously and strode across the hall to greet them with a charming smile.

"My fair lady Mortimer!" the king said in a polished accent. "You have come just in time to join the dance. May I be the first to introduce you to the quaint traditions of my realm?" He bowed resplendently.

Evie's eyes were like flint and she gave off a haughty manner, not submissive or impressed in the least.

"My lord, Lady Mortimer is my mother," she said curtly. "I am Elysabeth Victoria Mortimer, granddaughter of Duke Horwath, who defeated Atabyrion at the Battle of the Steene thirteen years ago. I did not come here to *dance*, my lord. I came here to *prevent* another war."

Her voice was commanding, imperious, and it sent a hush through the crowd more efficiently than the horn-man had done with his tune. The hush was followed immediately by a murmuring of anger and resentment, making Owen fear she had gone too far.

The king's eyes narrowed as the sweat continued to trickle down his face. Owen realized they were sequestered at the end of the hall that was farthest from the doors. It was quite a vulnerable position.

"Well—" the king said tightly, his face betraying strong emotions, none of them positive, "—you speak very *boldly* to a king, Lady Mortimer."

"Lady Elysabeth will do if you cannot pronounce my entire name," she said pointedly. "You are, by rights, the king of this realm. But remember, my lord, that the Duke of North Cumbria holds domains far vaster than this puny island."

He gritted his teeth at her audacity. "You are outspoken," he said evenly. "So my *cousin* Severn bids a little girl of his realm to come and lecture me on history? I fear him not, Lady *Mortimer*. For I hold in my court the true king of Ceredigion." He raised his hand and snapped his fingers, gesturing for the young man Owen had previously identified to approach.

Owen's stomach twisted with concern at how Evie was handling the situation. She, an earl's daughter, was treating herself as equal to the King of Atabyrion. She was establishing her authority as emissary of a realm that dwarfed the size of Atabyrion and could afford to treat it with impunity. It was a highly offensive approach, and Owen hoped it would not destroy her standing.

The pretender approached. Tall and athletic, he looked to be a few years older than Owen and Evie. He had the Argentine chin, but he did not share Severn's dark looks. No, his hair was gold, and he was every bit as handsome as Eredur was purported to have been. The girl in the white dress was on his arm, her expression serious and concerned, troubled. She seemed to understand the language of Ceredigion, or so her appearance indicated.

"I bid you greet Eyric Argentine, true king of Ceredigion, and his wife, Lady Kathryn, the Earl of Huntley's daughter," Iago said, his voice full of hostility. "They were wed this morning. It is their wedding celebration you are interrupting so rudely with your provocations."

Eyric—or was it Urbick?—was not dressed like the others in the room, and his more formal attire, although almost indistinguishable from the uniform of underservants within Kingfountain palace, was probably the finest outfit in the entire island kingdom. Even the earl's daughter's dress—the white one—was inferior to Etayne's and Justine's and far less fashionable. The wealth in the kingdom had obviously not recovered from the loss of the original city and a long history of conflicts. They were not in a position, financially, to wage war on Ceredigion.

"We meet at last!" Evie said with a false cheerfulness, turning her iron gaze on the would-be prince. "Why, it was only a few weeks ago that I dispersed your ships and defeated the rabble you called an invasion army. Yes, my pretend lord. Those were my forces that ran you out. And you didn't even have the courage to land yourself." She turned back to Iago, her face flushing with anger. "No one in Ceredigion believes this young man is their true king. We have a true king, anointed and crowned. Even if this young person *were* Eyric Argentine, the line was judged to be illegitimate by law, as my lord's lawyers can prove and attest. So can his 'sister,' Lady Elyse. You provoke my lord king to wrath by such impertinence, Prince Iago. You do so at your peril. I have come to negotiate a truce with you. Perhaps I have wasted my time."

The young man, Eyric, strode forward a step, his face flushed with fury. He set aside his new wife's hand from his arm and stood next to King Iago, towering over him. Owen was tempted to test the young man with his magic, but to do so would risk exposing his ability to anyone in the hall who shared it.

"You *dare* to speak of my uncle as the true king of Ceredigion," Eyric said, his voice quavering with emotion. "Perhaps you have not heard the tale of how I survived his attempt to *murder* me."

Evie looked at him coldly, unmoved. "I have read it, *sir*. But as I said, no one in Ceredigion believes it." She turned back to Iago, not giving the young man any more of her attention. "My lord, we have evidence of this young man's true parentage, confessions written and received. He is an imposter, and you provoke Severn's sword of war by harboring him in your realm. It affronts us, in a most grievous fashion, that you have not only supported his false claim but endorsed it by arranging a marriage between him and the daughter of one of your nobles. Believe me, my king *will* come and fetch this young man in person if he must. And your hall will shake for it if he does."

As Evie spoke, Owen scrutinized Lady Kathryn, and his heart pained for her. This was her wedding day, and she believed she had wed the future king of Ceredigion. It was clear from the hostility in the air that they *all* believed the boy's tale to be true. But what Owen did not know was whether they also had been tricked by Tunmore's magically persuasive words.

Iago folded his arms proudly. "I have no doubt, Lady Mortimer, that my cousin has arranged any number of people who are willing to swear Eyric was a pig keeper—"

"A fisherman's son, but close enough," Evie shot back.

Iago ground his teeth. "I know this man's sad tale, and I am not the only ruler who believes it. Severn the Usurper will soon discover that he is the only ruler who *doesn't*." He took a step forward. "Do you think I fear your threats? If Severn attacks me, he will be invaded by four other kingdoms in his rear. You know he will. We all believe Eyric to be the true king. That bit about illegitimacy? The story the king has spun about Eredur's previous secret marriage?" He snorted. "*That* is the deception. Severn has barred his niece from her true rights, even as he's sought to woo her into his bed. Eyric has been in hiding because he was too young to fight his uncle. But he is a man grown now. When people see him, they will give their loyalty to their true king. And then the people of Ceredigion will hurl that crouch-back into the river to be dashed to pieces!"

"Let me handle this, Cousin," Eyric said, gripping the king's shoulder. He stood in front of Evie, his bearing tall and firm and regal. "I am who I claim to be. I *am* Eyric Argentine. My brother was murdered in the palace at Kingfountain. But I was taken by a remorseful servant to the sanctuary of Our Lady and smuggled to Brugia. The time has come for me to reclaim what is rightfully mine. And I promise you this, Elysabeth Victoria Mortimer. One day you will kneel before me as your king."

He is Eyric Argentine. But he is not telling the truth.

Owen felt the whisper from the Fountain in his mind, and it made him sick with dread.

CHAPTER SEVENTEEN

Lord Bothwell

Just as Iago's royal palace was on a much smaller scale than Kingfountain, so too were the accommodations. Many of the lords and ladies of Atabyrion had gathered for the royal wedding, and every inn, tavern, and barn was full. Evie and her escorts had been granted a single room in the royal apartments. A single, canopied bed filled a good portion of the chamber, along with a small dresser topped with a pitcher of water, a washing bowl, and a small mirror. The wainscoting on the walls was decorative, the trim carved and crafted into the weave pattern Owen had noticed in the great hall. The floor had thick rush matting, and there were broken boughs of pine at the threshold that crackled as they entered, releasing a whiff of sweet-smelling sap.

It was clear from the sparse abode that most of them would be sleeping on small mats on the floor. The bed would be reserved for Evie and Justine.

As soon as the large wooden door was shut, Owen began inspecting the room for loose panels and means of eavesdropping.

Evie started to pace, her face flushed with anger. "If I had not been here to see it firsthand, I would not have believed the Atabyrions could be so stupid."

"My lady," Justine warned in a wary voice. There was a changing screen in the corner, but there was no room behind it for Evie's gowns, so Justine began bustling around to find an appropriate alternative.

"I feel absolutely *terrible* for the Earl of Huntley's daughter," Evie went on, oblivious to the warning. "I'm disgusted by the machinations at work here. That poor girl! Her father has ruined her with this match. How could he be so shortsighted?"

Owen continued his inspection, listening to her rant as he worked. Etayne was doing the same thing across the room, and Clark had moved a chest over to the dormer window, high up on the wall, and tugged the latch loose so he could inspect outside. The sound of the falls rushed in with the fresh air.

"The girl's father believes he's making her Queen of Ceredigion," Justine said by way of explanation.

"Yes, but having them marry so soon?" Evie said incredulously. "He must have only arrived within the fortnight, mind you. Not long ago he sailed from Legault to attack us, and now he's already married to an Atabyrion. He's hopping around like a toad."

Owen chuckled at the comment and she stomped her foot. "It's not funny! That poor girl. She's beautiful, there's no denying it, and I can see why he'd be eager for a match to a wealthy lady, but what will happen to *her* once his claims are proved false? I wanted to box his ears!"

Owen knew that there was some merit to the man's claims, but before he could say as much, there was a subtle knock at the door.

Clark was still standing on the chest, so Owen stepped around the luggage to answer it. A middle-aged man stood there with a furtive look, but Owen recognized him as the man they had seen earlier, the one who had given the Espion sign.

"I am Lord Bothwell," the man said, bowing slightly. "The king has sent me to speak with the lady of North Cumbria. Is she disposed to have visitors presently?" His court speech was proper, and although his voice had an accent, Owen could tell he had trained in languages.

"Come in," Evie said, shooing away Justine, who was fidgeting with clasps to remove her jewelry.

Owen's first impression of Bothwell was that he was an oily man. He had lost the majority of his black hair, and he'd oiled what he had left and combed it down the back of his head. His eyes darted here and there, and although he was dressed in the court fashion of Atabyrion, his boots were clearly from Ceredigion. He wore a sword and dagger, but they were jeweled and seemed more ceremonial than battle worthy.

After the door shut behind him, he glanced quickly at each person in the room, as if doing arithmetic in his head.

"Ah," he said. "You will not find any traps or such here, my friends. This is the most secure room in Iago's palace. I chose it for you personally. My men are patrolling the corridor outside to keep out unwelcome entities." He smiled graciously. "It is an honor to meet my esteemed peers from Ceredigion. My lady, you were superb," he added with a flourish to Evie, bowing again. "You made a strong impression on Iago, not an easy feat to accomplish."

Evie folded her arms, frowning. "The *impression* I was trying to make on him was that he's being an utter fool."

"Oh, he *is* that," Bothwell said with a chuckle. "He's foolish, quick-tempered, too generous, and so far . . . an intemperate king. But he's young still. I must give him liberties based on that fact. Your presence in Edonburick has caused a storm amongst the nobles. You will see. You treated him not as a sovereign lord, but as a peer. Even your ship—the *Vassalage*—is a veiled implication." He chortled. "Well done. Well thought out." He tapped his fingers together with delight. "I get ahead of myself. First of all, introductions."

He bowed deeply. "I am Severn's spy in Iago's court. I am also Iago's closest friend and confidant. He really is that stupid. A few flattering words and he eats from your hand like a squirrel. As his advisor, I can come and see you as I please to deliver news and let you know how your negotiations are faring." He scratched his cheek. "If you require anything while here in the palace, let me know immediately and it will be taken care of. Iago has put me in charge of your comforts and ordered me to spare no expense, while in truth, the boy is nearly out of money! The royal coffers are practically empty, and without the nobles' support, he would not be able to pull off the attack he plans to make before year's end. You should know he's plotting an invasion of Ceredigion, though, quite frankly, he cannot afford to sustain it longer than a fortnight, if that. It will be a raiding party, no more. Nothing serious."

Evie glanced at Owen before returning her gaze to the oily man. "You're Iago's advisor? His trusted confidant? And you are telling us this? This is treason."

Bothwell looked a little startled. "Of course it is, my lady. I could be hung from a gibbet if Iago knew. Believe me, he's not that smart. Master Mancini more than compensates me for the risks I take and has offered me a position in Ceredigion should I become compromised. Truly, I am your ally in every sense of the word. Now, who is part of your entourage, hmmm?"

Clark stepped down off the chest. "The less you know, the better," he said. "My name is Clark."

"Yes, yes, I've heard of you," Bothwell said, bowing again. A growing feeling became more identifiable; Owen did not like this court intriguer. There was something about him—actually, there were many things about him—that disgusted Owen.

"And this is Owen Satchel," Clark said offhandedly. "He's one of Duke Horwath's household knights."

"So young to be a knight," Bothwell observed to Owen, bowing again. It was all the invitation Owen needed to reach out with his magic, letting it wash over Lord Bothwell like gentle rain. The man was more fit than he looked and he carried a blade hidden in his vest, which wasn't a surprise since he was a spy. Bothwell gave no indication at all that he knew his defenses were being tested.

"These two girls are ladies-in-waiting and will stay here. The rest of the lady's servants and lawyers will be residing on board our ship for now, as your inns all seem to be full."

"The crowds will soon depart Edonburick," Bothwell said confidently. "Once the wedding revels are over. In a few days, the palace will be quiet again and the servants can stay here. The king rarely stays at the hall, he's always off hunting or hawking or enjoying some other entertainment. If you two knights would fancy a tournament, he would be only too thrilled to call one."

"That won't be necessary," Clark said stiffly.

Evie stepped forward. "Tell us about the fisherman's son, Urbick. When did he arrive?"

Bothwell's eyes lit up. "Ah, I was sure you'd want to hear the story!" His voice took on a conspiratorial air. "He arrived less than a fortnight ago, but he was *invited* here by Iago before he left Legault. I tell you truthfully, every ruler wants to befriend this young man because they all hope to use him against your king. The boy's been in Occitania, Brugia, Legault, and now Atabyrion."

Evie shook her head. "But has he been tested? Has he been interrogated by those who would be in a position to confirm or dispute his claim?"

Bothwell shook his head and wagged a finger. "It's not that simple," he said with another oily smile. "First, he *looks* like an Argentine, does he not? I knew Eredur, and I've known Severn for years. He looks the part. He dresses the part. And his supposed aunt, in Brugia, has certainly taught him to *act* the part. He's been well trained, my lady. He can cite names, dates, and figures of importance, all from memory. More importantly, when you listen to his sad tale, as Iago did when he arrived, it makes you feel sympathy for him and animosity toward Severn. People want to help this young prince gain a crown."

Evie snorted. "Even if it's true, he was declared illegitimate by law. He cannot inherit the throne."

Bothwell steepled his fingers over his lips. "Laws are often changed, my dear. There are rumors even here in Edonburick that Severn will change the law to make his niece legitimate. That he is grooming her to be his successor *or* his queen. That is why he won't let her marry another man. Kings can do what they want."

He bowed again. "Now, I must be going. My visits will always be, of necessity, rather short. The king has invited you, my lady, to join him for a hawking trip on the morrow. He was captivated by you! There is a bend in the river called Wizr Falls that he would like to show you, and he hopes you may speak further now that Eyric is gone."

"Gone?" Evie demanded.

He waved his hand. "He's with his young wife now. One of her father's estates. Don't worry. He cannot leave Atabyrion without permission. The king conducts most of his business out of doors. Iago simply cannot sit in a chair for longer than a few moments. I will say it again. You've impressed him. He's not used to being treated as an equal, especially by a woman—a *younger* woman, no less. You are more than his match, my lady. Please try to convince him that invading Ceredigion would be a disaster."

"So the pretend prince will not be joining us?" Evie asked.

Bothwell shook his head. "No. They will be away from court for a few weeks, I believe."

"Do you know specifically where they are?" Clark asked pointedly.

Bothwell grinned. "Of course. And I can provide you a horse and directions if required. Believe me, there is nowhere in Atabyrion he can go that *I* won't know about. I'm at your service." He bowed yet again and excused himself.

After the door shut, Owen folded his arms. He had sensed none of the Fountain's magic during the conversation. Bothwell's style of spying reminded him of Mancini's. He didn't trust the man very much, but having such an ally would be helpful.

"I don't think I like that man," Evie said simply, wrinkling her nose.

"What did you make of him, Clark?" Owen asked.

The spy looked stern. "He's served Severn's interests for years. He's the one who told us Piers Urbick was here. He's been to Kingfountain several times, and from what Mancini tells me, he's quite jealous to live there. Atabyrion is too backward for his tastes."

Owen scratched the back of his head, chafing under the chain hood. "We have a bigger problem," he said. He looked straight at Evie. "I think Urbick may be telling the truth. He may very well be Eyric Argentine."

Stunned silence met his proclamation.

"How can you be so sure?" Evie asked after a moment, her voice quavering.

"I'm not," Owen said. He frowned. "But I felt something as he spoke. The Fountain spoke to me, but the message was not clear. He was lying about something, but I don't think he was lying about who he was."

"Oh dear," Evie said worriedly. "I've done it again, haven't I?"

Justine looked nervous and apprehensive. "Done what?"

Etayne had remained thoughtfully silent throughout the encounter with Bothwell. Her role was still supposed to be concealed from Evie, even though Owen had already told her.

"I did it to Dunsdworth once before. Deliberately offended him. Now I've done the same thing with the prince." She sighed. "But you don't think . . . Owen, you don't think Severn will step down for this rival, do you? This is going to lead to war, isn't it?"

Owen sighed deeply. "I think our goal now should be to prevent one."

CHAPTER EIGHTEEN

Wizr Falls

They had given Owen a brown stallion from the king's stables for their hawking expedition into the woods surrounding Edonburick. The land was a wild and savage place, pristine save for the trail cut along the river. Majestic snow-headed eagles perched in the tall trees. There were not a lot of game animals, but the noise of the horses had probably frightened them off.

Evie rode at the front of the column with Iago, who was spouting off incessantly about the wonders of Atabyrion—the majestic rivers, the fords, the lumber trade, how the speed of his hawks exceeded the falcons of Ceredigion. Owen rode comfortably in the saddle, next to Evie but slightly behind her, so he could hear the majority of what was said. In some ways, Iago's vigor for life, and love of conversation, reminded Owen of Evie herself. It was a bit annoying, actually.

Their horses were used to the rugged terrain, so they easily climbed higher into the mountains. The Ceredigic portion of the hunting party consisted of Evie, Justine, Owen, Clark, Etayne, and a lawyer named Sadger, and the Atabyrion contingent included King Iago, two of his knights, his birdmaster, a hunter, two lawyers, and several servants on mules hauling the food they would eat.

Owen listened with growing agitation as the dialogue continued, unable to participate in it at all since he was pretending to be a knight. He watched the woods for signs of trouble or ambush, the reins held loose in his gloved hands. He had been expending his energy looking for threats, and he was beginning to feel his power recede a little each time he used it. He still had plenty in reserve, but just being in a foreign land, with all its unique dangers and risks, was beginning to tire him. If he were not careful, he realized, he could drain his magic completely—something he'd never let happen before.

They spent the morning hawking, using the powerful birds to strike down smaller animals. Iago yelled with satisfaction each time one of the birds swooped down and caught something in its talons. His demeanor, while hunting, was all affability and good grace, as if nothing Evie had said the day before had troubled him in the slightest.

As it approached midday, they reached Wizr Falls.

Owen heard the falls before he saw them, and he had to admit, they did remind him hauntingly of the North. This waterfall started its descent in a series of steps, the water churning so violently it was nothing but froth and foam. The river twisted and turned at sharp angles along the way, cutting across the mountain path they had been following. The area was made of jagged, volcanic debris of various kinds. It was interesting to look at, especially the rocks that had naturally formed into thin columns and were crumbling in places like fallen tiles. The cliffs were fairly sheer and steep. Ferns and vegetation overhung the trail, forcing the horses to go single file through the narrow gaps leading up to the falls.

Wizr Falls was impressive, but then, the sight of so much water coming so quickly had never failed to strike Owen with awe. As they stopped to eat, he groomed Evie's horse himself, patting its withers and brushing it down, just as a knight in service would do.

"I must show you this part!" Iago said eagerly, grabbing Evie by the arm and pointing toward the edge of the narrow road leading to the falls.

Owen didn't want her out of his sight and noticed Clark's frown as well. They tied off the horses and hurried to follow the pair. Iago half dragged her through the brush.

"I've come here a hundred times if not a thousand," he said. "See the rocks hanging from the side of the cliffs? They look like Wizr pieces, do they not?"

"I can tell," Evie said, a little breathlessly. "They are like sentinels. They've not been carved?"

"Only by the river," Iago said. "They have always been here. Remnants of the Wizrs of old! I wish they existed today. Duke Maxwell claims to have a Wizr. It's all a bunch of rumors, of course."

Owen's ears perked up at the comment.

"We live in such drab and dreary days. It's all about laws and treaties now. In the past, during the age of King Andrew, when kingdoms had conflicts, they went to war! Sword against sword, that's how you managed things. I would have gloried in it. The past was truly the best of times. Our modern days are filled with blather."

"But war rarely solves problems," Evie countered. "It drains the coffers, grieves the mothers and widows."

"True, but plague and disease have much the same effect. There is always a new reason to weep. War is decisive. It is the ultimate test of manhood. It is a force, much like those churning waters. Ah, I love feeling the mist on my face!"

The wind had shifted, bringing some of the mist from the falls over to them. When Owen reached them, he saw them standing at the edge of the cliff, the river continuing far below them amidst a sea of rubble.

"Let's go farther down," Iago suggested, grabbing her arm.

Owen's heart leaped with fear. A little farther down from the crest was a series of boulders hanging over the river, each one wide enough for one or two persons. A slip would mean plummeting into a deadly chasm. The waterfall was to the right, almost bearing down on them with its never-ending flood.

Evie stared down at the boulders. "You've done this before?" she asked.

"Every time I've come here. The best view is from *that* one," Iago said, pointing to the farthest one, which was practically hanging off the cliffside. Owen's stomach shriveled at the sight. "Are you courageous, Lady Mortimer?" he taunted.

Owen wanted to rush down and shove the king off the cliff himself. He froze in indecision, wanting to speak up in warning, but he could already see the look in her eyes, the eagerness and daring that reached down to her very soul.

Iago let go of her arm and then ambled down the cliff like a goat, his footing confident and experienced. He went down to a lower stone and stood there, posing for her. "The rocks are a little wet, but you have sturdy boots. Come, I'll help you."

No, Owen willed her in his mind. Clark touched his shoulder and gave him a worried look that doubled as a question: *Should we intervene?*

But before Owen could say anything, she was scrabbling down the mountain after Iago. There was a grin on her face, an undeniable pleasure at braving something so risky. Sure-footed and fearless, she followed him all the way down to the shelf of rock overhanging the river. Iago held her hand as she descended the final part, and Owen realized he had stopped breathing.

"She's mad," Clark whispered.

"You're not far off the mark," Owen said, staring in bewilderment.

Iago looked up at Owen and Clark. "If you're too timid to join us, would you mind throwing a bag of food down?"

Owen needed no more goading. He ambled down the cliff himself, his heart in his throat, following the stair-like boulders and trying to ignore the screaming thoughts of what would happen if he fell. Well, he *was* Fountain-blessed. He didn't truly believe he'd die by waterfall.

When he reached one of the lower shelves of rock, near the one where Evie and Iago were sitting, he noticed the king was looking at him with admiration. Clark followed in his wake, his eyes wide with terror at the unnecessary risk they had taken.

"You have brave knights, Lady Mortimer," the king said to her, then nodded to Owen and Clark.

"The men of Ceredigion are fearless. The waterfalls of Dundrennan are even more impressive," Evie said mildly, acting as though the adventure were nothing out of the ordinary.

"So I have heard, so I have heard!" the king crooned.

"My name is Elysabeth Victoria Mortimer," she reminded him. "Lady Mortimer is my mother."

"And do you have your mother's eyes? I can't quite make out their color," the king asked slyly, his mouth turning to a charming smile. While he was shorter than Owen, he was about her own height and he could look her in the eye. Owen had always liked being taller than her. Hearing the familiarity in the king's voice made Owen want to punch him.

Lady Mortimer's eyes are green, Owen wanted to say smugly, for he had met her on occasion. She rarely ventured out of her own estate. The death of her husband had turned her into a recluse, and Evie's exuberance seemed only to drain her. She had none of her daughter's lively spirits. She was occasionally well enough to visit Duke Horwath in Dundrennan, but usually only for celebrations.

"It is your misfortune if you can't tell on your own," Evie said. Then she folded her arms and stared in awe at the rushing waters. "The falls are beautiful," she said.

One of the Atabyrion servants tossed a saddlebag down to King Iago, who caught it deftly. "Your meal, my lord!" shouted the servant.

Iago sat cross-legged on the rock and greedily opened the saddlebag, withdrawing a trove of food—crispy capon, grapes, bread and cheese, a jug of mead—which he proceeded to assemble on the rock before Evie like a Wizr board.

Owen heard a noise and turned back to see Justine standing on the cliff, white-faced and staring at Evie in mortal dread. She looked like she wanted to come down, but was too terrified to consider it. He was about to rise and help her, but Clark jumped up and ambled up the cliff to assist. She took his sturdy hand gratefully, her face quivering with fear as she painstakingly came down the edge of the cliff, rock to rock.

"Thank you," the girl whispered to Clark, her eyes grateful but still round with fear. She sat by Owen, trembling, her back pressed against the rock behind her, keeping as far from the edge as she could. A little flush came to Clark's cheeks and he nodded to her before returning to the edge, letting one of his legs dangle over it.

Justine glanced at Clark one more time, then looked away shyly.

Owen noticed.

Another servant threw down a second saddlebag of food. Owen caught it and began to distribute the meal while listening in to the conversation happening just below them.

"Now, I must ask you this, my lady. How the devil can you serve such a man as Severn?" Iago pressed. "Does it not sicken you what he did to claim the throne? I was young when I inherited, and the nobles hated my father, but they would have *never* allowed my uncle to rule instead."

"You mustn't understand our history very well," Evie said. "It's been naught but bloodshed and war. You say you crave those things, but it's a sad legacy. To answer your question, you seem to have completely misunderstood my master. I've studied the history of our kings, and he is no worse than many, and better than most. Let me cite some examples."

Clark bit into a crunchy apple, snapping away Owen's attention. His insides squirmed as he watched someone else pay devoted attention to Evie, so he was not hungry himself. There was an emotion called jealousy with which Owen was becoming intimately familiar. It felt as if a man were stabbing his insides with dull blades. Seeing Iago sitting so close to the edge gave him all sorts of fanciful hopes that he would see the man slip and fall.

He offered some bread to Justine and she accepted it, though she nibbled on the crust with little enthusiasm due to their precarious perch.

Evie was explicit. "First, the king's treasury is overflowing. He has made wise trading decisions, taxes the wealthy and the poor fairly, and spends less than he earns. There is very little debt in the kingdom, and when he incurs it, he pays it off before the interest is due. He has chartered several colleges and has increased the education of the people."

"He's bribing them to like him," Iago quipped.

"Not true. The people don't like him," Evie said emphatically. "He knows this. But he acts in their best interest regardless. He is just in his decisions, using the Assizes and the lord justices to ensure fair trials. He has pardoned many convicted of treason."

Owen had often been chosen as lord justice. His cheeks burned at the hidden compliment Evie had slid his way.

Iago lifted a finger. "But I have heard that his temper is nigh *uncontrollable*. That he flies into rages of passion, even in front of his servants. They say his wit is as cutting as a dagger. Do you deny it?"

"It's quite true," Evie said. "He does have a temper. It is his weakness, to be sure. But when you consider the lies that are said about him, the ceaseless interference with his kingdom's affairs, and the disloyalty shown to him, yes—he does get upset by this. He's a man, just like any other."

"He's a monster," Iago said with a snort.

Evie shook her head. "No, he isn't. He's misunderstood. He did not murder his nephews. One of his lords was behind that, in an effort to discredit Severn and put another man on the throne instead. Surely you must respect that he proved his right to rule in battle?"

"I do respect him for that," Iago said. "But while he may have won his crown by the sword, he can lose it by the sword just as well. I stand much to gain if Eyric becomes King of Ceredigion." He gave her a challenging look.

Evie returned the look with one of her own. "You stand to lose even *more* if Eyric fails. Wouldn't you rather have the friendship and support of a king in power? Think what it would do for your people. Think of the benefits that would come through an alliance with Ceredigion now, not later."

"I *am* thinking of it," Iago said with a hint of displeasure. "Eyric would be beholden to me, not me to Severn."

She shook her head. "You don't understand me. You stand something to gain if Eyric wins. But you risk even more if he loses."

Iago chuffed. "I risk nothing. The gain is all to my benefit."

"Not at all. You risk losing your life. Your crown. You have no wife. You have no child. If Severn comes to fight you, and he *will* if you continue to support this upstart, he will make Atabyrion his next conquest. He won't accept you as a vassal. You'll be destroyed, and someone else will be put in your place."

"You're threatening me?" he chuckled, almost amused.

"No, I'm warning you. You simply do not understand my king. He and my grandfather defeated Atabyrion before. They will do it again."

"That was my *father*," Iago drawled angrily. "Not me."

"And you are wiser and more experienced than your father was? Can you afford to wage war on Ceredigion? I'll say it again. Think what you are risking."

Iago shook his head. "I never do that. If I lived my life that way, I'd never step foot out of doors. We're sitting here on this stone because I'm *not* afraid of falling into the river. I think about what I might *gain*, not what I stand to *lose*. I've asked for an alliance with Ceredigion before, and Severn spited me. So I will treat with someone more amenable."

"What did you ask for?" Evie pressed.

"A marriage alliance. That is how you bind fates together. I wished to wed Princess Elyse. You can see I gave Eyric the girl he wanted. He had to have Kathryn the moment he laid eyes on her. I don't blame him!" he added with a dark chuckle. "And Eyric will give me Elyse. Even you must see the advantage in that! You're a clever girl, after all. And you know Severn will never grant me what I want."

Evie screwed up her nose a bit. Owen could see from the look in her eye that she was thinking very hard.

Don't say it, he thought. *Don't say it!*

Evie sat up straighter. "King Severn understands your situation. And he is prepared to enter into an alliance with you. A marriage alliance."

Iago leaned forward, eager. Their hands were almost touching, a sight that made Owen clench his teeth with fury.

"Not the princess? Oh, I see. I understand now. That's why he sent *you*." He leaned back, the realization flooding him with new ideas. New opportunities. Severn had baited the hook and dangled it now.

"I don't feel well," Clark muttered, his voice sounding queasy.

Owen glanced over and saw sweat streaking down Clark's face. He looked to be on the verge of vomiting.

"Maybe we should go back to the horses," Justine suggested. "I don't feel well either."

"What did you eat?" Owen asked the Espion, awareness striking him as sharp as an arrow shaft.

Clark's stomach clenched and he quickly rose, knowing now he was in peril. Owen saw the dizziness in his eyes, the unsteady shuffle of his boots.

And then Clark started to totter backward off the rock as Justine screamed.

CHAPTER NINETEEN

The Thief's Daughter

Owen shot out his hand and snatched at Clark's tunic before he could fall into the river. The Espion windmilled his arms, his face turning white with terror. Owen felt his own balance shifting and tried to dig the edges of his boots into the rock to steady himself. Then Justine grabbed Owen's shoulders, saving them both.

It was a heart-stopping moment. And the danger was far from over. Clark was always sure-footed and steady, but there was a feverish, pained look in his eyes. He had been poisoned; Owen felt sure of it, and from the look in Clark's eye, he knew it too.

"What happened?" Evie cried out, already on her feet.

Clark was safely back on the rock, but his body was swaying. Sweat dribbled from his pores.

"I'm sick too," Justine complained, her eyes darting back and forth as she gripped her stomach.

The Espion grabbed Owen's shoulder, his fingers digging in hard. "You saved my life," he whispered hoarsely.

"I haven't yet," Owen said with worry, realizing the dangerous predicament they were in. If Iago had ordered them poisoned, they were not safe in his hands or at his court. A spasm jolted through Clark and his knees buckled. Owen put an arm around Clark's shoulder to hold his weight, but he did not dare take his eyes off Evie as she climbed up to the higher rock to join them.

Justine choked back tears, her face full of misery at the sight of Clark's suffering. She was milk white herself, shivering as if they were in a winter storm.

"We need some help down here!" Owen shouted to the servants looking down from above. He shifted to his back to take more of Clark's weight and helped him climb up the next rock. The sound of the falls and the river was an ever-present reminder of what would happen if they fell. Some of the nimbler servants hurried down and helped by grabbing Clark's arms and hauling him up the side of the cliff. Owen turned back and extended a hand to Justine. Her palms were sweating, so he grabbed her by the wrist instead. She suddenly slumped, her eyes rolling back in her head, but he caught her around the waist before she fell.

"Justine!" Evie cried in terror and rushed forward to help, but Iago held her arm.

"You'll fall! He's got her!" the king said. Then he shouted, "Don't just stand there, oafs! Help him!"

Owen ducked under Justine and hoisted her up onto his shoulders, then climbed up to the next rock, where several servants met him, ready to take the load. Clark had already been carried up the trail, and as soon as he passed Justine off to the others, Owen rushed over to him. The servants had settled Clark down on the brush, and Etayne was already kneeling next to him, her ear on his chest. Moments later, Justine was laid down beside the other patient.

Owen's chest felt like a beehive that had been caved in. His emotions were swarming.

"They've been poisoned," Owen whispered to Etayne. His gaze was already assessing the servants, looking for an expression of guilt. The poisoner *must* be among them, he deduced. He probably wasn't the one who had thrown them the saddlebag, but he had intercepted it first. One of these men had tried to kill them. But which one?

He saw Iago helping Evie up to the trail, his hands gripping her waist, and he had to smother the rage that burned inside his heart.

"His lips are blue," Etayne muttered worriedly. She stuck her fingers into Clark's mouth, then turned his head to the side as he messily expelled everything he'd eaten.

"Get the bag of food he ate from," Etayne whispered to him. She hurried over to Justine and repeated the maneuver, making another mess. The servants backed away in disgust. Evie shoved Iago away and rushed to the side of her maid, her eyes glistening with tears of worry. Owen had a hand on his sword hilt as he approached the edge of the cliff.

Iago saw him coming and his eyes widened with fear. "I had nothing to do with this. I swear by the Fountain! For all I know, that lunch was meant for us." His face was twisted with worry and anger, which added credence to his tale. "Fetch my surgeon!" he called out to one of his knights. "I know it's bloody far! Start riding now!"

"Where's the saddlebag?" Owen said, and then saw it down on the rocks.

"I'll send someone down to fetch it. Toal! Down and fetch it. Now!" Iago snapped.

Owen turned back to the crowd gathering around the victims, his insides suddenly turning to ice. He realized that Iago had inadvertently saved his life. If Owen hadn't been so upset watching him and Evie, he would have eaten from the saddlebag as well. Then all three of them would have been sickened.

The king joined the crowd around the bodies and laid a hand on Evie's shoulder. "I don't know who did this," he said in a low voice. "But

I will find and punish him. I promise you that. No one besmirches my honor this way. You are here under my safe conduct. I'll flay the man when I find out who it was!"

Owen didn't care for the promises of vengeance. But Iago's reaction was exactly what he would expect from someone who was innocent. Justine and Clark were convulsing violently now. Their skin looked ashen, their lips blue. He stared at Etayne in wild despair and knelt down beside her.

Her eyes were focused and serious as she met his gaze. "I need my supplies," she whispered to Owen. "We've got to get them back to Edonburick."

"Then we ride at once!" Evie commanded, her voice shaking.

♦ ♦ ♦

Owen's frown felt as if it would be fixed on his face always. He stared down at Justine in her sickbed. Her cheeks were so waxy and pale she looked like a corpse, an effect that was only increased by the purple bruises under her eyes. Her lips were white, slightly parted, and her breaths were so far apart that she appeared for all purposes to be dead. Clark was in the next bed, his body still trembling as it fought off the poison trying to kill him.

Etayne was slumped in a chair between the two patients, looking weary and stern. Evie sat at Justine's side, stroking her hand.

"Do you think she will live?" Evie whispered to Etayne. "Tell me the truth."

Etayne stretched her arms and sighed. "I don't know, my lady. I've done all I can. I gave them both the antidote, but the poison was in their system for a long while. Her constitution isn't as hardy as Clark's. I think he'll make it." She reached over and took a cool cloth from the array of supplies on the small dresser. "Even asleep, he's still fighting," she said as she wiped his forehead.

Owen put his hand on Evie's shoulder to comfort her, and she turned into his abdomen and started weeping. He smoothed her hair, his throat tight. Justine had been their companion for years. She was like a sister to him, not a servant. It was not fair that she should suffer.

It was nearly midnight. The physicians and midwives of Iago had done their best to help, but it was Etayne's quick thinking and knowledge of poisons that had helped her identify which one had been used. There was no one else in the room with them. Iago had come several times to express his anger and sympathy, but Evie had no wish to talk to him or to accept his condolences yet.

Evie's tears started to ease as Owen rubbed her back, and after a while, she stifled a yawn.

"There is little else you can do, my lady," Etayne said to Evie. "Maybe if you were to lie down next to her and hold her? Help keep her warm?"

Evie nodded enthusiastically and quickly slipped onto the bed behind Justine, wrapping her arms around the pale, sick girl. Etayne rose from her chair and walked over to the open window, where she rested her elbows on the sill and stared into the night sky. The rushing sound of the falls in the distance reminded Owen of home.

Evie's eyelids started to grow heavy as she stroked Justine's hair, and before too long, she gave into the exhaustion of the day and fell asleep. Owen walked slowly over to Clark, who was still shivering and jolting beneath his mound of blankets. Though he was not inclined to climb into bed and snuggle with his friend, he was pleased to see the Espion's cheeks looked ruddier.

He then went back and bent over Evie, soaking in the sight of her chest rising and falling regularly, feeling tenderness and gratitude that she hadn't been harmed. He bent low enough to kiss the hair at her temple, grazing it lightly with his mouth, and then pulled away and walked over to the window. Etayne was still staring into the night sky.

"Thank you," he said sincerely.

She glanced at him, flushing a little at the compliment. "I might not have saved either of them," she said. "Save your thanks until morning."

He shook his head. "You did your best, Etayne. You knew what to do. That's why I'm thanking you. If you hadn't been there, I would have watched both of them strangle and die by the falls. At least now they have a chance."

She shrugged a little, turning back to face the open window. The moon was a thin sliver of light, just over a nest of trees. Then she turned to him. "It's going to be a long night, Lord Owen. Would you teach me a little about the magic? Can you show me how to use it?"

He was tired and weary, but he did not want to leave her awake all alone. Perhaps it was no coincidence that it was so late at night. After all, Ankarette had given him his first lessons in Fountain magic in the dark.

"I will try," he said wearily. "I'm not a very good teacher. The place we should begin is figuring out how you can fill your cup. Without that, you can't use the magic at all."

"Filling a cup," she said with a nod, listening to his every word with great interest.

"For me, it started when I was a little boy. I saw my brother stacking tiles in a row and then knocking them down. It utterly fascinated me and I began to mimic what he did. I could stack tiles for hours, every day. It was never a burden or a chore. I loved it." He chuckled. "I still do. As I've gotten older, I've found some of the same satisfaction from playing Wizr or reading. It's about strategy, I suppose. Plotting what will happen in advance. That is what gives me power with the Fountain. To know your power, Etayne, you must know your passion. Is there something you have always been fond of? Some work that isn't a chore or a trouble?"

"I have been giving this some thought since our talk on the ship, and I think I may have figured it out." But she looked abashed, as if she did not wish to speak the words out loud.

"What?" he asked carefully.

"I think you'll laugh," she said.

"Why? Is it strange?"

"I hate when people laugh at me," she said seriously.

"Then I won't. Tell me." He said it coaxingly, trying to put her fears at rest.

"I've always loved trying on clothes," she said hesitantly.

He wrinkled his brow and waited for her to say more, curious.

"You *didn't* laugh," she said, pleased. "I know it sounds ridiculous. When I was little, I used to pretend to be other people. I loved to put on different dresses. I'd imagine I was a baker's wife. Or a chandler's girl. An alderman's daughter. As I got older, I began to wish for more. My favorite was to pretend I was an *earl's* daughter." She looked down, flushing. "I've always taken a secret delight in studying people. How they walk. How they move. How they speak. I would practice playing a role in front of my little sister and my friends, and force them to treat me like I was something more than what I truly was—a thief's daughter."

Her mask fell away as she said those words, revealing her true self. Without the disguise, he could see years of bitterness and resentment, years of abuse and worry. Years of yearning to be someone important, to hide the shame of her past. Her confidence was gone, replaced by a look of self-loathing and contempt.

"How did you come to join the Espion?" he asked her softly.

Her lips pressed hard together. "My father," she said in a low, angry voice. Then she sighed. "I can't believe I'm telling you all this. No one ever asks about my story. They only want me to *do* something for them." She glanced at him. "Except for you. My father is one of those fountain-men at the sanctuary of Our Lady. I grew up with my mother and sister in a hovel outside the sanctuary, but my father had to stay there during the day for fear of the law. He used me to cheat people. He'd dress me up in fine gowns he'd stolen. He taught me how to watch the nobles, to act like them. All so I could steal from them. I even stole coins from the fountain. When I was twelve, I was caught by the Espion. They took me to Mancini." She frowned at the memory, her eyes guarded. "He offered me a chance to join them. He needed someone young, someone he could teach. Someone he could mold. Well, it was that or go into the river! To ensure my father and everyone else I knew would believe I was dead, Mancini shoved another body into the river. Then he sent me to Pisan." She shuddered at the word, her eyes blinking rapidly. After a moment, she collected herself again. "So you see, Master Owen, I'm more of a pretender than Eyric is." She sniffed, and then looked him in the eye. "I suspect that you are *pretending* as well."

Owen felt a coldness settle over him. He knew what she meant, but he wasn't going to say it. "Am I?"

She nodded with certainty. "I have a suspicion. Mancini never told me about you, you know. He told me about Ankarette, the greatest spy of them all, and how she had helped him become master of the Espion. But he never once mentioned you. After you and I met, I found myself wondering why. I think it's because Ankarette helped you both. When you were brought to Kingfountain as a young boy, I remember hearing about you. I think I even saw you once at the sanctuary. All by yourself. Then I learned about the little boy who could see the future in his dreams." She blinked. "That's not true, is it?"

Owen took a deep breath. This was so dangerous, talking to her. Yet she had secrets of her own, some of which he now knew. She had trusted him with the story of her past, something he realized she rarely, if ever, did.

Over the years Owen had missed his relationship with Ankarette—there had been no lies between them, and yet she had also understood and could relate to his powers. What if he lost Evie? Not having a companion to confide in and trust would make his life an utter misery. He shared Etayne's eagerness for friendship, but he felt conflicted by it, particularly because he knew she would be able to understand him in ways that Evie could not. Evie *should* be the one with whom he shared everything; Evie, who was not Fountain-blessed.

The feelings wrestled inside him like snakes, and he could not bring himself to say the words. But she was looking at him so imploringly, so desperate for anything resembling friendship, that he could not resist. He shook his head no.

Etayne breathed out. Her voice was very low when she spoke again. "That wasn't easy for you to admit. Thank you for your trust." Then she looked him in the eye, her face vulnerable and intense. "I swear by the Fountain that I won't tell anyone. I swear it."

"Thank you," Owen whispered. "I won't tell anyone about you either. You have my word."

She straightened her shoulders. "I will do whatever you ask, Lord Owen. Anything. Just teach me. If I'm truly Fountain-blessed, that is a secret I don't want anyone else to know. Especially Mancini."

Owen nodded.

She sighed, relieved. "How do you use the power then? How do you summon it?"

"It's difficult to describe," Owen said thoughtfully. "It just seems to happen naturally for me. I don't need to force it, but I do need to open myself to it. I can feel the Fountain all around me. It's like a river of rushing water, always flowing. When I want to access the power, I just open myself to it and let the current take me. Let me show you."

He let out his breath and opened himself to the Fountain's magic, letting it flow from him into her. There it was again, that sensation of his power draining away and not being replenished. This time, he wasn't trying to probe for her weaknesses. He just wanted her to feel what it was like. She closed her eyes, lifting her chin slightly, and sighed.

"I can feel it," she murmured. "It's like rain."

"Good," he said coaxingly. "Now try to use it. I don't know how the power will manifest in you, but let it flow through you, and then try to—I don't know—*direct* it back at me."

He watched as she stood there, eyes closed, hands pressing against the edge of the windowsill. She was concentrating, or perhaps meditating was the better word. It did not seem to be a strain or difficulty.

He remembered how Ankarette had tried to teach him about the nuances of the Fountain when he was a little boy. She had been so patient, so tender with him. He could tell that Etayne had experienced little tenderness in her life.

"Is that what she looks like?" Etayne asked. "I see a woman's face in my mind. It's coming from you. Is that Ankarette Tryneowy?"

Owen was startled. Was she reading his mind?

"Yes, I was just thinking about her."

"She was pretty," Etayne said, eyes still closed. He felt the flow of the Fountain magic shift, a ripple like a huge stone plunging into placid waters.

His vision rippled like the waves and he blinked rapidly.

The person next to him by the window wasn't Etayne anymore.

It was Ankarette.

"By the Veil!" Owen gasped in shock. It looked just like her!

The mirage vanished as Etayne opened her eyes wide in surprise. "What? What happened? I feel faint." She started to wobble and Owen had to catch her before she crumpled.

♦ ♦ ♦

There has always persisted deep enmity between Ceredigion and Occitania. Over the centuries, great wars have been fought to assert rights of rulership in Occitania. The greatest and most interesting war occurred nigh on fifty years ago. A young girl from Donremy in Occitania arrived at the court of the exiled prince of Occitania claiming the Fountain had spoken to her and that she had been instructed to take the prince to the sanctuary of Rannes and there crown him king. And she did. Never underestimate the power of those who are Fountain-blessed to achieve great things.

—Polidoro Urbino, Court Historian of Kingfountain

♦ ♦ ♦

CHAPTER TWENTY

Evie's Duty

Etayne's dizziness did not last long. Owen helped her into a nearby chair and quickly found some of the invalids' broth for her to drink. She took a swallow, blinking rapidly, and then took a longer sip.

Staring down into her eyes, Owen pressed, "Have you done this before?"

She shook her head. "That was the first time. I'm surprised how tired I got so quickly. Like I was plunged into a river. I struggled to swim in it. But if I practice, I think I can get used to it."

Owen nodded in agreement. "It can weary you if done for too long. But you are right, Etayne. If you practice, it will get easier and easier." He could imagine many ways such a gift could be used, especially by a member of the Espion.

"I think we should keep this a secret for now," he said earnestly. "At least until we get back to Mancini."

She smiled wryly. "I have no problem keeping this from him altogether. I can only imagine how he'd want to exploit it."

"True," Owen agreed. "It will be our secret then. For now. Can you try it again? Are you strong enough?"

She nodded vigorously and set the mug down on the floor. "I was startled, that's all. Help me feel the magic first. Can you summon it again?"

Owen did, allowing a gentle ripple of Fountain magic to swell inside him. She closed her eyes, immersing herself in it. He watched her eyes squeeze harder, as if she were struggling with some internal discomfort. Then a shimmer danced over her face and her features changed. This was someone different—a handsome older woman with dark hair and wrinkles at her eyes and cheekbones.

"Who are you now?" Owen asked curiously, feeling his excitement growing moment by moment. Yes, another Fountain-blessed would know she was using magic, but they would have no way of knowing how the magic was being used. This power she possessed was truly impressive. It was an obvious manifestation of her determined efforts to disguise herself. He had never read about such a power, not in all his studies.

The image shimmered and then vanished. Etayne's eyes were solemn. "That was my mother."

♦ ♦ ♦

By the next morning, Clark had roused from his fever. He was weak and pale, but the violence of the seizures had passed. By midmorning he was slowly taking in broth and managing to sit up on his own. Walking was impossible, but his strength was slowly returning.

The poison had devastated Justine, who had not stirred at all. The look of dread and misery on Evie's face was torture to Owen, as was the sight of his friend's suffering. Justine's black glossy hair was dull and fraying. Her skin, normally pale, had a greenish cast to it. Her cheekbones were sunken, and the bruises under her eyes gave her a frightening cast. Etayne had done everything she could, even forcing broth down her throat to bring her vital sustenance. But poor Justine was withering before their eyes.

Their Espion contact in Atabyrion, Lord Bothwell, arrived midmorning to examine the invalids. "I am greatly disturbed by this outrage," he said with unctuous concern. "I thought you would wish to know the results of my investigation."

Clark glanced at Owen from the sickbed, his brow furrowing with distrust and anger.

"What have you learned?" Owen asked, as patiently as he could. He had been up all night and was bone weary and sick at heart. His eyes darted to Evie, who was still sitting by Justine's bed, clasping her limp hand.

Lord Bothwell frowned. "You don't suspect that *I* was behind this?"

"At the risk of sounding impertinent," Owen said sharply, "it would help matters if you'd get to your point quickly and leave the suspicions to us. My lady's maid is very ill and our tempers are short."

"I see," Lord Bothwell stammered, looking rather waxy with sweat. "I assure you that I am doing everything I can to resolve this matter. It is fortunate you brought someone trained as a . . . midwife with you. Her skills have certainly been of great use. As I was saying, I have investigated the matter on behalf of Iago. He is most anxious to understand if one of his servants is to blame. There were two men under suspicion, and one of them has failed to arrive at the palace since the outing yesterday. His whereabouts remain unknown, but I feel confident he's our man. We are searching for him now, and if need be, we will torture him to get a confession."

Evie looked sickened by the notion. "Under torture, a man might confess anything. Find out what you can about him, but please, let's understand his motive before you become barbaric."

Bothwell was chagrined. "I thought it was the custom in Ceredigion. I beg your pardon, my lady."

Evie shook her head. "No doubt you have heard many rumors about our realm that simply aren't true."

There was a knock at the door and a servant opened it. "His Grace would like to visit the injured," the serving girl said, dipping into a clumsy curtsy.

Looking startled, Lord Bothwell bowed deeply. "As I was saying," he continued in a very different tack, "I see you are indisposed this morning and that further outings would not be appealing to you."

"You're here, Bothwell?" Iago said, entering the sick chamber with a jaunty walk and clapping Bothwell on the back. "I thought I told you to find out who poisoned our friends and bring them to justice?"

"I . . . I . . . I was merely taking the courtesy of telling Lady Elysabeth . . . M-Mortimer, that you had indeed entrusted me with that very duty—"

Iago looked perturbed. "Then get on with it and quit annoying her. Go."

The interaction made Owen appraise Lord Bothwell in a new light. His opinion of himself and his influence with the king was probably exaggerated. Perhaps it was possible that Iago was not as vapid as the spy assumed.

Iago came and stood by Justine's bedside, his face darkening with emotion. "Ah, I was hoping to see some improvement this morning. 'Tis not so." He glanced at Clark, who was struggling to sit up. Etayne hurried over to his side and helped him. "At least your knight appears to be recovering. How fare you, sir?"

"Much improved since yesterday," Clark replied with a hoarse voice.

Iago nodded with respect. "You do your kingdom honor. I wish you a hastened recovery."

"Thank you, my lord."

Iago turned back toward Evie, pursing his lips. "You look terrible."

Evie had not changed her gown or brushed her hair since their harried arrival from the outing the day before. "As you can see, my lord, my maid is quite indisposed," she said sharply.

Iago waved his hand. "I jest, that is all. I was told you waited up all night with your servant. Your friend, more likely than not. It is commendable. Would you walk with me? I think some fresh air would suit you."

Evie frowned. "I'm afraid I must decline. Justine is looking worse and I want to be here in case . . ."

"I was just going to take you for a walk around the grounds," he said. "We will not be far, I assure you, and we can be fetched immediately if her situation worsens. Come, my lady. Walk with me." He offered his elbow.

It was a sensitive and thoughtful gesture, and Owen begrudgingly admired him for it. Evie stared at Iago warily, looking conflicted about accepting his offer, but then she nodded brusquely and rose. After smoothing some of the wrinkles from her gown, she accepted Iago's arm and glanced at Owen, giving him a nod to follow, which he had already intended to do.

Owen looked at Etayne, who nodded in a silent agreement that she would stay behind with the sick ones, and he followed the two as they began their walk around the grounds. Iago pointed out different aspects of the building's architecture, explaining that the braided design of gold was called a Kiltec weave. Owen paid little attention to their talk, choosing to walk at a discreet distance and observe the scenery for himself. The sour smell of pipe smoke lingered in the air, mixed with the fresh fragrance of evergreen sap. There was much commotion on the grounds, woodsmen cutting firewood, blacksmiths grinding with whetstones, and a constant parade of children, ribbons, and barking dogs. There was nothing about Iago's clothes that set him apart from his people, nothing that proclaimed him the king of the land.

"You really do?" Evie asked the king in surprise, drawing Owen's attention back to the conversation, although he had missed much of it.

"Of course!" Iago answered, then lowered his voice. "I roam the mountain valleys often. How else am I to learn the troubles and needs of my people? Most of the folk outside of Edonburick have no idea what I look like anyway, and travelers are common. I've slept in many a hayloft and supped with plenty of pottagers and their wives."

"What is a pottager?" Evie asked curiously.

"One who tends a garden. What are they called in Ceredigion?"

"Farmers, I suppose," Evie responded. "I'd not heard that word before."

"The land is so rugged here," Iago said. "Everything grows at a slant. There isn't room for oxen and plow horses. Pottagers fix up the land as they may, growing leeks or squash or whatever will survive here. Leek soup is one of my favorites!"

Evie smiled at that. "And do you hear things about yourself that offend you while you're staying with a pottager?"

"Constantly," he replied with a jovial laugh. "But I never let on who I am. Iago is a common name in Atabyrion. The equivalent in your country is James. Hardly a cause for suspicion. Ah, here we are." They were approaching a roofed porch with a bench, a table, and a Wizr board. It was open air and set near a small flower garden surrounded by a stone hedge.

"You brought me all the way out here to play Wizr?" Evie asked with uncertainty.

"You don't fancy the game? Shall I teach you?"

Evie smoothed some hair over her ear. "I'm not very good," she feigned. "I lose all the time when I play."

"I will try not to take advantage of you then," he said gallantly and ushered her over to the bench. She sat down, placing her elbows on the table, and risked a quick look at Owen as Iago circled the table to seat himself.

Owen wanted to sigh dramatically, but he was afraid it would make her start giggling. So he feigned interest in the flower garden while staying within earshot.

"The pieces are carved out of wood, not stone," Evie said.

"I imagine the set is not as fancy as the ones to which you're accustomed. But the rules are still the same. You've chosen the light? I'll play the dark side."

Owen had to cover his mouth to hide a smile when she beat him in four moves.

"Well," Iago said, half-chuckling, half-incensed. "Shall we play again?"

"If you'd like," she replied meekly.

Then she beat him in six moves, using a technique Owen had taught her.

Owen risked a look at Iago, whose face was darkening. "You were being modest, I see."

"No, I *really* do lose most of the time I play," she answered.

Then he seemed to understand. "Ah, I see. I'd forgotten. You grew up with Lord Kiskaddon, the boy who's Fountain-blessed. Let me try this again. Please don't toy with me. If I'm going to beat you, I want to earn it." He reassembled the pieces.

She defeated him in eight moves.

"Humph!" he grunted, sitting back and staring at the board. "If you play this well, I'd fancy seeing a game between you and Kiskaddon."

It was all Owen could do not to cough on his sleeve. He turned his back to the pair of them so that neither would see his face.

"I'll be honest," Evie said. "He taught me to play Wizr. He's fairly skilled at this game."

"I would imagine," Iago said. Then his voice took a more serious tone. "What you told me yesterday, before the commotion. You said you were here to negotiate a truce between our kingdoms. That Severn was offering *you* as one of the terms." He paused a moment, choosing his words carefully. Owen's stomach plummeted. "It was *my* understanding, well . . . I suppose it's no more than gossip really, that you and Lord Kiskaddon were betrothed. Are you doing this to please your king? Or is it what you would wish?"

What Owen wished was that he could pick up a dirt clod and throw it at Iago's head. What could Evie say, knowing that Owen was standing so near? It was probably torturing her. At least, he hoped it was torturing her half as much as it was giving him pain. He bit his lip to keep from swearing under his breath, but he remained stock-still and utterly silent.

"That is kind of you to inquire," Evie said evasively, her voice sounding more and more uncomfortable. "But I would rather not discuss such personal matters over a game of Wizr."

"You could hardly call this a game of Wizr," Iago spat. "You have completely obliterated my self-confidence and my pride. I'll admit, I'm not all that fond of the game anyway. I would rather swing a sword at someone than move a few bits of carved wood around a board. They say that Wizr shows you how someone's mind works, though, and you've shown me that you are far smarter than I will ever be." He sniffed and sighed. "Well, Lady *Mortimer*, if you aren't comfortable telling me about your feelings, can you at least tell me something about Lord Kiskaddon? All I have heard are the inflated legends that grant him mystical qualities."

"They're probably all true," Evie said with the hint of a smile in her voice.

"Will you disabuse none of my illusions then?" Iago implored, exasperated. His voice sounded calmer when he continued. "I can see why he would be jealous of parting with you. You've only been here a short while, and I'm already taken with your vivacity, your wit, and your courage. Those are traits that I admire and never thought I would find in a . . . a . . . *lass from the frozen North*."

"We may be used to the cold, but our blood burns hot," Evie said.

"I already knew that. Now tell me something about Lord Owen Kiskaddon. I insist. Not a secret. Nothing too personal. What does he look like? What is his personality? Is he as rude as you are?"

Evie laughed at the question. "Very well, my lord, if it will please you." She took a moment, seeming to steady herself. Owen's ears were aflame, and he was frozen in place, feeling an acute sense of misery. "Owen's older brother was a hostage of King Severn's, and because of his parents' complicity in the plot to topple the king, he was thrown from the falls after the king's victory at Ambion Hill. Owen was then sent to

Kingfountain as a replacement hostage while the king and his advisors planned the fate of his family."

"He must have been terrified," Iago observed in a contemplative tone.

"He was," Evie said. "My grandfather, Duke Horwath, brought me to Kingfountain to be his friend."

"And your father, Lord Mortimer, died at Ambion Hill himself?"

Evie paused. "You knew that?"

"I do. That must have been very painful for you. Losing your father. When my father died, it affected me deeply. But please, go on."

The king was more sensitive than Owen had realized. He nudged a clump of grass with the tip of his boot, wishing a flock of squawking ducks would flap overhead to interrupt things.

"Well, I will just say that Owen and I became close friends. And we have remained close ever since." She paused, and he could hear the pain in her voice when she continued. "He is very dear to me still."

Owen felt tears sting his eyes and one of them escaped, streaking down his cheek before he knew it had come. He clenched his jaw and willed them to cease.

"Then your mission to Atabyrion comes at a great personal cost," Iago said in a low, sympathetic voice. "You have a duty to your king and a duty to your heart. All I can say is Owen Kiskaddon is a lucky man to have such a devoted friend. He is a powerful lord in your realm. Word arrived in Edonburick that he defeated the King of Occitania in a surprise night battle and sent him scampering. That's the equivalent of defeating someone in Wizr in only *two* moves, which is theoretically impossible. I would that I could meet him someday. What does he look like?"

"He's rather handsome," Evie said in a tone that implied, to Owen, that she enjoyed talking about him. "He has brown hair with a patch that . . . he never combs. His hair is quite unruly." Skating away from dangerous territory, she continued, "He is kind and thoughtful and very brave.

He stands up for those who are weak, and petitions the king to have mercy. The king knows he is loyal, and listens to his counsel and advice."

And Owen could tell she wanted to say, *And he is standing right there listening to our conversation.* But she did not.

Owen surreptitiously wiped the tearstain from his cheek, his heart burning inside his chest for the girl he loved.

"I guess I must ask you this," Iago said softly. "When someone has conflicting duties, they must choose one of them. Can I surmise that you wouldn't have come to Atabyrion if you weren't prepared to fulfill your king's wishes?"

"Are *you* prepared to release the pretender to my custody so that I might bring him back to Ceredigion?"

Iago sighed with pain. "I do understand conflicting loyalties," the king said. "I gave Eyric my sworn word that I would aid and protect him. If I broke that vow to him, how could you ever trust that I'd keep a vow made to you?"

"You made that vow hastily," Evie said pointedly.

"Indeed. If only you had come sooner. But there may be a way around it." His voice grew more serious. "If Severn were no longer King of Ceredigion, then you would no longer have to hold fealty to him."

As soon as he said the words, Owen's mind began to race.

Suddenly a serving girl came rushing up to the patio. "My lord, I beg your pardon! My lady! Your maid is sinking fast. Her breathing is troubled. There is fear she is dying. I was sent to find you."

Evie pushed away from the table and the Wizr board and started to run back to the sickroom. Owen was fast at her heels.

CHAPTER TWENTY-ONE

A Quiet Breath

As Owen stood to the side, watching Justine gasp, his heart was sick with sadness. Evie barely managed to hold back tears as she knelt by the bedside of her friend and companion and squeezed her hands. The Atabyrion doctor shook his head solemnly, giving the universal shrug of helplessness, and exited the room. Clark was sitting up unassisted now, and his look was dark and troubled as he stared at the pale girl. Standing beside him, Etayne looked haggard with exhaustion. The small band from Ceredigion was silent as they listened to Justine's quiet, labored breaths.

The king had not accompanied them to the sickchamber, choosing instead to give Evie space to grieve amongst her own people.

"Please, Justine," Evie begged, her face pinched with sadness. "You can do this! You can pull through! Please don't abandon hope. There was so much we were going to do together. Please try to live! You *must* try. If you'd only awaken, you'd be able to eat and build your strength." Evie wiped tears from her cheeks with the back of her hand, the other hand still gripping Justine's pale fingers.

Owen hated to watch Evie suffer. He took a step toward her and put his hand on her shoulder. She looked up at him disconsolately, trembling with pent-up sorrow.

"I can't bear to lose her," Evie whispered. "I cannot."

"I've done all that I know, my lady," Etayne said wearily. "Poison affects people in different ways. Clark was stronger."

"And I feel weak as a kitten still," Clark said. Then he stared down at the girl's sickbed once more, his mouth turning into a deep frown. "Poor lass."

"I can't give up; I won't lose hope!" Evie said with frustration. "Please, Justine! I *need* you! I need your comfort and your companionship. You are so dear to me. *Please*!"

The gasps were getting more pronounced. It was agony to watch her frail chest heave and sigh. The intervals between her breaths were punctuated by moments of stillness.

A timid knock came at the door. Evie looked furious at the interruption, so Owen walked to the door and opened it. Lord Bothwell stood on the other side, his face flushed.

"What is it?" Owen asked.

Lord Bothwell covered his mouth. "The . . . ahem . . . the individual we were seeking. Tell your mistress," he craned his neck to try to see around Owen, who blocked the view deliberately. "Tell her he was found. At the bottom of the falls. A fisherman caught him in his nets. There was a knife wound in his back. I suspect that means the poisoner is still at large. Do be careful, sir. Guard your mistress. It looks like her protection rests in your hands entirely now."

"I will indeed," Owen said. "Thank you, Bothwell." He started to shut the door, but the Atabyrion noble held it.

"If there is anything I might do to be of service . . . ?"

"Her ladyship would appreciate a moment to grieve in private," Owen said. Then he shut the door and blocked the man's view entirely.

Owen noticed the sound of the girl's rattled breathing had quieted. A final sigh escaped from Justine's lips, and then she was gone.

"No! No!" Evie said bitterly, weeping as a horrible flood of emotions buffeted her. Sobs and groans racked her chest as she buried her face against Justine's breast.

Owen felt the trickle of the Fountain bubbling up inside of him. He had not summoned the magic, but he felt it awakening inside of himself nonetheless. Etayne's head jerked up, her eyes meeting his with confusion. She felt it too.

"She's gone," Clark said with finality, his voice thick with despair.

Owen slid the door's bolt into place, moving almost unconsciously, and followed the flow of the Fountain to the bed. He could sense a presence in the room. Justine lay silent and still, her lifespark having left the waxy shell of her body. The true Justine was still with them in the room, however, and Owen could feel the comforting thoughts she was directing toward Evie, who was too anguished to feel them.

Stepping forward slowly, warily, Owen stood behind Evie, staring down at the body of her friend. Something was welling up inside him. The waters of the Fountain were churning now, lapping at him in waves. A shiver of fear ran down his legs.

Etayne stared at him, her eyes widening with awe. But she was the only one who seemed to sense there was something brewing.

Owen felt the shrinking edges of his magic expand for a moment, swelling as if the waters of a great river were filling him.

He stood by the bedstead, near Justine's head, gazing down at the untidy black wisps of her hair. He knew what he needed to do. From some deep well of memory, he could see a sickroom in Tatton Hall. Hear the sounds of grief coming from his parents. There was a stillborn babe with a downy fluff of white against his scalp. The blood-slick babe was cradled in the arms of the midwife. Ankarette Tryneowy—the queen's poisoner. She had used all her knowledge and the power of herbs to save him, but it had not been enough. But there was another power she possessed. A power that would drain her very essence.

Owen knew he would be weakened by it. He knew he would not be able to summon the magic again, perhaps for days or even weeks. That was a serious risk for all of them. But his heart was swayed by Evie's heartrending tears and his own feelings toward Justine. And more than that, he sensed it was the Fountain's will.

Trying to tame his nerves and fear, Owen moved closer. He planted one hand on Evie's shuddering shoulder and then stooped low over the bed. With his other hand, he smoothed away the dark hair from Justine's brow.

Evie lifted her head, her nose dripping, her face full of grief and sadness and a touch of confusion.

This was not something Owen had been taught, but somehow he knew what to do.

He brought his mouth down to hover just above Justine's cold lips. There was no heat emanating from her body, but he still felt her presence in the room and the flow of the Fountain inside him. Poised over her mouth, he felt the word and then said it.

"Nesh-ama."

Breathe.

Owen lightly kissed her mouth, and when his skin touched hers, the Fountain waters rushed from inside him and filled Justine. For a moment, Owen was lost in the swirl of the magic, his ears tingling as well as his fingertips.

Justine breathed in a long, shuddering sigh and her eyes blinked open.

Owen lifted himself, still feeling the magic rushing through him, and his eyes met Justine's. She knew. She had been dead moments before, but she had not gone back to the Deep Fathoms. He had rescued her from the brink, just before the plunge.

"Justine!" Evie gasped in absolute surprise.

Owen's legs buckled as all feeling of Fountain magic abandoned him. He was empty, completely hollowed out, and felt like he weighed no more than a feather. Darkness clouded his vision, and he fell.

♦ ♦ ♦

When Owen awoke, he had no idea how much time had passed.

He heard the sound of a snapping hearth fire. But it was the sound of a window opening that had awakened him. A sigh of air came in from the outside, bringing with it the distant rumble of the waterfall. One of the hinges on the window creaked gently, ever so gently. The sound made him worry.

Owen's eyes were as heavy as iron doors. He tried to shove them open, but all he could see was a slender slit of light. The room was dark, so it was well after nightfall. How long had he slept? It was the sickroom. He recognized the smell of it instantly.

A boot scuff.

Owen tried to turn his head, but it felt as heavy as an anvil. He managed to move only a few degrees. He was lying on a bed covered in thin sheets and sweating heavily. His chain hauberk had been removed. He could see it hanging over a chair next to the bed, glinting in the dim light. There was a blot of shadow by the window, darker than the rest of the room. That shadow was moving.

A frantic sense of panic bubbled up inside of Owen. He felt completely bereft of Fountain magic. His cup was empty, not a single drop remaining. He had *never* experienced that sensation before, for he had never let his cup run low since discovering he was Fountain-blessed. Now there was not even a whisper of magic. It felt about as wrong and strange as if his arm had been amputated.

Where was Evie? Where were Clark and Etayne? In the bed next to his, he saw Justine's black hair and her chest slowly rising and falling in deep slumber. There was no more anguished breathing. It was the clear, light sound of someone in deep sleep.

Memories came trickling back into his mind. Justine had died earlier, but he had saved her. Was it that morning? Or had more than a day gone by? There was no way he could tell except his stomach felt as empty as his store of Fountain magic.

The shadow slowly moved away from the now-open window and approached Owen's bed. He heard another soft scuff of boots on the floor, and the shadow stilled. Other memories came rushing back to Owen, filling him with panic. Bothwell had come and revealed their prime suspect was dead.

Which meant the person who'd poisoned the food was still at large.

And, as likely as not, Owen realized with further alarm, the poisoner was now sneaking up to finish his botched assignment.

CHAPTER TWENTY-TWO

Betrayed

The feeling of helplessness was terrible. Owen searched the room for a way to escape, but even if he found one, his limbs were sluggish and heavy, so bereft of strength that he could hardly move at all. He tried to speak and found that at least his mouth worked.

"I see you," Owen said in a low voice.

The shadow froze midstep. The deep silence was interrupted by the sound of the waterfall from the open window.

"As I see you," said a familiar voice from the shadows. The voice was no longer simpering, but Owen recognized it nonetheless. Lord Bothwell.

"Why are you here now?" Owen asked. He had to do something to stall him. Could he shout for help? How quickly would it take for someone to come? He could not defend himself, but did his enemy know that?

"Isn't it rather obvious?" Bothwell replied snidely. He started toward the bed again, keeping to the shadows, his hand gripping a dagger. "I was paid to help you, but I was paid even more to make sure you all die."

Owen felt a prickle of gooseflesh down his back. "All of us?"

"Well, especially Lady Mortimer. If she's assassinated in Atabyrion, it will more than provoke your king to invade. And that will draw his eyes away."

"Away from what?" Owen pressed, anxiety hammering inside his heart. He was utterly helpless.

The shadowed man clucked his tongue. "Things are not as they seem. Now, be a good boy and stay down so I can kill you properly. It'll be painless and quick. You have my word."

He took a few steps closer, and Owen saw a faint outline of his face. The act of subservient affability had been discarded. There was no question Bothwell intended to murder him.

"You weren't with us at the falls. Who tried to poison us?" Owen challenged, a bead of sweat dripping down from his forehead.

"It was supposed to look like an *accident.* A year ago, I hired a servant in Iago Llewellyn's household, waiting for an opportunity such as this one. You ruined it, and I had to throw him into the river. Ah, well, at least I can leave this backward land and return to a more civilized kingdom. Happy morrow, *boy.*"

Bothwell loomed over Owen's bedside, his face leering down at him in the dim light.

A dagger plunged into the side of the man's hip.

Owen registered that it was a woman's hand holding the hilt as the blade jerked free. He tried to roll off the bed, but he only managed to lift himself partway. His heart was hammering in his chest, and he felt tingles in his fingers and toes as fresh blood surged through him.

Bothwell jerked away and lunged toward the bed where Justine had been lying so still, his dagger out and ready. Only it wasn't Justine.

Owen saw a flash of black hair, but he instantly recognized Etayne's face beneath it. Her eyes were wild with passion as she kicked the poisoner in the stomach. He fell backward, then did a roll to get clear of her, but Etayne was ready. She sprang from the bed, dagger in hand, and charged after him. Owen kicked against the sheets, trying to free his legs, trying to do something. The air was rent with grunts and curses as the two poisoners fought on the ground in the shadows. He saw a dagger rise up in the light, then saw Etayne's hand grip the man's wrist. There was some violent cursing, a chair wobbled and tipped over, and suddenly Etayne was on her feet, backing away, dagger held out. Some of the black hair from the wig stuck to the sweat on her face. She positioned herself by Owen's bed, acting as a shield.

The grim-faced man rose, bent over with pain. "You are too young," he growled. "Too green. I have heard about you from the school. And surely *you* have heard of Foulcart. You're good with disguises, but I am better at knife work, and you know it."

"How certain are you?" Etayne asked warily, holding her dagger underhanded now, her arms close to her chest.

Bothwell took a faint step forward and then collapsed onto the floor face-first.

"Which is why I poisoned my dagger before stabbing you," Etayne said with a sneer.

Bothwell twitched and convulsed.

Etayne stepped on his wrist and then pried the dagger from his hand.

"You knew of him?" Owen asked, filling his lungs with grateful breaths. Etayne had made herself up to look just like Justine; she was even wearing the other girl's gown.

"We went to the same poisoner school in Pisan. He went by a secret name to hide his identity," she said, wiping sweat from her cheek. "He works for Occitania now, I believe. I'd never met him in person, or I would have recognized him."

Etayne picked up the fallen chair and hoisted the comatose man into it. She then proceeded to bind his wrists and ankles to the wood while his head lolled to the side.

"Is the poison you used fatal?" Owen asked.

"No. It's paralytic. I stabbed him in the leg to make it more difficult for him to fight, and also so the poison would go directly into his blood." She sheathed her dagger in a girdle strap and then came over to the bed and helped Owen sit up against the headboard.

"Thank you for saving my life," he said, looking at her with gratitude. She mussed with his shirt to arrange it.

"It was a gambit," she said with a shrug. "Clark is still in no condition to fight, and you were as weak as a newborn pup after the Fountain drained you. So we spread the rumor that you were ailing too, and Justine was too sick to be moved. I disguised myself as her and took her place. The earl's daughter is safe as well. I thought the other poisoner might use this as an easy chance to kill you both, and he did. Bothwell fell into my trap."

"I've never been so weak," Owen said, not certain how he felt about being used as the bait in her trap.

"I can help with that," Etayne said. First, she shut the window and barred it. Then she lit a candle to provide more light. Bothwell was starting to snore, his head still hanging low. The poisoner fetched some herbs from her bag and quickly added them to a cup of broth on the small dresser. She stirred it with a spoon and then came to Owen's side.

As she pressed the cup to his lips, he inhaled the aroma of chicken and vegetable broth and saw little lumps of lentil grain in it. She tipped it and he swallowed, tasting the salty broth and a hint of some herbs he recognized from his time with Ankarette. These were the healing herbs a midwife used. He had drunk a similar concoction as a child.

He took several deep swallows of the tepid broth, and when Etayne encouraged him to drink more, he managed to finish the cup.

"There," she said, using her finger to dab his wet mouth. "Your strength will return faster now."

It made him nervous and uncomfortable to feel her so close. She gazed at him, her eyes traveling along his scalp to the patch of white in his hair. For a moment, he thought she was going to touch it. Then she leaned away and set the cup back on the small dresser.

Etayne began rifling through the poisoner's pockets. She removed a vial that hung around his neck from a piece of twine and carefully sniffed the tip that was plugged by cork. Then she proceeded to remove a second dagger, along with all the rings from his fingers. The poisons must have been added recently, or Owen's power would have detected them.

Etayne discovered some papers hidden in a pouch secured to the man's chest with leather straps.

Bothwell's head snapped up, his eyes blinking. "Gaawww!" he moaned, his eyes wild with panic. He jerked on the bonds hard enough for the chair to lurch in place. Etayne put her hand on his shoulder to keep it from tipping over.

"If you fall forward, you'll break your nose," Etayne warned.

"You won?" Bothwell asked with disbelief. He looked absolutely furious.

She patted his cheek condescendingly. "Things are not as they seem. Now, be a good boy and stay still so I can kill you properly."

His eyes widened at her deliberate insult. "That was good, Etayne. Ooooh, just the right amount of venom to sting and burn." He struggled against the ropes, frowning angrily. "What did you use on me? Catspaw?"

"Veregrain," she countered.

"That was my next guess. Ah, I see. The first stab," he said with a grunt. "You waited until my back was to you."

She shrugged and tried not to look pleased. "You still serve Chatriyon, it seems."

Bothwell's eyes narrowed with resentment. "I serve those who provide the best opportunities. So should you," he said emphatically. "I don't care how much Mancini pays you. Chatriyon can best it. A girl with your talents would go far in Occitania. Kill the boy, though, he's listening in."

"I know," Etayne said. "I'm a little tempted by your offer. By a little, I mean not at all. Loyalty binds me."

Bothwell spat out an oath. "Don't mock me, Etayne. You are loyal to yourself. To your own interests. This is a better offer. If you want to still serve Ceredigion, by all means, do so *after* the usurper falls. Even better, be a spy for us from within the kingdom. Like Mancini is."

Etayne wrinkled her brow. "I found some papers on you." She teased him with them, waving them through the air. "What kind of ciphers did they use, I wonder?"

His eyes widened with terror. "Give those back."

Etayne clucked her tongue. "I beat *you*, Bothwell. Remember?" Owen watched as she opened the papers. "The formian cipher," she asked with an exaggerated sigh. "Really, you disappoint me."

He bucked against the bonds. "We didn't think *you* would be sent."

"Is that the *royal* 'we'?" Etayne asked sarcastically. Owen had picked up on the slip as well. He wished he could use his Fountain-blessed ability to study Bothwell again, but trying to tap into his magic was like blowing into a hollow jug. He was completely bereft of his power.

Bothwell frowned. "You don't know him."

"Don't be so sure," she replied, quickly scanning the encrypted message. She brought it closer to the candle. Owen watched as the young man began flexing his fingers, testing the strength of his bonds. Feeling himself reviving, Owen leaned forward from the bedstead, though the movement made him dizzy. He swung his legs off the side, but he knew it would be recklessly foolish to try to stand.

Bothwell's eyes were affixed to Etayne's face. Her look grew darker as she read.

"Who ordered this?" she demanded, slapping the paper across her hand. "Chatriyon? I don't think even he's that stupid."

Bothwell's eyes blazed.

"What is it?" Owen asked, his voice wary. The whole business of poisoners and death. It was like playing Wizr, except someone could remove your piece without entering the game.

Etayne turned and gave him a worried look. "A poisoner is going after King Severn."

Owen gasped in shock. He turned on Bothwell. "Who?"

The young man's frown was nervous. "I am only doing my part," he snapped. "There cannot be peace between Ceredigion and Atabyrion. It would be a disaster!"

"Answer his question!" Etayne insisted.

Bothwell's eyes darted from her to Owen. "If you release me . . ." he suggested.

"I'll release you into the river!" Etayne threatened.

Bothwell blanched. "There's no need to be nasty!"

Etayne shook her head. "Every moment we delay increases the jeopardy of my king. We are loyal to him, Bothwell. I assure you of that."

The poisoner snorted. "Then you are going to be startled when you find out he's no longer the king."

Owen wanted to start choking the man. "And who will rule Ceredigion? Eyric? The people don't know him. They don't trust him. His claim may be true, but he has been missing for too long. The people are prosperous. They will rally behind Severn."

Bothwell shook his head. "Perhaps you are right. But you don't see what is truly going on. You are missing the waterfall because of all the mist. You can hear it, maybe. But you cannot see it."

"Stop speaking in riddles," Etayne said. "Perhaps we can make this more simple. How about a dose of henbane? Hmmm? Or better yet . . . pure nightshade."

Bothwell's eyes bulged and he started rocking in the seat. "You may as well just kill me!" he snarled. "If I tell you, I am a dead man regardless!"

"But the best part," she said, "is that you won't even remember telling us."

"Gormless!" Bothwell cursed. He sighed. "I will tell you. I will tell you!" He shook his head, defeated. "It's probably too late for me anyway. Chatriyon doesn't want Eyric to rule. He's just a pawn. A distraction. Chatriyon's humiliated because of his defeat at the hands of that little prig Kiskaddon. You see, he was going after Brythonica to sate his ambition, but now he's changed his mind. Now he wants a bigger jewel. He wants Ceredigion."

Owen shook his head. "That's not ambition. That's madness."

Bothwell snorted. "That may well be true. But he's determined. He wishes to provoke Severn to war with Atabyrion by killing the Mortimer lass. Then he'll kill Severn by poison and claim the throne through a forced marriage with the crouch-back's niece. That's the plot, Etayne. That's all of it. He will rule Ceredigion through his wife. Tunmore's role is to persuade the girl. He's Fountain-blessed, if you didn't know. We've been poisoning her mother for weeks to help sour her on the old man. The fact that you are here in Atabyrion, Etayne," he chuckled darkly, "will only make it easier for Tyrell to get to the king."

♦ ♦ ♦

Every person who is Fountain-blessed demonstrates a remarkable power, and sometimes more than one. They keep their lore secret from the world, except for some general principles that I will speak on. The terms used to describe the two major ways in which they draw in power are "rigor" and "vigor." The term "rigor" implies severity and strictness. The magic comes through meticulous and persistent adherence to some regimented craft or routine. These individuals are iron-willed and self-disciplined to a degree very uncommon amongst their fellows. The term "vigor" implies effort, energy, and enthusiasm. To do a task out of the love of it, not for ambition's sake alone. These two concepts mark the twin horses by which the magic of the Fountain can be drawn. Why one individual may prefer one to the other or whether there is difference in the efficacy of these methods remains, to the rest of us, a mystery.

—Polidoro Urbino, Court Historian of Kingfountain

♦ ♦ ♦

CHAPTER TWENTY-THREE

Glazier

Bothwell was secretly removed from Iago's palace and confined to a cell in the hold of Evie's ship. It was Owen's intention to bring him back to Ceredigion with them and then challenge Mancini for further information about the Espion master's true loyalties. The man's news had rattled Owen, and the threat to King Severn made him anxious to fulfill their mission in Atabyrion and return home.

Owen and Etayne had both heard of Tyrell before, but in different contexts. Owen remembered his name in connection with the murder of Severn's nephews, while Etayne knew quite a bit of secondhand information about him from her time in Pisan. He was at least Severn's age, he had a reputation for hired murder, a handsome face, and a small gap between his front teeth. With any luck, it would help them find him.

After capturing Bothwell, Owen and Etayne filled the others in on the particulars of the plot. It was decided that Clark would return immediately to Kingfountain to warn the king and begin the hunt for Tyrell. Owen, Evie, and Etayne would remain behind to finish the tasks assigned to them as quickly as they could.

Etayne made more broth for Owen, who felt his strength and health returning. But his connection with Fountain magic was still not available to him. He needed to find some books to read, play Wizr, or do something else to fill his reserves, but those things required time—of which he had very little.

To focus his thoughts, he took a quick walk around the royal manor, stretching his legs and loosening the knots in his shoulders. His mind was preoccupied with the many threats bearing down on them, and as he wandered the grounds, he tried to piece together a strategy. In the past, it had always been easy for him to quickly get to the heart of a problem. Having been drained of his magic, he could hardly remember all the details of the Occitanians' murky plot, let alone create a plan of action.

About midday, a servant came and told him that Lady Mortimer wished to see him. He quickly complied and made his way to her room. His own body felt like a stranger to him.

As he entered the room, he saw Clark conferring with Etayne in the back corner while Justine was up and about, fussing over Evie's dress. Her recovery had been complete and dramatic. When she saw him, her cheeks flushed and she whispered into Evie's ear, who immediately turned and looked at him.

"My lady?" he said formally.

Evie beamed at him. "Justine is too shy to say it, so I will do so in her place. Owen, she knows she died yesterday, and she's aware that you summoned her back to life."

Owen looked at Justine in surprise; the girl's flush increased and she nodded emphatically.

"I don't see why you can't tell him yourself," Evie said with a hint of exasperation. "It's not as if you two have never spoken before."

"This is different, my lady," Justine said meekly. She seemed completely in awe of Owen now.

"I did what I could do, Justine." Owen saw she was growing uncomfortable, and he was beginning to feel that way himself, so he decided to change the topic. "Clark, when do you set sail?"

The Espion turned his gaze. "We will leave at high tide. There is a merchant ship leaving with timber that will give me a ride to one of our ships anchored off the coast. I hope to be back at Kingfountain by midnight. I was wondering if I should take Bothwell with me."

Etayne shook her head. "You are too weak still. Better to leave him here with us. There may be more information I can wring from him. And Owen wishes to discuss certain matters relating to our prisoner with Mancini. Besides, even in a cage, he's dangerous."

Clark pursed his lips. "I still think I should take him. If he can help us identify where the poisoner is hiding, it would save us time in catching him."

Owen could see the logic in both positions. Again, he keenly felt the lack of his magic. "I'd like to keep him close. I have no doubt he will try to escape. Etayne, I want you to find out where Eyric is staying. I think Bothwell mentioned earlier it was at one of the Huntley manors."

"I could ask Iago," Evie suggested.

Owen shook his head. "You weren't even supposed to know about this part of the mission. Iago is cleverer than he looks. If he knew I was here, I'd find myself in a dungeon somewhere."

"But shouldn't we tell Iago something?" Evie pressed. "The Occitanians are undermining the very alliance they made with him. They're counting on him to fail! Wouldn't it help our cause if he knew that?"

"I see where you're coming from," Owen said. "Sharing the Occitanian plot would sour his opinion of Occitania, but it wouldn't dissuade him from backing Eyric to topple Severn. You have seen how much Iago wants this war. I think it would do more harm to give him the impression that you were involved in our plot," he said. "My hope is to persuade Eyric to join us. But if we can't do that, we may have to resort to other measures." He gave Etayne a knowing look.

"I'd best be on my way to the docks then," Clark said, but he glanced furtively at Justine, who blushed furiously and looked down at the ground.

Evie noticed her friend's reaction. "There was something I left down at the ship," she said. "Justine, would you be a dear and walk down to fetch it for me? The blue gown with the silver trim. I've wanted to wear that one."

Clark's eyes looked hopeful. "I can escort her down to the docks, if you would like, my lady?"

Justine blinked with surprise, and a timid smile twitched on her mouth. "The blue damask one? I remember it. I would be happy to fetch it for you. If Lady Etayne will be your chaperone while I am away."

Etayne gave a deep, formal curtsy, but there was a wry gleam in her eyes.

Clark extended his elbow and Justine took it. Giving Evie a look that beamed with gratitude, she left with her escort.

Once the door had shut behind them, Evie sighed. "They are both so quiet that they'll likely walk the entire way in silence." She looked wistful for a moment and then turned to Owen. "I can't thank you enough for what you did for her," she said, her eyes softening. They looked more blue than silver or green today. She took Owen's hands in hers and squeezed them. "My heart nearly broke in half. And then you saved her. Thank you."

Owen felt abashed. "I wasn't sure what I was doing, and I'm far from certain I could do it again. But you're welcome."

Evie tugged on his hands. "You still have no connection to your magic? You look a bit forlorn today. Like a lost soul. Am I reading your countenance right?"

Owen nodded, feeling pain tighten in his chest. She read his moods so well, always had.

"I thought so. In that case, I think I have something for you that may come in handy. I asked Iago for this during breakfast and he had his glazier assemble it. It's one of the reasons I sent for you. Come look."

She brought him over to the dresser, where he noticed a wooden box. His heart began to pound as she opened the quiet hinges and revealed row after row of gleaming rectangular glass tiles.

"I thought," Evie said with delight, seeing his smile, "that this might help."

Owen almost started to tremble at the sight of the tiles. He felt like a man dying of thirst who had been given a huge drink to quench it. Or the parched ground the moment rainclouds appear. It was a visceral, greedy feeling, one of childlike wonder and excitement.

Evie lifted the box off the table, and in silent agreement the two knelt down, clearing away the floor rushes to provide a flat surface on which to stack the tiles. The glazier had provided an assortment of colors and a variety of shapes. As Owen knelt on the floor, he began fingering the pieces, and in a moment, he was eight years old again, kneeling on the kitchen floor. He could almost smell the baking loaves in Liona's kitchen and hear the sounds of servants bustling to and fro. The instant he started to arrange the pieces, he felt the trickle of the Fountain responding, the first drops of power drawing into him.

Evie helped by handing him pieces, a victorious smile on her mouth.

"Thank you," Owen breathed softly. They were bent so close together he could smell her hair. The scent seemed to draw in the Fountain waters faster, and for the first time, he realized that Evie was tied to his magic in some way. He could not dwell on the thought, though, for his mind was racing this way and that as his fingers deftly stacked the pieces.

After the box was empty, Owen let Evie knock the first set down. The glass made a different sound as it tumbled down, a tinkling sound that reverberated inside him, filling his heart with curiosity and delight.

For a moment, he was a child again; everything was simple, he and Evie knew they were meant for each other, and they spent their days holding hands and jumping into cisterns, eating honeyed wafers, and relishing the sun.

There was a knock at the door, interrupting the moment of pure joy. Owen rushed to his feet. He did not want the servants to see him playing with the tiles. Everyone knew that Owen Kiskaddon had a penchant for tiles and playing Wizr. If he were discovered . . .

The rapping on the door grew firmer and a muffled voice said, "It's Justine!"

Etayne unlocked the door and let the girl in, then shut it fast behind her.

Justine looked flushed and worried. She had been gone for perhaps an hour, though it felt as if only moments had passed. The blue gown was draped over her arm, but her face was animated with worry.

"I wanted to tell you quickly," Justine said, panting. "A ship from Brythonica just arrived in port. I was barely able to get back up the steps ahead of them. I think the duchess has come! They're on their way to the great hall."

Owen and Evie exchanged glances. *Brythonica?*

♦ ♦ ♦

In short order, Owen was back in his hooded hauberk and the tunic of Horwath. Evie had changed into the blue damask gown, the color of which mixed with her eyes in a lovely and elusive fashion. While Justine brushed out her mistress's hair, Etayne quickly returned the tiles to the box.

Owen could feel Fountain magic again. His cup was far from full; it was akin to the palace cistern when the water lapped at the lowest mark on the stone column measuring its depths. But at least he was no longer empty.

While Evie fidgeted with her dress, she launched question after question at Justine about the visitors, but Justine did not know for certain who had come. She could only repeat the speculation of those around her. Someone *thought* the duchess had come, but Justine had not seen any noble ladies disembark from the ship.

As soon as they were ready, they left Evie's room and headed to the great hall. Upon their arrival at Atabyrion, the hall had been crowded with guests for the wedding. Those guests had long since departed, and now the hall was mostly full of servants, guards, and a pacing and nervous Iago Llewellyn. When he saw Evie, he blinked with surprise and delight and came rushing up to her.

"I've only just heard the news myself," he said with an animated tone. "But an embassy from Brythonica has just arrived. This is a rare honor."

"That is what my lady told me," Evie said, nodding to Justine. "Do you know who it is?"

Iago shook his head. "I have no idea. The visit is completely unexpected." He looked agitated. "I can't find Lord Bothwell at all. No one has seen him today."

They kept their expressions guarded. It was a comforting relief for Owen to have his magic back. With it, he was so much more attuned to the expressions and demeanors of those around him. He hadn't realized how rich and layered his ability with the Fountain was until it was taken away from him. He also wondered if the Duchess of Brythonica had come, for he'd never met her and was curious to know more.

They had not been in the great hall long when the embassy arrived. A horn was sounded to announce the visitors.

"Lord Marshal Brendon Roux of the duchy of Brythonica!" the portly man shouted.

That was not the person Owen had been expecting. In fact, he was surprised to find a man of his rank and prominence on such a mission unless the intent of that mission was to declare war. He was the protector of the duchy, the guardian of the duchess.

Owen recognized him instantly. His short gray hair was combed in the Occitanian fashion, and he looked as stern and brooding as he had when Owen met him in Chatriyon's abandoned camp. He strode into the hall, a man with a cause and a mission, and frowned when he saw Iago and Evie standing together near the dais. And Owen realized with growing horror that the lord marshal might see through his disguise as a knight. It would probably be wise to remain out of the man's sight.

As if hearing Owen's private thoughts, the lord marshal turned to look his way. His eyebrows lifted, just slightly, and a look of recognition came into his eyes.

Hello, Lord Marshal, Owen said through his Fountain magic, gritting his teeth for not having acted sooner.

And he had the sinking suspicion that Roux had once again outmaneuvered him.

CHAPTER TWENTY-FOUR

Lord Marshal

Owen's stomach tightened into knots as he wondered whether the lord marshal would betray him to Iago. The king would be embarrassed and likely furious if he found out that Owen Kiskaddon was masquerading as one of Evie's protectors. Even more concerning was the marshal's presence in Atabyrion. What fate had brought Owen and Roux together again?

"Welcome to Edonburick, my lord," Iago Llewellyn said with a smug look. "I pray there were no sudden storms?"

"The only storm," Marshal Roux said with a firm, aggravated tone, "is the one you are about to call down upon yourself." He bowed stiffly as he reached the dais. With a casual nod, he bowed again to Evie.

"Have you met Lady Mortimer before?" Iago asked. "Shall I introduce you?"

"I have not had the pleasure of meeting Lady Mortimer's *daughter* until now," Roux replied with a subtle acknowledgment. "My lady, I bid you greetings from Lady Sinia, Duchess of Brythonica. I noticed, by your lack of a headdress, that you were not from Atabyrion."

"Indeed no, sir," Evie replied warily. "I have heard much about you."

"No doubt from Lord Kiskaddon," Roux replied with a shrewd look at her. "My compliments to the duke. I came this way, on my lady's orders, to speak to King Iago."

"Speak then, man," Iago said, frowning. "I mean to convince Lady Elysabeth to go hawking with me later. Would you care to join us?"

"I will be returning promptly to Brythonica," Roux said. "I've no time for such frivolity. We're on the brink of war, my lord. I have come to bid you to reconsider your allegiances."

Iago's frown deepened. "As did Lady Mortimer before you," he said with concern. "I believe I've been sufficiently *cautioned*, my lord. I'm surprised you took the trouble to come so far."

Roux stepped forward, his voice earnest. "You awaken a sleeping wolf," he insisted. "And a winter one at that. You know about the wolf in winter, my lord. It's easy to be brave when it is afar. But when you see its ears and hear its growling, you may feel differently."

Iago waved in annoyance. "I thought Severn's badge was a boar, not a wolf. A boar is the prey that *fears* the hunting dogs. Besides, a beast may howl, snort, or moan, but that does not mean I should fear it."

Evie's eyes burned green. "The King of Ceredigion is not a beast. I object to such talk."

"It's only a saying," Iago said calmly.

Owen stared at Lord Roux, his senses heightened to detect any glimmer of the Fountain's magic. He sensed nothing but the growing tension in the hall.

"I beg your pardon, my lady," Lord Roux said formally. "A poor choice of words on my part." He returned his focus to Iago. "If you invade Ceredigion, then you will be facing Brythonica as well. My lady's recent escape from Chatriyon's ambitions will not be forgotten so quickly. We stand ready to support King Severn."

Owen felt a surge of gratitude and respect for the marshal, but it was tempered by lingering wariness.

Iago scowled, his face flushing with anger. "Have a care, sir, about making more enemies. We both know that you won't leave Brythonica defenseless, not while Chatriyon is still licking his wounds. Kiskaddon may have outmaneuvered the Occitanians once, but when Chatriyon brings the full might of his kingdom to bear, the Duke of Westmarch will find his little tricks to no avail."

Lord Roux actually smiled. And it was a smile like a wolf's. "I think you and Chatriyon underestimate the duke's cunning," he said. "And his abilities."

"I know how to kill a Fountain-blessed," Iago said threateningly. When he heard Evie gasp, he looked at her with mortification. "My lady, that was spoken rashly."

"Indeed, sir," Evie said, her voice trembling with anger. She had color in her cheeks. "What is it about men? Cease all this blustering," she said, shaking her head. "Let me speak the truth here, for none of you will. My lord of Atabyrion. I can see why Lady Sinia sent Lord Roux to speak to you. He is a seasoned battle commander who has experienced the world and has successfully defended Brythonica despite substantial odds against him. You should hearken to his counsel. You are young and you are impetuous. I do not mean to offend you, my lord. You long to prove yourself in battle. The King of Occitania holds that same desire. You seek the glory and honor of the kings of the past, who won great renown on the battlefield. But think of the lives lost. Think of the suffering mothers and children who will lose their sons and their brothers. You play Wizr, but your side only has half of its pieces. You will lose."

Iago stared at her, his brow knitting with consternation. "What you say is true, my lady," he said with some emotion in his voice. Owen thought it was defensiveness. "I am impetuous, true, but fortune favors the bold. And you are correct in your reckoning that Atabyrion cannot face the full might of Ceredigion. But you will also recall that the game *ends* when the king is defeated, no matter how many pieces are left on the board. The true king of Ceredigion is my friend, my companion, and my ally. It is no crime to restore the rightful ruler to his throne. Then all the other pieces will obey him."

Iago's lips were trembling with anger as he turned his gaze back to Roux. "I am sorry you came all this way, Lord Marshal, to fail in your mission. I would suggest to the duchess that she reconsider *her* position. She's spurned the one man who could have made her a queen. And when Ceredigion is defeated, there will be no one left to protect Brythonica. You may suggest that *her* alliances are the weaker ones. Now, I intend to go hawking. You may go."

Lord Roux bowed stiffly, his face impassive. He turned to Evie. "Thank you for your candor, my lady. I would have a moment of your time before I leave?"

"Yes, my lord," Evie replied.

Iago snorted and turned away to a servant. "Fetch my horse. This hall is stifling."

In the commotion that followed, Owen noticed that many of the Atabyrions were looking darkly at the foreigners, their eyes full of anger and resentment. They wanted war. They wanted to fight. It would take more than words to dissuade them.

Evie motioned for Owen to join her and Lord Roux in a small alcove to the side.

The marshal's tone was deliberately low. "You risk a great deal being here, my lord," he said, though his eyes were still fixed on Evie's. "You do not lack for courage."

"Thank you," Owen said in reply.

"I appreciate you coming to try and help," Evie said. "I see the minds of the Atabyrions are fixed on conflict."

"There's a saying. He who complies against his will is of his own opinion still," Lord Roux said. "I've found that true in mules and men.

My lady, I must warn you. And in so doing, warn your king. I fear that dishonorable means will be employed to remove Severn from power. One does not hazard the misfortunes of war without some hope of success. With my fleet, I could burn this city to ashes and still have time to return and defend Brythonica. Iago Llewellyn does not realize how vulnerable he truly is if events turn out badly, as I believe they will. They underestimate Severn and his resources. Do not make the mistake of underestimating their desperation to be rid of him."

Owen sensed the implied meaning behind his words. "You believe there is a conspiracy to murder the king."

Lord Roux glanced quickly at Owen. "I do, although I have no proof."

"You have proven a faithful ally," Evie said. "I think it is time we departed Atabyrion. My mission here has failed."

Lord Roux looked at her and then at Owen. There was something in his eyes. Something he was not saying. Something he *wouldn't* say. "By your leave then," he said gruffly. And with that, he was gone.

Owen wondered what sort of weaknesses this man had. But he dared not use his Fountain magic in such an open place. Not only would it reveal himself to Roux, it would drain him again, and he could not risk that. Owen suspected gratitude wasn't the only motivation behind Brythonica's support of Ceredigion.

There was another part of the mission that was unfinished however. Just as Chatriyon was using a poisoner to overthrow Severn in preparation for Eyric's arrival, so was Severn intending to do the same thing with his enemy. He felt his mouth go dry. It was clear to him that Eyric had to be removed from the Wizr board, but he did not want to kill him. Besides, Severn had given him reason to believe he would not want his true nephew dead. If they were able to abduct Eyric and bring him back to Ceredigion, the balance of power would shift. Owen did not believe they could persuade him to come willingly.

And then a thought came to Owen's mind, a flash of insight. A strategy.

"My lady," Owen said to Evie in a low voice. "I have an idea."

"I'm anxious to hear it," she replied.

Owen saw the pieces coming together in his mind. The order of events that needed to happen. The way the tiles needed to stack in order for them to fall as he planned. "I would like you to ask Iago for permission to see Eyric Argentine."

"What for?" Evie asked, looking startled.

"To test his claims. Tell him you were given facts and details about his childhood. You would like to visit him tomorrow. I think he'll grant that request if he sends an escort with you."

"And what will you do?" Evie asked.

He smiled. "Etayne and I must get to him first."

♦ ♦ ♦

Owen paced nervously, wishing Clark were still around. He did not like leaving Evie unprotected. She and Justine were walking the grounds, waiting for Iago to return from his hawking trip. Owen and Etayne were together in Evie's room, where they were working on their side of the plan.

He heard the rustle of fabric from behind the changing screen as he continued to pace the room. The swirling events around him were like tide pools threatening to knock him off his feet with another wave. He was eager to be done with the role of imposter, eager to resume his identity and take action. Chatriyon was using Iago to use Eyric to topple Ceredigion's throne. But Chatriyon's goal was to claim the throne for himself through marriage to Elyse. Owen saw the pieces aligning on the board. Iago was vain and proud, but he did not see the machinations happening in the background. Just as Owen realized there were some pieces on the board that *he* was not seeing.

"I'm almost finished," Etayne said. A few moments later, she emerged from the changing screen wearing one of Evie's gowns and a set of her jewelry. For an instant, seeing her wearing Evie's clothes made his heart quicken with desire. Oblivious to his gawking, she made her way to the small dresser topped with a mirror. Next to the dresser was a trunk—one of Etayne's. The King's Poisoner opened the trunk and began to rummage through it until she found what she needed, a dark brown wig. She had already removed the one she wore regularly, the long blond one, and she replaced it with the dark one. Looking at herself in the mirror, Etayne began to apply powders and stubs of charcoal to her face. Owen watched with growing fascination as she dabbed color to her lips and cheeks, transforming before his eyes. He could *feel* the ripples of the Fountain draw into the girl, increasing in intensity as she became lost in the moment. Etayne's movements became more dreamlike as she stared at herself, applying little dots to mimic the blemishes and blots that were on Evie's skin. After a time, she seemed to be acting unconsciously, and Owen could sense her losing herself in the act of disguise. It was the same feeling Owen had while stacking his tiles. It was fascinating and—honestly—more than a bit alluring to watch her transform. He forced the thoughts from his mind, trying to stay focused on their upcoming mission together.

She finished the last bit of color and then began mimicking Evie's expressions. Her eyes became animated and her hands began their almost-flapping gestures of excitement. "I love what you've done with your hair, Justine," Etayne said, her voice sounding hauntingly like Evie's, her tone and inflection matching. "I think mine is too drab. I wish I had a spot of white, right here, like Owen's. But alas, we cannot all have such dashing good looks." She grinned mischievously, looking at Owen in the mirror. He'd been staring too much, and she'd caught him at it.

"I do recognize you," Owen stammered with an approving nod. "But at a distance, I'd be fooled. You're taller than Evie, but I don't think anyone would notice."

"I made a few other adjustments," Etayne said slyly. "I've done what I can."

Owen shook his head. "No, you haven't. You haven't done it all. Now, I want you to try and summon Fountain magic. Here, in this room. I want you to make me believe that I'm *seeing* Evie. Like you did with Ankarette's image from my mind. I want to know if I can see through it if I try."

Excitement churned through Owen's body. There were so many possibilities, so many ways that Etayne's power could be used, and he wanted to know how deep her magic could go. She could be a formidable ally if she learned to harness her powers.

Straightening her shoulders, Etayne stared at herself in the mirror. "How do I summon the magic?"

"You did it before," Owen said.

"Yes, but it's not like a pump handle. Last time I was responding to you. You started it."

Owen nodded. "After Ankarette was gone, the king became my tutor in the magic. He sometimes needs to touch someone to get his magic flowing. That's not the way it is for me, but I learned this from him. Here, stand in front of me."

She obeyed. He blinked a few times, trying not to be distracted by her disguise.

"This is an exercise the king taught me. Hold your arm out like this. Not stiffly. Good. Now spread out your fingers. Close your eyes and imagine . . . imagine that you have a river inside of you, yearning to come out. The waters are going to come out of your fingertips."

"Do I touch you?" she asked, wrinkling her brow. His skin prickled in anticipation.

"No! Just . . . stand there, as you are. Sometimes it helps to close your eyes. Imagine the flow of water inside you. Release it, feel it flowing from your chest, down your arm, and out through your fingers. I'm not going to summon mine yet. I want you to instigate it this time."

He felt sweat starting to itch along his scalp from being so near her. He subdued his emotions, trying to maintain his composure. He was loyal to Evie. But this was a part of himself he would never be able to share with her. Not like this.

"All right," Etayne said. She closed her eyes, and he immediately felt the magic coursing through her.

"Can you feel it?"

"Yes," she said, smiling.

"Well done. Now, I want you to use it. I want you to become Elysabeth *Victoria* Mortimer. Convince me."

Etayne took a deep breath and let out a sigh. As she did so, Owen watched her transform before his eyes. She even looked smaller, shrinking slightly to match Evie's stature. As Owen stared at her, he felt her magic come rushing into him, trying to persuade him that she was Evie. He *wanted* to believe it. Seeing her made his heart ache with longing. But he felt the flow of magic parting around him, making him immune to the deception. She looked like Evie. But he knew she wasn't. His heart couldn't be fooled.

"Open your eyes," Owen said softly, relieved that her power was not strong enough to deceive him. It would have duped another Fountain-blessed, he was sure of it.

Etayne did so, and the magic wavered.

"Keep it going," he insisted.

The weakness dissipated and the illusion was maintained. Owen took her shoulders and turned her around to face the mirror. To face the reflection of Evie.

"Bless me," Etayne whispered reverently, her voice full of awe. "I can be anyone."

"You clearly are Fountain-blessed," Owen said in admiration. "Now, do you feel the edges of your magic? It's like a big, vast bowl. Is it shrinking? Do you feel yourself growing weaker?"

She nodded, trancelike. "But I'm not tired yet. It is like . . . swimming. I could do this for a while, but not forever."

"Good," Owen said. "The last time, you only held the illusion for a moment."

"I think it helps," Etayne said thoughtfully, "that I put on her dress and her jewels. That I tried hard to look like her. I can feel a difference this time. I also know Lady Elysabeth better now, having spent time with her. I could speak in her voice. I could act like her." She glanced at him in the mirror. "Did I convince you?"

Owen shook his head. "I can tell it's not real. But that's because I'm Fountain-blessed also. I can sense when others use the power. As you can."

"Like when you used your power on me," Etayne said slyly. "So what is your plan, Lord Owen?"

He stared at Etayne for a moment, feeling the final pieces click into place. "We're going to visit Eyric. The two of us. We're going there now."

CHAPTER TWENTY-FIVE

The Ardanays

The carriage jostled and rattled, making Owen queasy. He would have preferred riding horseback, which would have brought them to the Ardanays manor at a faster pace, but the carriage was part of his plan. It was a simple bow-curtained carriage, with drapes on the front and back sides, but those drapes were open so that passersby could see the stunningly beautiful Elysabeth *Victoria* Mortimer—who was actually Etayne, the King's Poisoner. Owen sat in the rider's box, close enough for them to speak. A servant with a whip rode on one of the lead horses and kept the pace over the lumbering hills. The land was thick with woods and forests, and the road was made of compacted earth with the occasional ruts.

Etayne was not using her Fountain magic yet, but her disguise was convincing enough at a distance. Riding alongside the carriage were two servants, also on horseback, whom Owen had bribed to accompany them as an escort and to handle the horses. He found himself staring longingly at their mounts. He chafed with impatience as they rode into the seclusion of the forests to one of the Earl of Huntley's manors, where the recently wedded couple were spending their holiday.

Owen's plan was simple, and it relied on the element of surprise. Word had undoubtedly been sent ahead that Evie wanted to visit the couple with the king's household the next day. Imagine the staff's surprise when a smaller entourage arrived a day early. Etayne would arrange for a private meeting with Lady Kathryn, giving Owen a chance to be alone with Eyric. Though he still did not believe Eyric would accept his overtures, Owen would attempt to persuade him to come willingly to Ceredigion. Meanwhile, Etayne would incapacitate Kathryn, take one of her dresses, and then emerge in her persona. Their hope was that she could succeed where Owen would likely fail. The carriage would take them to the docks, where they would stow Eyric aboard Evie's ship.

If Owen *was* successful in convincing Eyric, then Kathryn would be given the opportunity to come with them.

It was a bold plan. It was deceitful. And there were several dozen things that could go wrong. The closer they came to the Ardanays, the more he worried about them.

"Do you remember what Lady Kathryn looks like?" Owen whispered over his shoulder to the passenger.

"Vaguely," Etayne said. "I'll need to study her in order to get a grasp on her face and mannerisms. How long do you think you can keep Eyric occupied?"

"Long enough, I hope," Owen quipped.

The whip rider turned back. "There is the manor!" he shouted, pointing ahead with the whip handle.

The evergreen trees peeled away, opening to a lush green enclave surrounded by majestic trees and lawns. Instead of fences, there were large rough stones marking the path at intervals. As the carriage cleared the trees, Owen saw an imposing stone manor house set amidst the verdant splendor. The dirt road turned to the crunch of gravel as the carriage entered the drive, heading toward a large circular roundabout in front of the main door.

The manor was made of rectangular stone bricks, in differing shades of gray, giving it a patchwork look. The roofs were all sloped, and dozens of chimneys could be seen protruding from the roofline in various locations. The structure was only two stories high but very long, with an L-shaped wing jutting toward them on the western end. There were all sorts of vegetation clinging to the walls, including an untamed patch of ivy and wisteria vines. A turret with a weathervane rose prominently over the front path, which was bordered by large stone planter vases thick with gorse plants. The structure at the far western end of the manor was almost completely overgrown with ivy. Even the chimney was sheathed in green, but the windows had been cut around to provide a view. It was a charming, secluded place with lazy plumes of smoke coming up from some but not all of the chimneys.

As the carriage wheeled around the circle, coming to a stop on the side facing the front door, Owen gingerly jumped off the rider box seat and went around to open the carriage. He felt the trickle and churn of Etayne's magic as she assumed her full disguise.

The front door of the manor opened, and a thin, graying steward strode forward. His hair was still flecked with black, as were his eyebrows, and he had a thin, sour nose above a worried frown. His eyes were dark in color, and very serious.

Owen reached up and took Etayne's hand as she dismounted the carriage.

The steward reached them immediately. "We were not expecting you, Lady Mortimer, until tomorrow," he said in an agitated tone. He gave Owen a quick glance, but then shifted his gaze to Etayne.

"Tomorrow?" Etayne said blithely. "There must have been a misunderstanding. We have traveled quite far to arrive here today. Am I not welcome?"

The steward blanched. “Of course you are, Lady Mortimer!” he said. “I was just noting my surprise at seeing you so soon. My name is Lawson and I will attend you.”

“My name is Elysabeth *Victoria* Mortimer,” Etayne said sweetly. “Lady Mortimer is my mother.”

“Ah, my apologies. Welcome to the Ardanays!” He smiled, but the furrowed brow and intense look did not alter. He was extremely nervous, and Owen suspected it was not just because he was unprepared to receive visitors.

“If you will follow me,” Lawson said with a stiff bow, and proceeded to walk briskly back to the doors. Etayne glanced at Owen, a small frown of distrust on her mouth.

Owen felt the shifting of the gravel under his boots. He turned to the hired men, who had also dismounted. “Make the carriage ready,” he ordered softly. “Then rove the grounds in case you’re needed.”

The men nodded, and they began guiding the carriage around so it was ready to depart the way it had come.

Owen followed Etayne and Lawson.

The manor was furnished more decadently than Iago Llewellyn’s palace. It was obvious the Earl of Huntley had far more extraneous wealth than his sovereign. There were servants rushing to and fro, looking nervous about the commotion, but Owen saw half a dozen, no more. The manor was much smaller than Tatton Hall and Owen imagined the staff was smaller as well.

“How was the journey from Edonburick?” Lawson asked over his shoulder.

“Pleasant,” Etayne said simply, keeping her answer short and to the point.

The steward steered them to the right, and they were quickly guided to a waxed wood door. He rapped on it firmly and then twisted the handles.

It was a beautiful sitting room, with luxurious furniture and a huge bay window partially blocked by overhanging wisteria. The window curtains were open, filling the room with light. Eyric and Kathryn were already there, waiting for them.

Eyric wore a simple hunting tunic, the collar loose. He was not armed, for which Owen was grateful. He paced nervously, his hair unkempt. When they entered, his attention was fixated on Etayne, but there was nothing in his eyes to indicate he could see through the illusion.

"Lady Elysabeth," Eyric said with a bow. "May I introduce you to my wife, Lady Kathryn?"

Etayne did a formal curtsy, which was reciprocated by Lady Kathryn, who also bowed her head as if deferring to one of superior rank, even though they were both the daughters of earls.

Kathryn was no longer wearing a headdress. She had a beautiful green gown, modestly cut, and was not wearing any jewelry save for a wedding band on her finger and a simple set of earrings. Her hair, Owen discovered, was chestnut red. Her lack of a headdress was another clue that their arrival had surprised the couple. Her hair was braided into rings on the back of her head, but stray wisps fell across her brow.

Kathryn was a beauty, as the reports had said, but there was no trace of haughtiness in her expression. Her eyes were hazel and innocent, and he knew without extending his power that she had had a very sheltered childhood and life. Her lips were full and almost hinted at sadness. As she looked at her guests, her brows wrinkled just slightly, showing concern.

"The pleasure is mine, Lady Elysabeth," Kathryn said in a soft, quiet way. "You honor us with your visit."

"I am sorry for the misunderstanding," Etayne said airily. "I do not know how it happened, but such things do, I'm afraid."

"May I bring refreshments?" Lawson asked, looking at Lady Kathryn for direction. Owen noticed the subtle deference.

Kathryn nodded simply, and the steward left, shutting the doors behind him.

"While we are surprised by your sudden arrival," Kathryn said, "it is not unwelcome. This manor was a wedding gift. From my father. It is our new home." She smiled shyly at Eyric, who looked at her with adoring eyes. He walked up and took her hand, then brought it up to kiss her knuckles.

"I imagine you came here to threaten me," Eyric said to Etayne, his face darkening. "If that is your purpose, you wasted your trip."

Etayne smiled coyly. "Not at all. We have much to discuss, actually. But I'm afraid I must beg a moment alone with Lady Kathryn." Her voice pitched a little lower. "Along the journey, a most womanly matter suddenly presented itself and caught me by surprise. I must beg your help, Lady Kathryn."

Owen nearly smirked, but managed to keep his gaze neutral.

Lady Kathryn looked sympathetic. "My poor dear, of course. Come with me."

Eyric looked at his wife for a moment, but then smiled in understanding. "Clearly certain *matters* are of greater importance. I'll await you here, my love."

Kathryn and Etayne linked arms, their skirts swishing as they went to the door. Kathryn looked back at Eyric, gave him an endearing, tender look, and then escorted Etayne away. As the door shut, Owen could not believe how well his plan was working. Would all the pieces fall where he'd arranged them?

Eyric stared after her for a moment longer, looking absolutely besotted. He sighed and clasped his hands behind his back. He glanced at Owen, though he only saw him as a knight, an escort. No one of importance. Certainly no one worth conversing with.

"My congratulations on your marriage, my lord," Owen said innocuously.

Eyric started to pace again, the look of love beginning to fade into one of worry. He had a careworn look, the face of one who was hunted and weary of the chase. He was strong, young, and very good-looking. There was no doubt in Owen's mind that Kathryn was already as much in love with her husband as he was in love with her.

Eyric glanced at him again. "Thank you," he said absently, his brow furrowing.

Owen slowly sauntered over to the window, looking out at the grounds below. It was a beautiful scene, and the puffy clouds made it even more idyllic. The trees swayed in the gentle breeze. He could smell the wisteria through chinks in the panes. Then he saw one of the men he'd hired walking around the manor, surveying the grounds. The man looked at Owen as he passed, and nodded to him discreetly. Owen smiled and nodded back.

"Do you know what Lady Elysabeth wants?" Eyric asked. "Not that you'll tell me, being her loyal servant."

"I'm not her servant," Owen said, gazing at the beauty of the trees. There were only a few years separating him from Eyric, but Owen felt the other man was much older. Though both had suffered, Eyric's life experiences had been even more painful.

Eyric's head snapped up. A wary look crinkled his eyes. "Who are you then? Are you . . . are you a poisoner?" His voice nearly throbbed with fear as he suddenly realized he was alone—and defenseless—with an armed man.

Owen gently reached out with his magic, letting the flow of the Fountain rise out of him. He studied Eyric, looking for weaknesses, and he saw him exposed like the words in a book. The deposed prince was a kindhearted man. He was clumsy with a sword, having never been properly trained. But his whole soul was riddled with fear, and it reminded Owen, darkly, of himself. Eyric was constantly aware of the threat of being caught. He was afraid of Owen, afraid a simple knight would be able to defeat him. He was afraid he would not be able to protect his wife.

"I am not your enemy," Owen said, shaking his head. He remembered something Ankarette had taught him. It was risky, but he decided to try it. If Eyric was terrified, he would not think calmly or rationally. Owen needed to try to dispel his fear and build trust with the young man. The fastest way to build trust was to be vulnerable.

"Who are you?" Eyric said, a little throb of panic in his voice. He glanced at the door, the expression on his face indicating he was deciding whether to escape.

Owen brought down the chain hood, freeing his mass of unruly hair. "You've been away from court too long to recognize me. I am Owen Kiskaddon."

Eyric gasped, whistling in his breath as if he'd been struck. "You're . . . you're Fountain-blessed!" He was starting to pant.

"I am," Owen said. "And you are not. I can sense that about you."

"Does Iago know? I don't think he does. He would have *told* me!"

"If Iago knew who I was, I'd probably be his prisoner," Owen replied candidly. "I'm trusting you with my secret. In return, I'd like for you to trust me. Tell me who you are. Do not lie to me. I will know it if you are," he added meaningfully. He was confident that Eyric was who he claimed to be, but the truth was so important he wanted confirmation from the man himself.

The young man stared at Owen, his face betraying his surprise. "You came all this way. You risked your very life to come here."

Owen nodded. "Your uncle needed to be sure. He couldn't trust the rumors or the reports. It is only too easy to deceive."

"My uncle?" Eyric said with a twinge of wrath. "Of course my uncle wants me. He wants me dead."

Owen shook his head. "He does not. I assure you. Tell me who you are."

"I am Eyric Argentine, son of Eredur. I swear it by the Fountain."

It is true.

"I believe you," Owen said. "The Espion reported that you were possibly a fisherman's son, Piers Urbick."

Eyric nodded. "The Urbicks protected me. They raised me. They were paid well to confess that I was their natural child."

"Why the deception?" Owen pressed, stepping away from the window. "Why pay them to lie about you?"

Eyric's eyes narrowed. "I don't have to tell you."

Owen shook his head. "Why not? What is going on?"

"More than you know" was the evasive answer. "More than Severn knows. He cannot be allowed to remain as king. He cannot wear the hollow crown. I must take it from him."

"I don't think that you can," Owen said simply. "The lord marshal of Brythonica was just at Edonburick, warning Iago that he will not support your uprising. And the people, Eyric, won't rally to you. Chatriyon is only using you to defy your uncle. He means to force a marriage to your sister and claim the throne for himself."

Eyric's look darkened. "I don't believe you."

"You are being used by both sides," Owen insisted. "Think, man! Chatriyon only wants power for himself, and Iago is using you to topple Severn for his own purposes. You are their puppet. Let me help you cut the strings."

"How?" Eyric said angrily. He frowned and started pacing, looking as if he wanted to grab one of the vases and hurl it down onto the floor. "If Severn gets his hands on me, he will finish what he failed to do all those years ago. I was a *child*!"

Owen stepped forward. "I understand that. Believe me, I do. I spent months living at Kingfountain, shuddering with fear, thinking the king was going to murder me or throw me off the waterfall. My father betrayed him at Ambion Hill."

"But you have value to him," Eyric snapped. "You are Fountain-blessed. Of course he would want to save your life. I am his rival. He sent you here to kill me. If I don't come with you, you are supposed to murder me. Can you deny it?"

Owen breathed in slowly, trying to calm his own emotions. "Only if you were an imposter," he said calmly. "Only if you were really Piers Urbick. But you are not. You are Eyric Argentine. When we first arrived, when I first saw you at Iago's court, you said who you were, and the Fountain told me it was true."

Eyric's eyes widened. "Then you know my claim is just. You know I am your rightful king!" A look of hope sparked in his eyes. "If you help me regain my throne, your place in my court will be unparalleled. Name your terms, and I will grant them, even up to half of my kingdom. With you on my side, Lord Owen, I can do this!" His eyes were lit from within. "I will reward you with anything you desire."

A roaring sound filled Owen's ears. The roar of ambition, which he'd heard once before, while Iago and Evie were playing Wizr. He saw the possibilities, the chance to have Evie for his own. Severn was reluctant to unite the two duchies, but Eyric would be happy to grant him such a boon. Owen had never felt so tempted in his life. He saw the road in front of him. But it would mean betraying Severn. It would mean betraying the man who had guided him and given him his current rank. The man who had sent him to Atabyrion to help Evie win the heart of another man. Owen's heart ached with pain. *This* is why men rebelled. *This* is how they fell.

"I am no kingmaker," Owen said, shaking his head slowly. "I've read enough history to know what happens to such people. If you want to be a king, you must do it on your own merits. I will oppose you. Vigorously."

Eyric breathed in through his nose. "Your integrity does you credit, my lord."

"Loyalty binds me," Owen said simply. "Reconsider your own claims. Your own ambition. When you were a prince, you were the Duke of Yuork."

"A title my uncle stripped from me!" Eyric spat.

Owen stepped forward. "But what if he restored it? You are his brother's child. I know, for myself, that he deeply regrets what happened to you and your brother. It was none of his doing."

"None of his doing? He usurped the throne from us!"

Owen shook his head. "Because of your mother. She tried wresting the protectorship from him—the protectorship your father granted to your uncle. I know the history, Eyric. We cannot undo what was done. But if you came to court, I am certain the king would not only spare your life, but he would also make you one of the nobles of the realm. You lack experience and training. You've been running for most of your entire life. Come with me to Kingfountain. I will speak on your behalf, and I give you my word, Severn is not the monster you fear him to be. Reconcile with him and you will gain more than what you have now. This is a beautiful manor. You have a beautiful wife. Lay aside your claim to the crown. Come back with me. I implore you."

Eyric was breathing hard and he had a wild look in his eye. Beads of sweat trickled down his temples. "If only you knew," he muttered.

"Knew what?" Owen demanded hotly.

Eyric looked up at Owen. "It is a secret I cannot tell."

The door to the solar burst open, and the steward could be seen directing guards into the room. "Take him! Take him at once!"

For a moment, Owen didn't know who they were going to seize. But then he saw the look of triumph in Eyric's eyes.

"You had your chance to join me," Eyric said. "Without you, Severn will fall. And when he does, you will lose everything."

♦ ♦ ♦

In my research of the history of Ceredigion, I have been reading the interesting accounts of the Maid of Donremy. Truly, she is perhaps the most notable Fountain-blessed these lands have witnessed in several hundred years. She was a peasant girl who came from a town on the border between Brythonica and Occitania. She turned the tide in the conflict between the protector of Ceredigion and the Prince of Occitania. One of the more fascinating aspects is that her rise to power occurred after she met the prince. The Prince of Occitania demanded proof that she was Fountain-blessed. She demonstrated her talent by visiting the sanctuary of Our Lady of Firebos. She reached her hand into the waters of the fountain and withdrew a sword. It was cankered with rust, but the rust quickly fell away with a little scrubbing. There were five stars on the blade. That is all we know about her sword. When she was eventually captured, she no longer had the sword. No one knows where it is. The Occitanians believe that if their kingdom is ever invaded again, another Maid will rise up with the sword and expel the invaders. I did find one rumor in my search. One reference claimed the sword was found not at Firebos, but at the island sanctuary in Brythonica.

—Polidoro Urbino, Court Historian of Kingfountain

♦ ♦ ♦

CHAPTER TWENTY-SIX

Refuge

A shower of glass and fragments of wood preceded Owen's departure from the bay window. He had deliberately placed himself there, realizing it afforded him the most expeditious way to retreat from the manor. Shouts from behind heralded the arrival of his pursuers, and he wasted no time in drawing his sword and dashing for the front of the manor, where, he hoped, they had untethered the horses from the carriage.

Using his Fountain magic, he sent a thought hurtling through the air at Etayne. *We must go. Now!*

As he rounded the corner, he saw that both of the carriage horses were free, and the servant with the whip was standing by them, his eyes wide with concern at the sudden commotion. The front door was wrenched open, and two men with swords emerged, coming at a sprint to head off Owen.

The servant with the whip blanched and fit his own foot into one of the stirrups and hoisted himself onto the mount, then started whipping it violently on the flanks to get himself as far away as possible. That left one horse for Owen and Etayne.

As he ran toward the confused beast, he realized he could be pulled out of the saddle before he had the chance to escape, so he changed his tactics. Instead of fleeing the two men, he charged them. Hours and hours at the training yard came rushing back to him in a whirlwind. He didn't slow down at all as he rushed toward the nearest man and raised his sword for a downward thrust. Changing tactics at the last moment to catch the man off guard, he leaped forward instead, his boot connecting with the man's stomach so hard the man nearly backflipped and landed on his face.

The other Atabyrion lunged at Owen, and their blades connected. Owen parried twice, then dropped low and sliced the man's leg at the knee. There was a jet of blood, but Owen was not trying to amputate his leg, only cripple him and prevent him from pursuing them.

Kathryn is drugged. The thought came from Etayne. *I'm going to poison Eyric's gloves to incapacitate him.*

No! Owen thought back. He stared briefly at the farthest part of the building, the one half-overgrown with foliage. *Get out here! Meet me there.* He knew that she could see the vision of it in her mind.

This may be my only chance! Etayne thought back angrily. *I cannot fail this mission!*

He could sense the determination in her thoughts. She had been trained by the very best poisoners in Pisan, and she did not want her first major assignment to bring her shame. Owen also realized, however, that if he left without her, it was probable she would be caught and killed. Ankarette had been tormented with guilt after accidentally poisoning the wife of her intended victim. Haste was dangerous.

Listen to me, Etayne! Owen thought back. He reached the horse and swung up into the saddle as the guards rounded the end of the manor and rushed at him. He slapped the horse's flank with the flat of his blade to get it moving. His heart was thundering in his ears at the closeness of his pursuers. *Get out here. Now! I'll circle back for you!*

No, my lord. I'll steal a horse and meet you at Edonburick. I can get Eyric. I know I can. Let me try!

Owen's mount was starting to gallop, and Owen had to hold tight with his knees and ride low against the horse's neck. One of the men sprinted after him. He was quite a runner, but even he could not outrun a horse. Owen stared back at him, smiling as the gap widened. The man quit the pursuit, hurling an epithet after him.

It's no good, Etayne. They know who I am now. We're leaving as soon as we get back to Edonburick. I'm not going to leave you behind. Now quit being stubborn and get outside! Don't make me come in there to fetch you.

He could sense a hive of black thoughts. *Yes, my lord.*

Owen circled back, bringing his horse into the trees for cover. He wondered whether he had done the right thing in revealing himself to Eyric. He grit his teeth, angry that the man was too afeared of his uncle to accept Owen's words. He was angry, but he knew he shouldn't be surprised. The man had been trained his whole life to fear Severn, to mistrust him. And now he had a beautiful wife who was the daughter of Atabyrion's wealthiest earl. What promises had he made to her? What promises had he made to everyone else? No, Owen realized that it had been naive for him to believe he had even the slimmest chance to change his mind. But he also couldn't stomach the thought of murdering him, especially since he knew the king's own feelings argued against it. He was an enemy to Ceredigion, but he was no traitor. He had a claim on the throne, if a weak one. Like Etayne, Owen was troubled by the thought that he'd failed in his mission. He had come to prevent a war. And from the way things were shaping up, he'd probably contributed to starting one instead.

Where are you? he thought, reaching out to Etayne. The trees ghosted past him, and the horse was tense and nervous, snorting angrily at its rider.

Silence.

Owen's heart thrummed with worry. He could see part of the estate through the trees ahead. He'd taken his mount into the woods on the side closest to the ivy-thick edge he had shown her in his mind. If he got too close, he would be seen. He reached out with his senses, listening, and heard the sound of men and horses. Through the trees, he could see Eyric was in the front of the manor, talking to the guards. Groomsmen were bringing up horses from the stables, one at a time. Owen wiped the sweat from his upper lip. Eyric was going to ride after him. He could hear the murmuring of voices, but at this distance, they were indistinguishable even to him.

Etayne! he thought again, gritting his teeth.

No answer.

His horse snorted loudly, and Owen frowned, hoping the sound had not been heard over the ruckus. "Where are you?" he muttered angrily, staring at the manor, feeling the hard saddle beneath him.

Then he saw her slipping out the rear door of the ivy-choked house. Suddenly there was a scream and a shout. "Over here! There's one of 'em here! She just left out the back! Hurry!"

The men milling around the entrance came running. One of the guards was mounted, and he kicked his beast into a trot.

Owen saw Etayne slip into the woods, wearing a pale white gown, Atabyrion in style. It was one of Kathryn's gowns. He clicked his tongue and whistled, and her eyes darted over to him. A look of relief crossed her face, and he met her partway. Reaching down, he took her hand and swung her up into the saddle behind him.

"Why didn't you answer me?" he snarled at her.

She shook her head, her expression darkening. "I couldn't hear you. My magic . . . my magic failed." There was an exhausted look on her face and she swayed a little in the saddle. Now he understood. She had expended her power in trying to maintain her illusion for too long. Her capacity would grow with time and practice. He realized that if she'd stayed behind, she would likely have fallen unconscious.

"I'm glad you listened to me," he said with maybe a bit too much self-satisfaction.

"In the trees! Over there!"

"I see them!"

The voices startled Owen and Etayne.

He sighed. "Hold on to me tightly. I want to get to Edonburick before Eyric."

Etayne nodded and wrapped her arms around his waist, tightening her grip on her wrists. "Thank you," she whispered. The look in her eyes was revealing, vulnerable. He smiled at her and turned away, wondering what she was thinking. In truth, he was afraid of what the look meant. She was the daughter of a thief, a sanctuary man. He was the Duke of Westmarch.

And his heart belonged to an earl's daughter.

♦ ♦ ♦

"I don't understand why you must depart so quickly," Iago said as they walked down the many wooden steps leading to the docks. Owen was a few steps behind, watching Evie and the king as they walked ahead of him. "Surely you can wait until tomorrow? I thought you wanted to see Eyric and Kathryn yourself?"

"I did, my lord," Evie said evasively. "But I received an urgent summons back to Kingfountain. I must depart at once."

Iago looked upset. "What does that mean? Why would Severn want you back so quickly? I was really enjoying our walk today and felt we were making strides. You're a remarkable woman. I was expecting your stay to be much longer."

"I must go," Evie said. She glanced back at Owen with worry in her eyes. She knew about the disaster that had unfolded at Eyric's lodge, so she was just as eager as he was to seek refuge back in Ceredigion. They did not have much time to take their leave. Iago looked like a disconsolate puppy. Owen wanted to kick him. Etayne had ventured ahead to tell the captain to make ready.

They reached the bottom tier of the docks. The sound of the waterfall made soft communication difficult, so Iago raised his voice. "When can I see you again?"

Evie looked flustered by the persistence of his attentions. "I don't know, my lord," she stammered. There was some noise from higher up on the platforms. Evie glanced up, and her face went pale. "Well, it seems you have some court business that requires your attention. I thank you for your hospitality."

Iago turned and looked back up the ramps. Men were waving down and shouting, but their words were lost in the noise. Iago frowned in annoyance. Evie was about to walk down the pier toward the ship, but Iago caught her arm. She stared at him, her eyes blazing with the fear of being caught.

"I wanted you to know," Iago said, stepping toward her. He gently took her hand with both of his. "That I have given sincere thought to Severn's offer. Of a truce between our kingdoms. I can't tell you how tempted I am."

The words sickened Owen. He grit his teeth, scowling, wanting to be away from Atabyrion and their peculiar customs and fashions. He wanted to be back in his own realm, his own kingdom, wearing his *own* badge. Iago wasn't looking at him, but he stared at him heatedly all the same.

Evie was silent, her cheeks a little flushed.

"I am bound by honor to help Eyric. I wish I had met you prior to giving my oath. But I promise you, Lady *Mortimer*," he added with a devious grin, "that I consider you a friend. That I will speak on your behalf when Eyric rules." He brought her knuckles to his mouth. His look was suddenly vulnerable as he gazed at her. "You have the most bewitching eyes," he murmured softly, and Owen nearly rammed him off the pier into the fish-soiled waters.

"I truly must go," Evie said, trying to pull her hand away.

Iago nodded and released her hand. She started to turn and leave. Then, in an act of pure impetuousness, he strode up and caught her shoulders, brought his mouth down on hers, and kissed her right there on the docks, in front of everyone—in front of Owen. It was one of those claiming kisses, the kind that makes girls swoon and invokes murderous jealousy.

Startled by it, Evie quickly pushed him back. "My lord!" she scolded, her cheeks stained with crimson. "That was . . . presumptuous!" She wiped a hand over her mouth.

"I know," Iago said, grinning like a fool. "I'm reckless. I take risks. And I wanted you to remember me. Farewell, my lady. Until we meet again." He bowed graciously.

There were some whistles and catcalls from the docks and—much to Owen's vexation—Iago Llewellyn seemed to bask in them. When Owen looked at Evie, she was staring after the king.

She sighed and shook her head, and she and Owen started up the ramp. She gave him a pointed look. "*That's* how it's done properly, by the way," she said to him.

Owen was mortified. His heart burned with feelings too savage to describe. His ears were hot, his cheeks flushed, and he knew he would never scrub the memory of that kiss out of his mind. It was Evie's first kiss. He knew that. And it had not been with him.

As the captain ordered the sailors to shove off, Etayne approached them worriedly. She wore a cloak to cover the gown she had taken from Lady Kathryn.

"What is it now?" Owen asked with concern, seeing the look in her eyes. They had separated as soon as they arrived in Edonburick from the Ardanays and had not spoken since.

"I went down into the hold to check on Bothwell," Etayne said softly in his ear. "He was gone. I found Clark in the cell instead. Bound, gagged, and unconscious."

Owen's eyes widened. "He's down below? He never made it back to Kingfountain?"

Etayne shook her head. "I assume not. Which means Severn may already be dead."

CHAPTER TWENTY-SEVEN

Seasons

On board the ship *Vassalage*, sails billowing with the wind, Owen paced as he watched Justine tending to Clark's injury, a particularly nasty gash on the back of his head that had left him unconscious and with a hazy memory. Etayne's look was dark with worry and dread about the escaped prisoner. Poisoners were renowned for their sense of revenge, so she had much to fear from the man who had escaped.

Clark sat on a barrel in the hold, wincing with pain. The lantern swayed with the rocking motion of the ship. Evie watched in worried fascination as Justine treated the Espion.

"You can remember nothing else?" Owen pressed, trying to subdue his agitation. He felt as if they were being thwarted at every turn, and he did not like the thought of being outmaneuvered in any game, let alone the realities of life, especially not when his king's life was at risk.

Clark tolerated the pain of Justine's ministrations with perfect patience, although his fingers were digging into the barrel lid and the tendons were standing out on his hands. "I didn't see who hit me. Someone was crumpled on the floor in the yonder cage." He motioned with one of his hands. "I called out to rouse him, and then I was struck from behind. The next thing I knew, I awoke bound and gagged, with thunder in my head. I know I missed my transport back to Ceredigion. The captain surely left without me when I didn't show up." He frowned with melancholy. "After this, I'll be assigned duty to watch over Dunsdworth again," he complained bitterly. "And I deserve it."

"Nonsense," Owen said, rubbing his chin.

"The important thing," Evie said consolingly, "is they didn't kill you."

Justine's head jerked up, her eyes blinking wildly. She flushed a bit and then started back to work.

"Thank you, lass," Clark mumbled to her.

"It's quite all right," Justine replied, looking embarrassed.

"Someone has been playing us for fools," Owen said after a lengthy pause. "The problem is, there are too many people who wish us harm. The king has too many enemies."

"Including his nephew," Etayne said darkly.

Evie looked at the poisoner. "Tell me more about what happened when you went to see Eyric."

Feeling restless energy rush through him, Owen thumped his fist against one of the deck struts. He glanced at Etayne, whose eyes were downcast. She believed she had failed in her mission. He could tell she was also worried about what Mancini would do to her. Owen was more concerned with finding out the true allegiance of the leader of the Espion.

"I believe Eyric is who he says he is," Owen declared. "And I know that Severn would not have wanted him to be murdered in Atabyrion." He shook his head firmly. "That Eyric survived is nothing short of a miracle from the Fountain. I've known the king half my life, and he is still troubled by the murders of the princes. And Lady Elyse will be thrilled to learn that her brother is alive. No, we did the right thing in sparing his life."

Etayne's eyes, and the expression on her mouth, spoke that she felt otherwise. "Yet he's going to invade Ceredigion to claim the throne. You can have no illusions about that."

"I don't," Owen said, agreeing with her. "Just as I believe Iago Llewellyn will join him in the invasion. We've wounded his pride, and he *is* a proud man." The last comment he fired at Evie.

"Also a desperate one," Evie said, taking the blow without retaliating. "His kingdom is nearly bankrupt; his nobles are all scheming. But Iago doesn't understand the might of his enemy. He's like a man who gambles on a throw of the dice. He risks much to gain much, but he doesn't realize that the outcome isn't up to chance. It's a matter of mettle. And I don't think Iago's matches King Severn's. But I understand why he's facing the hazard. In his mind, the opportunity for reward is too great. The chance to get out from beneath the thumbs of his nobles."

Owen didn't like the man personally, but he agreed with her assessment. "Well, as Mancini likes to say: Two can throw the dice in a game of chance."

"You can't throw dice if you are dead," Etayne said broodingly, reminding them all that the risk Severn faced wasn't just on the battlefield.

The comment made them all sulk in despair for a moment.

"I've done all that I can," Justine said after a moment, wiping her hands on the towel she had used.

"Thank you, my lady," Clark offered in a humble tone.

She smiled at the praise and then followed her mistress back toward their private room. Evie motioned for Owen to join them and he did. The steps leading out of the hold were steep and narrow, and it was dark when they reached above deck. The stars were shining through the windows like a swarm of tiny fireflies. They conferred with the first mate, who informed them that the journey back would take less time because the wind was at their backs. He hoped to reach Kingfountain before dinner the following day.

Evie's chamber seemed much too small to Owen. Everything about the ship was cramped, like the cage in the hold, but the physical size wasn't the real issue. Owen was restless. He felt his life was becoming more confined and restrictive, and he longed to burst the bands of duty and obligation, to be free. But he would not risk losing everything he had acquired in a rash act of rebellion. *Loyalty binds me.*

"You're agitated," Evie said with a sigh. Justine started to help her remove her jewelry.

"It's not every day you get to see another man kiss the woman you love," Owen said with bitterness.

Evie sighed. "That was . . . unfortunate. Please don't think I enjoyed it."

"There has been precious little in this journey that I've enjoyed," Owen said. He wanted to kick himself for being dramatic at such a time. "Forgive me for being sullen."

"I can't blame you," Evie said, the wrinkle of a smile tugging at the corner of her mouth. "You've had to endure Iago talking about you in your very presence! You've watched him flatter and dote on me day after day. That was an unfair burden to place on you."

"Let's not pretend that *your* discomfort was not as great as mine," Owen said, deflecting her sympathy. "This has not been an easy mission for either of us. I'm sorry if I've not been as attentive as the King of Atabyrion."

Evie looked at him and shook her head. "You will always be my closest and dearest friend, Owen. Your pain is mine. And I don't want another moment to pass between us without you knowing how deeply I care about you and your feelings." She sighed, her look growing more troubled. "Do you think . . . do you think Severn will force me to marry him? If he invades Ceredigion, I cannot imagine that Severn would still want an alliance."

Owen chuckled. "Then here's to hoping he does!"

"Be serious," she chided. "You know he cannot win. He's too brash and self-confident to realize it. He doesn't know the man he is provoking. But do you think Severn will still make me marry Iago? I'm too close to the situation to see it objectively."

"And you think I am not?" Owen said, suddenly very serious. "Losing you is my greatest fear. I'm sorry, but I don't think Iago

Llewellyn deserves you. He *needs* you, and not just for your connections and your inheritance. He needs your wisdom and prudence. The advantage is all on his side. You would bring him the stability that he most desperately needs. I have no doubt his efforts to woo you were sincere, if not selfishly motivated."

Evie flushed at the compliments. "You are kind to say those things."

"They're true," Owen said with a grunt. The pain in his heart was swelling, making it almost difficult to breathe. He tried some levity. "I have a difficult time picturing you wearing one of those fancy Atabyrion headdresses, though. You would look quite silly."

She started to laugh and it was music to his ears.

They stared at each other a moment, feeling the healing balm of shared pain. She wanted him to hold her. He could see the need in her eyes, but he also saw her unwillingness to act on it. Owen needed no more coaxing than that. He crossed the small room to her, startling Justine, and Evie rushed into Owen's embrace. He hugged her tightly, pressing her against him, feeling her body trembling in his arms. Her hair smelled sweet, and he could feel its softness crushed under his forearms. Her cheek pressed against his chest and throat.

"What will happen to us?" she whispered, her voice thick with tears.

"I don't know," Owen said, feeling as if his heart were wrenching into two halves. He held her for a long time, just enjoying the moment—the sway of the ship, the feeling of comfort that came whenever his love was near. He wanted to kiss her—to tilt her head up and kiss her—but not while he was consumed with the memory of Iago's lips having claimed hers first. At least he had the satisfaction of knowing the kiss would be tainted for Iago when he learned that Lord Kiskaddon had been in his realm.

"It's getting late," Justine said, looking forlornly at them both.

Evie backed away, a little shy look on her face. She smoothed the wrinkled front of her gown. Her eyes were more blue at that moment.

"What did you make of Eyric and Kathryn?" Evie asked curiously. "When you met them at the Huntley manor?"

Owen thought for a moment, bringing the memories bubbling back up in his mind. "I have no doubt they are very much in love," he said. "There was something special about seeing them together. It may have been a political match, on the surface, but I have no doubt the two care deeply about each other. And I believe that Kathryn has confidence in Eyric and his story. Their love was touching."

Evie seemed pleased by the words, but then a worried look replaced it. "What will happen if he does become king?" she whispered.

"What always happens when a king is thrown down," Owen answered ominously. "It's rare for the king's favorites to stay in power. Your grandfather would lose his title. And so would I. We have much more to lose if Severn falls."

"And you don't think that Eyric would be willing to accept something less than the crown?"

Owen shook his head. "I offered that to him and he rebuffed me. He cannot trust Severn. Not after all he has been taught about his uncle. He fears the man. He probably even hates him. No, I don't think Eyric will be swayed with the promise of being the Duke of Yuork again. He wants the crown or nothing."

Evie's face went dark with anger. "Then he will likely lose everything."

"Or we will," Owen said flatly.

Her lips pressed into a firm line. He'd seen that look on her face before. The look of determination that was a warning not to defy her.

♦ ♦ ♦

The next day, the sky was veiled in thick, gray clouds. Owen craned his neck, feeling an icy bite to the wind. He needed to go to his room for a cloak soon. Every sailor chafed his hands and blew on them, looking hard pressed to tug on ropes and tie knots in such cold.

Owen went to look for Evie, and he found her and Justine talking to the captain above deck.

"How far off is Kingfountain?" Owen asked, staring at the churning sea as the *Vassalage* sliced through it.

"It's yonder," the captain said, a strange look in his eye. The captain had a small scar on his left eye, slicing down his cheek. It was faint, and Owen hadn't noticed it before.

Owen raised his hand to his brow to get a better look at the land ahead. He started with surprise.

"This is unusual," Evie said, shaking her head. "I've never seen Kingfountain swathed in snow this early in the season. Winter is still two months away."

The palace of Kingfountain and the trees on the grounds were shrouded in a thin blanket of freshly fallen snow. Owen had been there in winter before, but he had mostly spent his winters in Westmarch, where it didn't get as cold. This was an unusually early winter storm.

"Have you seen the like before?" Owen asked the captain.

He shook his head. "Not in my twenty years at sea," he said. "I've never seen Kingfountain so white this early."

A memory stirred in Owen's mind. He felt the supple churn of the Fountain along with it.

It was something Severn had said during breakfast to Dickon Ratcliffe one long-ago morning. Owen had been close enough to hear the conversation. The memory had always nagged at him.

"Remember the eclipse, Dickon? The eclipse that happened the day my wife died? I was blamed for that too." Then his voice had shrunk to almost a whisper. "That, however, may have been my doing. My soul was black that day. And I *am* Fountain-blessed."

It is true, whispered the Fountain.

The first flakes of snow began to fall silently on the deck.

CHAPTER TWENTY-EIGHT

Perfidious

A servant took the snow-dusted cloak from Owen and shook it over the threshold. The interior of the palace of Kingfountain was lit with braziers, filling the air with a smoky haze that gave the scene a surreal look, the stuff of dreams. It was a relief to be back in Ceredigion, but with such dramatic changes happening all at once, it felt almost as peculiar as Atabyrion. As Owen marched toward the throne room, he encountered Mancini along the way. The very sight of the man twisted his mouth into a sour frown.

"Your return could not be more expedient," the spymaster said. He looked stressed and sleep-deprived. "That you returned at all counters our worst fears that mischief befell you in Edonburick."

"Mischief *did* befall us," Owen said angrily, breathing in deep mouthfuls of the warm air to soothe the coldness from the journey. "Justine and Clark were poisoned. I would have been a victim too, but I did not partake of the food on that particular outing. We caught and then lost the poisoner. You should know that it was Lord Bothwell. He went by the name of Foulcart at the poisoner school."

"Bothwell?" Mancini said. "He betrayed us? After all I've paid to win his loyalty?"

Owen was impressed by how surprised Mancini sounded. He would keep his suspicions about the spymaster to himself until he had a moment to confide them to the king.

"How is the king? I sent Clark ahead of us to warn him of the Occitanians' plot to poison him and deceive Lady Elyse. Clark was waylaid and knocked out. We've had our share of troubles, Dominic."

"They sent a poisoner?" he said with surprise. "We've seen none of that, and I have the Espion investigate those who request work at the palace. The king is quite hale, but he is not well. You know about his niece? How did word reach you so quickly that she fled?"

Owen gave him a wry look. "I *am* Fountain-blessed." He was relieved to hear that Severn was still alive.

"Then make it stop snowing, please," Mancini quipped. "The common folk fear the river will freeze over. You can imagine the consternation that is causing at the sanctuary."

"Whatever for?" Owen asked.

"You know the legend of Our Lady. That the rights of sanctuary will last until the water stops. Because that waterfall has *never* stopped flowing, not in a thousand years at least, it's believed the rights will last into perpetuity. The sanctuary men are thinking they will lose their protection. Superstitious fools."

Owen shook his head with scorn. "How long ago did Elyse flee? And how did she get away? Was she abducted?"

"No, I don't believe she was abducted, although I cannot be totally certain. She vanished the day after her mother's funeral."

"The queen dowager is dead?" Owen exclaimed. "I learned in Atabyrion that she was being slowly poisoned."

Mancini shrugged helplessly as they approached the doors leading into the throne room. The doors were closed, and the guards posted on either side of them bore spears. The spymaster gestured, and they saluted and then opened the doors.

"She died not long after you departed. She'd been sick for many months. Her death was a terrible blow to Lady Elyse. It's my belief that Deconeus Tunmore used her death and the girl's subsequent grief to persuade her to accept Chatriyon's proposal of marriage. She was smuggled from the sanctuary in disguise and then boarded an Occitanian merchant ship set to sail that morning. You can only imagine the king's fury at such a betrayal. I *told* him to keep her on a shorter leash. Any leash! But he trusted her, swore she would never abandon him. Well, she has, and I can't blame her, considering her reduced prospects and his unwillingness to take her for a wife. He is angry, lad. Angrier than I have ever seen him. It's a boon you are here, for he listens to none of us."

Owen swallowed as he crossed the threshold, his insides churning with worry. Mancini took a position near the fireplace, close enough to be within earshot. He saw Severn slumped over in his throne, a man who looked exhausted and full of turmoil. His hair was grayer, or so it seemed from his unhappy demeanor. He sat in brooding silence, teasing his bottom lip with a black-gloved hand. Light from the torches exposed his unshaven chin and untidy hair. He was wearing the crown, which was unusual, for he seldom wore it outside of ceremonial occasions. The metal band around his head seemed to be made of dull iron instead of gold.

Owen approached the dais and then sank to one knee. As he looked up into the king's eyes, he saw the caged inferno hiding behind the steel. That he was sitting so still belied the explosions roaring inside him. His eyes shifted to Owen, and for a moment, it seemed he did not recognize him.

"Owen?" the king asked hoarsely.

"I've returned, my lord," he replied. "But I fear not soon enough to prevent such mischief." He wished Mancini would leave so that he could vent his suspicions, but this wasn't the right time.

"So you've heard?" the king said flatly, his voice tight with control.

"My lord, I heard about the plot in Atabyrion," he answered. "I tried to send word, but I have failed you."

The king's expression changed. He rose from the throne like a puppet on strings. "You? I have been plagued with doubts and torments. I feared that even *you* were in on the plot. Or that you would be destroyed yourself. And yet here you are, kneeling. Rise, my friend. You needn't kneel to me ever again."

Owen slowly stood, staring at the king, feeling the depth of the man's emotions. "What happened?" he pressed, keeping his voice low. There were no servants in the great hall. It felt like a sepulchre.

The king came off the dais and put his arm around Owen's shoulder, leading him to the furnace-like hearth. Owen was quickly drenched in sweat, but the king seemed immune to the heat. Severn stared into the flames, his mind tormented.

"With her mother's failing health," the king started, "she came less frequently to the palace. It did not alarm me. It was only natural she would seek to comfort her mother in those final hours. She came to me once. It was late at night and she looked so tired, so sad. There was little I could do to offer comfort, for I hated her mother and she hated me. But I said no harsh words and offered only sympathy for her grieving. Elyse"—her name seemed to burn his tongue, and he flinched—"asked if I would ever force her to marry. I'd long ago promised I would never do that, so I repeated my pledge. She was quiet, and then she asked if I would ever let her marry at all. She said that she understood any child born from her womb would be perceived by some as an heir to the throne." He stared deeply into the flames, butting a clenched fist against his mouth.

"What did you tell her?" Owen asked, wiping a trail of sweat from his cheek.

The king's eyes were haunted. "I told her the truth. That I couldn't let her marry. Not yet. And then I told her that *she* was my heir. That she would inherit the throne if anything happened to me." His lips curled into a grimace. "The next morning, she was gone."

He whirled away from the heat, his face livid with passion. "She abandoned me for that *whelp* Chatriyon, who promised to make her his queen. That sniveling upstart who wears hose and garters and has never killed a man with his own hands, his own knife! He thinks to lay claim to Ceredigion through her. He thinks that I will just lie down and let their boots dash me to pieces." The look in his eyes, the tone of his voice was terrifying. "I will *not* be easy meat for their feast. This boar has tusks, and I will gore them all."

"My lord," Mancini said guardedly. "We haven't heard Lord Owen's news. What of the pretender, Piers Urbick? Is the king's enemy dead?"

Owen looked from the spymaster to the king. "I'm convinced he is being truthful. My lord, hear me out. I know Mancini's spies have found people claiming to be his parents. I think that is a purposeful deception. I've met with him, my lord. More than once. He is not Fountain-blessed. Neither is anyone around him, at least not from what I could perceive. When we arrived, we were in time to join the wedding celebrations."

"Wedding?" Mancini gasped.

"Yes. Iago Llewellyn matched him with the Earl of Huntley's daughter, Lady Kathryn. They've been married less than a fortnight now. All the nobles of Atabyrion believe Eyric is who he claims to be, an Argentine. Your nephew. I believe he is as well."

Severn stared at Owen in surprise. "How did he survive? Why has he not tried to come back before now? You must recognize his very claim is highly questionable!"

"If you were to meet him yourself," Owen said, reaching out and gripping the king's shoulder, "I think you would come to the same conclusion. He's terrified of you, my lord. He believes what they say about you. I tried to persuade him to return with me. In fact, I was planning to kidnap him, but Kathryn's steward must have overheard our conversation, for he sent men to capture me. I fled with Etayne, and we returned promptly. I don't think Iago will be pleased when he learns about my duplicity."

"I don't give a care about how he feels," Severn snapped. "You were wise to flee instead of being captured. I would have paid any ransom to secure you, Owen. Now I can save my gold and conquer Atabyrion and Occitania with it instead."

Owen shook his head. "You don't need to attack Edonburick. Iago is going to come here. He's desperate to prove himself a man, and he's reckless. I think he was tempted by your offer. He is . . . fond of Elysabeth. But I think he hopes he can still have her once Eyric is wearing the crown. They are coming to invade."

Severn frowned. "Let them come. Let them all come. I can defend my kingdom. And if these little ewes want to wet their swords in blood, I will give them all the blood they can stomach. They can watch their men perish and their manors burn. They can hear their mothers weep."

"There is more," Owen said fervently. He could feel the rage seething inside the king. Best to deliver all the bad news at once.

Severn cocked his eyebrow in disbelief.

"They have no wish to face you in battle," Owen said. "It turns out that our Espion at Iago's court, Lord Bothwell, was a poisoner trained in Pisan under the assumed name Foulcart. His mission was to kill us all and foment a war between Ceredigion and Atabyrion. From him, we learned about another plot to murder you. A poisoner hired by Chatriyon is here in the palace. According to Bothwell, the King of Occitania doesn't want Eyric to rule. I think he's right. He's just using Eyric and King Iago as a distraction to keep you looking north. Lord Roux of Brythonica confirmed as much. *He* came to Edonburick to warn Iago not to oppose you."

"Roux was there?" Mancini said with shock. "I don't believe it!"

"He came in person," Owen said to the king, nodding back to the spymaster. "I recognized him, and he recognized me. I think he's Fountain-blessed, my lord. And he said the duchess is still our ally."

Severn gazed at Owen in awe, his blazing anger finally beginning to cool. He reached his hand around Owen's neck in a fatherly gesture. Then clapped him on the back. "You have done well, my boy. You have done your king good service and honor. And for this, I will reward you. If you revealed yourself to Eyric, you took a huge risk. But I can see why you did it. You tried to persuade him, did you not? You tried to convince him to return willingly."

Owen nodded. "I did. I promised him a duchy. The same duchy he once held as a child."

Severn smiled. "And I would have honored your pledge. Instead of gaining a duchy, he will lose everything. I wish his father-in-law well, for he will be supporting these children with his own treasures. Oh, the irony of it galls me! He could have become my legitimate heir if he had proven himself an ally and friend. But he gropes for a prize he is not tall enough to reach. He's a child." The king shook his head. "And a disobedient one at that. I feel cheerful for the first time in days. I am hunted and oppressed. The wolves are yapping at my heels. But I have true subjects. I have warships and an army. And my enemies will learn that when they rouse the wrath of a beast they fear, they will feel the bloody tusks. To war then. I welcome it."

He slung his arm around Owen's shoulder and led him back to the throne. He nodded to Mancini. "Now fetch me Horwath's granddaughter. I'm in need of her grace and good cheer. I daresay if she asks me to build a fishpond in the great hall, I may just do it!" The king laughed, probably for the first time in weeks, and clapped Owen on the back. "Well done, lad. Well done." Then his face grew more serious. "Oh, and Mancini. Have Tunmore join us from the tower for supper. It's been two days since he's eaten. I'm sure he's hungry."

Owen's smile faded as he realized what the king meant. Tunmore had *already* been dragged out of sanctuary.

CHAPTER TWENTY-NINE

Grave Secrets

Owen and the spymaster Mancini walked side by side, moving deep into the palace's Espion tunnels to the towers where the prisoners were kept. The dark corridors were frigid and Owen saw little puffs of mist as he exhaled. A deep sense of foreboding had settled inside him, thicker than the winter clouds shrouding Kingfountain.

"You finally persuaded him," Owen said, trying to master his anger. He still distrusted the man, but for the moment, he needed Mancini to believe they were on the same side.

"Persuaded whom to do what?" Mancini asked. "Be clear, young man. I do a lot of persuading every day."

"You know what I meant," Owen snapped. "Abducting Tunmore from the sanctuary."

"We should have done it years ago," Mancini said dismissively. "The man's been scheming from Our Lady all the while. Why should he be protected from his treason?"

"How did you do it?"

Mancini shifted the lantern he was carrying to his other hand and lifted it higher. "There are men in that place who do anything for enough coin." *Such as you*, Owen thought darkly. "I had someone distract the sexton while half a dozen men waylaid Tunmore. He was carted out under a tarp, trussed up and gagged, and brought straight to the palace." He snapped his fingers. "Easily done."

"How did you convince Severn to do it?"

Mancini snorted. "I didn't need to persuade him at all. Once we discovered what had happened with Elyse, you should have seen his fury. I don't think I've ever seen him rage like that, not even when Ratcliffe turned traitor. Her betrayal was particularly personal because he had put so much trust in her." The Espion turned and gave Owen a knowing look. "Even you betraying him would not have cut him to the quick like this. He needed vengeance. And it was Tunmore who turned her mind to Chatriyon."

"I'm surprised Severn didn't throw him into the falls," Owen muttered.

"As we both know, that particular method of execution cannot be relied upon for the Fountain-blessed. No, the king has had Polidoro investigating all the details of the execution of the Maid of Donremy. He wants to make sure Tunmore stays dead."

The bleak feeling within Owen worsened. He did not have much pity for Tunmore, but something felt entirely wrong about forcing the man from sanctuary. Violating an ancient tradition out of petty revenge did not sit right. While Owen believed that some of the folk customs about the Fountain were merely superstitions, he knew for a fact that the Fountain was real, and he felt a queer sensation that it was offended.

There were Espion guards waiting for them at the end of the corridor.

"Good evening, Master Mancini," one of them said.

Mancini handed his lantern to one of them. He glanced at Owen. "I change the guard regularly, and we inspect his cell every hour. The man hasn't slept or eaten in two days."

Owen felt a throb of pity.

"He's quite uncomfortable, per the king's commands," one of the guards added with a cunning smile.

"Tonight, the king would like Tunmore to join him for supper."

The other man chuckled. "What will he serve him? Rat stew?"

"With a side of kidney pie," Mancini snapped. "Open the door."

A guard unlocked the heavy iron door and a drafty breeze came through. Together, Owen and Mancini started winding their way up the tower. The wind keened and moaned up the black shaft. It sounded like the pained moans of a man, a thought that made Owen shudder.

"Do you think Severn will release him?" Owen asked Mancini.

"Pfah, no! Nor would I advise him to. No, the man is going to die. Severn is implacable in that regard. He's a changed man, boy. When Elyse betrayed him, something jarred loose. Or should I put it another way? His disposition altered rather suddenly and dramatically."

"How so?" Owen pressed, feeling the weight of his conscience grow heavier. He had sworn his loyalty to the man Severn *was*. What if Elyse's betrayal had scarred him so deeply Owen could no longer serve the man he had become? All of Owen's wealth, his status, and his holdings were due to his loyalty to the man. Was he willing to risk all of that? Was he willing to betray his king?

"In many ways, many ways," Mancini said. "For starters, his first impulse was to assassinate Chatriyon. But now that his temper has cooled, he's determined to destroy him in person. He is planning to invade Occitania and shatter the lad's kingdom. It may take him several years of austerity to finance such a venture, but he's determined to depose him. To yank the crown from his head. All while Elyse watches helplessly. He will never trust her again. I don't know if he will trust *anyone* again after this. Confound it, is that the wind or Tunmore's moaning?"

He seemed to have finally noticed the noise himself.

When they reached the top of the tower, there were two more guards pacing nervously in front of the door.

"He's been moaning like a madman," one of the guards said worriedly. "I've warned him to shut it or we'll gag him, but he's gibbering. He's gone mad, he has!"

"Open the door," Mancini said sternly.

The guard wrestled a key into the lock and opened it.

The tower loft was ice cold. All the windows around the cell were open and snow hung in thick clumps throughout the freezing chamber. There were no beds, an empty brazier had been knocked over, and other than a filthy straw pallet, the only furnishing was a foul-smelling chamber pot.

At first, Owen could not see Tunmore, but the moaning brought his attention to the man standing on a previously unnoticed bench by a double window. His arms were gripping the window ledge. He was making a terrible sound, his eyes filled with despair.

"What are you . . . get down from . . . what are you doing, man?" Mancini shouted against the wind.

Tunmore had sleet sticking to his face. His hair was spiky, and his skin had a grayish cast to it. There was a wild look in his eyes when they came to rest on Owen.

"Chaaaah!!!" he groaned, recognizing the young man instantly. "It's not too late! It's not too late! Thank the Fountain! It's not too late!"

Owen stared at Tunmore without comprehension. "What is the matter with you?"

"I am a dead man. I've seen the waters. I've seen the Deep Fathoms, so I thought it was too late. But you are here. *You* are Fountain-blessed! The Dreadful Deadman is coming! He returns to Ceredigion! He must wear the crown, boy. He *must*!"

"What nonsense are you babbling about?" Mancini asked angrily.

Owen felt something reach into his heart and clench it. A cold hand, a knife. "Who?" Owen demanded. "Eyric Argentine?"

Tunmore's face twisted with pain. "He's *not* the Dreadful Deadman! You will know. You will know him! You are part of him! You serve him. You've always served him! Be loyal to your *true* king, Kiskaddon."

"King Kiskaddon!" Mancini shouted in surprise, but Owen knew the spymaster had misunderstood.

There was a feverish look on Tunmore's face. "It's not too late! It's still not too late! The chest! Boy, the chest! You must move it or all is lost! Take it to the fountain at St. Penryn. The waters there will quiet the curse. Do it, boy! Before *all* here perish!"

"He's raving," Mancini said with a whisper.

"Who is the Dreadful Deadman?" Owen asked, taking a step toward Tunmore. "Do you know?"

"He is coming! He is returning! As it was, so will it be. You are his champion. The true king . . . !"

His words were cut off by a roar of wind that jolted the castle tower and brought in flurries of ice. Owen shielded his face from the sting of sleet.

"Take him!" Mancini shouted to the soldiers. "Grab him before he jumps!"

But it was too late. Through squinted eyes, Owen watched as Tunmore toppled over the window ledge. He raced over to the window, staring in shock, his heart thundering in his chest. The wind knifed against the keep towers, sending swirls of snow with it. When he looked down at the inner bailey, he saw a crumpled body spread-eagled on the flagstones below.

"He killed himself?" Mancini shouted, grabbing Owen's shoulder. The spymaster gazed down at the body, shook his head with revulsion, and then ordered the soldiers to hurry down and conceal the body.

Owen felt dizzy from the great height, and the deconeus's words had shaken him to his core.

"What was he raving about?" Mancini asked in a troubled voice. "I couldn't hear the last words. Did he name you . . . did he name *you* king, lad?" The grip on Owen's shoulder tightened. "I thought he did. He was a deconeus. Was it a prophecy?"

Owen could see Mancini's mistake, but he was too confused and heartsick to know what to say.

"He was delirious," Owen finally answered, shaking his head. "You drove him mad by putting him up here."

But the young man remembered seeing the chest in the waters at the fountain of Our Lady. A chest that he had first seen in the cistern waters beneath the palace. He was confused and shaken, but something told him Tunmore's words were not meaningless ravings.

"So he was trying to do more mischief?" Mancini asked. "Trying to sow the seed of rebellion in you? I wouldn't put it past him. That man was a cunning eel. He said something about St. Penryn. That's a sanctuary in Westmarch, isn't it?"

Owen wished the spymaster hadn't heard that part. "Yes," he answered. It was a fishing village along the coast in a deep corner of Owen's domain. He had heard curious tales about that place. Fishermen routinely dredged up strange items along the coast—shields, rusted helmets, and horseshoes.

There was a history to the land of Penryn. Owen did not know much about it, having spent so much time in the North. But he knew of two people who did know a great deal about history. He had to see Evie and the court historian, Polidoro Urbino.

But first they needed to tell the king that his enemy had fallen to his death from the tower and would not be joining him for dinner.

♦ ♦ ♦

In my time at Kingfountain, I have found no legend more commonly known but ephemeral than that of the first king of Ceredigion. Chasing this legend is like chasing a ghost. Very little has been documented, and most of the documents that do exist date back centuries and are duplicates of earlier sources. The legend depicts a time in the distant past. A time when powerful Wizrs walked the land. A time when bravery was accounted as the foremost virtue. It was an era when a young man, a Fountain-blessed boy named Andrew, united a fractured kingdom and stopped the wars and bloodshed that tortured Ceredigion. This young man became a great and mighty king, perhaps the mightiest of kings, and he had Wizrs who advised him. It is said that he had a magic Wizr set. A set that, if played, would predict the outcome of battles and determine the destiny of nations. King Andrew was so wise that he never lost but one game, a game he played against his bastard son. King Andrew was defeated shortly thereafter, flooding the world with darkness. But there was a prophecy by the great Wizr Myrddin that Andrew would one day return. The prophecy is called the Dreadful Deadman.

—Polidoro Urbino, Court Historian of Kingfountain

♦ ♦ ♦

CHAPTER THIRTY

Leoneyis

Owen knelt on the floor, arranging the final pieces of a massive tile tower that was so delicate it was already starting to wobble. He felt Fountain magic seeping into him, replenishing him from the earlier drought. Justine was working on an embroidery nearby, but she occasionally glanced over at him and Evie on the floor, their heads nearly touching as they concentrated on the final pieces.

He had shared with Evie every detail of his confrontation with Tunmore in the tower. Speaking the words out loud had allowed him to sift through his thoughts, arranging what he knew and did not know. He knew he lacked all the pieces to solve the riddle.

"How did Severn react to Tunmore's death?" Evie asked, handing him the final tile.

Owen shook his head. "He was surprised but not sorrowful. I would almost say he exulted in the man's downfall."

"But you didn't tell him what you told me. About the chest."

"No, and neither did Mancini. I'm sure the Espion will be watching the sanctuary. But Mancini thinks the Fountain is a superstition.

He can't see the treasure. Now that Tunmore's gone, I might be the only one who can. I think Mancini took Tunmore's words as the ravings of a madman before committing suicide."

"But you think there's more to it," Evie said softly. Her eyes were shifting colors at the moment, moving from silver to blue to green. She was deep in thought.

"It is so frustrating!" Owen complained. "All these hints and secrets are maddening. When I faced Eyric, I could tell he had been told something. A legend? A secret? I'm not sure what it was. But it influenced him greatly. And he tried to influence me to join him. But how could I without knowing more? I don't relish being someone's fool."

"I know," Evie said sagely. She reached out and patted his hand. "No one does. You're wise to be wary about what Tunmore said. He implied that some sort of imminent danger was coming and you were the only one who could prevent it. That would naturally make you curious, but it could well be a trap."

Owen looked into her eyes. "He literally gave his life because of this information. It was like a burden he had been carrying, but he told me what I must do without explaining why. If I listen to him, if I carry the chest to St. Penryn, won't that implicate me in a greater plot? Yet if I tell the king, what will he say? He is Fountain-blessed himself. Will he seek the treasure?" Owen frowned and tried to tame his frustration. "I remember something Ankarette said. That Dunsdworth's father could see the treasure in the waters but could not claim it. It drove him mad and he drowned himself."

"You nearly drowned yourself trying to get it too," Evie reminded him.

"No I didn't!"

Evie shook her head, exasperated. "I remember it very well, Owen. I was worried about you. You were under the water for so long. There was something *wrong* about what you were doing. I could feel it."

He continued to frown at her, but there was some truth in her words. "I don't know what to do, Evie. I'm so confused. Our kingdom is about to be invaded by three men, Eyric, Iago, and Chatriyon are going to fight us—and one another—to lay claim to Severn's crown."

"Iago doesn't want the crown, but go on," Evie said simply.

Owen squelched the sudden pang of jealousy. "Well, the man wants *something.* My point is that we're about to be invaded. But there is something else happening as well. Something we can't see. Another player moving on the board. It has something to do with the past, but it's affecting us today. And at the center is this myth about the Dreadful Deadman. I've told you about the whispers I used to hear from the Fountain about the Deadman. I still hear them. Somehow *I'm* part of this prophecy."

Evie blinked. "Are *you* the Dreadful Deadman?" she asked him.

Owen stared at her. "Why do you ask that? Of course I'm not."

"Think on it, though. You told me the story long ago. You were stillborn. And then you came back to life. Just like you brought Justine back from the brink in Edonburick. This power you have, Owen. This is not a superstition. It's real. I've seen it. Maybe *you* are the fulfillment of that prophecy."

Owen continued to stare at her, his heart beating wildly in his chest. He was feeling the flow of the Fountain all around him, *in* him. Then he heard its whisper.

You are not the Dreadful Deadman. But you will be one of the first who will see him.

A shudder rippled through Owen, and Evie looked at him in alarm. "What's wrong?" she asked.

"I'm not," he said, shaking his head. "But the Fountain told me he's coming. That I will be one of the first who sees him."

The room grew quiet and still. Even Justine had stopped her needlework. Her eyes were dark and serious, as somber as the overriding mood in the palace.

"I can't tell Severn," Owen whispered. "Not yet. I need to know more myself."

Evie nodded. "Let's go see Polidoro. He's been studying the myths of King Andrew since he arrived. I know nothing about St. Penryn, as I said earlier, but I imagine he might." She paused, then said, "I don't think you should tell him about your 'visions,' if that's the right word. He feels a great depth of loyalty to Severn. I'm not sure I would trust him entirely."

"That's good advice. Let's go see Polidoro. Would you do the honors?" he asked, motioning toward the starter piece that would knock them all down.

Evie smiled and obliged.

♦ ♦ ♦

Polidoro Urbino was an interesting, intense fellow. Tall and rail-thin, he had skin that was well leathered from the elements, silvering brown hair that was always neatly slicked back, and intelligent eyes. He wore the court fashions of Pisan, which were more gaily colored than Severn's favored black, and he had a reedy voice that made him sound always breathless. He was a man of many flowering words, great curiosity, and it was obvious that he was completely in awe of Evie. Owen gave Justine a warm smile and nod as she sat down on a nearby chair.

"I tell you Lady Elysabeth *Victoria* Mortimer is the wisest creature in all this vast kingdom," he crooned, pumping Owen's hand vigorously as a pleased, rapturous smile stretched his lips. He bowed to Evie with a deep flourish. "King Severn has a jewel in his kingdom to be certain. I was just going over the court records of the Maid of Donremy, an interesting tale. I know you'll like to read them as well, my dear. I am so pleased you took the time to visit this lowly court historian. If I can be of any service to you whatsoever, you know you only need ask."

Evie was smiling a little from the barrage of flattery. Justine rolled her eyes. "Master Urbino, there is something I'd like to ask you. I think your knowledge would help settle a dispute I have with Owen."

Polidoro bowed again. "I am yours to command, my lady. The two of you make an excellent pair, if I might say so." He straightened and tapped his lip. "I've always been struck by you. What point of conflict could exist between such kindred souls?"

"It's a geography question, actually," Evie said. "Owen told me that the sanctuary of St. Penryn was in Westmarch, but I disputed that it was once laid claim by Occitania. Can you settle the matter for us?"

Owen loved how deftly she had posed the question.

"St. Penryn, St. Penryn," the historian muttered, tapping his lip. Then he clucked his tongue. "I'm afraid, my dear, that neither of you scores the point on this match. You are both wrong."

Owen looked at the historian curiously. "I've seen the map of my duchy, sir, and I'm quite certain I saw St. Penryn on it."

Polidoro shook his head and offered a wizened smile. "No doubt you saw the *sanctuary* there, but did your map also show the land of Leoneyis? Of course it didn't. It's all underwater now."

Owen felt a jolt in his heart. "What did you say?"

The historian nodded vigorously. "The kingdom is gone. Leoneyis is part of the King Andrew legend. It's where King Andrew was slain by his bastard son. Well, not slain to be exact. He was mortally wounded, unto the point of death. They put his body in a boat and sent it over the falls. Shortly after, the land of Leoneyis was flooded. Only a few souls survived. The sanctuary of St. Penryn was on higher ground, and the people who had fled there survived. It's one of the reasons sanctuaries offer protection today! Fascinating, isn't it?"

"You are saying that the history of the sanctuary privileges of Our Lady go back to this time?" Owen asked. The story was hauntingly similar to the vision he'd experienced as their ship entered the harbor at Edonburick. He wondered how many more drowned cities existed.

The historian shook his head. "No, those practices existed before. Those who survived the great flooding helped reinforce the belief. I've heard that fishermen off the coast of Westmarch continue to draw objects from the drowned households out of the waters around there. There are dealers who specialize in that trade. I've heard that buyers in Brythonica pay enormous sums."

"Brythonica?" Evie asked before Owen could.

"Indeed. The duchess is a great collector of historical artifacts. I thought everyone knew that. Did you know that one of King Andrew's greatest knights was from Leoneyis? He was banished to Brythonica for having an affair with the king's wife."

"Can you tell me where you found that history?" Evie asked, her tone one of intense curiosity.

"It's not *history*, my lady Elysabeth. To be sure, there are many who claim King Andrew was real, but there is no evidence whatsoever that he was a real king. These legends are entertainment. That is all. But if you are interested, I would recommend an Occitanian poet. I think I have a translation somewhere in here, and when I find it, I'll bring it to you."

"Thank you, Master Urbino," Evie said with a pleased smile.

"So you see, you both were wrong. While St. Penryn is technically off the coast of Westmarch, it is actually considered part of Leoneyis. It is where King Andrew met his fate, and they say—" he added with an amused chuckle, "—it is also where he will return again. I hope you found the tale diverting."

"Indeed," Owen said, giving Evie a meaningful look. The three young people left the historian's chamber, listening to him chuckle and hum to himself as they walked away.

Owen pitched his voice low. "The treasure in the cistern had an ancient look to it."

Evie shot him a dangerous glance. "Do you think it came to be there after Leoneyis flooded?"

"I think I would like to find out," Owen said. "Assuming, of course, that the cistern hasn't frozen over yet."

"I don't think it's that cold," Evie said.

"Where are we going?" Justine asked worriedly. "I don't like the sound of this."

Owen looked at Evie. "Have you ever told her?"

Evie shook her head. "It was *our* secret. Remember?"

Owen turned to Justine. "Are you afraid of heights?"

CHAPTER THIRTY-ONE

Cistern

A trail of footprints in the snow led to the edge of the cistern opening in a walled-off portion of the palace of Kingfountain. The air was chill, and thick flakes of snow came down like autumn leaves. As Owen stood at the lip of the cistern and gazed down, he saw the water was much deeper than it had been in their younger years. The reservoir was well stocked.

"It looks colder than the Vairn River near Dundrennan," Evie said, stifling a shiver.

"You are both quite out of your senses for considering this," Justine warned. "The water is absolutely frigid! You won't be able to spend more than a few moments in it without catching a chill. And how will you get up again?"

Owen nodded to an ivy-strewn portion of wall. "There is a door over there and steps leading up to it." He sighed as he stared nervously down at the water. "It *does* look cold."

"My lady," Justine said, shaking her head. "This is ridiculous. Your grandfather would not approve. Come away from the edge."

Evie gave her a rebellious look. "Be a dear and fetch us some blankets. I think we'll need them."

"You're not going to—"

Evie reached out and took both of Owen's hands. "Together? Like we did before? Ratcliffe is dead, so I don't anticipate anyone will drain it on us."

Owen took a shuddering breath.

"Someone *is* trying to kill you," Justine said, her face going white. "Please, my lady, don't do this!"

"Go," Owen said, squeezing her hands. Standing across from each other over the hole, they stepped off at the same moment and plummeted into the cistern.

The shock of cold was worse than the Vairn. Absolutely worse. It made Owen nearly gasp as sharp needles of freezing pain stabbed at him from all sides, soaking into his clothes. His vision went black for a moment, and he feared he'd passed out from the shock of it. He kept himself still, trying to let the momentum of the fall bring him down to the bottom. He craved a fresh gasp of air, his lungs were screaming for it, but he felt the solid thump of the cistern floor against his boots much sooner than expected. Of course. He was much taller now than he had been as a child. Already the air in his chest was making him start to rise again, so he let out a few bubbles and blinked rapidly, trying to see through the blur of the water.

The treasure was still there.

He saw open chests spilling over with coins. There were battered shields with strange markings on them, the crests unfamiliar. Were these truly from Leoneyis? He felt a tug on his hand, and Evie motioned for him to swim back up.

He needed to bring something away, something to show her that the treasure was real. That *he* could see it, even if no one else could.

He spied a long weathered box, about the size of a sword, with straps and buckles holding it shut. There was a symbol branded on top of it. It looked vaguely familiar.

Take it. You will need it.

The whisper came from the Fountain. Owen felt himself rising again and breathed out a few more bubbles of air. He broke his grip with Evie and used his arms to swim toward the box. His muscles cramped with the cold and he felt the edges of his vision growing black. Gritting his teeth, he kicked hard and tried to close his unresponsive fingers around the box. He could not get a grip. His freezing fingers just wouldn't respond. But Owen was determined. He used his forearms to scoot the long box toward him and managed to clamp it against his side with his left arm. Using his right, he paddled back toward the surface. The weight of the box and the lack of air in his chest threatened to suck him back down, but he surfaced moments later, gasping for breath and chattering with cold.

"O-v-v-er he-ere!" Evie stammered. She grabbed at his shirt and the two quickly swam to the stone steps.

"Are you all right?" Justine cried from the cistern hole above. Her voice was edged with concern and panic. "I'm going to fetch help!"

"No!" Evie shouted. "J-Just f-fetch some blankets!"

"I'll be right back!" Justine shouted and vanished.

"Th-that was c-cold," Evie whispered, shuddering violently.

"I liked th-the last time . . . better," Owen offered with a smile. His fingers were working a little better now. "Do you see this? I'm not imagining the box?"

"No, it's real," Evie said, nodding vigorously, her eyes wide. "Let's g-get out of h-here first. We n-need a fire."

Owen didn't object. Pressing the box against his body, he gripped her arm with his other hand and helped haul her up the stairs. The Espion latch was a bit tricky with his numbed fingers and trembling body, but he managed to get it open. He had to butt his shoulder into the door, and the force of it made them stagger into the snow, clutching each other. Evie looked as pale as the weather and her lips were faintly blue.

Their teeth were chattering too much to talk, and each time they exchanged a look, they both started laughing. It reminded Owen of their childhood, of chasing her around the edge of the fountain before she fell into it. Maybe she had the same memory. Her eyes carried the same mischievous glint he had always fancied in her.

When they reached the open doorway leading back into the warm corridor, the one they had used to reach the cistern, he helped hoist Evie up. Justine was already approaching with blankets, and she scolded Evie thoroughly as she wrapped her up.

Owen handed the box down through the window and then struggled to climb through himself, his body shaking so violently it wouldn't obey him. He ended up tumbling onto the floor in a heap, his belly tight with laughter.

"Get up off the rushes, Master Owen," Justine said, an amused look belying her frown. She swaddled him in a blanket as well, and they started quickly back to Evie's room. There was a servant girl stoking the fire when they arrived, and both of them collapsed in front of it, savoring the cascading blasts of heat. The servant girl looked at them askance, and it was all it took for Evie to burst into giggles again. Owen could not help but join her.

Justine paced behind them, folding her arms. "My lady, we *must* get you out of those wet clothes at once. You've ruined your gown. Come to the changing screen. Master Owen, you can sit in those wet clothes for all I care."

"I'll be fine," Owen said, trying to subdue his laughter. Evie smiled and paused to squeeze his shoulder before rising and hurrying over to the changing screen.

"If your grandfather only knew," Justine said in a scolding whisper.

"You'd better not tell him," Evie said. "You are the only other person who knows about our secret place. It needs to *remain* a secret, Justine."

"You know you can trust me."

"Don't open the box yet!" Evie called from over the screen height. "I can hear you fidgeting with the straps! I'm almost done."

She was right, of course, so Owen forbore what he had been doing until she hurried out from around the changing screen. Justine was trying to cover her head with a towel, but Evie shooed her away and rushed over to kneel at Owen's side, wet hair dangling in front of her face in a deliciously tangled way.

"You look like a half-drowned mouse," Owen said.

"You *are* a half-drowned mouse," she quipped back. "Open it!"

There was a firm pounding on the door and then it immediately opened. Both turned in shock as Mancini hurried into the room. There was no time to hide the box.

"There you both are," Mancini said angrily, striding forward. "Look at you both! It's as if you've been swimming . . . in . . . the . . ." His voice dropped off as he recognized the truth of his forming statement from their guilty looks, Owen's soaked clothes, and Evie's wild hair.

"What is it?" Owen asked, angry that the spymaster had caught them so quickly.

"It's cold as death out there and you two were *playing* in the cistern again?" He gaped at them, but then his shrewd eyes saw the box lying before them. "What is that you have there? What's in that box?"

"I don't really know," Owen said. "We haven't opened it yet. Why are you here?"

"Because you were seen tramping about the palace soaked to the bone while I was trying to summon you to see the king! Jack Paulen arrived with news of the blizzard from East Stowe. The king wants to see you at once, Owen. I have news to share as well. But what is in that box? It looks long enough to hold a sword. Open it. Where did you get it?"

Owen didn't fully trust the spymaster, but he was not sure how he could refuse.

"Go ahead, Owen. Open it. We didn't do anything wrong." Evie gave Mancini a look of unconcern. She was a great actress sometimes.

Owen bowed forward, his curiosity piqued, and started unfastening the leather straps holding the box closed. The leather was surprisingly hard for having been submerged underwater for who knew how long. The buckles were rusty, but the rust flaked off easily, revealing shiny metal. Evie worked on one of the straps while he did the other, and soon they were loose. Owen bit his lip as he studied the markings on the box. Upon closer inspection, it looked like a raven's head. Wasn't that Brythonica's symbol?

Owen pried open the lip of the leather-bound box, and the hinges groaned a little and sloughed off rust as it opened.

"A scabbard," Mancini said with a tone of disappointment. "That's all?"

It was indeed a scabbard, devoid of a blade.

But it was not just any scabbard. It was made of leather, wrapped around a wooden sheath, hand-stitched with a wide belt fashioned into it. The hilt guard shared the same raven's head sigil design as the box. The scabbard was scuffed and bloodstained. A few strands of leather had been tied into decorative knots. It was a beautiful work of craftsmanship and it looked quite old. A metal chape ended it with a filigree design.

Owen reached into the box and hefted it. The leather felt warm in his hands, which surprised him considering the cold place where it had been hiding. The interior of the box had no water stains, no sign of seepage, which also did not make sense.

"Just a scabbard," Owen said. What sword had this scabbard held?

The sword of the Maid, came the answer.

"Where did you get it?" Mancini asked, his tone questioning and stern. "The cistern?"

Justine gasped and covered her mouth. Evie rolled her eyes in disgust.

"That answers *that*," Mancini said, chuckling at the girl. "When you were children, you said something about there being a treasure in the water. I didn't believe you. I was there when the cistern emptied. I saved your sorry carcasses from the falls. Let's not forget that. But there was nothing on the cistern floor. Not even a florin."

"But there *is* treasure on the floor," Owen said, turning and looking up at the spymaster. "Only, you cannot see it."

"But you can."

Owen nodded.

"Is that what Tunmore was raving about then? Did he leave a treasure in the fountain at Our Lady?"

Owen didn't want to answer, but he knew he should. "He did. I've seen the chest. But not open. It's not long, like this one. It's about this size." He held up his hands about shoulder-width apart.

Mancini rubbed his mouth. "This is all very interesting and quite curious. I'm not one for superstitions, as you know. But I seem to have heard a legend or two about swords and fountains." He glanced at Evie. "You know the ones."

Evie nodded. "The greatest is the legend of King Andrew. He was a baseborn son of a duke. He drew a sword from a fountain and used it to claim the throne of Ceredigion."

Mancini nodded curtly. "And the other?"

"The other was more recent. The Maid of Donremy drew a sword from a fountain in Occitania and used it to defeat Ceredigion. No one knows what happened to these swords . . . or if they were the same sword."

The spymaster pursed his lips. "Very curious. Well, lad. Best you dry off and go see the king. Paulen is here, as I said, and the king wishes to consult with you on his strategy for defending the realm. I'm going to pay a little visit somewhere, and then will join you. I won't be long."

Owen didn't like his tone of voice. "Where are you going, Mancini?"

The spymaster gave him an enigmatic look. "Never you mind. You keep your secrets too, my boy. I'll meet you in the throne room. Tell Severn I have news about the poisoner Tyrell. Etayne is closing in on his trail. He came aboard a ship from Brugia five days ago, it seems. I'll have more news later. It's best not to get his hopes up."

Mancini stared down at the empty scabbard and sniffed. "Pity it wasn't the sword itself. The king could use a legend in his favor right now. He could certainly use a miracle."

CHAPTER THIRTY-TWO

Fall of the Espion

Before going to the throne room, Owen changed into dry clothes. He belted the new scabbard to his waist and slid his sword into it. He wondered if there would be some manifestation from the Fountain when he did so, but there was not. Still, it should have been impossible for the leatherwork to be in such perfect condition after being submerged for so long.

Though his hair was still damp and mussed, Owen made his way to the throne room. Jack Paulen was still there, and the king was pacing with great agitation.

One of the things Owen did not like about the Duke of East Stowe was that the man was significantly taller than him. He was slightly taller even than the king, and had a handsome face and dark brown hair that was long and wavy. Jack was twice Owen's age, with a younger wife and two small children. The badge of his duchy was the Bear and Ragged Staff, an emblem he had inherited from his ancestors. The bear was muzzled, and a chain connected it to a long tree trunk covered in stubs where once there had been branches. The bear was facing the trunk and its two front paws were extended, holding the beam upright. It was a symbol denoting power and strength, the ability of man to subdue a fierce and primal creature such as the bear. Although Jack had every reason to be agreeable—he was a handsome man and one of the few dukes of the realm—he had adopted the sardonic temperament of Severn.

The king stopped his pacing when he caught sight of Owen, but he was still full of brooding energy. "There you are, lad. You took your time coming."

Owen let the comment pass. He bowed his head formally. "Mancini said there was news."

"There is. But, curse this storm, it was delayed because of the roads. Jack rode in from East Stowe and I'll let him tell you."

"Hello, Jack," Owen greeted, nodding.

The Duke of East Stowe gave Owen an angry scowl. They had never been close, for Owen's loyalty was bound to the North and Duke Horwath, but nothing in their past would explain such open animosity. "The roads were pitiful, my lord," he said, addressing the king rather than Owen. "It was hard going and cold. But I knew you would want to hear the news immediately."

"Cut to the quick, man," Severn snapped angrily. "I want to get Owen's opinion."

Jack's eyes narrowed at the slight. "If it pleases Your Grace." He looked at Owen again, seething. "News from Atabyrion. Seems you and the Mortimer lass rankled feelings during your visit. The king just told me that *you* went with her. I hadn't known that." Again, Owen sensed his resentment. "One of our trading ships arrived with news that Iago Llewellyn has summoned his nobles to court and they are stuffing provisions onto ships. The call has gone out to the warriors to come down from the hills and gather at Edonburick. The Earl of Huntley is the foremost among them. I heard you ruined one of his manors."

Owen snorted. "Only a window. What else?"

The duke sighed with a shake of his head. "News from abroad is always exaggerated. I'll try not to repeat the sin. They tried to stop our ships in the harbor, but this one fought its way through. They were fired at from harbor defenses and took serious damage, but they escaped. Clearly Iago didn't want them to warn us, which implies, as I told the king, that Atabyrion intends to invade immediately."

Owen shifted his gaze to Severn, who was nodding in concurrence. "That's what I think as well, Owen. Is that also your interpretation?"

Owen folded his arms, letting out a sigh. "I agree with you both," he said tightly. "We warned him not to."

"You did? Or Lady Elysabeth?" Jack asked, the challenge clear.

"She did, of course. But I spoke to Eyric myself. The King of Atabyrion invested too much into the alliance. Eyric married the Earl of Huntley's daughter. He is the noble with the most treasure in the kingdom. I don't think we can avoid a war with them."

Jack sniffed. "My thoughts exactly. My lord, I have ships patrolling the coast of East Stowe. We have strong captains and can cast a wide net. I say we don't even let the Atabyrions touch our sand. Let's fight them at sea."

Severn listened to him, but then he turned to Owen, which made Jack glower.

"Did you warn Stiev Horwath?" Owen asked the other duke. "They could just as easily strike the North as East Stowe."

Jack blinked with surprise. "But the Duchy of East Stowe is the closest to Atabyrion. I . . . I thought—"

"In other words, no. You didn't," Severn scoffed. "You came running here straightaway to get the glory of telling me the news, but you thought about your own duchy instead of the kingdom."

Jack's face went pale with rage and humiliation. He was flummoxed.

Owen intervened. "No, he did the right thing by coming here straightaway. In such a moment, I would have overlooked it as well."

"Not likely," Severn snorted, and Owen wished the king would keep his barbed tongue behind his teeth.

"Regardless," Owen said with a cough, trying to change the tenor of the conversation. "Duke Horwath needs to be told immediately."

"Agreed. I'll send his granddaughter. A little snow won't stop her. You should hear the common folk complaining about this storm. It disgusts me. I've enjoyed seeing the palace shrouded in white."

Owen noticed that Jack was still fuming, his eyes flashing angrily at the king.

"I agree. It makes sense to send Evie to the North immediately to warn her grandfather."

"I'm not going to wait here and do nothing," Severn said, starting to pace again. "If Eyric wants my crown, he'll have to wrench it from my head while I'm lying in a pool of my own blood. I'm not afraid of Iago or my brother's son. He would have fared far better had he listened to you and come to my side. I think I should go to the North. They are the most loyal to me, and the people would come in droves to protect the kingdom if we're attacked."

Owen shook his head.

"You disagree?"

"We don't know where the Atabyrions will strike. And I've had no dreams to offer guidance. My advice, my lord, if you'll heed it, calls for a different strategy."

The king beamed. "That's why I summoned you, lad. I wanted you to plan our defenses."

"But my ships are already defending us!" Jack said petulantly.

The king only sneered at him, not bothering to respond.

Owen gave up trying to save the other duke from himself. "And your ships are probably too spread out to communicate with each other. Iago will come with a fleet and he will slice through your net. His people are sailors, and they are warriors. They will strike hard. Eyric is convinced, my lord, that you will be killed upfront to make way for him.

Occitania sent a poisoner to accomplish this! Better to keep you moving. Go to Beestone castle. It's in the heart of your realm."

"It's closer to Westmarch," Jack sniped.

"I'm pleased you know your geography, my lord," Owen said. "Since we cannot predict where he will land, we must stand ready to respond as soon as he does. Let Iago try and put one of our cities under siege. Let him see what happens."

The king smiled grimly. "Then we collapse around him on all sides."

"First we cut off his escape," Owen added. "Trap him inside our realm. And then we teach him the cost of betting foolishly."

The king's smile turned into a smirk. "I like your thinking, lad. So your plan is to return to Westmarch, gather your forces, and stand ready. All the dukes will do the same. Wait until Iago lands and then—" He suddenly clapped his hands together, letting out a sharp noise that startled Jack. "Like a fly caught between two hands."

Owen felt a queasy sensation in his stomach. In his mind flashed the quicksilver thought of Iago kissing Evie. Well, if Iago were dead, the rivalry between them would end. But still . . . it felt unfair that Iago was being maneuvered into attacking Ceredigion only to fail as part of a larger conspiracy. The King of Atabyrion was operating under imperfect knowledge.

"What vexes you?" the king asked Owen, his brow narrowing.

Owen shook his head. "It's something I cannot say," he said, struggling to put his doubts into words. "Give me a moment to think on it."

"By all means," the king said. He came up and slapped Owen's shoulder affectionately. Then he turned to the duke. "Sail back to East Stowe, my lord. If this blizzard keeps up, the roads will be difficult. Call your retainers, those who owe you loyalty, and prepare for war. Go."

It was a firm dismissal, and Jack Paulen bowed stiffly, his complexion showing the hue of his jealousy and resentment. He stared at the king with eyes full of wrath, taking Owen by surprise. The look was beyond humiliation; the man's eyes were full of murder.

"I would speak to you about Mancini," the king said to Owen, his back already turned to Jack. Owen could not rip his eyes off Jack's face—the emotions there were boiling hotter and hotter. He felt a trickle of warning from the Fountain and realized its power had been seeping into the room.

The king seemed to sense it as well, for his head jerked up and his hand dropped to his dagger hilt.

Owen stepped around the king and walked briskly over to Jack, putting his hand on the man's shoulder. "What are you doing?" he asked in a low voice.

As soon as he touched Jack's shoulder, he felt as if the waters of the Fountain had been diverted—like a river splitting off around a boulder. Jack blinked suddenly, the anger purging from his expression.

"I . . . I'm not feeling well," Jack stammered, his forehead suddenly rimmed with sweat beads. The power of the Fountain was emanating from the doorway of the throne room. It was rushing toward where Owen and Jack were standing, but the power of its intention was broken now that Owen was standing there. He remembered Etayne saying that Tyrell was Fountain-blessed.

"It's coming—" Owen started.

"—from the doorway," Severn added.

Both of them drew their weapons and started toward the closed throne room doors.

"Open the doors," the king commanded the soldiers standing guard there.

The rushing sensation from the Fountain vanished in an instant.

The guards yanked on the door handles and pulled them open. As the doors opened, the air filled with noisy commotion. Servants and soldiers were running up and down the corridors in absolute confusion. There was a mass of bodies, so many it was impossible to discern who had summoned the Fountain's magic, but as Owen reached the opening, he sensed the residue of the magic on the doorframe itself.

Clark broke out of the crowd and rushed forward, his face grave and streaked with sweat.

"What's going on?" Owen shouted above the ruckus as the Espion came into the room and shoved the doors closed, muffling some of the racket.

Clark pressed himself against the doors. "My lord," he said, facing the king. "The people were rioting in the streets. The palace doors have been barred and sealed, and your guard is being summoned."

"For what cause?" Severn snapped, his eyes piercing and fierce. "Bring me my sword! What has happened?"

Clark leaned back against the door, panting. "My lord. Mancini is dead. He went to the sanctuary of Our Lady. He had several Espion with him. When he arrived, the deconeus denounced him. He said he had broken the privilege of sanctuary by abducting Tunmore. He said . . . he said you *threw* Tunmore from the tower window yourself!"

"That's a lie!" Owen shouted.

"Tell that to the mob," Clark said, gesturing with his head. "They grabbed Mancini and hauled him to the river."

Severn's face was aghast. He mouthed the word no.

Clark nodded vigorously as Owen felt his own stomach tighten with horror. "The mob threw him into the river, my lord. He went over the falls. A friend of mine saw him go over the edge. Now they are marching on the palace. We must get you out of the city. The mob is coming here next!"

CHAPTER THIRTY-THREE

Retribution

When Owen looked at Severn, he saw the king's implacable will turn his face to stone, sending ripples of the Fountain into the room. The king's eyes were like flint and his mouth twisted to a deep frown.

"If I abandon my crown to a mob," Severn told Clark in a tight, barely controlled voice that quickly rose to a shout, "then I do not deserve to wear it. By the Fountain, I will make this rabble kneel in obedience!" He grabbed Jack Paulen's tunic and jostled the man. "Go through the castle and rouse every man with the spleen to fight. Every butler, every knave, even my woodsman Drew. We're to gather in the courtyard and open the gates." He turned to face Owen. "I want my armor and my horse. They will not evict me from this place willingly. Will you stand with me, lad?"

Owen admired the king's bravery and courage. He had no idea what was going to happen, but his instincts told him Severn was right. If he fled from the mob, he would not be allowed to return. But there would be blood spilled. Mobs responded to force, not sugared words.

"Loyalty binds me," Owen said gravely, gripping his own sword hilt.

"This is the proof of it." He glanced at Jack who was quailing with fear. "Why are you still standing there, man?" he barked, and the duke hurried to the doors.

Owen turned to Clark. "Summon every Espion in the palace and arm them. We fight with the king or so help me, every last one of the spies will drown with us. No one leaves the docks. Not a single ship is to set sail. Lock down the harbor, Clark. Now!"

"It will be done," Clark said darkly and rushed from the room.

Moments later, a few of the more levelheaded servants arrived, bearing armor for the king and Owen. Severn was impatient with his squires, but they managed to help him shrug on the hauberk and plates despite his constant epithets. Owen donned a hauberk and hood himself, wearing his own badge this time. While the king was finishing his preparations, Owen went to the open doorway, his eyes drawn to smudges on the lintels. There was a stain on the wood that had not been there before; it looked like some bloody mixture had been dabbed over it. It was out of place and ominous, and he called over a servant to fetch some soap and water to clean it.

He spied Evie approaching him from down the hall, her face flushed. Justine trailed behind her.

"The city is in an uproar," she said passionately. She paused at the threshold by Owen, then stared at the king. "He's going to fight them?"

"And what would you have me do, my lady?" Severn snapped, his every motion accompanied by a clang of the metal armor. "Surrender to mob justice? If I'm going over the falls, at least I'll drown if I'm not shattered to pieces."

Evie stared at him. "The people are afraid, my lord. They are superstitious because of the snow. They think you caused it by taking Tunmore out of sanctuary!"

"They may think many things that are unreasonable and foolish," Severn shot back. "The only thing they'll understand is force."

He looked at Owen. "The time has come."

Evie caught Owen's arm, but her gaze was pinned on the king. "Don't just kill them, my lord. They are panicked, frightened of the early winter storms. Try to appease them first."

Severn's face twisted with anger. "They think I'm a butcher," he said with a voice full of loathing. "Well, even the sheep flee from wolves."

"You are not a wolf," Evie insisted. "You are a man. A misunderstood man. Do not support their fears through actions that seem to confirm them. Let Owen speak on your behalf if you are too angry! He was in the tower when Tunmore jumped! He was a witness."

"They'll not believe us," the king said, shaking his head. "Men believe what they will. I do not fear them. I don't fear death." He snorted, his eyes flashing with fire. "I would welcome it." But then he paused, giving consideration to her words. "If they won't listen, I will *compel* their obedience."

"Do that, my lord," Evie said, releasing Owen's arm. Her cheeks were flushed. "We only detest that which we do not truly understand. You can be very persuasive, my lord. Try that first. Try your gift of words first."

The king sighed. "My gift only works one to one. I'd never be able to persuade so many."

"At least you can try," Evie pleaded.

The king gave her a pitying look, as if he thought she was quite naive. He glanced at Owen to solicit his thoughts.

"I trust her judgment," Owen said. "The worst that can happen is the people drag you from your horse and throw you into the river. Any less than that is a victory. But if you are going into the river, so am I. We may even survive it."

The king grinned at the words. Then his face hardened. "Well said, lad." And he marched out of the throne room, sword in hand.

♦ ♦ ♦

The courtyard teemed with soldiers wearing the badge of the white boar. There were a few who had Owen's badge and even fewer who bore the badge of East Stowe. When the soldiers had learned the king intended to suppress the uprising personally, they had taken courage and rallied behind their master. Muddy snow had built up on the flagstones, and stable boys were using muck rakes to drag it clear. Fresh snow fell in gentle waves, sticking to the black tunics and giving them a silvery cast.

Owen's mount shifted nervously and snorted with the cold. Noise from the mob could be heard beyond the portcullis, louder than the distant roar of the waterfall. Severn sat on his warhorse, his face firm and resolute. He wore a helmet that had been fashioned to hold the crown—the same battered helm he had worn at Ambion Hill. But while Owen's father had made a different decision on that fateful day, Owen rode at the king's side.

Evie was also there, much to Owen's annoyance, with a group of men wearing her grandfather's badge. She would not be kept away from the action, and she'd insisted that the presence of a lady might help prevent violence.

"Open the doors!" the king shouted over the ruckus. "But do not raise the portcullis. Not until I command you." He looked to his right and then to his left. "When I give the order, we charge. Your swords are sharp. Your courage is tested. These are our countrymen, but they will yield or they will perish. The choice is theirs."

"Aye, my lord!" shouted the gate captain. Four men on either side helped haul the doors open, revealing a tangled mass of men. As soon as they saw King Severn astride his horse, their roars turned into screams. Rocks came tumbling into the courtyard. Clubs and staves rattled the iron bars of the portcullis.

The king shouted at the mass of angry faces, trying to be heard, but the mob only grew louder, more truculent. Some of the men were heaving at the portcullis, trying to winch it open with their brute strength.

"They won't even listen," the king said with a snarl of contempt. Owen saw his hand start to lift, ready to give the signal to open the gates and attack. His stomach roiled with despair at the imminent slaughter. The mob was ferocious, true, but how many had survived a battlefield before? How many were used to the pain and disfigurement that armed warriors could inflict?

Then Evie's horse charged forward toward the gate, and Owen watched in horror as she positioned herself in front of the king. Her action completely startled everyone, including the rioters; those in the front ranks quieted somewhat when they saw her.

"Foolish girl!" Severn muttered, nudging his stallion forward as Owen did the same.

"Stop this!" Evie said in a clear, strong voice. "Stop this at once! Go back to your homes before there is violence. Think of your families! Think of your children and your sisters! Retreat from the palace immediately, and none of you will be harmed!"

"The king has broken sanctuary!" someone screamed and instantly the flashfire of shouting went up again. Yells and jeers came from the crowd, the noise so loud it drowned out any further chance for Evie to be heard. Owen felt a throb of pride and a twinge of panic. She was totally fearless . . . and totally exposed.

Someone threw a club through the gate and it struck her stallion's foreleg. The beast reared in surprise, and Owen watched as Evie tried to cling to the saddle horn. Then the horse's hooves slipped on the ice and both beast and girl went down. Owen gasped in shock, unable to move quickly enough. He swung out of his saddle and rushed to her side.

She was so still on the stones, her face so pale, and his heart spasmed in pain and panic as he knelt beside her, lifting her head and cradling it in his arms.

The winches of the portcullis were groaning, and Owen saw the iron teeth lifting from the holes. Suddenly the mob was turning in fear, pressing against each other to escape the wrath that would hail down on them. The sound of archers loosing strings came from the battlement walls, and then a swarm of arrows began to descend on the mob. Owen cradled Evie's head, his heart breaking with despair.

Bellowing with rage, the king was the first through the portcullis, followed by rows of battle-tested war horses. The white boar pennant fluttered in the snowy breeze. Owen caressed Evie's hair, his chest heaving with emotion. Was she dead? He pressed his ear to her mouth, trying to hear or feel even a puff of air amidst the chaos around him.

He would use every bit of his magic to save her life. He began summoning Fountain magic, drawing it inside him. Was her skull broken? Was her neck? There was no blood he could see, but he felt the knot of a bump on the back of her head.

Owen felt her lips kiss his ear. "I'm fine, silly boy. I've fallen off horses before."

He lifted his head and looked down at her, her eyes gray in the low light. She blinked quickly, and a smile stretched across her mouth as she awoke in his arms.

He could not believe she was even speaking, not with her cheeks so pale. Evie sat up, holding Owen's shoulders and drawing her legs in toward her chest to keep from getting trampled by all the horses charging through the gates. The thrum of bowstrings continued to sound and a cheer went up from the soldiers who were now chasing the mob away.

She put her hand on Owen's cheek. "Go to the king. Go right away."

Owen shook his head. He felt a hand on his shoulder, but he didn't even look to see who it was. "I won't leave you," he said with determination.

She blinked and gave him a look that said he was being foolish. She let her hand linger on his cheek. "I fell off my *horse*, Owen. This is not the first time. I'll be all right. But you need to go to the king. To rein him in before he massacres all of them." Her eyes burned into his.

"He's in a rage now. Stop him before he goes too far." She smoothed her thumb along his bottom lip. "Etayne will help me. I'll be all right."

Owen glanced back and saw it was Etayne's hand that was on his shoulder. As he watched, she stepped forward and applied a compress to Evie's wound to stanch the bleeding.

"I'll take her back to the palace," Etayne promised.

A conflict raged inside of Owen, but he knew Evie was right. She was always right. And in hindsight, her intercession had disrupted the riot. Although it was an accident, it had caused the rabble to start to flee, struck by the shame of their conduct.

He stared down at Evie, his heart nearly breaking. "I love you," he whispered.

Evie closed her eyes, smiling as if savoring something delicious. Then she opened them again and patted his cheek. "Finally," she said with a contented sigh.

♦ ♦ ♦

I had not expected to be at court when such momentous times unraveled. The more superstitious denizens of the city, riled up I believe by the sanctuary men, who are natural criminals, tried to overthrow the monarchy by literally throwing Severn into the river. Their attempt met with a disastrous failure as the rebellion was snuffed out by the heavy snows and the steel courage of Severn's knights. Order has been restored to the city, and people are keeping to their homes. The grounds of Our Lady have been deserted by all but the deconeus and the sexton. The lawless men who have lived under the auspices of the grounds' protection have fled, and skulk in taverns and dark holes. The king, at this very moment, is with Duke Kiskaddon at the sanctuary. News of this event will spread quickly. One cannot know the consequences.

—Polidoro Urbino, Court Historian of Kingfountain

♦ ♦ ♦

CHAPTER THIRTY-FOUR

Our Lady

The violence was over, the rioting quelled. The streets were deserted and the trampled snow had crimson stains that sickened Owen. He did not know how many had died, but the memory of the freezing corpses would haunt his dreams.

He had never seen the interior of the sanctuary of Our Lady so empty. The black and white tiles in the main foyer that had always reminded him of a giant Wizr board were now littered with debris from the hundreds of inmates who had fled the sanctuary, carrying their belongings and dropping many in their haste to exit. Owen nudged a book with a broken spine with his boot. The sight only added to Owen's worry and despair.

"My lord sovereign," the deconeus said in a tremulous voice to the king. "What is your intention regarding worshipping at the sanctuary of Our Lady? The grounds are despoiled. Men were . . . were *tromping* in the fountain waters to seize as many coins as they could before fleeing." His voice was heavy with grief.

Owen slid the broken book out of his way and joined the king. The deconeus and the sexton were aged men, and they looked crushed and defeated in their cassocks and robes.

"Spare me the gloom, gentlemen," Severn said with a sardonic edge in his tone. "And do not pretend to think I don't know what really happens here." He gestured to the wide, empty space. "The sanctuary has always been an illusion. A dream."

The deconeus's suffering expression turned grim. "You meddle with something you do not comprehend, my lord."

"Do I?" Severn said with a tone of exasperation. "You curry the people's fear to hold dominion over them. I did not raze the sanctuary, deconeus. The villains you harbor here *fled* of their own accord because they did not believe the Fountain would protect them from me."

"They did not believe it because you had your Espion kidnap the Deconeus of Ely!" the sexton said in a tone that was almost a shout.

Severn skewered the man with his gaze, and Owen took a step closer. He did not believe the king would shed blood in the sanctuary. But he was not completely convinced. The sexton was a fool for speaking so boldly.

"The deconeus was a proven traitor to Ceredigion," the king said venomously. "And you've been harboring him these many years while he continued to plot with our enemies in Occitania. How long have you known about his efforts to lure my niece away? You cannot suppose I would hold you guiltless for such treachery."

The deconeus's eyes blazed with naked fear. "I knew nothing of that!" he gasped.

"I find that terribly difficult to believe," Severn said with a cluck. "For all I know, you're an integral part of this conspiracy. You've been waiting for me to fail, to fall. Oh, don't bother denying it, either of you!" he scolded when he saw they were about to object. "I've stayed my hand in punishing treason long enough. I have been too gentle."

The sexton looked as if he were about to swoon.

"What's to become of us?" the deconeus asked hoarsely.

Severn sneered. "You'll have to wait for the Assizes, now won't you? Unfortunately, your meddling has thrust me into the middle of a war. Atabyrion will invade, and I have no doubt that Chatriyon will use that as a pretext to take back the land Lord Kiskaddon wrested from him. If my enemies think I'm unable to fight two battles at once, they completely underestimate me. I had Mancini fetch Tunmore, but I did not throw him from the tower. You think I'm that great a fool? The gibbering coward leaped to his death. Lord Kiskaddon is my witness, for he was *there* and saw him do it. Mancini is dead, thanks to you, at a time when he is sorely needed. I will not forget this, gentlemen. Trust in that." He looked up to the vaulted ceiling, examining the silver light streaming in from the stained-glass windows. "I will post soldiers at the gates of the sanctuary. This is a place of worship and you've made it the lair of thieves and murderers. I will let the people worship here, for now. Let them salve their consciences by tossing coins for their crimes in the fountains. But each night, you will dismiss the visitors. Each night, it will remain empty at the peril of your lives. My men will lock the gates." He gave them both a stern, angry look. "Is that clear, gentlemen?"

"Yes, Your Grace," choked the sexton, bowing meekly.

"Indeed," said the deconeus.

"Leave us," Severn snapped, and watched as the two old men shuffled away, their shoes clapping on the tiles.

Severn walked to the edge of the main fountain and gazed into the waters. As Owen joined him at the edge, he could see the mud and debris from the boots of the men who had trampled inside the fountain to steal the treasures. His heart wrenched with pain. He looked for the chest he had seen there earlier. He remembered exactly where it had been. There were two scraped gashes in the mud showing where it had been dragged to the edge of the fountain.

It is already gone. Another Fountain-blessed must have taken it.

Owen gritted his teeth with frustration. He placed his hands on the rail, staring into the dirty water and feeling naught but disgust.

"Was I too harsh, lad?" Severn asked, putting his hand on Owen's shoulder. "I was so angry, so *very* angry. I could have thrown them all off the bridge. But I didn't because you were here. You have a calming effect on me. So many of them were men who have long defied my laws and flaunted the protection of the sanctuary." He stared up at the statue of wisdom at the head of the fountain. "I do not think that was the intention when this place was hallowed."

"What are you going to do with the deconeus?" Owen asked. He didn't bother mentioning the sexton.

The king had a faraway look in his eyes. Then his lips began to quiver with wrath. "I suppose that depends, lad. It depends on whether I survive this conflict. Iago and Eyric are goading me to go after them, but it is Chatriyon who is pulling the strings. Occitania is our ancient enemy. He's stolen my niece, and I will never forgive him that. Never. She deserves to be a queen." Owen watched the emotions battle across Severn's face. That he missed Elyse was obvious. But he was pained by her betrayal, and the wound was festering.

"She didn't betray you, my lord," Owen whispered. "I'm certain of it."

His eyes flashed with anger as they met Owen's gaze.

"It was Tunmore's fault," Owen said. "You know about his gift. He was Fountain-blessed with writing. Your niece is an exceptional person. I know both of us admired her. Elyse was the first person who offered me friendship when I came to the palace. But you were in an impossible situation with her. You could not marry her yourself for fear of impropriety, but she deserved more than to simply be remembered as your brother's bastard. Her situation was becoming more and more hopeless. And then her mother died, probably by poison. All these events crowded together and made her vulnerable to being twisted and manipulated by someone with power. Someone who was desperate."

Owen saw the tears in Severn's lashes, but the force of the king's will was too strong for them to fall. "She should have come to me," he said thickly. "She should have come! I trusted her more than any person alive.

Even more than *you*," he added blackly, his jaw quivering. "If she could betray me, then I can no longer trust anyone. My brother Eredur knew I would never falter. He knew that loyalty bound me." His frown was so heartbroken that Owen grieved for him. "I have no one like that. Not anymore. Well, I wish Elyse well with her new husband. A husband she will not keep for long, for I intend to crush Occitania and bring it as a vassalage to Ceredigion. I will do the same with Atabyrion. If they think I'm a monster now, they will not like what they have made me become."

Owen's heart cringed at the words. "You are *not* a monster!" he insisted, but he could see what was happening to the king. The constant pressure to be someone he was not was winning out. How uncanny Ankarette's discernment of Severn's character had been. The king was altering, irrevocably. It was like a tile that had been tipped from back to front. But this tile would not be easily set aright.

"Hear me now," Severn said, turning to face Owen with ruthless determination in his eyes. "I will go to Beestone to prepare to defend my realm. I take your counsel and value you as the masterful strategist that you are. I'll let Iago strike me, but after I give him a fleeting taste of victory, I will crush his raiding party and make him beholden to me. Unless I feel like killing him. I command you to go to Westmarch and hold the territory you've won from Occitania. I want you to take Etayne with you."

"But what about the poisoner coming after you!" Owen stammered in surprise.

The king's gaze was stony. Maybe he secretly hoped he would die. "I've lived under that threat for years. We foiled the plot here. All the Espion reports suggest he fled the city during the chaos. He's probably skulking back to Occitania. It's you that I'm worried about now. If Chatriyon comes himself, you will order her to poison him. You must defend Westmarch alone, Owen. I will not be able to spare the men to come to your aid. You do this, lad, and you will prove you are worthy of my trust. May the Fountain weep for you if you fail me."

Owen felt the push of the king's will against his mind as the king's fingers dug into his shoulder. He knew the king was in earnest. And for the first time since he was a boy, he felt his life was at risk from this man.

Swallowing, Owen rested his hand on his sword hilt and steeled his courage. "I will not fail you, my lord," he said solemnly.

"Then go at once. Do not waste a moment. Get you to Westmarch."

Owen felt conflicted. He wanted to see if Evie was recovered, but the look in the king's eyes showed that he was testing Owen. Duke Horwath had lost his own son, Evie's father, in the Battle of Ambion Hill. Yet instead of going north to comfort his daughter and granddaughter, he had gone to Tatton Hall to fetch Owen. He knew this is what the king was expecting of him, although he would not say it.

"Send word for Etayne to join me, my lord," Owen said with determination, swallowing his rising discomfort. "I leave at once."

The king gave him a proud look. "Bless you, lad. May the Fountain bless you."

With the king's hand on his shoulder, they walked across the black and white tiles to the door of the sanctuary. As they crossed the threshold, Owen noticed that all the clouds had fled and a deep blue sky filled the horizon end to end. The snow and icicles were already starting to drip and slough.

"The storm has passed," the king said with a touch of irony in his voice. "That's all it was. Just a storm."

But Owen had the distinct impression that it was something else that had caused the snow to abate. Something involving the chest that had miraculously disappeared from the fountain of Our Lady. And he also had a suspicion of where he might find it next, as well as the person who had taken it there. He would be going west, but not to Tatton Hall or to see the mayor of Averanche in the new territory he had won.

No, Owen would be going straight to the sanctuary at St. Penryn.

CHAPTER THIRTY-FIVE

St. Penryn

The air had the chill of winter. Owen walked through the camp of his soldiers at dawn, hand on his hilt. His sword was sheathed in the braided leather scabbard he had withdrawn from the cistern waters at Kingfountain. It gave him a strange feeling of peace. The sky was gray and shallow wreaths of snow encircled the grounds. He could hear the sound of the surf crashing nearby.

Leaving his pavilion and the warm brazier inside behind, he trekked toward the water, following a sandy footpath overgrown with scrub. His mind was full of worries and doubts, of tangled plots and subtle machinations. This felt like a game of Wizr, only he could not see all the pieces on the board and shadowy hands were moving them.

The footpath ended abruptly, pitching steeply before a wash that led to the crashing waves below. The churning sea was impressive and came in undulating waves that crashed against jutting stones covered in seaweed and urchins. The beach was flat and gold, the sand fine and smooth. To the north, he saw the sanctuary of St. Penryn a short distance away. The sanctuary was built against the cliffside, a tall, stocky structure with many arches on each face. Thick balustrades offered support, and the main facade had twin towers on each side, set within a triangular-shaped roof.

Owen perched one boot on a boulder and stared at the structure. The stones it was made from were variegated bricks, giving it an almost mottled look. It was an ancient structure, in existence long before Ceredigion had become a kingdom.

It was also where Owen was setting his trap.

His mind wandered to Evie, as it so often did. His final words to her had been his declaration of love. The words burned in his chest, along with a sickening dread that Severn would continue to keep them apart. Part of him hoped that Iago Llewellyn would be slain in the coming battle. It was an ungenerous thought, but he did not regret it. The more he pondered the possibility of losing Evie to that man, the sicker his heart felt.

So many tiles were being arranged. But they were being arranged by someone else, someone who knew the pattern and knew the goal to achieve. The more Owen thought on it, the more he suspected that perhaps it was Marshal Roux of Brythonica who was behind the mist and shadows. Owen had long suspected the man was Fountain-blessed. Surely the Duchess of Brythonica would bring the most able and intelligent men to her service, men capable of impressive deeds. Roux had been there the night of Owen's attack on Chatriyon's army. He had come to Edonburick with a message of warning at exactly the right time to catch Owen and the others. But might there not have been another reason for his visit? Bothwell had escaped after that point, after all. Owen had not reasoned this out before, but he thought it possible that Tunmore might have been an ally of the marshal's. Did the sheath bear the mark of the Raven because the treasure was connected to Brythonica? If so, then it would make sense that Roux knew about and would try to seize the chest himself. But as far as Owen knew, the marshal had never tried to conceal his comings and goings, and no tangible link existed between him and the others. Tyrell, on the other hand, was a skilled poisoner, and Bothwell had identified him as the man who had been sent after the king. There was more evidence indicating he had been the thief, but that did not mean it was the correct answer.

Owen stared at the walls of the sanctuary, frowning deeply. He was convinced that the chest Tunmore had hidden in the sanctuary of Our Lady of Kingfountain had been brought to St. Penryn. The snow that hung thick on the sanctuary walls and the tents of his camp was a further testament to his intuition. The storm had moved to the coast next. He knew with an unshakable certainty that something in that chest was making it happen. Even though it had remained hidden in the palace for years, the unfolding of recent events had done something to trigger whatever was hidden inside it. A force powerful enough to affect the very weather.

The sound of approaching boots pounded up the footpath and Owen turned, catching sight of his herald, Farnes, in the mist. Dawn was creeping in slowly. The sound of a gull's shriek split the air.

"There you are, my lord," Farnes said with a sniff, rubbing his arms to ward away the cold. "I was told you'd wandered off this way. Best to stay closer to your men, I think. These cliffs can be treacherous."

Owen shoved off the boulder he had been leaning against and met Farnes a few steps farther down. "What news, Farnes?"

"You wanted to be told when the Espion girl arrived. She's in your tent right now."

"Thank you," Owen said with a nod. He was anxious to see Etayne, hoping for news about Evie's health.

"And word has also arrived from Averanche," Farnes continued, a gleam in his eye. "You were right, my lord. They have word of Occitanian troops marching toward the city. You have several hundred men holding the city's defenses. They can hold the city until the rest of our army arrives."

Owen shook his head. "We're not going to Averanche, Farnes. That's exactly what they want me to do. I'm keeping my army near St. Penryn."

Farnes wrinkled his brow. "What on earth for?" he said with confusion. "There are no enemies here. And no fortifications either."

"Not yet," Owen said with a smile.

Farnes looked even more confused. "Did you have a . . . a dream, my lord?"

Owen rubbed his mouth. "You could say that. We stay here. Let Chatriyon hammer away at Averanche for a while. He'll be watching his back the whole time. And I don't think that's his true goal anyway."

Owen started down the footpath toward his pavilion, Farnes at his heels. The men were murmuring from their places among the patches of snow. There were no inns or taverns nearby. The conditions were rather deplorable, but these were men of Westmarch. He could see the looks of respect and determination in their eyes as he passed them on his way back through camp.

His fingers and toes felt wooden from the cold, and Owen stretched his fingers beneath his gloves, clenching and opening his fists. After bidding Farnes to linger outside, he ducked inside the warm interior of his tent, feeling the heat sting his cheeks.

Etayne was kneeling in front of two large saddlebags, undoing the straps. As he entered, she turned and saw him, and a slight flush crept onto her cheeks, followed by a hesitant smile.

"She is on the mend," Etayne said, preempting his first question, and he was grateful to her for that.

"Thank the Fountain," Owen sighed, rubbing his forehead. "In all likelihood, it looked worse than it was."

"I stitched it myself," Etayne said. "She'll have a small scar on her brow, but only if you look for it. When I left Kingfountain, she was preparing to ride North."

Owen started pacing, feeling edgy and anxious. "Did the king give you your orders?" he asked gruffly.

Etayne inclined her head. Her face was deadly serious, but she nodded once. "I was expecting to find you still at Tatton Hall, but they said you'd ridden on to St. Penryn." She stood and smoothed her dress. "This is a desolate place to bring an army. Why here?"

Owen wished he could discuss his plans with Evie, but she was not there. Etayne had shown herself to be loyal thus far and he believed she would tell him the truth if his reasoning were off.

"Can I trust you?" he asked her in a low voice.

Etayne's countenance changed and she stepped forward. "I would do *anything* you asked of me," she answered sincerely. He sensed an invitation in her words, but he sidestepped it.

"How is your strength with Fountain magic right now?" he asked her. "Have you recovered from our journey to Atabyrion?"

She nodded resolutely. "I grow stronger day by day."

Owen flashed her a smile. Then he tapped his mouth, deciding he would trust her with the entirety of his plan. Ankarette had said that the most important skill was the gift of discernment, of being able to judge the motives and intentions of another. In his dealings with Etayne, he had learned that the thief's daughter had been so mistreated and distrusted that she craved approval and attention. Owen had given that to her by treating her as a person and not an instrument. He had noticed her growing attachment to him, her loyalty. With Mancini's death, she was no longer bound to anyone else. He was certain she would be more loyal to him than she had ever been to the spymaster.

He looked deeply into her eyes. "I believe Iago is going to strike soon. Not here, but in the North or the East. I think East Stowe is his most likely destination, because he would not want to attack Evie or her grandfather directly. One of the duchies alone could repulse Iago's attack, let alone two. So the threat isn't going to come from Atabyrion. It's going to come here."

Etayne looked thoughtful. "How so?"

"Iago's attack is a diversion," Owen explained. "It draws our forces away and opens up Westmarch. I think this is where *Eyric* is going to land. This is where he will lay his claim to the throne of Ceredigion. This is where King Andrew died." He pointed in the direction of St. Penryn. "This area was once dry land, Etayne. There was another kingdom here. A kingdom called Leoneyis. It's now underwater, covered by the sea."

Etayne's lips twisted with surprise and horror. "They were all drowned?"

"Indeed," Owen said, continuing to pace. "There was a prophecy that King Andrew would return. This was where he was supposed to return, to save the kingdom. The prophecy is called the Dreadful Deadman. Eyric is not that man. But many believe he is. They are bringing him some relic of magic to turn the tide. Perhaps even literally. Occitania is a part of the plot, though I'm certain Chatriyon has his own ends in mind. And I believe that Brythonica might be as well. I don't trust Marshal Roux. Something is happening here that I don't understand. Something no one will explain. So I plan to be very unpredictable. And I plan to set a trap to lure Roux into revealing himself. If my instincts are correct, he is not in Brythonica right now. He is coming here by ship." Owen used his forefinger to stab his empty palm to emphasize it. "And we will be waiting for him."

Etayne's eyes were wide. "Owen, you said that one duchy would be enough to stave off an invasion from Atabyrion. But the last time you faced Chatriyon, you were not alone. You had Duke Horwath with you. Now you're talking about facing Occitania and one of its strongest duchies by yourself."

Owen nodded. "I know. I'll be a tempting target, don't you agree?"

"You'll be crushed!" Etayne said, blinking worriedly.

He smiled. "Not if they think I'm on their side," he answered in a quiet voice. "Ankarette once told me this story. It was about one of the previous kings of Ceredigion and how his nobles revolted against him. They raised an army to defeat him, and the king's son, a prince, negotiated a truce. He was so convincing that he was able to disband the rebel army. And then he destroyed it. They may try to do the same thing with me. I have no intention of trusting Chatriyon or Eyric, but I will make them both believe that I do. Eyric offered me power. I plan to accept it."

Etayne smiled at him, her eyes filling with light. "You are crafty."

He bowed to her. "But I need your help, Etayne. I need you to *become* someone else in order for my plan to work. May I look in your saddlebags, please? I am hoping you brought something. Knowing what your mission was, I was counting on you to bring it."

Etayne's eyebrows lifted and she smiled, one of her knowing, beautiful smiles. "I think I know who you want me to be. And yes, my lord. I did bring her dress."

♦ ♦ ♦

One can scarcely credit what one hears these days. But if rumors be true, then King Iago Llewellyn has indeed invaded Ceredigion. His troops landed in Aberthwist and began burning villages in a direct course toward Kingfountain. Refugees have been spilling from East Stowe. Some are heading south to Kingfountain, but most are rallying north to where the king's army has encamped. If that were not enough, there are reports from Westmarch that the King of Occitania has attacked our holdings there and that Duke Owen has turned traitor and has been in league with Occitania all along. As I said, I can scarcely give credit to such reports.

—Polidoro Urbino, Court Historian of Kingfountain

♦ ♦ ♦

CHAPTER THIRTY-SIX

Duplicity

Owen rubbed his bleary eyes, listening to Farnes as he hastily explained the news from Averanche. The reports were bad and getting worse and Owen's army was restless with inaction. They wanted to fight, to attack, to do anything but camp in the frostbitten wastes of St. Penryn.

Farnes's hair was unkempt and he stroked his fingers through vigorously. "Averanche can withhold a siege for a few days, a fortnight maybe, but if there is no hope of being relieved, they will turn back and seek terms with Chatriyon!"

"We will lift the siege," Owen said forcefully, staring at his herald with determination. "But they must hold as long as they can. How much food do they have?"

Farnes shook his head. "The provisions will hold for a fortnight easily. Captain Ashby isn't worried about that and he is rationing the stores. He's more worried about the locals betraying us. The lord mayor, for example."

Owen stroked his lip. "I trust Ashby. He'll follow orders. Have supplies run by sea to support the castle."

"Yes, but it's only a matter of time before the Occitanian ships blockade the city," Farnes insisted. "When shall I tell him you are coming to relieve them?"

"I can't say when, Farnes. The situation here is risky. I know Chatriyon is trying to lure me to Averanche, and I'm not going to snap at the bait like a codfish! He's distracting me from this place. This is where Eyric is going to land. I know it. I'm determined to wait like the patient hunter."

"But when, my lord?" Farnes pleaded. "If those under siege lose hope of rescue, they will falter. The Occitanians have brought in a mighty host. They will retake the city, and once they've done so, they'll challenge Westmarch. Would it not be more prudent to pull out our men by ship and bring them here? We could face Chatriyon from our own lands."

Etayne's voice interrupted. "Lord Owen will not abandon those who put their faith in him," she said scathingly. "Chatriyon would show no mercy to the lord mayor and those who surrender the city."

Owen was surprised at her remarks and he glanced at her, seeing through the disguise she wore. But even her tone and accent were convincing.

Farnes flushed. "I meant no disrespect, my lady," he said, flustered. "It's just that we risk running out of time. Your troops here are restless. The action is to the west, not here. The longer you wait, the more you risk."

"I'll not abandon Averanche," Owen said. "You send word to Ashby. Tell him to hold the city to the last man. I won't fail him."

Farnes pursed his lips. "Very well, my lord." He nodded, bowed, and exited the tent.

Owen was pacing, feeling the tension roiling in the pavilion. The fate of Ceredigion was hanging in the balance. From the reports he'd received from the king's army, Severn was letting Iago venture deep inland, letting him think there was little opposition, in the anticipation that he would extend himself too far. And then Horwath would cut off his retreat and Severn's army would come thundering out to trap Iago between them. Owen had no doubt that Severn would win.

He walked to his table and stared at the map there, running his finger along the coastline between Westmarch and Occitania. There was a V-shaped wedge of water at the crux between the two kingdoms. That water had once been the kingdom of Leoneyis. Owen looked at the outline of Brythonica and shook his head. Where was Marshal Roux? What was he doing? It felt like he was waiting in the shadows, waiting for Owen to move first. The thought made him grit his teeth with frustration.

"You look worried," Etayne said softly, coming up next to him. Even her perfume reminded him of her.

"I can't stay here much longer," Owen sighed, stabbing the map with his finger. "If Eyric doesn't arrive soon, I'll have to go to Averanche and lift the siege. You were right . . . I'm not going to abandon it. But I can't help but think that I'm being *forced* to step forward. Something isn't right. And it has to do with Brythonica and the duchess's true allegiance."

Etayne smiled at him. "You also don't want to be wrong. I don't know any man who readily admits he's made the wrong choice."

Owen smiled knowingly. "That too. But I know I'm right. There is something important about St. Penryn. Something I don't know, but I can smell it in the air." He gave her disguise another appraising look. "You're not even using your magic and you look like her."

Etayne dimpled at the compliment and nodded gracefully.

Owen fetched a flask and took a drink of stale wine. Wincing at the taste, he set it back down in a hurry. "Tell me more about this poisoner. The one who fled Kingfountain during the riot."

"Tyrell," Etayne said. "He crossed from Brugia in a ship, disguised as a sanctuary sexton, and visited Our Lady. One of the sailors remarked on the gap between his teeth, so I knew it was him. He stayed in an inn on the bridge between Our Lady and the palace. By the time I found his dwelling, he had already infiltrated the castle. He was the one who started the riot and spread the rumor about the king throwing Tunmore off the tower. I know he's Fountain-blessed. I felt him use his power."

Owen nodded, frowning. "And what would you say his power is?"

She wrinkled her nose. "His power is causing hatred. There is a potion he uses. I have a report that he carries a box of some lotion, which he spreads on doorways. Those who pass the doorway begin to feel a keen hatred for the man in his sights. He assassinates by poisoning the minds of others, causing *them* to murder his target. It's clear his target was Severn, as we suspected. It wasn't just the storm that was making the people riot. He spread some of his ointment on the gates of the sanctuary as well."

Owen stared at her. "Poor Jack was being affected by it. I thought he wanted to kill the king, though it made no sense."

Etayne looked at him shrewdly. "Thankfully Fountain magic doesn't work on you, Owen, or *you* might have been tempted to kill the king."

Owen chuckled softly. "So you almost had him in Kingfountain when the riot started. He may have removed the chest from the sanctuary and taken it here to St. Penryn."

"Or so you believe," Etayne prompted. "What about Marshal Roux?"

"It can't be both of them, can it? My suspicion is that Tyrell did it and he's trying to get the chest to Eyric. It will make a difference somehow. It's important in some way I don't understand."

"Why don't you just go into the sanctuary and take it back now?" Etayne asked.

Owen shook his head. "Because I'm going to figure this out, Etayne. I'm tired of being in the dark about our enemies and their plans. If I pretend to be on their side, they may expose the entire plot to me."

The sound of boots came rushing up to the tent and Farnes burst in, flushed. "My lord!"

"What is it?" Owen snapped.

"Eyric's ship just docked at the sanctuary! Four fishing vessels. He's at the sanctuary right now! You were right!"

Owen felt a throb of hope in his breast. "Get word to Ashby," Owen said. "Tell him I'm coming straightaway."

♦ ♦ ♦

Owen carried a torch to light their way as they walked down the main road to the sanctuary of St. Penryn. There were Espion hidden all along the way, as well as in the area surrounding the sanctuary, and they were the ones who had alerted Farnes of Eyric's landing. Owen missed Clark, but he had been assigned to protect Evie and get her and Justine safely back to the North. Owen did not think he minded the assignment, for it would bring him close to the woman he cared about.

An Espion by the name of Victor waited in the gloom, wearing beggar rags and shaking a cup. Owen paused and rifled through a coin pouch for some money to toss in.

"How many?" Owen whispered. Etayne wore a thick silver mantle covering her dress and hair. She faced the sanctuary so he could only see her profile. She looked like an apparition in the mist.

"One hundred men, if that," the Espion wheezed, jiggling the cup as the coins clinked into it. "They raised a battle standard from the spire of the sanctuary. The Sun and Rose. Men are coming in from all quarters, drawn to it. He has a boat ready to flee, though, and soldiers are guarding it with drawn swords. Oh, and his lady wife is with him."

"Kathryn?" Owen asked in surprise. "What about the Earl of Huntley?"

The shabby Espion shrugged. "No sign of the earl."

"Thank you," Owen said, then tugged at Etayne's elbow and started toward the sanctuary. He felt the magic of the Fountain begin to trickle in around her.

"Not yet," he cautioned. "And stay close. If Tyrell's there, I want him to think I'm the one who's causing it. They all know I'm Fountain-blessed."

The pathway wound its way up to some steps, which they mounted as they rose toward the grounds. A stone fence surrounded the sanctuary, while a wrought-iron gate speckled with flakes of rust commanded the entrance. They entered the gate and Owen began to summon his magic as the sound of their footfalls echoed on the pavement.

There were others carrying torches on the grounds, and the wind and sea fog blew in sharp gusts, threatening to tear away Etayne's hood. She gripped Owen's arm with one hand and used her other to keep the cowl in place.

The sexton awaited them at the main doors.

"Lord Kiskaddon, Lady Elyse," he greeted warmly, but there was a nervous edge to his voice. "They are expecting you both. Follow me to the fountain."

As they cleared the threshold, Etayne brought down her hood. Owen could feel the magic flowing from her, as innocuous as the breeze. She looked exactly like Lady Elyse. She was wearing one of her gowns, and her hair was in the fashion favored by the king's niece. Owen made himself appear agitated and nervous, and he continued to glance back the way they had come, as if suspecting treachery. Etayne's disguise was perfect.

There was a circle of light near the fountain's edge, and the lapping of the water helped prevent noise from carrying. Owen recognized Eyric immediately, only now he wore gilded armor and a sword belted to his waist. The pommel gleamed and the polished armor fit him well. Standing next to him was Lady Kathryn, holding on to his arm. She looked beautiful, but also very wary and nervous, and her eyes scrutinized them as they made their approach.

There were several men standing with them, including the deconeus and warriors from Atabyrion with their braided locks and rugged looks.

They stared at Owen with open dislike as he approached. Standing just behind the deconeus was another man, wearing the robes of a sexton. He had a noticeable gap in his front teeth. He was tall, with reddish brown hair and freckled skin. The robes could not hide his muscled gait. He looked like he was from Legault, and Owen could sense the power of the Fountain flowing from him. The man stared at Owen and Etayne shrewdly, a small frown quirking his mouth down as they approached.

A decorative table had been brought to the edge of the fountain, and Owen saw the chest on the table, the lid open and cast aside. His heart pounded with curiosity. They were all gathered around the box, but they'd turned as Owen and Etayne made their approach.

"Sister!" Eyric breathed with pure delight. Kathryn released his arm, and Eyric rushed forward, embracing Etayne with all the fervor of a man who had not seen his sister in a long, long while. Etayne fell effortlessly into the role of rejoicing sibling, and even shed some convincing tears as she hugged her long-lost "brother." Owen almost felt guilty for the deception, but he knew it would not work with the poisoner Tyrell.

Owen came forward and took Lady Kathryn's hand. He bowed graciously. "I beg your pardon, Lady Kathryn, for shattering the window in your manor before I left. I hope you can forgive me."

She gave him an intense look, not showing any emotion other than nervousness. "I do not consider it inappropriate given the circumstances. You had deceived us, Lord Kiskaddon. I trust you have not come to deceive us again."

Her words stung Owen's heart, especially considering how vulnerable she appeared at that moment.

Eyric swept up Etayne and twirled her around. "My dear, *dear* sister!" he crooned, shaking his head. "I would recognize you even if fifty years had passed. This is she, my love," he said, looking back at Kathryn. "I would have known her anywhere."

Lady Kathryn's mouth turned down. "If you say so, my lord husband." Her voice was skeptical.

"What brings you to St. Penryn?" Eyric demanded almost gleefully as he took Etayne's hands. "We weren't expecting you here. It's a welcome surprise, to be sure!"

Owen patted Kathryn's hand and then met Tyrell's gaze. The poisoner looked quite uncomfortable, almost writhing in his disquiet. Owen finally allowed himself to look into the open chest.

It was a Wizr set, but it was far from ordinary. Owen could feel the presence of the Fountain's magic just from looking at it.

The board was small, roughly the span of both of Owen's hands from end to end with his fingers spread apart. The board was made out of grayish-brown stone, and while the darker squares were marble, the lighter squares were some other polished stone. The figurines of the set were the typical pieces, except they were each hand-sculpted into small, squat depictions. The king, for example, sat on a throne—like in Owen's set—only each piece was carved with a face and an expression. One of the kings was leaning forward, resting his chin on his fist. The pieces were each highly detailed and looked to be centuries old, showing some wear and cracks. The board was already assembled, but it seemed to be in the midst of a game. Many discarded pieces were settled in the little slots around the sides of the board.

Tyrell's face twisted with anger as he watched Owen regarding the pieces. "My lord," he said with alarm. "You'll have time to visit with your *sister*. You must make your move. Play the game."

Owen felt something twist inside his stomach.

Eyric was enraptured by Etayne, gazing at her with adoring eyes, completely unaware of the tension around him. He kissed her knuckles and laughed softly. "Will Chatriyon still support me, Sister?" he pleaded. "When I heard you had married, I began to wonder if he wanted the throne of Ceredigion for himself. Lord Owen said as much to me earlier."

"The game, my lord," Tyrell said with a cough.

Eyric waved him down. "I haven't seen my sister in over a decade, Tyrell. A moment."

Owen watched with pride as Etayne masterfully mimicked Elyse. Even her voice was identical.

"My lord husband," Kathryn said in a pleading tone, looking more and more concerned.

Her words broke the spell. Eyric turned to look at his wife, then nodded obediently. He returned to the table and gazed down at the set. Owen could not determine any order from the way the pieces were positioned on the board, but he could tell by looking at them that both sides were evenly matched and in defending postures. He quickly memorized the pieces on the board, trying to parse any patterns from the previous matches he had played.

"Your move," Tyrell repeated with agitation.

"But I don't know this game very well," Eyric said with unease, staring down at the board. His hand hovered over the pieces.

"What is this game?" Owen asked, standing shoulder to shoulder with Eyric as he gazed down at the box.

"You'll *see*," said Tyrell with venom. "My lord, it doesn't really matter what piece you choose. We just need to see if you *can* move the pieces."

Owen felt a prickle from the Fountain in his mind.

He cannot. But his wife can. In her womb is the Dreadful Deadman. Protect the heir.

Owen blinked with surprise and noticed for the first time that Kathryn's hand was gently pressing her belly.

CHAPTER THIRTY-SEVEN

Loyalty

Etayne cast Owen a nervous look. He didn't know if she had heard the Fountain's voice or not. He was reeling from the revelation that the Dreadful Deadman was an unborn child, the son of Eyric Argentine. And he felt the imminent burden that would fall on his shoulders. He would need to protect this babe as Ankarette had protected him.

Reaching his hand toward the chest, Eyric tried to move one of the pieces of the Wizr set. But the piece resisted stubbornly, and Eyric's face crinkled with concern as he applied more pressure.

"It's not moving," Eyric said worriedly.

The poisoner Tyrell frowned, seeing the failure as evidence of something. "It's because you are not recognized as the king," he said. "You have claimed your uncle's throne, but you have not won it yet. Once you wear the hollow crown, you will be able to move the pieces, my lord. Not until then." Tyrell swiftly took the lid and shut it over the Wizr set.

Lady Kathryn took her husband's arm, giving him a worried look. "So it is true. You must earn the right to rule through conquest. My husband, I fear for you."

He gave her a tender look and then smoothed a strand of hair from her brow. "The Fountain will aid me, Kate. Look at all the allies it has already brought." He glanced back at Elyse and Owen, on whom his gaze rested. "Have you come to join me now?" he asked. "You spurned my offer before. I would welcome your support most ardently, my lord duke. Did my sister persuade you?"

Owen knew he had to control his expression. It was difficult when so much was happening around him. He tried to sound sullen. "The king changed when Lady Elyse forsook him. He's a different man now. He violated the sanctuary of Our Lady, and the people nearly threw him into the river." Owen risked a glance at Tyrell, trying to judge his reaction.

"I have persuaded Lord Owen," Etayne said, her voice and tone mimicking Elyse's perfectly, "to join our cause. I knew you would not trust his offer of assistance without assurance. Welcome home, my brother. The crown is rightfully yours."

Eyric's lip trembled with emotion. "I would take back what is ours, Sister. Uncle Severn besmirched our name, our family, and our inheritance. He sent the Espion to kill my brother and me, and Lord Bletchley ordered Tyrell, who is Fountain-blessed, to do the deed. But the Fountain forbade him from killing me. Instead, he smuggled me to Brugia. It is time to remove that monster from the throne before his madness infects the entire kingdom. He ought never to have worn the crown."

Etayne stroked Owen's arm. "Only Lord Owen has been able to quell his rages. I could not, in good conscience, continue to stand by him as he changed. Brother, I must return to my husband in Occitania."

"Before you leave, my lady," Tyrell said, his voice full of warning and disbelief. "I suggest, my prince, that you ask your sister a question. Something only you and she would know."

"Tyrell, it *is* my sister," Eyric said with a snort. "I recognize her as if we'd never parted."

Owen knew Tyrell sensed Fountain magic, but he probably could not determine whom it was coming from.

"I know Princess Elyse as well," Owen said. "I was raised at the court of Kingfountain. Believe me, Master Tyrell, I'd know if she was an imposter."

"I'm sure you would," Tyrell said acidly, his eyes churning with rage. Owen felt the Fountain boiling inside of him.

Lady Kathryn's eyes wrinkled in concern, and Eyric patted her hand. "There is no need to fret, my love. The danger is real, but I believe the people will rally to me now that Severn has violated sanctuary. They will flock to me in droves, like sheep needing a patient shepherd. You are my queen."

Owen wanted to get his hands on the chest. It was sitting on the table, teasing him with its vulnerability. It was a riddle and a mystery, and he wanted to solve it. But he had no doubt that Tyrell would never allow it.

Kathryn's eyes were doubtful. "My husband, your uncle is a cunning and shrewd man. He sent Lord Owen to deceive us once. Why would he not do so again? I feel"—she paused, her hand tightening on her stomach—"we can trust him, but I worry what will happen if you are caught. I could not bear to lose you." Her look was so tender and loving that it made Owen regret what he was about to do.

"If I am caught," Eyric said, dropping his voice lower. "We already discussed what I would do. What I would say. Have courage, dear one. It is time to cast the die. Iago Llewellyn may rid us of this monster once and for all. We must march against him now, while the tide is in our favor. We won't get another chance."

It was true.

Eyric turned to Owen. "Where is my uncle's army?"

"He's in the North."

Eyric nodded firmly. "That was always his greatest bastion of support. But I was once the Duke of Yuork. The people there will forsake him as everyone else has done. He was never meant to rule Ceredigion. It is time we rectified that mischance."

"Hold me," Kathryn murmured worriedly, coming into her husband's embrace. The couple lingered that way, and Owen's heart wrenched inside his chest. He had to look away, and his gaze found Tyrell's. The man's face was twisted in rage. It was easy to guess at the cause: His efforts to stir up contention had failed because Owen's magic deflected the magic of others. He was impotent in Owen's presence. And he knew it.

"Come, my lord," Tyrell insisted, almost whining. "Let's summon your soldiers. We have two hundred men so far and more will come every day. The sooner we march, the sooner the people will rally to the Sun and Rose."

"I perfectly agree," Owen said, stepping forward. "I have a pavilion a short distance. Why don't you and Lady Kathryn join us for a meal?"

Eyric shook his head. "My lady will not leave sanctuary until I return to bring her to the coronation. The Fountain will look after you in my absence." He tipped up her chin and gave her a lingering kiss. Lady Kathryn blinked back tears.

"I will return for you, my love. I swear it." He turned to Owen and Etayne. "Let's gather at your camp then. I'd like to speak to your men. I hope to help them see the rightful cause they undertake."

"My lord, I don't think that's wise," Tyrell said, shaking his head.

"Come, Tyrell. I've lurked in shadows for long enough. It is time to face the light." He gave Kathryn one last look before shifting his attention to the deconeus. "Your Grace, I leave my most precious jewels in your hands. Guard them well."

"I will, Your Majesty," the deconeus said with a plump smile.

Lady Kathryn gave Owen an imploring look. He was about to turn away, unable to bear her gaze any longer, but she caught his sleeve.

"Thank you," she whispered. She blinked quickly. "I know you risk a great deal, Lord Owen, and I will not forget your kindness. The daughter of the Earl of Huntley is grateful. My father will reward you handsomely."

Owen's mouth was dry. "Thank you, Lady Kathryn. But I do not do this for the reward." He looked into her eyes, knowing the memory of the trust he saw there would haunt him the rest of his life. It did not matter; he had a duty to perform. The Fountain had told him to protect Eyric's son. It had not told him to defend the father. But despite that, it was still an agonizing conflict.

Tyrell hefted the chest under his arm and they started to walk together out of the sanctuary. Owen sensed he had a dagger concealed behind the chest. But the man was not wearing armor, so he was quite vulnerable to blades himself. The night was cold and misty. Men came quickly with torches, and a rabble of Atabyrion warriors drew in around them as protection. Some cheered Eyric's name and others hoisted banners with the Sun and Rose. Eyric raised a fist and smiled. He was a handsome man and he looked like a true prince.

The call of a night bird came in the distance.

As they reached the gates, Tyrell cast furtive glances into the gloom, looking weary and sick with nerves. "My lord, where are your other guards? Should we not fetch them?"

"It's only a meal, Tyrell," Eyric said with a grunt. "I'll be staying with my lady at the sanctuary tonight. Once the soldiers hear my speech, the word will spread faster. Trust me, old friend."

Tyrell was growing frantic. He knew crossing the gate was dangerous, but he seemed to sense the tide had turned against him. Owen stared at Eyric, willing him to leave.

"It's cold," Etayne said with a shiver, bringing up her cowl. He wondered if her disguise was in danger of slipping.

"Of course," Eyric said, hooking arms with her. "Let's get you back to a brazier. Come, Tyrell. Quit skulking. Let us go."

"My lord," Tyrell moaned. "I have an ill feeling . . ."

Eyric snorted again, shaking his head at the man's foolishness, and then pulled Etayne with him as they left the gate. Tyrell lingered at the threshold, clutching the chest to his body. His eyes burned into Owen's with wrath and heat, but Owen merely gave him a confused expression, shrugged slightly, and followed Eyric. Tyrell gritted his teeth and left the sanctuary.

Their boots crunched on the gravel path heading back into the mist toward Owen's camp. His heart, though tortured, felt a quick surge of hope. It was going to work. *A little farther, just a little farther!*

The beggar man sat at the side of the road with his cup, shaking it and making the coins inside rattle. "Alms, my lords! Alms!"

Eyric opened his purse and produced a crown. "Here you are, my good man. Your fortunes are changing."

The coin thunked in the cup. "Thank you, my lord. So are yours."

The Atabyrion warriors slowly lowered their torches and tugged free their tunics, revealing the badges of Owen's house beneath—the bucks' heads on a field of blue.

Owen turned to the deposed prince coldly. "I arrest you by the name of Eyric Argentine."

The look of shock and horror on the prince's face would also be seared into Owen's mind forever.

"How . . . how!" Eyric gasped, his jaw quivering.

The chest thudded onto the ground. There was a flash of movement, and Owen saw Tyrell's dagger plunging toward his heart.

Etayne caught the thrust and jammed the flat edge of her hand against Tyrell's throat to crush his windpipe. She torqued the wrist, and Tyrell went face-first into the ground as some of the Espion rushed forward to restrain him. Seized by a hateful rage, he choked for air and thrashed against his captors.

Two of the Espion, one of them the beggar with the cup, grabbed Eyric.

Etayne pulled a vial from her sleeve, uncorked it, and quickly tipped the liquid into Tyrell's mouth as he gasped for breath. Owen watched her do it. He had ordered her to do it. He would not risk taking another poisoner captive, especially not one as skilled and deadly as Tyrell.

"What are you doing! What have you *done*!" shrieked Eyric, struggling against his captors. Realizing he had been duped, he started to sob hysterically. There would be no civil war. The embers of hope, which had burned so bright just moments before, had been crushed underfoot.

The choking sounds coming from Tyrell grew more spasmodic as he realized what kind of poison was in his mouth. Etayne backed away from him, her disguise gone, but except for her haughty, cold expression, she still resembled Elyse.

In moments, Tyrell hung limply. There was a hiss and a sigh from the Fountain as he died.

Owen walked over to the chest Tyrell had dropped onto the sand and picked it up. He was surprised at how heavy it was, but it fit under the crook of his arm. Etayne looked at him, her eyes glinting in the torchlight.

"What . . . what are you . . . going to do with me?" Eyric stammered, his cheeks pale.

"I'm going to turn you over to your uncle," Owen said dispassionately. "After we've dealt with Chatriyon. Trust me, sir, I'm not going to let you out of my sight."

Eyric's lips twisted with rage. "You, you are just like him!"

Owen shunted aside the truth in the words. He didn't want to falter, not at the final moment. It was too late to change the course he had chosen. He could only hope he was doing the right thing. "You should have heeded my warning in Atabyrion. What you will get now is much less than what you *could* have had."

"I am the rightful king of Ceredigion," Eyric said quaveringly.

"No," Owen replied flatly. "You were only a pawn."

CHAPTER THIRTY-EIGHT

Wizr

Owen carried the chest under his arm until they reached his warm pavilion. He was thrilled by the victory and frankly amazed it had gone off so well. He had been concerned that Tyrell would try to do something rash when he realized his gift of rancor was useless against Owen.

"Well done, my lord!" the beggar-clad Espion said, grinning broadly.

Eyric came into the tent, looking haggard and worried, and was followed by Etayne, still wearing Lady Elyse's gown.

"Your work isn't finished," Owen said. "I want you to keep the Espion stationed around the perimeter of St. Penryn. Anyone who arrives to join the rabble is to be arrested and sent to Beestone castle."

"Is that where you're taking the pretender?" the Espion asked, giving Eyric a derisive look that made the man bristle with anger.

"Oh no," Owen said with a chuckle. "He's coming with me. I'll present him to King Severn myself after I've lifted the siege of Averanche. What about the boats?"

The Espion nodded vigorously. "We did as you ordered. The boats from Atabyrion are no longer seaworthy, my lord. By morning, our ships will have blocked the waters to St. Penryn. No one comes or leaves without your express permission."

"What about my wife?" Eyric asked, anger throbbing in his voice.

Owen turned to him. "What about Lady Kathryn?"

"Will she be coming with us?" Eyric asked, fidgeting.

Owen wrinkled his brow. "I don't think she's going to leave sanctuary. Do you?"

Eyric shook his head. "I didn't know if you would still respect that privilege. Will you?" he asked with a taunt.

Owen ignored the question and turned back to his captain. "Get word to Ashby that we're on the way. We ride before dawn. Leave sufficient men to guard St. Penryn. And get word to the king that we have his nephew in custody."

"Aye, my lord."

"Leave us," Owen said, setting the chest down on the nearest folding table. Everyone other than Eyric and Etayne left the tent.

The deposed prince looked defeated as he slumped onto a camp chair, massaging his eyes dejectedly. "Why did you murder Tyrell?" Eyric said with a tone of sadness.

"One could hardly call that murder," Etayne rebuffed. "He was coming at Owen with a poisoned dagger!"

"He was only trying to *save* me," Eyric sighed. "Save me from my own stupidity." He lifted his head and gave Etayne a scowl. "You are good, Poisoner. I could have sworn you were my sister. Even now, you resemble her, but I can tell the difference. Back at the sanctuary, you completely deceived me. I'm fortunate you didn't use a knife when you embraced me."

Etayne gave him a cold, triumphant smile and bowed graciously.

"So Tyrell was the one who rescued you from Bletchley?" Owen asked.

Eyric nodded bleakly. "He used his strange power to goad a henchman into smothering us. But Tyrell used a powder on the pillows. One that would make us fall unconscious." He stared at the ground, his eyes haunted as a shudder went through him. "I will never forget the sensation I experienced when that man shoved the pillow against my face. I couldn't breathe, but there was something noxious, some smell. I passed out. They threw our bodies into the cistern beneath the palace." He shook his head. "I could hardly swim. My brother couldn't swim at all. He never revived, and drowned there." His voice fell off.

Owen stared at him, feeling the truth of his words.

"Then what happened?" Owen prompted.

Eyric looked up at him, his eyes bloodshot. "Tyrell came for me. He was grieved that my brother was dead. There was a boat in the cistern. He snuck me to the sanctuary of Our Lady and then onto a ship bound for Brugia. I was a prince no longer. But I was promised that I would return one day. Just as the prophecy of the Dreadful Deadman promised. A king who was dead returning again."

Owen rubbed his own jaw. "But you're *not* the Dreadful Deadman."

Eyric shrugged with melancholy. "No. I'm just a dead man now." He covered his face with his hands, his shoulder buckling with stifled sobs.

"Your uncle isn't going to kill you," Owen said. "If you had come with me from Atabyrion, you would have fared much better. He may, in time, have grown to trust you. Perhaps even made you his heir."

Eyric looked up at him then, his eyes welling with tears. "You think I believe that? I've heard what he's done to my cousin Dunsdworth. I would rather go over a waterfall than endure such dishonor."

Owen sighed heavily. "Your uncle would have restored you as the Duke of Yuork. But now you've attempted twice to invade his kingdom and depose him. Hardly grounds for trust."

"I have no reason to trust his word!" Eyric snapped. "Nor *yours*, for that matter. You came to Atabyrion to dupe me. You have finally succeeded. Well done, my lord," he added contemptuously. "But my wife is wiser than I am. She will stay in St. Penryn. She will stay there just as my mother endured sanctuary. She will stay there until the . . ." He caught himself, realizing he was about to make a blunder. But Owen already knew the secret. The Fountain had told him.

"Until what?" Owen pressed.

"Nothing," Eyric sulked.

"Until the babe is born?" Owen asked softly, and Eyric's head jerked up in utter astonishment.

"What sort of Wizr are you!" the man gasped.

Owen stifled a knowing smile. Etayne's eyes were wide with surprise, but she said nothing.

"I *am* Fountain-blessed," Owen said in an easy tone. He fetched a cup, but then stared down at it suspiciously, wondering if he were in danger of being poisoned. His thoughts went to the king, who had lived for years under the dark shadows of that fear. He set the cup down and walked over to the chest. Eyric's eyes widened with alarm as Owen unlatched it and raised the lid.

As he stared down at the Wizr set, Owen felt the power emanating from it. Just looking at the ancient relic made him feel wary and vulnerable. The positions hadn't changed since they'd left the sanctuary, he noticed. The carved faces on the pieces were full of emotion.

"What is this?" Owen asked, trying to discern any patterns in the arrangement. The one he discerned the most quickly was a series of pawns blocking each other, as if two master Wizr players had been scrupulously defending each piece, not wanting to surrender. The Wizr piece from the dark side was missing, which usually meant the game would come to a quick end. But the darker side had managed a defensive strategy to prevent the light side's Wizr from moving easily across the board. As he studied the pieces, he felt the rushing sensation of the Fountain.

A touch on his arm startled him, and he blinked and looked away from the game. Etayne was staring at him worriedly.

Owen shuddered, feeling vulnerable to a power much greater than his own. He closed the lid of the box.

Etayne stared at him fixedly. "Are *you* the Dreadful Deadman?" she asked.

Owen blinked with surprise. "Why would you say that?"

"The way you were looking at the Wizr set. It was like it was speaking to you." He shook his head, but she still continued, "It was uncanny. And everyone has heard your story. How you were brought back to life as a babe. How you were the youngest person to be discovered as Fountain-blessed in all of Ceredigion. Are you the king everyone is waiting for?"

Owen was amused by the reasoning. "I am not," he answered truthfully. The Fountain had told him Eyric's son was the one. That knowledge twisted inside him, as did the directive he had been given to keep the heir safe. He gestured back to the chest. "What is this?"

Eyric's countenance fell. "I cannot say."

"You cannot say, or you will not say?"

A wry smile quirked on Eyric's mouth. "If you let me return to the sanctuary, if you let me return to my *wife*, I will tell you. Do not keep us apart."

Owen shook his head. "Impossible."

Eyric shrugged meaningfully. "Then I will not help you. There is *power* in that game. If only you truly understood it."

Owen realized he was being goaded. He changed tactics. "What do you know of your sister? Did she go to Chatriyon willingly, or was she abducted?"

The other man threw up his hands. "I cannot say. Lord Marshal Roux warned Iago that the alliance between Occitania and Atabyrion would come to naught. That man is cunning and wise. If we had harkened to him, none of this would have happened."

"If you had listened to *me*," Owen said angrily, "a better outcome would have befallen you!"

Eyric frowned. "I have not spoken to my sister. I do not know why she did what she did. But I believe she did it willingly. It was her only chance to escape the prison my uncle crafted for her. It *was* a prison, my lord. No matter how gilded the bars. If my sister had not been so loyal to our mother, she might have left long ago. She did not want to abandon her, as so many had done." His voice throbbed with emotion. "You cannot imagine how my family has suffered."

"It seems to me to be suffering resulting from bad choices," Owen replied. "Your mother tried to prevent Severn from fulfilling his *duty*. Surely she realized that Severn was loyal to your father. That his loyalty defined him in his own mind."

Eyric gave a solemn frown. "I don't think she realized the depths of it, no. Or what he might do in order to secure his own interests. He's not blameless, Owen. And neither are you for supporting him. You're his little lapdog. His little Fountain-blessed *pup*. Wait until he starts kicking you like a dog too."

Etayne stepped forward quickly, as if she were about to slap Eyric across the face.

"Etayne," Owen said, forestalling her. "I think our guest is tired. Fetch him a drink."

Eyric's eyes widened with terror.

♦ ♦ ♦

The disheveled prisoner was soon snoring on a pallet covered in fur blankets. Owen sat on a camp chair and pressed the bridge of his nose, trying to decode the mysteries he could not solve. Etayne had changed out of Elyse's gown and was wearing one of her own, a much simpler design. She came up behind Owen and put her hand on his shoulder, using her thumb to dig circles into his tense muscles.

"What do you make of him?" Owen asked her, giving her a glance over his shoulder.

She didn't bother concealing a sneer. "He's a puppet, Owen. He may be of noble blood, but someone else was controlling him."

"Who, though?" Owen said. "Tunmore claimed that he saved him and had him shuttled away first to Brugia and then to Legault. Yet who was Tunmore serving? Everyone believes Eyric is Eredur's son. Yet, it's as if they want him to rule Ceredigion because he's an idiot."

Etayne laughed softly. "Not everyone is as smart as you, my lord. Including *our* king."

There was an implication in her tone. Owen shifted his gaze to her face and saw the look she was giving him. It was a look of total and complete surrender. A look that said, *You could be the King of Ceredigion. I could help you.*

It was a temptation, and he felt its cracklings awaken inside him like sparks on kindling. But he knew he would never be able to look Evie in the eyes again if he succumbed to it. Her look, her offer, her fingers soothing him—all of it made him wholly uncomfortable, so he rose from the stool and started pacing. Her hand lingered in the air for a moment before she lowered it. His thoughts became muddled with traitorous impulses, but he shook his head, trying to master himself.

"Who do you think the king will choose to replace Mancini?" Etayne asked softly.

Owen had almost forgotten about that. "Poor Dominic," he said. "When I first heard he had been thrown into the river, I wondered if it was a lie. But you saw him go in?"

Etayne nodded. "There was no way I could have saved him," she said. "It happened so fast. I think Mancini came to the sanctuary looking for something. But when he arrived, the deconeus denounced him with hostility and rage. I imagine it was Tyrell's doing, now that I think on it. It matches with what Eyric told us." She took a step closer to him. "I don't regret that Mancini is gone. It seems he was part of this plot as well, in some unfathomable way." Her eyes were full of meaning, and Owen suspected that something dark had existed between her and the

Espion master. "Do you think, my lord, that the king will choose you?" There was hope in her eyes, a questioning hope.

"I have no idea," Owen said with a depressed sigh. "That may all depend on whether we *survive* the next fortnight." He looked at her seriously. "I will serve my king however he wishes. I am not like Mancini," he said reassuringly.

She nodded. "Indeed, you are not. He was very . . . selfish." And she left it at that before turning away. Her back was to him when she spoke again. "I don't think the king intends to let you marry Lady Elysabeth," she said over her shoulder. "I know Mancini was persuading him against it. The king will use you to expand his realm. Even if it breaks your heart."

Owen had the sensation of being a castle gate struck by a huge battering ram. He jolted at her words, not wanting them to be true, but fearing that she was right. It rattled him to his core. But he felt helpless, unable to prevent the separation between him and Evie without destroying the king.

"How do you know this?" Owen whispered hoarsely.

She glanced back again, almost shyly. Her hand smoothed her gown in a nervous gesture. "I overheard them discussing it."

"And they did not know you were there," Owen said, trying but failing to conceal a sad smile.

Etayne shrugged. "When Eredur ruled Ceredigion, he had his brother do many unpleasant things. Things that were required under the circumstances. Things that tested Severn's loyalty." She turned and looked him in the eye. "He will do that to you, my lord. He will test your loyalty to the breaking point."

Owen gritted his teeth, feeling his cheeks flush with heat.

Etayne's eyes narrowed coldly. Her voice was just a whisper. "But remember this, Owen. I am loyal to *you*."

◆ ◆ ◆

We anxiously await news. The king's army has faced Iago Llewellyn at the village of Taunton. They fought during a blizzard. We have no word yet who won the battle. Some have said the king was betrayed and fell. Not since Ambion Hill has such uncertainty hung over this realm. If the Duke of Westmarch had been at Taunton, what would have happened? But the duke has joined forces with the army of Occitania. The betrayal of Owen Kiskaddon to his king will live in infamy.

—Polidoro Urbino, Court Historian of Kingfountain

◆ ◆ ◆

CHAPTER THIRTY-NINE

The Queen of Ceredigion

Staring at the map, Owen felt his pulse quicken and his stomach twist with dread. Although he was physically tired from the hard journey back to his army, the news awaiting him was ominous. He stared at the map again, wishing the situation were only a dream. Like one of those nightmares that forced him to blink awake, heart hammering in his chest.

"How many does Chatriyon have?" Owen asked again, swallowing thickly.

"At least twenty thousand," Captain Stoker said. "We have four . . . almost five thousand. They continue to hammer away at the defenses of Averanche, but the Occitanian army is poised for battle. Their camp is disciplined, and they have guards day and night."

Owen stared at the map. Surely Chatriyon was not leaving things to chance. He was bringing the brunt of his army into action following his defeat. This wasn't a border skirmish. This was a full-out war.

Owen tapped the map, which was covered in metal markers to indicate the size and composition of the various forces at play. "And the

Brythonican troops, you say they have blockaded the harbor as well and have troops encamped here . . . and here?"

"Aye, my lord. Marshal Roux leads them."

"And his soldiers are right there, betwixt us and Chatriyon's? He could be on *either* side," Owen added darkly. "Have we had any messages from him?"

"Only one. The lord marshal sent his herald with the missive that Brythonica stands with you. My lord, if you attack the Occitanian line, it would give Roux the perfect opportunity to flank us."

"I see that plainly," Owen grunted. "How many men does he have?"

"Two thousand. Possibly three. And he may have more soldiers in the ships in the harbor."

Owen gritted his teeth. "And there's no way to tell?"

The Espion in charge, a man by the name of Kevan, shook his head. "We can't get close enough. Roux's fleet is preventing us from providing any relief to Averanche, and if there are additional soldiers on board, they are rotating them with the crew so that we do not know. My lord, this is clearly a trap. Ashby's men are cut off in Averanche. I advise we draw back to Westmarch and choose the ground we defend. Better to lose five hundred than risk losing them all."

Owen looked at Kevan and scowled. "I won't abandon Captain Ashby."

Captain Stoker looked angry. "Nor do I recommend it, my lord. If the king's army were coming up the road behind us, perhaps we would stand a chance, but he isn't."

"The king is facing Iago Llewellyn amidst a storm," Owen said, rubbing his lip. The tent flap moved and grim-faced Farnes entered, looking as if he had been blown in on an ill wind.

"What is it, Farnes?" Owen asked his herald.

"The Occitanian herald just arrived. You remember him. Anjers."

The last time they had faced each other, Anjers had tried to bribe Owen into relinquishing his campaign. The soldiers in his tent scowled.

He wished Etayne were with him, but she was guarding Eyric in another tent, making sure he was not privy to their plans.

"Send him in," Owen snapped.

In a moment, Anjers arrived, ducking low enough that he did not smack his head on the tent flap as he'd done before. He wore his garish Occitanian finery and had a sneering look on his face as he approached.

"Back so soon?" Owen quipped.

Anjers flushed with anger. "Still so smug, Lord Kiskaddon?" he replied in a saucy tone. "Then surely you have not yet received notice of your king's death at the Battle of Taunton." He rubbed his hands together, giving Owen an imperious look. "Her Majesty Queen Elyse is now the lawful ruler of Ceredigion. She bids me command you, on pain of death, to join your forces with ours as she marches on Kingfountain to seize the city."

Owen could see the troubled looks on his captains' faces. He kept his own expression carefully neutral. "I find it incongruous, my lord, that *you* would hear of this before I did. Whence came this sorry news?"

"It came," Anjers said disdainfully, "from our poisoner. You know the man, I am sure, for he duped you in Atabyrion. Birds travel faster than horses, my lord," he added condescendingly. "We will march with you or *through* you. If you wish to preserve your rank and your lands, then you will submit to Queen Elyse's authority at once. To do otherwise would be an act of treason."

"Is she truly amidst your army, Anjers?" Owen asked. "Perhaps I would be persuaded of this fanciful tale if I could actually see and speak with her."

"By all means! You are most welcome to come with me to see her," Anjers said. "But do not think us mad enough to trust her amongst those who would wish to do her harm. Or *pretend* to be her," he added with emphasis. "What is your answer, my lord? I grow impatient with this dallying. Will you submit to your rightful queen?"

"I will gladly submit to my *rightful* queen," Owen replied with a bow. "When there *is* one to submit to. Thank you for your pains in delivering the message. You will receive our response shortly."

Anjers sniffed, clipped his heels together, and bowed to Owen before departing from the tent. As soon as he was gone, Owen let out a pent-up breath.

"Is the king truly dead?" Stoker asked in a strained whisper. "I cannot believe he would lose to that Atabyrion peasant!"

Owen put his fists down on the map. He had studied warfare since he was a child. He had read the accounts of all the major battles in the last few centuries. All of his instincts screamed that this was a trick. If Severn had died, the Espion would have gotten him a message. But with Mancini dead, it made sense that there would be confusion and chaos in the way messages were handled and delivered.

He stared at the pieces on the map, looking from his small cluster of pegs to the Occitanians' enormous army. In a straight battle, the odds were not in Owen's favor. He had not chosen the ground. His supply lines would get longer and longer the farther he went from Tatton Hall. Owen grimaced, feeling the weight of the decision on his shoulders. If Severn were dead, then continuing to fight would be construed as treason. Besides, Elyse would make a better ruler than Eyric, a man who no longer knew his country or his countrymen. He would submit to Elyse, but only after he had seen the king's corpse.

"What should we do, my lord?" Stoker pressed anxiously.

"Out," Owen said sharply. "I need a moment to think. All of you—out!"

The captains abandoned his tent, leaving Owen in the muddled silence of the camp. He stared down at the map and opened himself to the Fountain's magic. How could he turn this situation to his advantage? A nighttime raid would be predicted and prevented. Chatriyon would not be duped the same way twice. He could try to send Etayne into their camp to murder the king, but they would undoubtedly be expecting it. He rubbed his throbbing temples, feeling the trickle of the Fountain as it rushed into him. He stared at the emblems on the map representing the Brythonican forces. If the alliance with Brythonica were real, then having Marshal Roux there would actually help his cause. But he could not trust that the lord marshal was a true ally. He had been involved all along, working toward his own unknown motives, ever since Owen's first encounter with the Occitanian army. And then there was the uncanny way he always seemed to know where to be and when . . . No, Owen could not trust him. But he could test him.

The Fountain filled Owen's mind. It was like he saw a Wizr board mapped out in his mind. It almost felt as if Ankarette were there in the tent with him, leading him from the Deep Fathoms. He felt his throat catch and thicken with tears. She was the one who had taught him about Wizr, who had shown him how to defeat an opponent quickly and decisively. But she had given him another lesson in the game. When an opponent threatens you, the best way to respond is not by reacting to the threat but by turning the game around and delivering a new threat.

The way you won a game of Wizr was by capturing the king.

The strategy unfolded in Owen's mind, blooming like a flower kissed by the first rays of the sun.

♦ ♦ ♦

Owen watched Etayne's face for her reaction as he explained his plan to her.

As she grasped the full scope of it, her eyebrows lifted. "You're going to march against the capital of Occitania, the city of Pree?"

Owen nodded. "I won't need supply lines, because my men can feed off the wagons that Chatriyon is sending to support his own army. More importantly, it pulls him after us, away from Kingfountain. It buys Severn time."

"But what if Severn truly is dead?" Etayne asked, still dumbstruck.

"I don't believe he is," Owen said, shaking his head. "We would have heard. We need to give the king time to bring his army down here. Then we will have caught the Occitanians between us. And by marching on this side," Owen said, pointing to his map, "we keep the Occitanians between us and Roux's men. There's no opportunity for him to flank us. If he's on our side, it actually pinches the Occitanians between us. They won't be expecting it."

"But we only have a few thousand men," Etayne said, shaking her head. "This plan is full of risks, Owen."

"A smaller force defeated Occitania years ago at Azinkeep. Surely they won't have forgotten that. I'm going to leave behind a column to block the road, then I'll have the men come around in circles to make it seem like reinforcements are arriving constantly. War is all about deception, Etayne. If we're going to face this army, I want to do it on ground *we've* chosen. On *our* terms, not theirs."

"You are either mad or brilliant," Etayne said, shaking her head. "When will you do this?"

"Now," Owen said. "Roux always seems to be one step ahead of me. I hope to catch him off guard this once. Tell the captains to come in. We're leaving camp right away. We'll leave all the tents up to disguise what we're doing. I want to start marching while there is still daylight left."

The captains were amazed to learn that Owen was planning such a bold maneuver, but they assured him the army would be ready to move quickly. Clouds from off the coast began to churn in the sky, promising fog or a sea storm. Owen strapped his sword to his waist, wearing his hauberk, and nodded to his flag bearer. Farnes had been sent ahead to advise the Occitanians of Owen's decision not to join forces. But he would give them no warning as to his plans.

His stomach churned with worry as he watched his army begin to march in thin columns. There was movement in the Occitanian forces—the troops were lining up for battle, assembling soldiers to form the vanguard. The wind whipped up, making the pennants and flags flap sharply. The air smelled of mud and filth. Owen could not remember the last time he had bathed.

He led the column with his captains, some mounted archers going off ahead to clear the way. The Espion had chosen a road through a small wooded area where the army could divert from Averanche and join the main road to Pree.

A few splattering drops of rain began to strike against Owen and his steed. The clouds were black and roiling in the skies overhead. Soon it became a downpour. Owen marched on grimly, trying not to let the weather foul his mood. The roads became muddy and clogged within the hour, and the men began to grumble.

Lightning forked across the sky in the distance, followed by the distant rumble of thunder.

They reached the main road to Pree, which was able to accommodate a much larger column. They were now at the flank of the Occitanian army, cutting off their supply lines and blocking their way to their capital. Owen felt as if a giant hand were looming over his head, releasing a Wizr piece and saying in sepulchral tones, *Threat.*

Moments later, a soaked and bedraggled Espion came riding up to him from the road to Pree, having scouted ahead. "My lord!" he called above the torrent. His face was spattered in mud.

"What news, man?" Owen shouted.

"The supply wagons are stuck in the mud yonder," he replied, pointing down the road they traveled. "Enough of them to feed us a good while. But there's a problem, my lord. There are several thousand Occitanian soldiers coming up the road from Averanche right now to stop us from claiming it! They'll be on us within the hour!"

Owen felt the queer sensation that the next move would be against him.

CHAPTER FORTY

The Battle of Averanche

Owen's first battle was amidst a rainstorm in a valley near Averanche. The Occitanian army had not stood still while Owen's men had marched past them on another road. The tiles were starting to fall, and there was no way of stopping them now. Owen had his archers line up to block the road and send volley after volley at the advancing troops. Rain may have dimmed their vision, but it was nearly impossible for the archers to miss with so many coming against them. Behind the archers were his spearmen, row after row, ready to charge.

Once the battle began, it was impossible to control or predict the course of it.

Owen felt the sick reality of combat, all the glory of it reduced to angry men trying to bash in one another's brains. The number of Occitanians seemed unending, wave upon wave of them hammering a rocky shore. There was no going back, no retreating. The muddy road was stained crimson with the conflict. These were not men; these were soiled wretches who cut and smashed against shields and pikes. Owen soon lost count of how many he had killed, but his sword felt like it was part of him. The years of training, the grueling hours in the yard had finally come to fruition. He was exhausted, but he was relentless, urging his men to continue on and on, to endure the hardships that rain and steel inflicted on them. His throat was burning for a drink, but there was no time. He had to be everywhere at once. Whenever someone charged at him, he would focus on the attacker for a moment, use his magic to read the other man's weaknesses, and then parry his blow and dispatch him quickly. He felt power surging inside him each time he struck, and his blows seemed to wield an unbelievable power.

Owen wiped the mud and rain from his face, staring at the onslaught that continued down the road. His men were grim-faced and terrible as they held their position on the road amidst a field of corpses and wounded men.

"My lord!" someone shouted, coming up behind him. It was Captain Stoker. The captain's sword was dripping with blood.

"How many are there?" Owen snarled as the next phalanx approached. His horse shied from a groaning man, and Owen had to cling tightly to its reins as it almost reared.

"My lord!" Stoker said, his face jubilant. "The Brythonicans! They're attacking the Occitanians from behind! They've trapped Chatriyon between us! That's why we're being hard pressed. We're all that stands between them and safety!"

Owen coughed with surprise. Marshal Roux was attacking? Attacking Chatriyon's army?

"Be you sure, Stoker?" Owen asked forcefully. He wanted to believe it. But he didn't trust it to be true.

"His banner is the Raven!" Stoker said, nodding. "His men are in the field! They started as soon as Chatriyon turned on us. It helps even the odds a bit, my lord! In this tempest, it's difficult to tell friend from foe!"

Lightning split the sky overhead, sending crackles of thunder across the heavens. Owen raised his arm up to shield his eyes and an arrow struck his arm. Pain exploded from his elbow down to his wrist. His entire arm went numb, but his mind reeled in shock as he recognized that if he hadn't lifted his arm at exactly that moment, the arrow would have pierced his neck . . . or worse.

"My lord!" Stoker shouted in surprise.

The arrow shaft felt like a hot poker in his arm, and he swore in pain. Was his arm broken? He was thankful it wasn't his sword arm. An archer had singled him out. Then a strange numbness started to stretch down the length of his arm and move up to his shoulder. He felt his body start to stiffen.

Poison. It was in his blood.

Owen turned to Stoker, blinking rapidly. "Etayne! Get me to Etayne!"

A shroud of black seemed to drape across Owen's face, and he felt himself tipping out of the saddle. He was falling. He struck the muddy ground face-first and began choking in it.

♦ ♦ ♦

It sounded to Owen as if he were amidst a hive of bees. There was light beyond his lids, and he felt tugging and jostling. Suddenly all of those bees were stinging his left arm. There was something in his teeth, and he bit down on it as the needles of pain in his arm worsened.

He shook his head, trying to rouse himself, and then opened his eyes. Etayne was crouching over him, and they were inside a small tent filled with the rattling sound of rain striking the canvas. The sensation of being in the beehive faded as he came awake.

"Hold still," Etayne said, working feverishly on his arm. He looked down and saw that the needles he imagined to be figurative were literal—she was stitching his arm with catgut thread and a needle that looked as blunt as a shovel.

With his other arm, he removed a half-bitten arrow shaft from his mouth. "That hurts!" Owen rasped, his voice so thick with weariness it croaked.

Etayne shot him a concerned look. "It was moonflower," she said. "The arrow tip was coated in it. Enough to kill you . . . and quickly. Thankfully, I know the cure."

"What has happened?" Owen said, trying to sit up, but she shoved him back down on the cot.

"The battle is over," she said, giving him a private smile. "You won."

"How could I have won if I wasn't even there?" Owen said, shaking his head. He tried to sit up again, but she pushed him back down.

"Rest, Owen. If you try standing now, you're more than likely to end up on the floor in a puddle of vomit. Hold still while I finish the sutures."

Owen eased back down, scowling and wincing as she continued her work on his arm. When she finished, she dabbed ointment around the wound and then bound it with linen strips that she tied off with tiny knots. He noticed a bloodstained arrow on a camp table nearby, and the size of the head made him shudder.

"Is my arm broken?" he asked.

"No, but the arrow went deep," she replied. "Let me give you something for the pain."

He shook his head. "I'll deal with the pain. I want my wits about me. Where is Captain Stoker?"

"He's talking to Marshal Roux in your tent."

"Where is that?" Owen asked, looking around. "Where is Eyric?"

"This is the tent where I was hiding Eyric. He's in your tent now, with Stoker and Roux. You've won, Owen. You've defeated the Occitanian army. Do you know how many ransoms you will get for this?" She looked at him with delight, shaking her head. "Do you know how *wealthy* you will be after this battle? How many lands you will be entitled to?"

"Where is Chatriyon?" Owen demanded.

She shook her head. "He was never here. He sent all his marshals and captains to defeat you. He feared for his life. He's been in Pree all along."

Owen tried to sit up again, and this time Etayne helped him. His arm was throbbing with pain, making him regret his refusal to take a potion. He blinked swiftly, realization slowly sinking in. The battle was over. He had won.

"Let me find where they put that shirt for you," Etayne said. Owen only then realized that he was stripped to the waist. His battered and stained hauberk was crumpled on the floor of the tent. There were rags stained in mud and dirt strewn about and a basin of filthy water. He looked down at himself and saw that he had been cleaned. Etayne seemed to notice the reason for his scrutiny and she flushed slightly, then hastened to find a shirt for him to wear.

She helped him put it on, being especially delicate with his arm as he struggled to get it into the sleeve.

"Thank you," he said as she finished tying the crossweave at his neck. She brought out a padded vest, which was much easier to put on, and helped him stand. His legs were wobbly and his head spun for a while, nearly making him fall, but she was there to keep him steady.

When he was finally standing without wavering, she looked him over critically, arranging his clothes a little to make him look more like a lord and less like a mud-spattered peasant. She then strapped the scabbard and sword to his waist, her hands deft and efficient. He was uncomfortable with her standing so near, dressing him.

"I meant to thank you for saving my life," Owen told her, trying to catch her eyes even though she was refusing to look at him.

She shook her head slightly, ignoring his words. "It's still storming. You need a cloak."

Once again, he sensed that she felt more for him than friendship and gratitude. He thought it only fair to disabuse her of the notion that they could ever be together. But doing so now, just after she had saved his life . . . well, it would feel a bit coldhearted. He grunted as a throb of pain burst to life in his elbow.

She fetched a cloak, draped it over his shoulders, and lifted the cowl over his head. Once she was also equipped to face the rain, she took him through the rain-drenched camp to the command pavilion. Outside the main doors were two battle standards, the Aurum and the Raven. Both were dripping.

Owen ducked his head as he entered the tent. It was dusk, and the pavilion was full, but he immediately spotted Captain Ashby and the mayor of Averanche inside. He also recognized Marshal Roux, who was still wearing a mud-spattered tunic over his armor. The marshal gave him an almost reproachful look, as if it bothered him that Owen had come to the meeting so late.

"It is good to see you hale, my lord," Roux said warmly, though his eyes were wary.

"Thank you, lord marshal," Owen said. "Your intervention, once again, could not have been better timed." Even though that had decidedly worked in their favor on this occasion, there was still something about the Brythonican that set him on edge. He noticed Eyric sitting silently at the edge of the tent, listening to the conversation.

The marshal bowed stiffly. "The duchess keeps her promises," he said.

Captain Ashby came forward. "My lord, the lord marshal has been supplying Averanche for days. His ships brought casks and kegs to make sure the city was well provisioned. It was a siege, but we ate like kings! I wanted to get word to you that we could have held on much longer, only we could not get past the soldiers at our gates."

Owen felt a prickle of guilt for having distrusted the Brythonicans so much. But even after hearing about their generosity, he felt uneasy.

The lord mayor looked particularly relieved. "We are grateful, Lord Kiskaddon, that you kept your word and did not forsake us. The people of Averanche long to welcome you back into your city. If I may suggest that you move from your camp to the castle to get out of this storm?"

Owen smiled when another loud crackle of thunder followed the mayor's words, causing him to stiffen in surprise.

"I thank you, lord mayor, but must decline," Owen said, shaking his head. "I long to get out of the wet, but we must ride back at once to bring tidings of our victory to King Severn. You may be sure that a celebration of our victory will be held in due time. At such an event, I hope we can have the pleasure of the duchess's company?" Owen gave Roux a serious look.

The marshal's face was perfectly composed. "She rarely ventures from Brythonica, Lord Kiskaddon. As you can imagine, her situation is fraught with peril, and there is a considerable risk of her being kidnapped and made a hostage. She has authorized me to negotiate the peace terms and ransom distributions on her behalf, though she is wont to be generous to our allies from Westmarch. I am certain we will find an equitable arrangement?"

"Indeed," Owen said, feeling his curiosity about the duchess grow. His left arm started to throb painfully, and he felt sweat bead up on his brow. He wanted this conversation to be finished.

Marshal Roux studied Owen's face for a moment, so implacable. "We will depart then and seek shelter at the castle, as the lord mayor's guests. If you permit it."

"I do," Owen said with a nod.

"We would be most gracious hosts, my lord," said the mayor, grinning eagerly. He seemed the kind of man who relished having powerful guests.

"Captain Ashby," Owen said. "Provision the garrison to remain behind. Captain Stoker, have Farnes begin tallying the noteworthy hostages. Once it's done, bring word of them to me at Kingfountain. The king's nephew and I," he said, looking Eyric in the eye, "will join him."

Marshal Roux inclined his head and was about to leave.

Owen stopped him with a gesture. "My lord, have you heard anything about the battles in my realm? Anjers insisted that Severn was dead, but I'm convinced it was a trick."

The lord marshal's brow furrowed slightly. "I pray the Fountain that your king is safe," he said cryptically. "I have no spies in your realm, my lord. We would appreciate the same courtesy in return." There was a slight tone of reprimand in his voice.

"My best to the duchess," Owen said.

The lord marshal nodded. Then his eyes wandered over to the chest containing the ancient Wizr board. His lips pursed. "You may wish, my lord," he said in an undertone, "to leave certain *valuables* in places where they cannot be easily stolen."

He then ducked under the tent flap and left. Owen was curious about his choice of words. As his captains prepared to leave the pavilion and enter the storm once again, Owen crept over to the chest. He carefully removed the lid, afraid the Wizr set inside might be missing. The pieces were still there, undisturbed.

Except for one.

His mouth went dry as he realized a move had been made. One of the pawns on the white side had been replaced by the Wizr piece. His heart started pounding violently in his chest as he stared at the gleaming piece. It was on the left-hand side of the board. The pawn was now sitting in one of the adjacent trays for discarded totems.

Had someone come into his tent and *moved* the piece? Or had it moved all by itself?

♦ ♦ ♦

King Severn Argentine returned to Kingfountain with his triumphant and frostbitten army. There is no doubt his life was preserved by the Fountain and that he is truly the King of Ceredigion. He defeated Iago Llewellyn's forces with the help of his loyal friend, the Duke of Horwath, who cut off Iago's retreat and captured him along with his chief nobles, including the wealthiest one, the Earl of Huntley. The prisoners are being held at the royal castle while preparations are underway for Iago to marry Lady Elysabeth Victoria Mortimer, who will become the Queen of Atabyrion and seal the new alliance between our kingdoms. An alliance that has been purchased with much blood. We now await the arrival of Duke Kiskaddon, who conquered the massive Occitanian army that came to invade Ceredigion. His success ranks as one of the most decisive, improbable victories since the defeat of the Occitanians at Azinkeep. All rumors of his defection and treason have proved false.

—Polidoro Urbino, Court Historian of Kingfountain

♦ ♦ ♦

CHAPTER FORTY-ONE

The Queen of Atabyrion

It was a brisk autumn day when Owen rode his weary stallion beneath the portcullis of the palace of Kingfountain. The cheers from his ride through the city were still ringing in his ears as he dismounted in the bailey. Eyric sat stock-still on his mount, gazing up at the spires and towers of the palace with a look that combined nostalgia and fear. Owen's left arm ached from his wound. Etayne had changed the dressing regularly, and it was strapped to his chest with some leather as he rode. The cloak he wore concealed the crooked bend of it, and he could not help but harbor the dark thought that he was slowly, ponderously, turning into a shadow of Severn himself.

One of the groomsmen offered a hand to Eyric, who at first blinked at the disruption and then took the hand and dismounted as well. Etayne appeared behind him, her eyes assessing the various onlookers for any sign of a threat. With a nod, Owen bade her to keep an eye on Eyric, and she gave him a subtle motion with her head to acknowledge it.

Although Owen's stomach craved refreshment, he felt so worried and nauseous he would not be able to eat. Word had reached him of the king's alliance with Iago Llewellyn—and the price of that alliance. He was haunted by the grim reality that he was losing Evie forever. He had clung to the hope that his victory against Occitania would be enough to sway the king into granting him his heart's desire. But every league he had crossed to return to the palace had filled him with fresh despair; his worst fears were about to come to pass.

"My lord," Justine's voice said at his shoulder. He had not seen her approach, but that was not surprising, for he was in a fog of misery. She looked mournful, which only pushed the knife deeper into his heart.

"She is here?" Owen asked hoarsely. "The wedding arrangements are underway?" He desperately wanted to be contradicted.

Justine flushed a delicate pink. "They are, my lord. She asked me . . . she wants to speak with you herself. Before you see the king. She's at your secret place. Waiting." Justine looked as if she wanted to say more. He saw tears in her eyes, and then she reached out and put her hand on his arm, making him flinch with pain.

"I hurt you!" she gasped. "I'm sorry! That's your wounded arm. I'm—"

"It's not your fault," Owen said, shaking his head, trying to banish the memory of the pain. "I will go at once."

Owen knew that Severn would be expecting him in the throne room. He should go there first and deliver his report in person. But he had to see Evie. He had to listen to her words himself. As he started across the yard, he caught sight of Etayne. "Wait for me outside the throne room," he told her.

She nodded and hooked arms with Eyric, who was shuddering with fear as he crossed the threshold of his childhood palace.

Owen had a thought and caught Etayne's arm. "Take him to Liona first," he whispered to her. "Let him see a friendly face."

He stared back across the yard at the yawning portcullis. The last time he was here a violent mob had been pressing against the gates with the intent of throwing Severn into the river. The memory hit Owen like a spike of pain: Evie facing down the mob and trying to persuade them to relent. Evie falling. He had held her in his lap, afterward, as the blood flowed from her brow. It was the last time he had seen her or touched her. He had seen an unusually large number of armed soldiers wearing the symbol of the white boar while passing through the city. There was a curfew now where there had not been one before. They were preparations in case of another riot.

Owen's throat tightened painfully, but he swallowed and entered the palace. When he reached the corridor leading to the cistern, he found the door at the far end ajar. He tried to control his breathing, but he felt as if he were about to plunge over a waterfall. He pushed the door open gently, gazing out at the place where he had shared so many memories with her.

Evie was pacing near the edge of the cistern hole. She was wearing a dark green gown with silver stitching. He would have recognized the sound of her leather boots anywhere. Her hair was long, with little braids woven together in an intricate and exquisite pattern. As the sound of the creaking door reached her, she spun around to look at him.

The worried look in her eyes was the final affirmation that his life with her was over.

"Owen," she murmured, and he saw tears dance in her lashes as she rushed to him.

He took her into his arms, crushing her against him, feeling his own tears burning down his cheeks. His heart ached with a torment that was different from when Ankarette had died. This was a new sort of death. He didn't know how to endure it.

Owen felt her tremble and sob as she clutched the front of his tunic, his one good arm wrapped around her shoulders. His left arm was in agony, but the pain was nothing compared to what was in his heart.

He stroked her hair, feeling the softness, savoring it. "Say the word, and I will take you from this place. Say the word, my love, and I will take you far, far away. I cannot *bear* this, Evie! It hurts. It hurts so much."

"I know," she replied with a shiver in her voice. "I would be lying if I said otherwise." She pulled back slightly, pushing some hair behind her ear and dabbing her dripping nose on her sleeve. "But this must be, Owen. This must be. We must both learn to accept that life isn't fair. That not all our dreams will come true. That sometimes we must be parted from those we cannot live without." Her face crumpled into a look of misery. She struggled to keep her composure as tears streamed down her face. She took a steadying breath. "I choose this, Owen. This is not happening against my will. I care for . . . I care for Iago. He sincerely loves me, I know that. I think he can make me happy." She glanced down for just a moment. "I *think* I can make him a better man . . . a better king. But I cannot be happy to see you grieve like this. It will be a torment to me, Owen. I am willing to endure it. But you must . . . please . . . you must try! You must try to care for someone else."

Owen hung his head, ashamed that she was handling her emotions better than he was. He tried to wrestle his heart into submission. "How can I pretend?" he whispered thickly. "How can I pretend this will ever stop hurting?"

She shook her head and stroked his arm, his good arm. "It won't *stop* hurting," she said softly. "Not a day goes by that I don't miss my papa. But it lessens in time. And so will this. We are still young, Owen. I'm not doing this because I'll become a queen. I would rather have been a . . . a duchess." She squeezed his arm. "I'm doing this because it is my duty. It is *our* duty. Loyalty binds us. Isn't that what we've been taught for so long? When I heard the rumors that you had forsaken him, I could not believe them. I knew it was a trick, a deception. I knew you would not do that to him." She gave him a look of adoration. "Not my Owen. Never *my* Owen." She shook her head. "But you are mine, no longer. I will be Elysabeth *Victoria* Mortimer Llewellyn. We can do this, Owen. We must. He needs you. Go to your king. Submit to his will, as I have done."

Owen reached out and took her hand. Her fingers were so soft and warm. It was holding her hand that had given him the courage to jump into the cistern waters. She had taught him everything he knew about bravery and fidelity. And love.

"As you command, my lady," Owen whispered huskily. He pressed her knuckles to his lips. If she could endure this, then so could he. As he turned, he spied Justine standing in the doorway, sobbing.

He walked past her, pausing only to pat her shoulder and push her to join Evie in the cistern yard. Owen did not want her to be there when he went to see Severn.

♦ ♦ ♦

Etayne was waiting with Eyric outside the throne room doors, which were closed. The man looked positively greensick. The poisoner saw Owen's crestfallen look, and her expression filled with shared pain.

"He is waiting for you both," she murmured in his ear. "Everyone else has been ordered out."

Owen nodded and took Eyric by the elbow. The guards gripped the massive handles of the doors and pulled them open. Something told Owen that Severn would be pacing inside, and indeed, that was the first thing he noticed. The king was chafing with obvious impatience and agitation.

Eyric, for a moment, couldn't move, until Owen tugged on his arm. Severn turned immediately, his expression a mixture of excitement, worry, and triumph. His black garb was a contrast to Eyric's more princely raiment. The king wore his battle sword as well as a dagger in his belt. Eyric was unarmed, a defeated rebel.

"My lord king," Owen announced in a firm, controlled voice. "The rebel Eyric Argentine was captured, and I bring him to you for justice."

Severn folded his arms, giving Eyric a dispassionate look. The king's demeanor softened, his brooding looks settling into place.

"Welcome back to Kingfountain, nephew," the king said flatly.

Eyric summoned his courage. He was trembling with the weight of the moment. "I am not your nephew," he said in a quavering voice. "My lord, I will confess the truth to you. My name is Piers Urbick. I am from Brugia."

Owen felt a heavy wall of blackness settle on him. As if an unbearable weight had been heaped on his shoulders.

Say nothing, the Fountain whispered to him.

Severn's expression changed to one of confusion, and the first glints of anger shone through. "Piers Urbick?" he said in challenge.

"It is true, my lord," the young man offered meekly. "I am an imposter, trained at the court of your sister to deceive you and the rest of the kingdoms. Long have I sought to escape this disguise. I was chosen because I bear a resemblance to the Argentine family. Perhaps my mother had a dalliance with your elder brother during his exile in Brugia. I was taught what to say. I was promised a kingdom. Your kingdom." He bowed, his knees trembling.

Owen knew Eyric wasn't telling the truth. Every word out of his mouth was a lie.

Say nothing.

Severn looked outraged, his anger blasting white hot in his eyes. "You mean to tell me, lad, that you've been duping us all along? That my *sister* persuaded you to seek my throne unlawfully, illegitimately, and through lies and deception, you managed to convince a king to marry you to one of the noblest daughters of his realm!" His voice continued to rise until he was shouting. "That this is all a sham? You may be my nephew, my *bastard* nephew, if that! And you come to Kingfountain to seek pardon for these heinous falsehoods!" The king whirled around, his eyes sparking with inner fire. "I ought to throw you into the river myself," he growled with such wrath that Owen thought he might do just that.

Eyric shrank from the words, wincing away from the king. Owen felt the trickling of the Fountain, felt the waters of it seeping inside the king as he lashed out at his nephew.

Why would Eyric lie? Owen could not fathom the logic or fear that had driven him to such a blatant falsehood, but then he remembered Lady Kathryn's eyes, the way her hand had touched her abdomen.

It is your duty to protect the heir, the Fountain told him. *The Dreadful Deadman will return. If you tell the king, the babe will perish. You must hide him. You must protect him.*

Eyric collapsed to his knees, his voice throbbing with anguish. "I beg you to have mercy!" he pleaded. "Dread sovereign! I implore you. I was coerced by ambitious men. I did not want to deceive everyone, but I was carried forth by the unfolding of events. I beg for mercy!"

Severn eyed the prostrate young man with disgust. "Take him out of my sight," he ordered Owen. "If your marriage to that young woman was performed under such a lie, then the marriage is not valid." He snorted scornfully. "She married you because she thought she had married a prince. Well, I thank you for taking the trouble to bring the Earl of Huntley's daughter to Ceredigion. Her father has been frantic to hear word of her. I shall tell him that his son-in-law was nothing more than a sniveling coward and an imposter. Well, if she wanted to become Queen of Ceredigion, there is *another* way."

Eyric's eyes widened with shock. "You are a monster," he breathed out. Owen felt the heaviness of the Fountain still, and it prevented him from speaking out on Eyric's behalf. He saw the king's mind shifting, tottering, shutting.

Severn sneered. "If that is what everyone expects, then I shan't disappoint them any longer. I have no family left. No niece. No nephew. No sister." His eyes were glaring with wrath. "I won't kill you, lad. But you will come to wish I had. You are my prisoner." The king turned to Owen. "My lord duke, I give you charge of the Espion. Have young Urbick assigned to Dunsdworth. Have them both guarded day and night. I forbid him to share a bed with the woman he seduced and deceived. Have Lady Kathryn brought to the palace. I should like to meet the beauty of Atabyrion who came to be queen. And I should like to hear him confess his duplicity to her face."

"My lord, I beg you, no!" Eyric started, and Severn held up a hand to silence him.

"Take him away."

Owen was sick at heart. He stared at the king, feeling animosity roil in his heart. Was this how Stiev Horwath felt? Was this why he was so often silent?

Owen grabbed beneath Eyric's arm and pulled him up. Eyric's face was white with despair, his hands trembling. When Owen reached the door, he gave Etayne orders to see to the man. Then he paused, and turned as the doors were shut once again.

Severn stood by the fireplace, shaking his head. A strange expression was on his face. An almost giddy look.

"My lord, may I speak to you?" Owen asked.

The king glanced over his shoulder, looking surprised Owen had not yet left. "You've seen the girl, haven't you? Lady Kathryn? Lord Bothwell tells me she is a beauty. Soft-spoken, demure. He could not say what color her hair was because the fashion in her country is to wear headdresses." Severn looked almost distracted in his thoughts. "When you bring her, I don't want her wearing Atabyrion fashions. Have a gown made up for her. Let Etayne do it. She should wear black, as if she's in mourning. Black, but I want the cut to be the finest of any princess. Yes, I want her to wear black. It's appropriate, after all."

Owen's horror grew as the king spoke. He was not himself. Something had altered him. Was it the threat of being thrown in the river? Was it the stress of facing another Ambion Hill? Or had it been his niece's betrayal? Perhaps he was finally feeling the stress of all his miserable years of loyalty to his brother.

The thought shocked Owen and made him sick inside.

"What did you want?" the king asked peevishly.

"I just wanted you to know," Owen said, feeling a strange sensation in his stomach. He would not tell Severn that Kathryn was with child. He felt the heavy weight of it pressing on him, but he knew it was a secret he had to keep, just as he had kept so many other secrets from the king.

"To know *what*? Speak, man! You have errands aplenty to attend to. Aren't you grateful for the new office? The new trust I have put in you?"

Not in the least, he refrained from saying.

"My lord, I just wanted you to know. To hear it from my own mouth. I loved her. I truly, deeply loved her."

Severn wrinkled his brow. "The Mortimer girl. Yes, I know."

Owen felt the stirrings of hatred begin in his heart. "You knew?"

The king nodded and folded his arms. "Mancini saw it first and then I noticed it myself. Yes, you were fond of the girl. But you are barely a man, Owen. There is much you have yet to learn."

Owen was struggling to control his temper. "You knew . . . and yet you allowed Iago to have her? Your enemy?"

The king shook his head. Then his face became cruel. "You don't think I know what you're feeling? Finally someone else understands what *I* had to endure. What *I* had to go through! My Nanette, the daughter of the Duke of Warrewik. She and I were much like you and the Mortimer girl. I loved her deeply, as Warrewik ensured that I would! And then he sold her off to form an alliance with the Prince of Occitania. She was to become their queen." He gave Owen a look of fierce loathing and rage. "She was wed to our enemy. And when they returned to Ceredigion with an army, hoping to break my brother's crown, I destroyed her father and her husband. That's when I realized I was Fountain-blessed. When I was able to persuade her to love me in spite of that." He came forward, and Owen felt the magic of the Fountain rush to life inside the king. He gripped Owen's shoulder, and the pain in his elbow howled with the pressure. The magic of the Fountain flooded him, but it could not penetrate him. He stood steady against it, immovable.

"You will understand what I had to endure to be loyal, young Owen," the king snarled. "You will understand what it feels like to be hated. To be despised. You will learn the cost of loyalty as I did. Then we'll see if you can smugly talk of love as if that were the single most important thing in the world, the only consideration regarding the destiny of kings and fate! The people love you now. But they will hate you. And then we will see if you do not become the very man that I am!" His eyes were losing focus and appeared to be gazing at something far away. "Yes, they wanted a monster, and now they will get one. And I will make the world howl for it!"

CHAPTER FORTY-TWO

Winter

Flakes of snow floated down like leaves, blurring the view from the window of the solar. Owen stood by the glass, wishing that his heart were made of ice. The door creaked and Duke Horwath entered the chamber. His movements were slower. Maybe it had always been like that, but the man looked so much older to Owen's eyes. Old and weary.

Owen guessed that his expression was sufficiently desolate, for Horwath's face frowned in sympathy. He came forward and stood by the window, his arm coming around Owen's shoulder.

"We'll both miss her, lad," the duke said gruffly. There was pain throbbing in his voice. "I would like it if you came by Dundrennan now and then. You never need an invitation. Maybe an old soldier can help."

Owen felt a pulse of gratitude, but it was quickly snuffed out by his misery. "The ceremony is over. The ships have embarked. Will she return, my lord?"

The duke let out a deep, sad breath. "I doubt it. Unless the king calls for her."

Owen steeled himself, trying to keep afloat. "I'm not sure he will. She always told him what she thought. I don't think the king will appreciate that now."

Horwath nodded sagely. "He's changed. Something within him finally broke. As I said, you need no invitation." He clapped Owen on the shoulder, careful to avoid his injured arm, and turned to leave.

"You're riding out to Dundrennan tomorrow? In the storm?"

The old duke nodded. "This isn't a storm. I've ridden in worse. Many were slain in the battle. I have widows to see. The dead to honor." He gave Owen a heartfelt smile. "Maybe a lad to comfort."

Owen did not think he would ever smile again. "Safe travels, my lord. Do you have any advice on running the Espion?"

Horwath stroked his goatee. "I think you learned enough from Ratcliffe and Mancini on what *not* to do. If I read the king's mood right, he's ready to take the game to the other side of the board." His eyes narrowed wisely. "Be careful. Study the history of the time of the Maid. It may teach you what happens when kings overreach."

With a sardonic smile, Owen nodded to Horwath and watched him leave. His elbow throbbed dully, but it was healing, and he no longer needed the sling to secure it. The flurry was growing thicker outside, making it difficult to see what was happening in the bailey down below. Owen thought about Lady Kathryn and what he was going to say to her. He knew what needed to be done, but it would require her cooperation, and she was not likely to trust the man who had deceived her husband.

He walked out of the solar and started down the steps to the main floor. There were servants everywhere removing the decorations from the wedding celebration of Iago and Evie. He caught himself. Iago and *Elysabeth*. He had to stop thinking of her pet name. It hurt too much when he did.

Dodging around some girls carrying rolls of fabric that had been used to festoon the great hall, Owen retreated to the room of the Espion masters called the Star Chamber. It was near the king's bedchamber. The room was large enough to fit several chairs. Everywhere there were desks, quills, ink, chests filled with coins for bribes, and one wall was lined with hooks holding keys to all the various locks within the palace. The plush chair was larger than Owen needed it to be, but he sat in it, staring at the mound of letters and missives that arrived daily from ships and couriers across the realm. Like shoveling snow. The walls of the Star Chamber were thick, and Owen bolted the door, signifying that he did not want to be disturbed. He leaned his elbows on the desk and buried his face in his hands, wondering if he had done the right thing. If he had assisted Eyric in overthrowing Severn, would it have changed the fate of the realm? Could he have done so against his conscience? Would knowing what the king had become have changed his decision?

He thought of Evie on a ship sailing for Atabyrion. He imagined Iago by her side, claiming her mouth in a kiss. A searing pain lanced through his heart at the thought. No, he couldn't think on that! He would drive himself mad. His shoulders trembled with stifled gasps as he tried to control himself.

They would have children. What would she name her son? Would she name him Andrew as so many did, choosing the famous king as a namesake? Or would it be a dearer name?

Owen didn't hear the sound of the secret door opening. The fire in his heart was too loud. But he sensed a presence in the room. He heard the rustle of fabric. The swish of a skirt.

Then he felt the soothing ripple of Fountain magic.

Owen turned his neck slowly. There she was. Ankarette Tryneowy. Of course, it wasn't her. It was Etayne, but she *looked* like Ankarette. There was that same tender smile, those wise and sad eyes; even the smell reminded him of her.

"I wondered how best to comfort you," Etayne said softly as she walked forward, the skirts shushing on the carpet. "I could have looked like *her*." She shook her head. "Other men would have asked for that. But you aren't like other men. I could never make you *believe* I was her. You'd despise me, and I never want you to despise me. Who then to comfort you?" The look on Etayne's face was so full of compassion and sorrow. She put a soft hand on his shoulder. "Let me comfort you, Owen. As *she* would have. I found the letter she wrote you. I searched all the secret places until I found it."

She handed him a small square of paper, folded over.

Owen stared at her in surprise, feeling his emotions churning relentlessly.

With a trembling hand, he took the paper and opened it.

To my dear Owen:

Before I die, I wanted to write this for you. I'm sad to be leaving the palace of Kingfountain behind forever. This tower has been my haven for many years. There are sad memories here. But good ones as well. Life is like that, you will come to learn. When I am asleep in the Deep Fathoms, I will cherish my memories of you. I wish I could see you grow up and the man you will become. Someday you may be called upon to do something that is against your conscience. I leave my final advice for you. If your master demands loyalty, give him integrity. But if he demands integrity, then give him loyalty. I love you, my little boy. I willingly give my life to save yours. Someday, you may be asked to do the same for another.

Your friend, Ankarette

His eyes blurred with tears as he read her final words. The grief in his heart was unendurable.

"I can see why Mancini didn't want you to read that," Etayne said. She smoothed her hand over his hair, then sat next to him on the stuffed chair, pulled his head down against her shoulder, and gently stroked his hair.

He felt the illusion of her magic all around him. But just this once, he surrendered to it and pretended the queen's poisoner was there with him.

EPILOGUE

Owen had never witnessed a woman giving birth before. He was really of no use at all, for he felt sickened and disgusted by the entire ordeal. He had heaved his stomach out in a bucket near the door, and the sounds of Kathryn's pangs made him light-headed and utterly dizzy. He was truly the world's greatest fool to think he could hide such an event from the awareness of King Severn. At any moment, he suspected guards wearing black tabards with the white boar emblazoned on them would come pounding on the door of the sanctuary of St. Penryn and seize the child.

Owen heard the sound of footfalls and feared the worst. A knock came on the door, and Owen drew his sword and pulled back the latch with wobbly fingers, ready to fight. It was the deconeus.

"How fares the lady's labor?" the deconeus asked nervously.

Owen glanced over his shoulder at Etayne, who knelt by the bedside, offering Kathryn sips of broth and potions to help her keep up her strength. "I could not tell you one way or the other," Owen answered truthfully.

The deconeus seemed to notice the blade and backed away. "Forgive my intrusion, my lord. I swear to you, by the Fountain and by the chest you hid here, that I will not reveal you. There is no one here at the sanctuary right now, my lord. Not a soul." He glanced heavenward. "But there looks to be a squall blowing in from the sea. Are you sure you wish to risk the babe's health by riding in a storm? He is to be our king."

"May the Fountain make it so," Owen said, shutting the door in his face when he heard Kathryn moaning in agony again.

He leaned back against the door, blinking rapidly. He had the Espion chasing ghosts all over the realm at the moment. He had even concocted a possible threat from his imagination—both to give himself an excuse to be away from the palace and to keep Severn distracted. The king was desperate to see Lady Kathryn, to get to know her, to woo her. Owen wiped his mouth, remembering all the lies and tricks he had used to forestall the inevitable.

Lady Kathryn had stayed in sanctuary for five months. At first Owen had reported that it was her fear of Severn that kept her away, followed by the excuse of a long illness. And then she went into labor early—months early—and it was all Owen could do to get Etayne and himself there without drawing the notice of the other Espion. Etayne had trained as a midwife, and she had been practicing over the months in anticipation of this birth.

Owen's job would be to bring the babe to a safe haven, a place where the child could be raised in anonymity. The arrangements had been made with the help of Duke Horwath, though the story Owen had told the duke was not true. He'd spun a tale of a young widow who had lost her husband in the Battle of Averanche, a woman who was carrying her husband's child but couldn't afford to care for the babe without a husband. He had promised to find someone to raise the child to be a soldier like his father—to teach him honor and duty and loyalty.

Owen knuckled his brow.

Kathryn lay still. A solemn silence fell over the room. He saw Etayne swaddling the bloody infant. An infant who made no sound.

Kathryn was gasping. "I . . . I can't . . . hear. I can't . . . hear . . . him. Is it a boy . . . truly?"

"He's a boy," Etayne said in a solemn voice. A voice full of dread. Owen met her gaze and knew the truth. He could see it in her eyes.

The babe was stillborn.

Owen's heart wrenched with pain. He sheathed his sword and approached the bed, feeling the dizziness threaten to knock him down.

"Let me . . . see . . . him," Kathryn gasped.

Etayne looked heartsick. She wiped splotches of blood and goo from the babe's puckered face. She held the boy as tenderly as the mother herself would have, gazing sadly down at the face, the cold, limp face. Owen saw the tears well in Etayne's eyes as she pressed a kiss to the babe's forehead.

"Let me . . . hold him," Kathryn pleaded.

Etayne offered the child to his mother. Sweat made her auburn hair cling to her forehead. She was utterly spent and exhausted from the difficult labor. Her black gown was hanging over a chair, and her white chemise was soaked with sweat and blood. Owen watched Kathryn's face twist with emotion as she stared down at the little child in her weak arms.

"No . . . no!" she moaned. "It can't be!" Sobs began to rack her chest.

Owen stared at the babe. And then he knew what he needed to do.

Fighting his doubts, he approached the bedside and took the babe from the weeping mother. Etayne stared at Owen, her eyes widening with the realization of what would happen.

The babe had been born . . . dead.

Just like Owen.

The prophecy of the Dreadful Deadman spoke of a dead king who came back to life. Owen felt the power of the Fountain well inside his heart. He could hear it in the crashing surf beyond the sanctuary walls. He could feel it in the storm clouds scudding across the sky.

Owen cradled the tiny infant in his arms, staring at his waxy skin. He felt the love of the mother radiating from the woman below. He remembered watching as Eyric suffered at Kingfountain, a prisoner bound by bitter fate in companionship to Dunsdworth, maintaining a lie so that his offspring might be kept safe. Owen felt a spark of hope as he stared at the little babe—the hope that a better reign might soon come to the land.

Owen brought the babe's face close to his lips. He didn't remember the words. But somehow he knew what to say in a language he'd only spoken once. He felt the power of the Fountain gushing from him as he whispered it.

"Nesh-ama."

Breathe.

The tiny eyelids of the quiet king fluttered open.

AUTHOR'S NOTE

There is usually some basis of fact in my books and this one is no exception. During my studies of the Wars of the Roses in medieval England, I learned about the mystery of Perkin Warbeck and how he claimed to be one of the lost princes murdered by Richard III. Because this story is set in an alternate universe in which Richard III won the battle instead of Henry VII, I thought it would be even more interesting to explore how Warbeck's claim to the throne would be received by the uncle who purportedly murdered him. It created some great tension for the story and some guidance on the plot. For those interested in learning more, I'd recommend Ann Wroe's book *The Perfect Prince: The Mystery of Perkin Warbeck and His Quest for the Throne of England.* One of the elements of the book that has haunted me was what happened to the child of Perkin and Lady Katherine, the Earl of Huntley's daughter. Historians don't really know. Why is it that we authors are attracted to such mysteries?

I've mentioned many times a fondness for middle books. I don't know if I will be able to say that about this one because I've never cried as an author as much as I did writing the concluding chapters of this book. If you feel you've been put through some form of emotional torture, I have been there right alongside you. I'm deeply involved in the lives of the characters.

There is a story told about the sculptor Michelangelo. As he was chiseling the statue *David* out of a huge marble block, a young boy asked him, "How did you know he was in there?" For me, writing books is a similar process. It feels sometimes like I am bringing to life a story that has always existed. This was part of the story that needed to be told. In our lives, we don't always get what we deserve or what we want. But how we deal with those misfortunes mold our character.

As with this second book, time will leap-frog again into the future for book three, where the ramifications of the decisions made here will play out. You will also learn more about the mysteries that have been eluding Owen for so long. Get ready for some surprises ahead in *The King's Traitor*.

ACKNOWLEDGMENTS

I would like to thank many who helped this series move forward. First, to my early readers who dealt with the emotional trauma in this book with great equanimity! Robin, Shannon, Karen, and Sunil. My wife and oldest daughter were also great listening ears as I discussed what to do with this book and the tortures Owen would face. I'd also like to thank my amazing editorial team for their enthusiasm about this series! That would be Jason Kirk, Courtney Miller, and Angela Polidoro (who got an intentional cameo in the book because her last name coincided with the actual sixteenth-century historian Polydore Vergil, a source I used during my master's thesis as well as in writing this series).

ABOUT THE AUTHOR

Photograph © Kim Bills

Jeff Wheeler took an early retirement from his career at Intel in 2014 to become a full-time author. He is, most importantly, a husband and father, and a devout member of his church. He is occasionally spotted roaming among the oak trees and granite boulders in the hills of California or in any number of the state's majestic redwood groves. He is the author of The Covenant of Muirwood Trilogy, The Legends of Muirwood Trilogy, The Whispers from Mirrowen Trilogy, The Landmoor Series, and *The Queen's Poisoner*, book one of the Kingfountain Series. He is also the founder of *Deep Magic: The E-zine of Clean Fantasy and Science Fiction* (www.deepmagic.co).